WORLDS END

WORLDS END

BOOK FIVE IN THE CROSS AND THE CROWN SERIES

BY

SARAH KENNEDY

www.penmorepress.com

ISBN-13:-978-1-957851-16-7(Paperback)
ISBN   :-978-1-957851-15-0(e-book)

BISAC Subject Headings:
FIC014000FICTION / Historical
REL053000RELIGION / Christianity / Protestant
FIC031020FICTION / Thrillers / Historical

Cover Illustration
emilysworldofdesign@gmail.com

Address all correspondence to:

Penmore Press LLC
920 N Javelina Pl
Tucson AZ 85748

Praise for The Cross and the Crown Series:

A great many things are happening in *The Altarpiece*: there is mystery, action, and even some romance. Kennedy has managed to create some interesting characters in the sisters of Mount Grace, particularly in Catherine, who is both intelligent and resourceful. She finds herself torn between her vows to the church and her desire for more in life. . . . Kennedy also deserves credit for approaching the period from the refreshing perspective of the devout. *Historical Novels Review*

The energy in the language conveys the urgency of a fraught moment in history with prose as bright and dazzling as Catherine's illuminated manuscripts. Kennedy's command of her characters and subject matter is impressive, and *The Altarpiece* is a very promising beginning to Kennedy's *The Cross and Crown* series. *Per Contra.*

Having chosen William Overton, Catherine Havens Overton now struggles to manage her wifely duties in his house, where her extraordinary gifts in physic and healing are feared as witchcraft as well as sought after by all, creating a difficult and dangerous situation. Filled with drama, suspense, vivid scenes and larger-than-life characters, *City of Ladies* fast becomes impossible to put down. Author Sarah Kennedy is clearly as gifted as her main character, almost supernaturally at home in the 16th century as she combines the striking vocabulary of the time with her own poetic talents to create a rich and original tapestry of language. Such writing! Sarah Kennedy brings a lost world blazingly to life. *Lee Smith*

Sarah Kennedy reanimates lost perspectives of Tudor England in her second story of Catherine, a former nun displaced by Henry's dissolution of the religious houses. With a scholar's imaginative sympathy, Kennedy restores humanity to Mary Tudor and the vulnerable women sheltered by Catherine. With a poet's sensual worldmaking, Kennedy conjures up the textures, temperatures, aromas, and emotions of daily life in a country undergoing dizzying upheavals of beliefs and convictions. In City of Ladies Kennedy takes her place with Daphne du Maurier, Anya Seton, Rosemary Sutcliff, and Hilary Mantel as writer of superb historical fiction. *Suzanne Keen*

Sarah Kennedy opens magical windows into the world of Tudor's England and brings it to life in vibrant colors and unforgettable reverberations. She reinvents the genre of historical fiction of that period giving voice to women of all ages, social classes, and economic standing. She writes with astounding detail of material culture and deft psychological insight about the experiences of women from the royal sisters to maids and confidants amidst whom the feisty protagonist Catherine Havens sparkles in the full richness of her empowered self, in the delicious shades of her moods, intelligence, warm motherhood and sensuality. This third novel in the series soars to new heights and we follow the heroine breathlessly on her suspenseful, sometimes reckless, always riveting journey. *Domnica Radulescu*, author of *Train to Trieste* and *Black Sea Twilight*

"[A]n excellent novel" *Minneapolis Star Tribune*

The religious tensions of Tudor England are the dramatic focus of the historical novel *Queen of Blood*. Catherine Havens is caught in the middle of divided loyalties as the Wyatt Rebellion ignites. You will feel the anguish of Catherine, a former nun, now married, with an oldest son who is a fervent Protestant, opposing the new Catholic queen. The London streets, rife with suspicion and fear, come vividly to life in this latest entry in Sarah Kennedy's engrossing series. *Nancy Bilyeau*, author of *The Crown, The Chalice,* and *The Tapestry*

Chapter 1

November, 1558, Yorkshire, England

So the queen was dead, and long live the queen. Out with the old, and in with the new, if Elizabeth Tudor could be called new. She was young, anyway, and, thanks to her sister Mary, the English knew already how to suffer a woman on the throne. She was the only Tudor they had any more.

And so Catherine Davies, once Catherine Overton, originally Catherine Havens, who would have been, if she'd arrived into a family of Protestant wedded bliss, Catherine Bridle, perched at her desk in her stone house, the message still booming in her head with the artificial self-importance of its deliverer's poor theatrics, and stared out at a sullen, grey sky. A dark bird slipped by. Mary Tudor was dead, already cooling for the tomb. Probably stinking, unless the cold weather was keeping her fresh, like a cabbage in a cellar. Catherine chortled. There would be revels in London, no doubt, and many a young nobleman would be smirking into his mirror, examining the turn of his tree-trunk legs, to see if he might appeal as a husband to the new queen, but they were nothing compared to the dancing of Catherine's heart, here in faraway Yorkshire, as she counted the ways she would begin again, now that she had won her battle against the departed queen. Hail to Elizabeth.

"Ann!" Catherine called. She waited. Pots clattered downstairs in the kitchen. Then her oldest and most trusted friend, Ann Smith, now Ann Goodall, clunked unevenly up the steps. Her right leg would be giving her trouble again. It always complained when the weather turned dismal.

"She's dead, isn't she?" said Ann at the doorway.

"So it seems." Catherine swallowed the giggle that tortured her throat. "The messenger claimed it, anyway. He seemed to have spent a long time practicing his part."

"Will you write to Elizabeth?" Ann had grown stout as a badger in the last few years, and she settled herself, wiping her hands on her apron, before Catherine. Her hair, long gone silver, sprayed out around her cap. "And are you going to tell her how far you've fallen, thanks to her sister?"

"Fallen? I still hold body and soul together well enough," said Catherine. "At least our house isn't being taken down around our ears, like some I could mention. We can order some new rooms onto the back, and they'll be ready before I can fetch our men home. But fetch them I will."

"Them? Both of them? Well, you are in a hopeful mood. It's back to kneeling to the Tudors, then, is it? You had better practice your curtseys. And scrub your face better."

"At my age, I'll probably fall over and break a bone if I so much as bend one knee," said Catherine. She put a hand to her cheek. It felt clean enough. "But I will do it. I'll kneel like no courtier has ever knelt before. I will shine at kneeling, so brightly that little Elizabeth will be dazzled into saying that they can come back to England. We had better begin with a new wing as soon as the weather allows, just on the possibility that they return on their own." She reached for the accounts. The ledgers needed putting in order, so that she could leave them.

"And what happened to your beloved plan for a city of ladies? You have that now, as good as. You're free to do as you like. And you're going to bring men back into your life? You'll choose it?"

"I'm done with all that business," said Catherine. "It was a silly notion, the idea of a girl. A Tudor's a Tudor, and a monarch a monarch, whether it's in skirts or breeches. There was a time when I would have given my right hand to help Mary Tudor. I was a fool. Let's have the men home."

"Well, you'll do as you will. You always have," said Ann. "Have you ink enough?"

"Yes." But Catherine suddenly felt the urge to plead a headache and simply go to bed. She could write to Elizabeth tomorrow. Now that she thought of it, she did seem to detect a definite pressure behind her right eyebrow, and she pushed her finger against her forehead to see if the pain would step out and show itself. But it didn't emerge, not really, and she didn't want to get undressed so early. The days were short enough in November as it was.

The black bird circled back, a couple of other ravens having joined the fray, all of them harassed by a couple of sparrows. They argued their way past the windows, then off into the fields beyond the house, and Catherine wondered briefly if she should sow it in something besides corn this year. Maybe she'd start some apple trees. Maybe she'd put down some roses. She still had enough sheep to keep her income comfortable. Why not have some flowers in the summer to celebrate her triumph over Mary? Over time itself?

Her haunches ached from the seat. Her breast suddenly bubbled and heaved, and she could not determine whether it was glee or dread. She thought she might weep and rubbed fiercely at her eyes. Was she perhaps coming down with a fever? Maybe she should retire for the day and let her excitement settle.

"She's dead," said Catherine. "Mary Tudor is dead." She almost giggled again. She stood and thought she might faint.

Ann had been pulling the heavy door closed, but she stopped. "It'll be a different world now." Catherine nodded, and then she was down on the floor, and then Ann was beside her, tugging her skirts away from the hearth flames. "Calm yourself. You're sure it's true? The last time a cry went up, they said she was having a baby."

"She was always claiming to be having a baby. But this man came from London," said Catherine.

"And now Elizabeth will be queen," said Ann. "I can scarcely believe it."

Elizabeth. That shrill, bitter child. Now a woman, but a woman always almost in motion, so bright and slender, so tightly wound that she seemed a spring sapling clustered with butterflies. Half the world scorned her, and the other half wanted to make use of her. It was impossible, had always been impossible, that she would ever be anything but a dear trade on the marriage market. But who would have had her then? After the scandal with that Thomas Seymour fellow. And then the talk about Robert Dudley. Now, all that talk would be nothing. Now, anyone would pay to have her. Her gaze might drive a man to his knees. It might start a war.

Elizabeth would be the queen.

"If no one poisons her first," blurted Catherine. "Her sister has paved the way for her, but she had better run her head into that crown before some upstart cuts it off."

"Or some priest," said Ann. "What happens to these new convents now?"

Catherine worried at the nap in the carpet until she pried loose a thread, then scoured the spot with her finger. She flipped the tuft of wool into the fire.

They both knew enough about the women who, under Mary Tudor, had taken impromptu vows with others and set up housekeeping together. Many of them taught children. Some of them made lace or embroidered. Catherine's stepdaughter Diana was one of them, and she gave music lessons to young girls. She lived with a pack of other unmarried women down in the city, somewhere near the old Blackfriars. Catherine sent them money every month or so. "I will write to Diana. She will want to come home."

Ann said, "It's snowing again," and Catherine knew she was suffering from achy joints. The cold would descend tonight, savage and relentless in these days when the sun barely cleared the southern horizon.

The afternoon was dissolving quickly into night, and the far border of her fields, hedged by gorse, had already been eclipsed by the gloom. Perhaps she would buy a few more cows and let them graze instead of planting at all this year, Catherine thought, and then caught herself before she spoke. Her imagination was running free of her reason, and she felt a cold stab of fear through her breast. She felt a little mad. She didn't want to become one of the muttering old women she saw on the roads. Ann was watching her.

"Write to Elizabeth first," said Ann. "You need to know where you stand."

Catherine almost laughed, remembering the time she had spent at Hatfield House when Elizabeth was a child. Catherine had often dictated the child's diet, and she briefly wondered if Elizabeth ate any heartier these days. "Yes," she said.

"But, Catherine, relax about the men. See what Diana has to say. Wait a bit. Let things set themselves into order first."

"I will write as soon as I can," said Catherine. "I will go to the court and Elizabeth must agree. She will. I will search our men out myself. It will be a sort of quest. I will ride home victorious. It might even please me, to see her again. Elizabeth is not her sister, and it can't be any colder there than it is up here." She was babbling, and she bit her lip. Then she felt the old weight at her heart. She'd felt it every time she'd thought of a Tudor in the last few years. It felt almost like joy, but she knew it was the burden of someone else's authority pressing on her lifeblood. "Oh, it will be terrible, to see a court again, I know that's what you're thinking. But I will crawl on my knees until she agrees. She cannot say nay. I have been dear to her, Ann. I have been dear to Elizabeth. She will welcome me, and she will say yes to my request, and I will have my husband and my son again. Diana can come, too, and she'll be happy to have her father home. She misses him, as much as I do. I'm sure of it. I will rescue them. We will all be a family once more."

The weary light hunkered further into the darkness.

"If you say so," said Ann, and she shut the door as she went out.

Chapter 2

Catherine wrote a note to her stepdaughter before she allowed herself the luxury of the bed, but by the following morning, she'd already decided to ride to London herself. She discarded the paper onto the embers in the hearth and began again, with a letter to Elizabeth.

As she was finishing up with a satisfactory little flourish of ink, Ann opened the door. "Will you eat?"

"Yes, I'm starved this morning," said Catherine. "Call the girls in."

Ann lifted a grey eyebrow. "Is that letter for Diana or Elizabeth?"

"Elizabeth. I mean to go to London and find Diana myself."

A girl entered the room, scrubbing at her eyes. She was tall and brown-haired and wore stockings, but no shoes. And no cap. She'd scorned headwear since she was old enough to remove with her own hands anything from her hair, unless she needed it against the cold. "Mother, why are you going to London?" she said. "It's winter almost." A small frowsy terrier stuck its head between her ankles.

"Come here, Alice," said Catherine. "Your feet will freeze right off. And must I tell you again to wear your cap?"

Catherine's younger daughter yawned and picked up the dog. "Not even Toby wants to go out in this weather. Or wear a hat." She collapsed like a bundle of sticks onto the rug beside the fire. "When will breakfast be ready?"

Catherine pushed back the stray fine hairs at the girl's temple. But she was no girl anymore. She was almost a young woman, with eyes as blue as a summer sky. Her older sister's had grown darker as she got older, and they almost matched Catherine's own, though they were bluish where Catherine's still offered a hint of green. But Alice's gaze only got brighter. "Alice, the world has changed. The news will be good for us."

Alice sat up and gathered her legs beneath her. "Tell me. What's happened?"

Catherine looked at Ann and breathed. "We will have a new queen in England."

"There's a girl baby? And fat old Mary died having it?"

"Alice, that's no way to talk," said Ann. "The walls have ears, even in Yorkshire. You know that. Be still and let your mother tell you."

Catherine said, "Queen Mary is dead, yes. There's no child. Elizabeth will be the queen. Do you understand what that means?"

"It means Father will come home, doesn't it? That he will no longer be in disgrace."

Catherine nodded. She expected her daughter to leap up, to shout, to cry out. But she just stroked her little dog and chewed her lower lip.

"Does he want to come home?" she said.

"Of course, he does," said Catherine. "Every father wants to come home to his child, and he is my husband."

"I don't remember what he looks like." Alice regarded her mother doubtfully with a sidelong challenge. "Do you even know where he is?"

Catherine glanced at Ann, who shrugged one shoulder. "Well, we will have to find him," Catherine said. "And Robbie, too. Wouldn't you like to see your brother again?"

"He is no brother to me. I hate him," said Alice flatly. "He hates us, and so I hate him. He can stay wherever he is. Father can come home, I suppose, if he wants to. If he wants to stay hidden, then we will continue on as we are without him." She gathered up the dog and rubbed her fair face against its brushy fur. "I want to eat."

Ann said, "Run down to the kitchen and ask for a bite. We will be down just after you. We need to speak to your sister."

"She's gone out already, with Reg. Something in the village," said Alice.

Always something in the village. And she, a woman alone, to attend to all of it. Well, not for much longer. Catherine sealed the letter and tucked it into her bodice.

Alice said, "Who do you write to?"

Catherine considered. "The queen. I will take it with me."

"The queen? You're riding to London to see the queen?"

"Only if she will have me," said Catherine. "I need to speak with your sister."

"She's out. I just said."

"No, your eldest sister. Diana."

"She is only half my sister, and she doesn't care about us, either." And Alice left, still lugging the dog under one arm.

"I suppose we had better eat," said Catherine. She looked out the window. The sun was barely a whimper of light against a menacing sky. "When do you think Reg might return?"

"Who can say?" said Ann. "He's my husband, not my servant. And don't expect me to go running after him. He can make his way home when he will. And he will, when he's ready."

Catherine could feel Ann's eyes on her back, but she didn't turn until she heard the door close.

Downstairs, Catherine found her elder daughter, Veronica, already at the broad oak table. She'd just ridden in with Reg, and sat, dirt streaking her sleeves, with Alice, who now had the dog in her lap. Veronica frowned at the animal over the dishes. "Can you not command him to stay on the floor?"

"He stays on the floor when we eat in the dining hall," countered Alice. "In the kitchen, he's as good a man as any." Reg hovered in the back doorway, knocking frozen mud from his boots. "Tell her, Reg. Toby has better manners at his supper than many a day labourer."

"Don't be speaking ill of working people," said Reg. He and Veronica had been in the village since before dawn, he said. The blacksmith had been kicked in the head while shoeing a big, hot-tempered colt, and had been lingering, untended by anyone but his wife, for three days before silently slipping away in the night. The weather was so cold that they could find no one to dig the grave, and so Reg had done it himself, with Veronica managing the tools. "And don't anyone be speaking ill of the dog, either," he added. "I'd rather eat with Toby than with many a rich man."

Alice simpered and snuggled her mutt, Veronica shook her head, and Ann, pouring the ale, said, "I recall a certain young lady who sneaked kittens in from the stable inside her bodice during the winter months." Veronica was forced to smile and duck her head. Alice, in silent triumph, doled out scraps of crust to Toby.

Catherine and Reg sat at the same time, Catherine saying, "Have you heard the news then?"

"They've been singing it out all over the village. I thought the old gal'd see us all into the ground," said Reg.

Catherine burst out a wicked grunt of laughter, then bit her cheek. "Your wife's just been scolding Alice for a loose tongue, Reg. It's not to be joked of. Death, I mean."

"No, it's not. I've seen enough of it for this morning. But I thought you'd be happier than anyone to see her go, and I don't care who hears me say it," said Reg. He reached for the bread, elbowing Toby's nose aside. "She was no friend to you, Catherine, if you'll pardon my saying so, even after all you did to help her get a child to stay in her."

"No. But she was the queen." Catherine put a chunk of white cheese into her mouth, and it tasted like a slab of chalk. She hadn't helped Mary at all, and she'd grown sick of the endless false hopes of a baby. She'd even held nightshade over Mary's cup twice, and it was only the coward in her that had kept her from dropping it in. She'd finally left Mary's service, and Mary had, as a fine favour, taken her big house away from her and suspended most of her court allowance in return. "I didn't expect her to die so soon."

"That husband of hers probably did her in," continued Reg. "Grief. And never having a child."

"Is that why she died?" asked Alice. "Truly, can a woman die because of a bad husband and not having children?"

"Some can, I suppose," said Catherine, "but it is the grief and shame that takes their lives, not the lack of a child. Think of your sister Diana. She has no husband or child, and she seems content."

"Well, she is no queen, and Diana has always been a solitary sort, at least since I've known her," said Veronica.

"A queen's got to have a child," said Alice.

"Yes," said Catherine.

"But Elizabeth's got no child, either. And she doesn't even have a husband. There will be another rebellion if she can't find one," said Veronica.

Catherine sighed and looked to Ann, who said, "She'll get her one if she wants one. She'll buy herself one."

"Oh," said Alice. "I would rather buy a horse than a husband."

Veronica snorted into her cup of ale. "You'd have a softer ride," she said, and Catherine cut her a sharp look. She muttered a "very sorry," though she clearly wasn't.

Catherine said, "Speaking of Diana, Reg, what do you think of riding with me to London? I need to see her. She will want to come back home now, go with me to find her father."

"You're going after him?" said Reg. "Do you know where he is?"

"The queen," said Ann. "You need to see the queen. Remember?"

"The queen?" said Reg. "I have no need to lay eyes on a queen, but I will go with you to London. Now, for her father, that's a different story. He could be at the far end of the world, for all we know."

"Or he might be within a boat's ride of us," said Catherine, "waiting to be summoned home."

Reg bit into the heel of his bread and gave it a good working over with his jaws before swallowing mightily. "I might enjoy having young Diana with us again She plays the lute like an angel. I want to see how she's faring with these nuns of hers. Ann?"

Ann shook her head. "My old bones enjoy a fire more than a saddle. I will stay with the girls. You two get a couple of the men and go rescue your lady without me. And I will hear all about this queen of yours when you return."

Chapter 3

To London, then. Roads from some dream, easily recalled but hazy and unfamiliar in the present day. Snow and cold mud, the horses' ear-hairs clicking with accumulated ice, Catherine and Reg hunched into their pilgrim wraps and pressing southerly. They had elected to leave the servants at home, Reg certain that he was man enough to guard himself and one woman, and they could ride quickly, far into the dark, and be in the saddles again before dawn. Before a fortnight was out, they approached the city once more.

"West, toward Blackfriars," Catherine said, once they spied the cathedral's blood-hued hulk, brooding under the starry sky. She trusted to her murky memory of Diana's descriptions of her dwelling to carry her far enough to see a sign.

Reg blew his nose, rubbed at his beard, and nodded. "Let's hope they have a stable."

Once in front of the old monastery, though, Catherine had to admit that she was no longer certain of her way. London menaced her. No longer the city she recalled in fond, mostly fantastical, memory, and now not one she wanted to be lost in. They stopped at a familiar-looking tavern for directions. The horses, at least, had luck of it, as the keeper had room for them with his own animals, and plenty of hay, for a price. "I could do with some of that myself, if I don't get some meat into me," said Catherine, and Reg laughed, for the first time since they had set out. Fortune favoured the human creatures of God, as well, because the tavernkeeper's wife said that the house in which Diana lived was almost within jumping distance. So Catherine's mind hadn't deserted her completely, after all. The tavernkeeper sent a serving girl to fetch Diana, if she was available, and Catherine collapsed onto a bench.

"I will eat before we visit, if you don't mind," said Reg. "And drink, too, with my feet in the fire if they'll let me."

Catherine agreed, and they were provided with a table inside the glowing circle cast by the hearth. Heaven seemed to be smiling on them, indeed. Hot stew was placed before them, and fresh butter for the bread. Then the oak door squealed open, and Catherine saw a face. The person was walking toward her, fast, and pushing back her thick hood. Catherine stood. It was. It was her stepdaughter, Diana, waving at Catherine, calling her name and then folding her into her wool-winged arms. It boded well for her quests.

"We have just this minute arrived here, to seek you out," said Catherine. She wanted to push back Diana's cap and feel her hair, but Diana would never allow that. She satisfied herself with cupping the younger woman's face between her hands. "You look well."

"You look well," Diana said. "I thought I was having a fit, or a dream, when the girl told me who'd arrived, but here you are. You looked nigh-frozen, and I thought I had better see if it was truly you, and get you to a fire. But you have discovered one already."

"We couldn't see our fingers before our faces for weariness," said Catherine. "Sit with us."

Diana Davies sat, though so daintily that her buttocks barely seemed to skim the wooden bench. She was dressed all in grey, and with her winter-pinked face looked like a mourning dove. "I am glad to see you, Mother. England will not be our friend any longer, you know. Nor yours, perhaps. I think the Catholics will burn again."

"As the Protestants did under Mary. But I may find a better friend in this queen than in her sister. I mean to prevail on her to let your father come home."

Diana nodded. "We have decided to go somewhere over the sea."

"We?" said Catherine. "Who? Away from England?"

"Yes," said Diana. She waved, and a man who had been standing outside by the window entered the tavern. "This is Father Andrew. He has been my priest for more than a year now. He has got us passports and will accompany us. We have two more sisters who want to travel with us. Come in, Father, just for a moment. We will not stay long."

Father Andrew, in his priest's plain garb, reminded Catherine so much of her own, dead father that her vision splintered, like a pane of stained glass, and she closed her eyes.

"Mother?" said Diana. "Are you sick?"

Catherine opened her eyes and saw only the face of her stepdaughter before her. From Diana's eyes radiated thready, nervous wrinkles, which Catherine had never noted before.

The priest bowed but did not sit. "It was God's work that these women have been doing, and we mean to continue in our ways."

"Yes, God," said Catherine absently. Then she twisted her hand into her stepdaughter's. "But, Diana, why all the way over the sea to do God's work?"

Diana untangled herself and settled out of reach. "This new queen, of course. Elizabeth. She will not be a friend to the true religion, as I said. You know this. We cannot trust her. We mean to be nuns, in the old tradition, and we will be forced to bow to the English church if we remain. We will not endure another change. We cannot. So we are going. We will be nuns in fact."

"Where?"

The priest said, "We mean to go almost to Rome. I have already sent ahead for our arrangements to be made."

Catherine felt a twitch in her breast, a longing tug at the back of her tongue to say she would go, too. A convent near Rome. But then Diana grabbed at her old-fashioned hood, pulling it snug over her hair. She looked frightened at the simple, warm room in which they sat.

Reg was appraising the priest. "Is this your doing? Do you know what you're doing, carrying English women all the way to Rome? You say you've got passports to go?"

"This is my decision," said Diana. "I am leaving this place. It is ruined now, and there is nothing for me here. We will go, passports or no."

"And what about your father?" said Catherine. "We don't even know where he is. It may be a long journey. I came to bring you home so that we can seek him out together."

"This is my father now," said Diana, indicating the priest. "If my father had wanted to know me, he could have written me a letter. Even one. In all these years." She blinked, but though her eyes brightened, no tears followed. "He wrote you at least once or twice, didn't he?"

Catherine nodded. "Not for years now, though."

"But me? His own daughter? His elder child? Never. Not one. It's as though he forgot us, because of Mary Tudor. I am no queen, but I was still his daughter. You were his wife." Diana's words had gathered heat, and Catherine leaned forward to touch her arm. Diana retreated further. "Do not apologize for him, Mother. He knows which end of a pen to use, wherever he is. He has known where we are. At least he's known where you are."

"I cannot make excuse for your father," said Catherine. "But I don't know what his circumstances are."

"Let us leave this vile place," said the priest. "It's nothing but sinners. To breathe the very air is a transgression."

Diana stood. "Come with me, to our house. There's room enough, and you can meet the others. You, too, Reg. You can lodge with Father Andrew."

Reg's face soured a little at this particular welcome. "I will have to see if the tavern can stable the horses."

"There's a stable behind our house," said Diana.

Reg rearranged his face into a smile. "Well, then, I suppose I will pay our reckoning and fetch them over."

The priest said, with a waft of patient sanctity, that he would wait for Reg, and Catherine walked with Diana over the road and down a few doors to a narrow, self-effacing house that leaned against its neighbor's shoulder. "Are you sure there is enough room?" said Catherine.

"Enough for anyone," said Diana.

They did enter a large enough eating room. Two women sat at table and rose when they came in. Diana said, "This is my stepmother, Catherine. She has come at a sorry time of the year, but here she is. Mother, these are the sisters of whom I spoke, who will go with us. This is Mary Jones, of Wales, and Mary Smythe, of Cornwall." The pair lowered themselves again, side by side, and Catherine fancied that they must be sisters of a closer kin than a nunnery. She remembered the twin Marys of her own convent, Mary Margaret and Mary Frances, from when she was a girl, and laughed aloud.

"What's the joke?" said Diana.

"Nothing," said Catherine. "A silly memory cast up by my weariness, that's all."

The present Marys were whispering to each other. Catherine took the bench across from them and tried out a pleasantry. "Tell me about yourselves."

Mary of Wales leaned forward and everyone scooted closer to the table. "We will be nuns, and that is all there is to us. Diana has told us that you were once in the convent. England has left us. There is no hope anymore of the return of the true religion. This place will burn with its evil. It will sink into the sea with the weight of its offences."

The other Mary added, "And the daughter of the Boleyn sits on the throne. A whore queen from a whore mother. No. That can't be borne."

Catherine said, "A woman cannot choose her mother."

"No matter," said Diana. She sat at Catherine's side. "She has that woman's blood in her, and blood will out. She will be the heretic her mother was, and we cannot abide bowing to a heretic. Not again. Not this one."

Catherine saw the fine wrinkles around the mouths of the Marys in the light of the candles. They were older than Diana, probably already on the fading side of thirty-five. But they were all too young to have taken vows during the old times of the Church. "You were never nuns before."

"We were raised by women who had been," said Mary of Wales. "Our own mother put us out to service when we were barely able to walk." Ah, so they were indeed blood kin. "Happily, the house had also taken three former sisters, and they raised us as their own. We have heard the stories. We know what heretics do to true women of God."

"Let our talk be of the future," said Catherine, forcing a bright note into her speech. "Perhaps the world will smile on this new queen."

"She is the daughter of the Boleyn," said Mary Smythe of Cornwall again. "Heretic daughter of a heretic mother. A whore. Whore of Babylon. She has bad blood and she will turn God against the English again. She will enflame the entire people. Our future is elsewhere."

Reg and Andrew came in, then, and Catherine said, "Can I fetch us more ale?"

"Through there. The kitchen," said Diana. "Many thanks."

Catherine went, and behind her came Reg. She almost dropped the fragile vessel as she filled it. "I think Diana has lost her wits," she whispered. "Those others are almost mad with hatred of Elizabeth."

"That Andrew has got a fire lit in him, that is truth," said Reg. He took the jug. "I don't think you'll persuade her to return with us."

"I'll send to the court tomorrow. If Diana knows that her father can come home, it may change her mind." They rejoined the others, who were in prayer at the table. Catherine waited until they raised their heads. "I am sorry to speak her name again, but I must petition Elizabeth for a passport. Where can I send a query?"

Diana said, "You could send to Hatfield. She may still be there. She has her people everywhere."

"Her spies," said Mary of Cornwall.

"Can someone carry a letter for me?" asked Catherine.

"We have a boy," said Andrew. "Send to Whitehall."

Catherine located the message, now bedraggled, wet, and sorry-looking, in her pocket and passed it over. "I think I will retire, if you can show me my room. It has been a long road."

Diana took her up a strait, dark staircase to a tall, dark door, and opened it onto a cramped, dank room. The narrow bed occupied almost an entire wall. A haphazard pile of books bowed toward the opposite wall, and the volumes seemed in danger of toppling into the middle of the straw mattress. "This is where I stay," said Diana. "You may share with me."

Catherine nodded, the tongue swollen in her mouth from grief. Diana had always been a tidy mouse of a girl, but this room could barely contain the two of them standing. A poor nun's closet. "That bed will not hold both of us," she said. "You see how I have spread in my old age."

"I will make a pallet for myself on the floor. I have done so before, for guests. It does my soul good to mortify the flesh."

Catherine wanted to demur, but her bones itched for rest, and she thanked her stepdaughter. But, after Diana left the room, she lay a long while awake. Begging a favour of Elizabeth Tudor. The reversal of fortunes bit at her heart—she had once been among the women the child pressed for affection and approval. Now the girl was the queen, and Catherine felt her declining years settling upon her like a sodden mantle.

And, lo. It was morning again, late morning, and Catherine had slept, deep and dreamlessly. Diana was nowhere to be seen, and the pallet, if she had made one, had been rolled away, out of sight. And there, an answer to Catherine's request by the early afternoon, when Catherine had barely gotten her clothes on her back and some bread in her belly. It was carried in by a bored young man who sniffed like a hound who'd found the shrubberies unworthy of his inspection. He tossed the message down and left immediately. But the letter was not from Elizabeth Tudor. It was signed by someone whose name Catherine could not decipher. The letter itself was brief and the script differed halfway through, so it had clearly been written by a lesser scribe, who'd probably passed it on to someone even lower than he was. Catherine wondered briefly who had really signed it, but no matter. She had her passport. She was free to travel abroad. The writer, almost as an afterthought, had added at the bottom of the paper that any lands made confiscate to the Crown would remain with the queen. It said nothing about whether she could bring her men back to England. Catherine was wished well and the missive was signed with a fiddly embellishment that looked absent-mindedly self-important.

Catherine turned the paper over, but there was nothing more. Well. She could go, at least, without fear of punishment. Diana would surely want to come, too, since the permission hadn't been given expressly by the queen. They could find her a convent, if that was what her heart yearned so deeply for. She waited, grateful at the solitude of the empty house and wondering at her disinclination to seek out her stepdaughter.

Reg returned just as Catherine had finished her scraps of evening meal by herself in the kitchen. Diana, with the Marys, entered the house briefly and offered up some prayers together, and Reg beckoned Catherine to stay as they departed again. Reg said, "I've been to the taverns we used to know. I threw the name Benjamin Davies around and got me a few bites. One man said that he went to Calais, but he left there a long time ago, before the fighting even began. Some said it was years back. I asked where he'd gone, and then I got little more than some glances to the right and left of me."

"No one would say anything? Even to you?" asked Catherine.

"They said bits and pieces," said Reg. "One man said he'd heard a report of a man like Benjamin living in Rome for a while, but another man said no, there was nothing for a wool trader from England to do in Rome. He said he'd gone to the Lisbon ports and was making his fortune there."

"Lisbon!" said Catherine. "It's almost to the end of the world! Why so far?"

"Nobody would confirm anything, yes or no," said Reg. "Someone said that there was work on ships and that he went for a sailor."

"Benjamin a sailor? I can't imagine it," said Catherine.

"Nor me, neither," agreed Reg. "He always liked the feel of solid ground under his feet."

"He might have hired on as a farmer," said Catherine. She tried to piece together the image in her mind. Benjamin was probably still strong enough, even in his sixtieth decade of life. He'd always had a thick back. But the picture broke apart and fell away. "The disgrace of it," she said. "No. He would aim to work his own land."

"If there's land to be had," said Reg. "Don't know if he could raise enough capital to buy. He would want to buy."

"And no one would discuss it further?" asked Catherine.

"I saw some dark looks thrown about," said Reg. "I said, 'What do you know of the man?' but no one would answer me straight. They'd just say 'Well, there's work for such as want to work,' or some nonsense. One man said to me that he'd leave it be, if it was his own master, and let the devil take him. But I didn't know him and he didn't know me. He looked like a drunkard."

Catherine rested her chin on her hand. "I have a message from the court, or someone who claims to speak for the queen. I think I am free to go find him."

"You will see Elizabeth now?"

Catherine shook her head and dug the letter from her pocket. "I have not been invited."

"This does not sound friendly," said Reg, skimming the message. "But it is not a refusal."

"Let's leave this place. I will speak to Diana when she is free of these two spectres and persuade her to come. She doesn't own much to carry. Then we will say our good-byes and one journey will be ended."

WORLDS END

"And another must begin," said Reg.

Chapter 4

They stayed three days, Reg trailing through old haunts seeking out any news of Benjamin and Catherine wandering the old streets with Diana. On the last day, they stopped in front of a church, and Catherine found herself unable to say exactly where they were. Diana halted at the door, and Catherine gazed upward, at the eye of the diminutive rose window at the front. She could not move away. Her chest thumped and her ears tolled softly. She could faint, crumple into genuflection right here on the street. Diana's voice beside her said, "It holds you?"

Catherine said, "Yes. It's small, but how it stares upon me."

"Maybe it tells you something," said Diana.

"I want you to come home. Then go with me to find your father."

"Mm," said Diana. "I know. But maybe you shouldn't go, either. Perhaps God wants you to go somewhere else."

"I will go to your father. But, standing here, I feel afraid. I don't understand why."

"We're all afraid," said Diana. "Put your trust in God."

"I've always trusted God. It's my duty to go and find my husband. I have thought on this for years."

Well, then, go you will. But prepare yourself for what you may find."

"What do you mean?"

"I don't mean any one thing. I just say what I think. It doesn't matter. No one considers my words anyway."

Catherine turned to look at the young woman's face, to see if she observed a prophet's light there, but Diana was already walking away from her, into the porch. And still the great eye held her, and Catherine feared that it might, mystically, close and she would fail in all of her quests. Or that it was, in fact, an unseeing eye and she was staring into emptiness. She followed Diana, but stopped again at the threshold.

Diana was waiting, and she turned. "You grow old," she said. "Come, you need God, not a journey to who-knows-where. If you must leave England, leave with us." She held out her right hand.

"You won't go with me to find him? You're in earnest?" said Catherine.

Diana dropped the hand. "I will not. Not to seek Benjamin Davies."

Catherine thought she heard singing inside and hesitated. She longed to hear it closer. Standing here with the cold sunshine on her back, with the scent of winter fresh in the air and a translucent half-moon hanging like a smiling old friend in the sky, she felt herself pulled back to childhood. She set one foot inside the door, and the dark interior drew her forward. The singing ceased, and she seemed to hear a prayer. The voices struck her ears in a strange cadence of downward tones, a low harmony. The voices were men's. It was almost a chant, almost another song.

Catherine was tugged by the tow-line of Diana's devotion. "Will I never clap eyes on you again?" she said. "I'll carry a letter to your father if you'll take the time to write it."

"My Father is here," said Diana. "Andrew will be my father on this earth."

"I will see you in heaven then," said Catherine.

Diana murmured, or hummed a note. "Only the godly will see the kingdom of heaven. The Protestants are heretics, and we have done our best to bring them home to the true God. Now they will have their Elizabeth, and we must shake the dust of the past from our soles and go on. That includes Benjamin Davies. I thought you knew, Catherine."

The name stung. Diana had been in the habit of calling Catherine "Mother" for years. "I understand, Diana. But we've meant a great deal to each other, you and I. We've been a family."

"Our Lord asked, 'Who is my mother?" said Diana. "And "where is my mother?'" She gestured behind her. "My family must be with the other nuns, and we must live in the sight of all that is good."

"And will you remain sequestered then, all of your days? You're a young woman yet."

"Old enough to know my mind," said Diana. "I can't be hemmed in with God surrounding me. My cell will be the world, and my robes will be my home."

"Very well," said Catherine. "God be with you, then, Diana."

"God is always with me. May He shine a light on you and bring you back to Him. And may He guard you in this journey of yours, if you insist upon making it. May its end find you in a holy place." She pivoted and walked back into the sunshine, Catherine trailing behind.

That night, Catherine said to Reg, "We must leave in the morning. I've failed."

"I've found nothing more to help us. I'm ready," he said.

And the next day, before the sunlight had hooked its claws into the housetops, they were on their horses. Diana stood in the doorway, pinioned by the two Marys, in front of her featureless house and waved a good-bye. She was dressed in her usual sober grey, her face invisible except for a pink chin-point and a tightly-clamped mouth, inside the heavy hood, and the Marys were a couple of attending crows in abstemious black.

Catherine said, one more time, "Are you certain that this is your path?"

"I am," said Diana. "And I will pray for you as you follow yours." And with that, Diana stepped back, into the house. The Marys followed and shut the door.

Catherine almost leapt from her horse to follow, but her elbow was seized. She pulled from the pressure, but the hand held on, and she turned. Reg said, "We must be on our way."

They turned their horses northward and were gone from the city of London before the sun reached its feeble zenith.

The ride home loosened Reg's thoughts, and his talk was all of the Lisbon ports and how best to get there. Of boats and the sea, of sailors and their complicated ways and superstitions. Catherine had never heard so much talk about rigging and hulls and suns in the mornings and she didn't know the source of Reg's knowledge, so she pointed her nose toward Yorkshire and let the words colour the grey chambers of her mind's eye. And by the time they knew their own roads again, she had fallen under his spell and become chatty, wondering how long the journey might take and what the look on Benjamin's face might be when they found him.

And so, days later, when they turned into their own front courtyard, Catherine's imagination was brightened anew by her hopes, and the grisaille tones of Diana's life and her impenetrable mood had faded. Ann and the girls were at their sides before the horses had stopped, asking about the queen and the city, and she was on familiar ground once more, throwing her reins to her groomsman and shaking them off until they promised to feed her before she fainted of hunger.

So, at dinner, all the news. She would begin again. First, Catherine would write a letter, this time bound for Lisbon, to tell her husband that she was on her way to bring him home to England. Her husband's banishment was almost at an end, anyway, and he would be on fire to see her again. The queen was dead. Let her pronouncements die with her.

Second. She would commence the expansion of the house. She could almost see, from her new roof, the old, grand one that Mary Tudor had seized to pay for her disasters in Calais. It had then been handed over to some fop of a hanger-on who'd never been bothered to live in it. The last time Catherine had ridden that way, she'd been astonished to find the walls already stripped at the corners and doors, almost the entire south side gone. The great Overton house looked like a great grey sheep, partly shorn on the one side. Those bits of wall were probably propping up someone's cow shed. She could push out the back wall of her own house and add some rooms. She'd take some of the stones herself to do it. Why not? Every farmer and his dog had done the same. No one would stop her.

The family chattered around her, and Catherine fell into private reflection. Diana had not receded entirely from her thoughts, and she had to admit that there was much to be said for the state of respectable widowhood. Everyone here in Yorkshire seemed to have forgotten that she'd ever had a man called Benjamin Davies. But she had. No. Diana was wrong. She would escort him back in a noble style. She might even drive him past a palace or two.

It had flitted through her mind now and then, though she had never given voice to it, that perhaps she was a widow in fact. Perhaps Benjamin lay dead in the earth somewhere that she would never find, and she would wander as hopelessly as a wayfarer without a map, wondering endlessly if he were in the next town. But surely someone, one of the other wool merchants or a new drinking companion, would have known of Catherine, waiting in Yorkshire for him, and would have written to her.

"Catherine. Catherine!" Ann was holding out her mug for the ale.

Catherine said, "Forgive me. My head is splitting from the ride."

Ann said, "How many will you take with you on this venture of yours? And how many rooms do you aim to build?"

"As many as I need, to answer both of your questions."

"I must go," said Veronica. "You'll need a younger woman by your side."

"If she's allowed to go, then I will, as well," said Alice. "And Toby. He hasn't seen much of the world."

"You'll need men," said Reg. "I'll figure who can be spared from here to accompany me."

"Ann, you must come. Of course," said Catherine.

"You don't think that I want to go all the way across the world, do you?" said Ann.

"You'll stay here, on your own?" said Reg.

"I'm not alone. I'll have an entire household at my beck and call."

"You should go. We should go," said Reg. "Catherine will need our advice."

"My advice is that we stay home and wait to hear news," said Ann. "That's what I intend to do."

"I'm too tired to eat any more," said Catherine. "We'll make our plans in the morning."

But upstairs, Catherine stood between two candles and regarded herself in her biggest looking glass. She rubbed her throat, stretching the lax, grooved skin upward. Her eyes had faded from the fresh green of youth to almost grey. And her hair was grey in fact. She looked like fog, she thought. But past forty years of age, it was nothing but vanity to worry about wrinkles, and she let her skin drop. Benjamin loved her. And he was older, too. He'd probably say she'd aged in the court of Mary Tudor, and she would be able to agree. It would be a joke between them.

They would laugh, husband and wife once more. The queen was dead. Long live the queen. She blew out the lights and fell into her own, broad bed.

Chapter 5

The next morning, Catherine jangled awake, thinking that she was still in London. She sat up and let her eyes bring her mind back to Yorkshire. Downstairs, someone was opening the big front door, and she lumbered in her nightdress to the window and pushed back the curtain. The sky held the green cast of approaching storm. A brown horse, barely fastened to a boy by a slender tether, fretted out in the yard. The animal stamped and snorted, and the boy led it around in a circle. A sullen mule hunkered at the gate. The horse was magnificent, a stallion. The horse of a man with some wealth. Catherine could see its breath mingle with the boy's as they danced. Had he come from the queen?

"Madam?"

Catherine turned. Her maid perched on the threshold, the melting snow a lace mantle on her shoulders. Her skirt was tattered at the hem. Catherine should order her a new dress made. New dresses for all of the maids. Why not? It wouldn't do to have everyone looking like shabby old cats when Benjamin walked in.

"Who is that, outside?" Catherine said.

Ann came in behind the maid. "A messenger has stopped outside."

"He has a lovely horse for a messenger."

"So he does," Ann said. She put her hand on the maid's arm. "You go down and see that they are fed. He says he has a letter for you. Maybe Elizabeth has decided not to snub you, after all."

"Help me get dressed," said Catherine, and together they flung some clothes over her and slapped her hair up. "I didn't think of it precisely as a snub."

"But it was," said Ann.

"She's surrounded by petitioners. She doesn't have time to write letters."

"If you say so," said Ann.

"Who else would send a man in this terrible cold? And on such a beautiful horse? It looks almost carved of wood."

Ann snorted gently as they went out. "A Trojan horse?"

The man himself was already sitting at the big table in the dining hall, rubbing his red knuckles together and blowing on them, as everyone did this time of the year. Catherine said, "Forgive our country manners. This weather has driven us all to our hearths. Please, tell the queen—"

"The queen?" said the man. He was aflame around the nose and his blue eyes ran with the rheum of someone who lived his waking hours out of doors. "The queen is dead, and the new one is a girl, busy with her glass and her new clothes. I reckon she'd better get herself covered with a man quick."

Catherine stepped backward. "Where have you come from?"

"I've come from my own land, and I wish I had stayed there. Business in winter. I'm too old for it. But I have a letter here for—" he retrieved an envelope from inside his coat—"a Catherine Overton of Yorkshire. You she?"

"I am," said Catherine, though her living husband was named Davies. It wouldn't be from Benjamin. The message was greasy and battered, and the seal was an indecipherable smear of wax. Not from Elizabeth, either, obviously. She tore it open.

"Mother," it began, "I cannot travel, but I must see you. England is an unfriendly place. Come to me at Wittenberg if you will. I have something for you. I will not go there. Your Son."

Catherine thumped onto a bench, sick in head and gut. She felt as though someone had dashed cold water over her heart. She could not see when it had been written, or sent, if that dark smudge in the corner was in fact a date. "This is all?"

"That's what I was given, and that's what I've delivered, at no profit to myself."

"Who gave it to you?"

"Man on a boat. On the boat I was on. I was coming north for trade and he shoved it in my hand. This is no time of year for seafaring, I can tell you that. Or for trading. Wish I'd stayed in the south."

Ann said, "Give him something to eat, Maddie," and the kitchen girl heaped some yellow cheese and bread onto a plate and shoved it between his elbows. The man fell to, and Ann nodded toward the ale jug. Maddie dutifully poured a mug and slid it toward the plate.

Catherine dragged Ann out of the room and read her the message. "What do you make of this?"

Ann said, "I think if you want to find out, you'll have to go to Wittenberg."

And so, begin again. Not Lisbon after all, not now, but Wittenberg. Catherine could not see her way forward, and after the messenger had gone, she called up the family.

"Wittenberg?" said Alice, offering a piece of the cheese to her dog and wiping his whiskers with a linen napkin. "Where's that? And what about my father?"

"Wittenberg is in Saxony, I think," said Catherine. "Far across the German lands."

Reg nodded.

"Your father will have to wait. This letter, from your brother," said Catherine, "it seems urgent. He should be the first one we fetch."

"But he's banished. Forever," said Veronica.

"Forever may only be as long as a queen's life," said Reg. "Shall we go see to this thing he has for you, then? It's a shorter journey, though you'll have to wait for spring thaw."

Alice said, "Why go at all? Let my brother read about the queen on a lamppost and send whatever he's got in a package for Twelfth Night. He should be right sorry, for the way he's treated us. Let him be the one who begs permission to set foot back in England. And my father, too."

Veronica said, "Alice! Who's put such a bitter tongue in your head? A girl should remember her father, at least, with respect." She picked at a fallen piece of bread and rolled the fragment into grubby dough between her fingers. "Those that have fathers, anyway." Veronica's own father was long dead, but she'd treated her stepfather as a suitable replacement, at least before he left England. She glanced up. "But she's right. How long has it been since we've had a letter from your husband, Mother?"

Catherine said, "Three years?" Had it been four?

"Longer than that," said Veronica. Alice nodded and started to speak, but Veronica stopped her. "But I'm with Alice about Robbie. He can go to the devil for all I care. We're for Lisbon."

Now it was Reg's turn to admonish. "Don't speak of your brother that way. We don't know his circumstances."

"I don't care," said Alice.

"Nor do I," agreed Veronica.

Ann said, "That's enough, girls."

"We aren't girls," they both said at the same time.

Ann said, "Enough of all of this. I don't want to go anywhere, and I am sick to my death of hearing about it.

Now eat, all of you, before I feed the whole lot to that dog. You don't see him wasting his breath while there's meat on the table." Toby wagged in agreement, and Ann offered him a sliver of cold pork. She dipped a chunk of bread into the butter and gave him that, too.

Catherine pushed back from the table. "If I were a man, you would all expect me to pack up and be gone tomorrow. If I were a man, I'd carry letters across the world and eat at strange tables and have people doff their hats at me for doing it. If none of you will go with me, then I'll travel to Wittenberg by myself. I've never been over the sea, and I've got my passport."

"I'll go," said Veronica, "if you must undertake it."

"And I," said Alice. "That's flat. I'm too young to manage this estate by myself."

"And I," said Reg. "You must have a man beside you. Ann will come, as well, won't you, wife?"

Ann said, "How many times must I say it? You should all stay home, the men and the women alike. I've no wish to put my old haunches into a saddle or onto some flimsy boat. The holiday is nigh upon us. And it's too cold. You can't go anywhere before spring. I have nothing more to say on the matter."

And Ann was right about that. The holiday came and went, with the regular rounds of singing and gifts and feasting. They heard no court gossip in their remote village, and no one seemed to notice. The servants enjoyed a few days free from labour, having stocked the woodpiles in the waning days, and Catherine packed and unpacked or figured at her ledgers while the girls sewed and told tales about the confusions at the church, where neither priest nor parishioners seemed to know how they were to conduct the service now.

In January, Catherine sent a gift to the new queen: a long linen cloth embroidered in bright silks by her daughters. She'd ordered some gold thread for the embellishments, which Ann sewed on, to be sure that they were fine enough. She oversaw the stores of food and wine, even turning the heaps of cabbages and carrots herself while the maids forked new straw between the layers to prevent rot. Beer was ordered, and bread was baked. The cold would not relent, and the sun struggled to push its face through the clouds, which lay across the sky like doves' feathers.

Not a word more came from Robbie Overton, and nothing at all from Benjamin Davies. Not a line, not a message. The coronation of Elizabeth Tudor in London came and went, followed by the expected rumble of resentment against women who sat upon thrones and dared to dictate law to men. Catherine agonized and studied the skies, growing colder and snowier and the sun unwilling to budge from behind its veil.

She fussed all one day with a sheep who'd lambed early and came into her kitchen soaked through with urine and blood. She'd ruint her skirt, and the twin lambs, in a wooden crate in a corner of the kitchen, looked scrawny and half-dead. Alice was set to nursing them, but Catherine would have to do the nighttime feedings herself. They were speckled runts, both of them, but Alice was convinced that she could save them. The ewe, exhausted and torn, was barely grown herself and should never have been let into the lot with the ram last summer. The shepherd was shamefaced at the sight of the newborns, so downcast that Catherine had not had the heart to let him go.

"Every day is too long," she said to Ann, coming back to the kitchen in fresh clothes. "I can't spend the entire year minding sheep while my family waits for me."

"You can leave all of this for the glories of Wittenberg soon enough," said Ann. She spread her hands to the fire in the south wall of the kitchen.

"Robbie's waiting for me, and I want to see how his face changes when he learns that we have a Protestant queen again," said Catherine. She folded the skirt for cleaning. It could go into the scrap-basket afterward. "If Robbie has something to give me, why didn't he simply include it with the letter? Or at least tell me what it is."

Ann threw a couple of thin logs onto the fire and resumed her hand-warming. "Maybe it's something of value, something he didn't want to write down for anyone to see." Reg came in from the back, holding aloft a makeshift udder that he'd crafted out of some thin leather. He'd milked the ewe himself and held his finger over the hole.

"Value?" Catherine threw her arms out on either side of her. The scent of sheep-dung and old straw wafted from her. "How could it be anything of value?"

"I wouldn't say it's of value to anyone, except to those there," said Reg, indicating the lambs.

"We were talking about Robbie," said Ann, "not your udder. Whatever he has for Catherine."

Catherine continued, "The only thing worth anything that he's ever owned is land. And that's gone. Why doesn't he come home to beg it back? God knows he's wasted enough time and blood defending what he thinks is his." The bitterness stung her mouth with guilt. He was her son. She should feel more charity. But it was cold, and she was tired and, to be honest, disappointed in him. So many times she'd been disappointed with Robbie and had bitten it back. She was tired all the way into her bones. "Why doesn't he want to come home to see me and his sisters?"

Ann regarded the flames, and adjusted the lay of the logs with an iron poker as Reg held the bag out. Milk spurted from the hole. The wood in the fireplace sighed and settled, releasing a rush of sparks. They breathed out a new wave of heat, and Catherine enjoyed it for a few moments. A tiny, whining bleat, pitched high as a child's cry, reached them from the corner, and Alice said, "They won't take anything. It just runs down their noses." She'd been using an old clout dipped in the ewe's milk.

"Try this," said Reg. He held out the bag for her. "Make sure the hole goes inside of their mouths." As he bent to the crate, he turned and said, "What he's got can't be sent? If I were a wagering man, I'd say he wants you to come and fetch him home. Only thing that makes sense. He may be too embarrassed to say so. He always had too much pride. So we'll go." Then he said to Alice, "I'll hold 'em and you squirt this down their throats."

Catherine looked at Ann and laughed. The mirth shot through her, and she doubled over giggling like a girl.

"Catherine?" said Ann.

"I'm an idiot," said Catherine. She sat on the rug and wiped her face with her skirt. It was clean, but her underclothes still stank of sheep. Her hands smelt like wool, and she pressed them against her face and inhaled. "Reg is right. It's a ruse to get his mother to come to him. And here we stand, discussing these runts. We need to be on the road."

"Someone must care for the runts in the world," said Ann. "And you're not standing. You're sitting."

"So I am," said Catherine.

"If no one cared for the runts, we wouldn't have Elizabeth for a queen, and then where would we be?"

"Where indeed?" Catherine said. "We'd have the Scottish queen, maybe."

"That would please a few," said Ann, "and enrage more. I don't think your son will come home as long as we have a queen without a king. And I don't think he's clever enough to think of trying to trick you into coming to see him. But I think Reg has it when he says that Robbie wants you to have something that can't be sent on its own."

Catherine tried to picture Robbie, but what she saw was a child, then an angry young man, refusing to wave good-bye to her as he walked away. "Then what could it be? He's never owned anything. And what about Benjamin? Why doesn't he write?"

"I don't know," said Ann.

"If he were dead," Catherine blurted, unable to hold the thought in, "someone would have gotten word to me."

"If you say so," said Ann.

Alice stood, holding the bag in one hand and a flap of skin in the other. "The nipple part ripped," she said. The flap, held up, showed where the hole had given way. It was torn down one side.

"I'll fetch another piece of skin and make you another," said Reg. "They got some in their bellies before it tore. That's the important thing."

"They've eaten their fill," said Alice. Her face was lit with triumph. "Reg made them do it. They're going to live. May I have them? I'm calling them Snow and Icicle, because they've got white on their noses. Snow's got a big spot right here"—Alice touched her nose—"and Icicle's got a stripe between her eyes. They're asleep now."

Catherine looked at her younger daughter. She was always soft-hearted with animals, but people had to earn her trust. Toby, the ratty dog, had planted himself between her feet and put his head on his paws. "If they live, they'll be yours. But you mustn't breed them as young as their mother."

"Never!" said Alice. "They'll decide for themselves if they ever even speak to those dirty old rams."

Ann guffawed. Catherine said, "Very well, then. I'll feed them through the night."

"Wake me if they cry?" said Alice.

"Yes. Now off you go."

Alice, never a lover of the night, trudged off to her bed, and Ann said, "You're engaged now. You can't go anywhere until those lambs die or eat hay."

"They'll eat before Epiphany," Catherine said. "And then we are away."

"We?" said Ann. "No, Catherine, not this old woman. My place is here by the fire. You go on and tell me about your adventures when you return."

"But you must," said Catherine. "I can't do without you, not on such a long journey. I need your wisdom, Ann. I always have."

"You're playing upon my pride," said Ann.

"Perhaps I am. Is it working? I'm begging you," said Catherine.

"Those lambs are barely in the world," said Ann, "and more will follow."

"And they will thrive, here at home," said Catherine. "But you and I? We are going to Wittenberg."

Chapter 6

And so, a new quest, all swagger and purpose. There would be no disappointment. The house and the fields were in perfect, almost holy, order. Catherine had money in her purse and three live children. Other women lived in chaos and poverty. Other women had husbands at home, but they were brutal or cruel. Other women had sons who had slipped away and never were heard from again. Other women's children had died. God would be with her, and Ann would be, as well.

"Pack your things, girls," Catherine said to her daughters. And to Reg: "Choose the best of the servants. We need at least two with us."

They lost another early lamb, a big one. The men butchered it within minutes and covered Alice's two runts with the fresh skin to fool the grieving ewe. One after the other was pushed toward the wary mother, but she finally accepted both as her own, and they were released from their kitchen pen into the fold. Alice watched with satisfaction as they frolicked off, tails waggling and heels kicking up, and declared that they were still hers. The young mother who had lost them originally, now recovered enough to be outdoors, showed no sign of jealousy or regret, and joined the flock to sniff out the new grasses.

Catherine said to Ann, "You see? They are well with the world. And now you must keep your promise and come with me."

Ann said, "I did not promise."

"I think you did."

Ann sighed. "I can't remember. I'm an old woman who's lost her wits long since. I would rather stay home, where I belong. But I won't break a promise to you, whether I made it or not."

So they would go. Over the sea, into the strange lands of the world. This set Catherine's heart into its little jig again and she caught herself, too often, with her thumbnail between her teeth and took to placing her hands, palms down, on whatever table stood nearby to calm herself. The tiny rivers of her blood raised up over the bones of her fingers, and the skin puddled a little around her knuckles. She was younger than Ann, but these were an old woman's hands. Her mother's hands. And yet not without strength. She would succeed.

Catherine sought out her managers, Eleanor and Joseph Adwolfe. They were out in the back together, which was not unusual, in the sheepfold. Eleanor was scolding Joseph for muddying his shoes beyond cleaning, and Joseph, his coat pulled back to expose the damage, was protesting that they were worn beyond use anyway. They looked up when Catherine called from the gate.

"Your sons have done well with the sheep this year. I dare say we'll have a mess of twins when we return," said Catherine.

"You're determined to make this voyage?" asked Eleanor.

"We are," said Catherine.

"It's a long way with no assured outcome," said Eleanor.

"I think nothing in this world is assured," said Catherine. "We will need to take at least two of the men, and your sons' wages will be increased for the added work."

Eleanor nodded and directed her gaze to the open land.

Jack Adwolfe, the eldest of the four Adwolfe sons, waved from the field as he drove a new pair of lambs out with their mother, and Catherine said, "Jack's a good soul. I'll bring a couple more of the women from the village to look after Alice's dogs and cats and to help the kitchen girls."

Alice, behind Catherine, said, "Toby must come with us. That's flat." She dug up a clod of mud with her toe and dispatched it with a flick of her ankle. She watched the flock make way for the newcomers. "I'll carry him myself if I must."

Eleanor came up and twisted Alice's nose. "You and your dogs." To Catherine, she said, "Will Joseph and I be in charge of the books?"

"Yes, if you will," said Catherine. "And a greater share of the profits from the flock. Your boys must begin thinking of beginning their own families."

"A greater share will be most welcome," Eleanor responded. "Yes, that will do. And don't you worry, Alice. I'll feed the dogs and cats with my own hands."

"Very well," agreed Catherine.

Alice said, "When we find my brother, I mean to give him a tongue-lashing that he will not soon forget. In the kindest manner possible, of course."

"Of course," said Catherine.

Finding a couple of new housekeepers from the village of Havenston and speaking with a few servants about their added responsibilities proved to be the easiest of Catherine's tasks. She, along with Reg and Ann, stayed up nights plotting out a course, gathering goods for the trip, and sending letters to book passage on a boat and to inquire about guides when they reached that other, faraway shore. Reg planned to leave out of a port in the east, and Catherine wondered if they would happen upon Diana and her friends. "They'll go by

Gravesend," said Reg, as though meeting with them was reason enough to go another route.

Of the three of them, only Reg had ever been on a sea-going vessel, and he warned the women that it was not like the ferries and barges that they'd ridden on the Thames. Catherine had seen ships, when she sent her husband and son off to their banishment, and in her memory they'd loomed dark and fragile, great rickety contraptions that the first strong breeze would blow to pieces. She dreamt of storms and torn linen, men drowning and being eaten underwater by giant fish, like dogs but with fins instead of paws. She woke more than once clammy and terrified, doubting if she could force herself onto any boat at all. Then she saw the sun's brave face and her breast began its giddy dance again.

Veronica bounded out of her bed every morning and repacked her trunk. She did—or did not—need plenty of stockings. She would—then would not—purchase what she wanted in the cities, after she saw what the ladies there wore. How many hoods would she need? How many pairs of shoes? What if all of her shoes seemed dowdy or old? Perhaps she should take only what she could carry on her feet and exchange them along the way. Maids flew in and out of her bedchamber, carrying things to be mended, cut differently, or washed again.

"You act like a bride," remarked Ann one morning, as Veronica whisked into Catherine's chamber with three pairs of gloves. "Take them all. They'll squeeze into a corner. Or wear them, one on top of the other. It's bound to be cold enough, out there." She gestured vaguely toward the window. "Bring some for me."

"Ann!" said Veronica, tossing them onto the bed. "How can you joke? We can't arrive looking like country mice."

Ann regarded her own plain garments. "I'll be just what I am," she said.

"Don't forget the reason we go," said Catherine. "We are seeking your brother. Unless you are planning to shop for a husband along the way?"

"A foreign husband? No. Never," said Veronica. "I will marry an Englishman, if I marry anyone at all. I won't have a man who aims to drag me to an alien home and lock me up there."

"And yet you want to dress like a foreign woman?" observed Ann.

This set Veronica back on her heels, and she picked up the gloves again. "I'm ready to go, then, I suppose," she said, and left the room.

"Now if only you could prepare me as easily," Catherine said. Her own trunk stood almost empty. She took the pair of stockings that Ann had brought in with her and, folding them, laid them in. "I'm ridden by nightmares, and then I wake and can scarcely breathe. I've never been a pilgrim, Ann, and I don't know what to expect. But I want to see the world."

Ann said, "I never thought to venture past the village gate again in this life."

"But let's take this chance, Ann. We're old. We may never go anywhere again. Let's aim to see what can be seen."

"What if we appear to Robbie so different that he doesn't know us? I don't want to shame him by looking like—what did Veronica say?—a country mouse. Though that's exactly what I am."

"You're no mouse and you never have been, Ann Smith." She picked up a handful of stockings and threw them aside. "I'm sick of this waiting and planning. A woman's quest is always like this, going in circles and then sitting. I want to set out, into the world, and win. I want us to be like a couple of warriors. Lady knights." Catherine laughed. "We'll ride into Wittenberg and sweep Robbie back to us. Then we'll all triumph home together, riding the seas."

"If you say so," said Ann.

Chapter 7

Finally, the weather gave a nod to spring and they departed, though the morning was cold and the extra men, brought along to return the horses to Yorkshire, grumbled that they had work enough to do right here at home. Ann had to be forced even to eat her breakfast, but the girls were on fire to set out. "Take it in a bag if you must," said Alice.

Ann looked at her plate. "We have days of riding ahead of us. Unfamiliar roads. Lumpy beds. Lice. I feel as though I'm being driven into exile myself." She threw down her napkin. "I'm old. And I'm a coward."

"Come, I'll be beside you," said Veronica. "Now eat."

Reg had booked passage on a ship at Lynn, the only one that would accept the women, and though Catherine and the girls anticipated the sea with giddy chatter, Ann could not stop herself from listing everything that could go wrong in their absence as they mounted their horses. The sheep could develop disease in their hooves. Eleanor or Joseph might fall ill. The stores of vegetables in the cellar could run low. Rot could set in, or vermin, and ruin everything.

"The world might also end and see us all whisked to heaven," said Catherine. She had now developed a fierce lust to see foreign lands. If she had to go, she'd do so without fear. There was much to observe beyond England, after all.

"Or the new trees might—" began Reg, but Catherine cut him off with a look.

Still Ann fretted while Alice wondered what the shops would be like across the sea and Veronica wondered what the languages would sound like. They'd seldom been even to London again during Mary Tudor's reign, and they would need new, more fashionable things. Only Ann seemed at odds with the mood of the day. But as they set out, Alice holding Toby in a sling across her chest and Eleanor Adwolfe waving as they went, the roads were clear enough, and they encountered no thieves or storms. At nightfall, they found inns with beds enough for them all, with fewer bedbugs than they had feared. Catherine remarked, on the third afternoon, that England seemed happy to have its new queen. "Even the fields look to have washed their faces."

"They always look like that this time of year," muttered Ann.

They passed a sign that marked the way south to Cambridge, and Catherine thought upon that other university town, Oxford, where Mary Tudor had ordered the executions of all those men. How many had it been? She could no longer remember, and her forgetfulness shocked her. She'd burnt the pamphlets that described their deaths before Alice could see them, but Veronica had read them down in the village. She had no stomach for seeing men or women punished for their beliefs, especially when religion altered with the whims of whoever occupied the throne, and she wondered how friendly they would find Wittenberg, but she said nothing to interrupt Ann and Reg's argument about whether the bread last night had been fresh enough for the price.

They could smell the cold sea before they saw it, and Catherine's mind skidded backward to that day, so many years ago, when she had brought the other Veronica home to Lynn, where she had died. She'd forgotten the fishy, rotted scent, but she recalled the mud in the bay, grey and slimy, burbling with sea creatures that made Catherine's skin prickle with disgust. The sea at Dover, when Benjamin and her son left, had surely smelt fresher, but Catherine's heart had been shriveled with the pain of leave-taking, and she recalled mostly that the water looked oily and rancid and that her heart had been set so hard against Mary Tudor that she had felt that she hated the sea, as well.

And then they were in Lynn proper, and the icy wind brutalized their faces and hands. The town was busier than Catherine had imagined anywhere could be this early in the spring, and dirtier. She expected narrow lanes, but these were downright clotted with baskets and crates, knots of cowering, shivering children dressed in rags. Skinny dogs and cats slunk along the muddy verges, and Catherine stepped her mare around a matted terrier with a rat in its mouth. Frowning men and women shouldered past one another, most with bundles on their backs. Travellers? Catherine wondered aloud if they would find accommodations in such a crowded place, and Ann said the stink made her feel ancient and peevish. "I think we should go back home," she said. Catherine had lost count of how many times she'd said it over the last few days.

Reg was looking around. He motioned the other men in closer, around the women, and he took hold of Alice's reins down near the bit. Her horse shied at a nipping hound, and Reg pulled it down an alleyway. "Follow us," he shouted, and they all assembled, nearly on top of each other, around the pair.

"I should find us rooms," said Reg. "You two, Oswald and Mark. Stay here with the women. I won't go far without coming back to you first."

"Let me come with you," said Veronica. Her eyes were glassy bright, and Catherine knew her spirits were heated, if her skin was not.

"No," said Catherine and Reg at the same time. "Not safe," added Reg. "I can't look for a sign and keep an eye on you, too."

"I want you to stay beside me," said Ann. "I feel safer having a younger person with me."

That mollified Veronica, as Ann probably knew it would. It was probably also the truth. She pressed up against a sooty brick wall to let a man carrying a child pass by. Reg called, "Do you know where there are rooms?"

The man halted and shrugged with one shoulder. "There's rooms plenty." He nodded back toward the main road. "Most of them's leaving. They sleep on the docks, even, to get a boat out of this island."

Catherine followed his nod. He was right. Most of the people were heaving toward the harbour. She said, "We should go down and see that we have passage. There is light enough yet."

"I can hardly breathe," said Ann. "I feel as though I've got a herring up my nose. We could wait where there is air as well as here."

And so they returned to the road in a clump and scanned the people. Most were definitely huddling near the water. Catherine let Reg and two of the men go on ahead, and she set herself on one side of Alice. Ann settled into place on the other side and they fell in with the human wave.

The harbour itself was a chaos. Most people had surrounded the ships' crews and were shouting and waving bags of money.

"They aren't wearing their names on their clothes," observed Ann, who could not read them if they had been. "What do you suggest we do?"

"We'll have to ask one at a time," said Reg. He fished a paper out of his pocket. "We're looking for a man called Simmons."

"Well, we know it has to be a seagoing boat, not one of these little ones," said Alice.

But they all looked large to Catherine, until she got closer. Then they all looked as though they would capsize at the first eddy of a wave. She could already feel herself in a room under the water, and her throat closed up. Was there enough air for breathing down there? How did the vessels not fall down into the water?

Catherine's heart skittered a little in her chest. Their men were staring longingly at a tavern nearby. Ann and Reg were murmuring together, and Ann was shaking her head as they walked on. Veronica and Alice were sitting back in their saddles, whispering and gazing around at everything. The skittering danced faster, and Catherine was afraid she might faint. She turned her horse, desperate for something to indicate where she should go.

Then, blessedly, Reg returned. "Dismount and lead the horses. Our Captain Simmons is over there, and the boat lies that way. Very early in the year for easy seagoing, he says."

"That didn't stop him from taking our money, did it?" Catherine swung onto the ground.

"No," said Reg.

The sailors saw them before they saw the sailors, and, recognizing Reg, called out, "There's the one with the women." Reg clapped one of them on the back.

"Captain!" said the sailor. "This man means to bring a whole brothel with him."

Veronica shoved past them all, muttering, and stopped before the captain. "Might you be Simmons?"

"Me mother says so," said the captain, and one of the sailors said, loudly enough to be heard by all, "Women brings nothin' but sorrow to a ship."

Simmons regarded the group. "There's many women among you."

"They're kinfolk," said Reg. "We have paid."

"Well," said Simmons. "I reckon I have the room. Not what they're accustomed to."

The mouthy sailor stepped forward. "That many women will toss us to Poseidon indeed. 'Tis bad luck, I say."

Alice clicked her horse forward and halted beside her sister. "We wouldn't set foot on your old boat if we had a choice in the matter, and that's flat. How do you expect us to get over the sea?"

"You got a choice," answered the sailor. "Everybody in the world's got a choice. Women ought to choose to stay home, where they belong."

This riled Veronica, who put in her oar. "Women must go as well as men sometimes. Queens travel across the seas, and no one minds them."

"Queens is queens, not women," answered the man. "They got to go, but no man's got to like 'em." He shot spit through his teeth, narrowly missing Catherine's shoe. "Women's nothin' but ill winds pushing a ship toward disaster."

"Is this bad luck?" asked Catherine, holding up the money bag at her waist. "Your captain doesn't seem to think so. I don't expect that you stop that ill wind from blowing you into a tavern when you get your pay."

Reg put his hand over the bag. "Don't," he said, and Catherine, shamefaced, stuck it back into the folds of her skirt and waited in silence. Reg turned to the sailor. "We have our passage," he said, and the sailor withdrew a step, grumbling, "Every man's got to live."

"This is Captain Simmons," said Reg, bowing a little formally, and the captain, in turn, bowed to Catherine.

"You are all of one family?" Simmons asked Catherine. He was white-whiskered with eyes squinched so tight that she couldn't make out their colour. He seemed to have been staring into the sun for years. Catherine nodded her agreement, and he nodded back, almost as though he were mimicking her. "And a dog?"

"Just a little one," said Alice. She raised Toby for inspection.

Simmons regarded her with his wrinkled eyes, but he slid a finger under the dog's chin for a scratch. "I expect you women to keep yourselves to yourselves. You'll bunk together below decks. The men aren't happy about carrying you."

"So we hear," said Ann. The sailors had retreated and she shot them a look of scorn.

"You must understand," continued Simmons. "Many of the men consider it to be bad luck to have women aboard. And so many women." His hand rose as though they were hundreds. "I trust this is not a matter of flight from the new queen and that you all have the proper permission to go?"

"We have permission," said Catherine. "I have my passport here."

"Well, that makes you a singular group, to be sure. We have men and women falling over themselves to get out of England, but they don't sail on my ship without passports." He did not ask for the written proof. "You've come at a lucky time. Be sure that your trunks are down there." The captain pointed toward a mouldy-looking dock. "We are making for Amsterdam. We load tonight. Be assembled here before sunup."

"So soon?" said Ann. "We've come straight from our home. We thought we'd have a few days' leisure."

"Sky's promising clear weather. A rare thing in spring. You're all here. We go. Sort your business as you will." Simmons bowed again, a little bounce from the waist, and, nodding at Reg, walked away.

"This looks like a pleasant journey," remarked Ann. Reg put his hand around her arm, and she added, "If not for you, old man, I'd be riding the other way again."

Alice said, "No! Reg has got the passage for us! You must come happily, so that we're in the right spirits for adventure."

"Adventure, hmph," said Ann. "I expected something more exciting than a pack of drunkards who say the same old things about women. I'll show them some sorrow, if they want to see it so badly."

"Ann," said Veronica. "Don't spoil it for us."

At this, Ann sighed grandly. "Let's board that ship and sail the waves, then, if we must."

Catherine stared out to sea. The sky was mild, almost friendly-looking, and blue, striped with lazy clouds. It would be a short venture. She would find her son, and then she would find her husband. She would bring her men home. And then all would be well with the world.

Chapter 8

One last supper upon the solid earth, and Catherine found herself laughing into her cup about Diana's two sister nuns.

"What now?" asked Ann.

"I have drunk too much of this wine," said Catherine. "I was recalling Diana's Marys—and our own."

"That's nothing to laugh about," remarked Ann.

It wasn't, the truth be told. One dead, the other who knew where, perhaps wandering the length and breadth of England as a beggar. Perhaps the old queen had shown her some mercy, but Catherine doubted that. The Marys had been aunts to her own son and daughter, and yet she could only remember them with any charity when she imagined them as girls. It was a fault in Catherine, to be sure. "It was all a long time ago," she said. "Don't you ever wonder where Margaret is?"

"No, and I don't care where she is, as long as she stays out of my sight," said Ann.

"Are you talking about Elizabeth again?" asked Alice. "She sent you packing in London, didn't she, Mother? She knows she's a queen now and may do as she pleases. That sailor said that queens aren't women."

"Hush, sister," said Veronica. "People will hear."

Veronica was right. Catherine knew she'd retreated to her northern home in part to remove herself from a world of spies and rebellions, and as Mary Tudor's reign had grown bloodier with each passing year, Catherine had stopped reading the pamphlets and listening to the passing tradesmen. Mary was a Tudor, after all. She'd done what she'd thought was required, just as her father had done before her. Catherine had buried her nose in the dirt of Yorkshire. At least it smelt clean, and the only deaths occurred when they butchered animals for their meat or when someone was taken off by God. They'd prayed in the old ways again, but Catherine herself didn't oversee anyone but her own servants and she rejected the notion of telling tales about the villagers' attendance at Mass. The old priest seemed to agree, and kept himself gathered into his black robes, wary of restoring England to Rome on the word of a woman, even if she did sit on a throne.

"Can't we speak of our own queen, or the one who's dead?" asked Alice. "She's got her rump where she wants it. What can the likes of us do to her?"

"No more!" shouted Ann. She stood up, then buried her arms into themselves and her chin into her chest, shocked at herself. "We're still in England, and Elizabeth is the queen."

The innkeeper showed himself in a doorway at the far end of the room and wrung his hands. "Ladies, your voices can be heard all the way out in the road."

"No doubt," said Ann. "Don't mind me, Alice. Or you, Veronica, either. I'm crotchety as an old sow. I just want peace and quiet these days." She unwound herself and left, headed in the direction of the women's bedchamber.

Catherine watched the innkeeper, who was watching Ann's retreat. Alice perched upon the bench, perfectly still, her face bleached white. Ann was frightened, with good reason. Catherine rose and said, "The wine with such a rich dinner has loosened everyone's tongues. We'll go to bed soon. The people are all in different excitements with our island undergoing such changes." She pressed a few coins into the innkeeper's hand on her way out. "Please forgive us for our ill manners."

The fingers closed over the money. "High spirits. That's what it is. You mean to board ship in the morning?"

"At dawn. Before the sun is up, we'll be gone from here. We do have permission to go. From the court itself."

"That's good," he said. "I'll have a girl call you."

"The earlier, the better," said Catherine. The man nodded and stuck his hand into his pocket. The coins jingled softly, and she knew he would not say anything, at least not until they were out of sight.

Before the dawn extended even the first fingers of pink in the east, the innkeeper sent not only a girl to wake them but also two men to haul their remaining things down to the pier. Catherine paid him again, throwing in a few extra coins to mollify him, and they were ready to board before anyone else. Captain Simmons, watching the sky, said that the weather appeared favourable. "You don't get sick at sea?" he said to Catherine.

"I've never been at sea," she said. "Nor have my people, none but Reginald Goodall. He's warned us, but I have as stout a stomach as the next woman. I hope to sail well."

"No woman sails well," answered Simmons, "but we can hope you sail without making trouble."

The others were already lugging their last bags into a rowboat, and Catherine followed. It was a narrow thing, and she held on, sitting just behind Ann, with all the strength she could employ as they slid into the water and toward the larger sailing vessel. The boat heaved and the sailors thrust it forward. A pin from Ann's cap flew back and struck her on the cheek. She turned her head and closed her eyes and prayed until she felt them loll to a stop.

The ship loured above them, and Catherine allowed herself to be hauled aboard. The wind chased the clouds from every direction, and she sucked in her breath, only to discover that the air stank of rot and mildewed fabric. Then she caught the brief blessing of a fresh breeze that wafted at least the fishy odour away. They were shown where they would sleep. "If you can," chuckled the sailor, ducking into what looked to Catherine like a hole rough-sawn into the boards of the floor. Below, the stench was stronger, of men's unwashed bodies and putrid food. Catherine gagged and backed up the steps. The sailor laughed. She forced herself to descend once more, and was delivered into dark space with a couple of filthy mattresses that looked as though they had been retrieved from a dung-heap and flung in for their accommodations. It was not a cabin, not a proper one. It was not even a room. No window. A big cup in the corner that the sailor sneeringly informed her was their piss-pot. "And don't be expecting working men to dump it for you," he added.

Catherine was back on the deck as fast as she could scrabble her way up the steps. "I will manage," she said, hanging her arms over the wooden railing. She had been speaking to herself, but Veronica, beside her, said, "We will all manage. Look, Mother, at the water! I don't care what dungeon they house us in. I'll sleep up here, under the stars, if I must. Alice will join me, won't you?"

"Toby will make a fine seagoing dog," Alice said. Toby looked less sure of the situation and maintained his position between her feet.

Catherine saw the sea below, but she couldn't admire it. To her, it was green and oily-looking on the surface. The sun was rising, casting a sheet of bright yellow over the rolling waves farther out, and Veronica said, "It's beautiful!"

Catherine saw no such beauty, though she granted that the sea was marvelous, in its way. It was large, of that she was sure.

"I'll manage," she said again, and a sailor—she couldn't determine whether it was the same one who'd taken them below—snickered as he went by, dragging an armful of ropes. "I will," she said, though no one was listening.

Ann joined them. The serving men had stayed at the far end of the deck to pray. "Our Mark and Oswald aren't very sure now that this will be the adventure they thought it would be," said Ann. "I believe they wish you had left them at home. I may agree with them before we see land again." She gazed out, over the water. "It's a long way."

Catherine stomped the board, then kicked the hull of the ship. "This seems solid. Sturdy enough to hold our souls in, do you think?"

"I pray so," said Ann. "I wouldn't want them to row us anymore."

A sea-wind rocked them, ever so slightly, and Veronica lifted her face to it. "The motion is pleasant. And the air takes the smells away. I plan to enjoy myself."

"It's not for our pleasure, I can tell you that," said a passing sailor darkly.

Catherine was weary of the men's complaints. There was much to be sober about, and much to be mourned, but could her daughters not even feel the freshness upon their necks without one of the sailors casting it as a dire prophecy? "I look forward to going," Catherine said, landing a brave note with the last word. "I mean to see the world, if I can, before I die."

Ann, uncharacteristically, said nothing, and the sailor who'd been hauling the rope came by again. "Prepare your stomachs, ladies. We'll be off soon." He ground out his rat's laugh again and lumbered away. He spoke to another of the sailors, and together they guffawed out loud. The sails whipped out and riffled the wintry air like fresh laundry hung out to freeze itself dry.

"My stomach is fine," she said, loudly enough to startle Ann, who said, "Don't tempt the devil, Catherine."

Then Ann grabbed her. They were moving. Sailors were calling to each other, and Veronica shouted and waved at no one in particular. Their men prayed, loud as fishwives on a street corner. Ann let go of Catherine, balanced herself, and Veronica whooped to Alice, who scooped up Toby so that he could see better. Catherine's belly lurched and rolled. Her feet went liquid and she couldn't find purchase on the boards beneath her.

The shore already looked far, far away.

After watching for an hour or so, Catherine grew weary of the girls' trilling excitement about everything. Gulls were just birds, after all, and she'd seen enough of them already. She tried the mattress below decks, but the air was so dense, with a reek like something dead, that she rolled to her feet and wobbled back up. The others were in various states of delight and dismay, Ann and Reg, with their arms about each other's waists, holding on to the railing, Veronica and Alice shouting every time they bobbed over the tiniest of waves, the sailors grousing and scowling.

"I have never felt so sick," said Ann, turning away from her husband.

"We're hardly underway," said Reg.

"My guts are heaving," Ann said. She tried to move with the motion of the ship, but her thin soles slipped along the slimy boards, and she clung to the wale. Then she emptied her stomach over the side.

Catherine came to stand beside her and rested her chin on her hands. "I thought I would be the one casting up my breakfast."

"You're well?" whispered Ann.

Catherine shrugged. "As well as ever, I suppose. Not as much as my daughters are. I wish I'd brought a dog for myself."

Catherine's eyes burnt with the salt spray, and her face was a block of ice, but Ann was in a sincere torment. "Here it comes again," she said, and she leant out as far as she dared. When the spasm gripped her, she flung her head forward, and her cap flew off, tumbling through the spray and into the sea, followed by another spewing of hot bile. "Oh!" she cried, but it was far too late. A couple of sailors hooted as they watched the cap go, like some great soft fish, then float away, and Ann covered her hair with her hands. "Take me below," she said to Catherine. "I'd rather puke into a piss bucket than listen to them."

And she was not alone. As she staggered past, the serving men fell to their knees, not in prayer now but huddled over unstable vessels, crying for the motion to cease. Reg fetched two more buckets as Catherine and a dizzy Ann tumbled down the boards that passed for steps. She could hear the men, just above them, retch again, and Catherine squatted on the edge of her mattress, to hold Ann's head. She hoped the slop wouldn't drip onto the floor. It was slick enough as it was. "How does anyone endure this?" Ann said.

Veronica and Alice had followed them down. "I am well," Veronica said. "And Alice. And Reg. The sailors just shared a fat loaf of bread with Toby a few minutes ago."

"Don't talk of food," said Ann. She lay back and Catherine took a wet cloth offered by Alice. It smelt of sweat and mould, and when she tried to cover Ann's face with it, she flew up again, gagging. "That's worse than ever."

Veronica put the cloth to her nose. "It was the cleanest one we could find."

Alice sat beside Catherine, pushing the damp hair from Ann's forehead. "What's happened to your cap?" she asked.

"The wind took it," said Ann. "I feel better without it. But I suppose I'll have to find another."

And so they went over the sea, the sailors content that the weather remained fine and the passengers remained out of sight. The captain looked in on them twice, and he departed with a word of hope that they would soon see land. Catherine and the girls took their turns keeping Ann company, and she stayed on her pallet, with a rag over her face, willing her stomach into submission.

The greasy sea bucked and swirled about them, and Catherine stood as long as she was allowed by the surly sailors and watched its flow. Motion unmoving, and them cutting through it, the dip and tug of the hull like a great heart beating out a tune. Her father had taught her about the music of the spheres, and she had believed it, but this was a song in a minor key, an opposition of forward melody and a circular low note, the harmony repeating itself beneath their feet. She turned, once, and found Alice and Veronica staring at her.

"Are you frightened, Mother?" asked Veronica.

"A little," said Catherine. "I've wondered, now and again, that some men spend their lives on the water. But I begin to feel the answer."

Reg came up then and stood beside them. "And you, Reg," said Veronica. "How is it that you know such a lot about sailing?"

Reg laughed. "You've heard of boys running away to be sailors, haven't you? I ran away from sailing to be on the land. This was many years ago, mind you, many. Many." He drew his heavy jerkin around him and watched the water. "I was apprenticed out when I was smaller than you, Alice. But the work wasn't my fate. Or so I decided. One time, when we returned to the very port we've just left, I said 'God be with you' to the boat and walked inland. I looked for work in every parish and found it, at the last, with Robert Overton, brother to your late father, Veronica. And that was that for this young sailor."

"Does Ann know this story?" asked Catherine.

"Ann knows every pit and crevice of my life," said Reg. "Your husband knew, too, Catherine, and he often had a good laugh that I had gone from sea-dog to manservant without so much as a backward look. Now, I'd better find a place to toss my blankets, or every spot on the deck will be taken."

The sun was setting behind them, and Catherine's limbs suddenly went slack for weariness. "I'll climb in with Ann and help her sleep. You girls can't stay on deck after dark, do you hear?"

And despite the reek and the cold, Catherine, once under the musty blanket with her friend, fell asleep to the roll of the sea beneath her.

Once, she woke to singing, and sat up. Ann's guts must have been staying in their place because she was snoring softly, and Catherine listened to all of the sounds that ministered to her in the dark. Men's voices. The sailors, shouting out a melody to each other, in what sounded like joy. Her daughter Alice's voice, joining in. Then laughing and more singing. So Alice was still above. Alice would have won their hearts. Toby would howl any minute now. She stood and felt her feet slide along the boards and thought she would go up to listen. But as she gripped the doorsill, Ann sat up. "I think I am well enough to go, as well."

"Ann, you're weak as a new piglet."

"I'm fine. I want to go up," said Ann. But then she rocked forward one time and was lying on the flat mattress again.

Catherine sat with her until her eyes opened. "You fainted. You'll stay here, down in the bed, stinking as it is."

And so she did, while Catherine lay awake beside her, wondering where in the world they were. She stayed with Ann most of the next day, too, trying her with a little of the hard bread the sailors used, dipped in some ale, but Ann slept much and ate little. And so it went, Catherine down in the bed during much of the daylight and standing on deck in the middle of the nights, watching the stars and then returning to Ann's side.

In the dim, cold space, altogether without the regular rise and zenith of the day, Catherine quickly lost her bearing in time, and when she heard a call from above and opened her eyes to daylight filtering in from above, she was certain that they were all to be overturned into the icy waves. But, no, it was land they were calling out. Catherine threw off the thin coverlet and clambered up the wooden steps. Veronica and Alice and Reg were waving and shouting. Toby was wagging. They could see Amsterdam, they crowed. They had arrived.

Chapter 9

"This is land?" Catherine said at first. "Where? This is a city on the water." She saw, far beyond her, what might have been homes and shops, but they were teetering over lakes and rivers, snaking every which way. It could be a phantom of the light. It could be a dream. Shouldn't they have sailed further in, she wondered, to reach a real port? She laid her palm across her brow, suspecting she'd sucked in a fever with the sea air and was imagining a floating city. If there were men and women out there, they would have to be walking on water.

But they moved ever closer, and soon enough her family's chests were already being dropped into another of those wretched rowboats, and she could now make out a rickety run of planks. "Ann!" she called, and got her feet under her to wake her friend.

As they made their slow way to the pier, the town solidified before her eyes. It was not made of smoke and water, after all. People were gathered here and there, just as they would in England, and passersby entered the shops without concern that they might tip into the sea and be drowned. Veronica called, "Look at the skinny houses!" and she and Alice went skipping off the boat like a couple of children.

Catherine took one of Ann's elbows, Reg the other. "Can you walk?" said Catherine.

"I believe so," said Ann. "But I've never seen so strange a place. How can people live with the sea at their very doors? This is lower than the fens. Reg, why have you steered us here?"

"The captain is the one who steered us," said Reg, "but this is a city of the future. Come on. There's plenty to see."

"This is our time, Ann," said Catherine. "It's come, or we've come to it. We must go forward."

"Yes. Your quest. But must we go forward into the very water?" said Ann. She hesitated, then allowed herself to be half-carried, half-accompanied, by Catherine and Reg. They disembarked in a tight knot, arms linked, their serving men, seemingly recovered from their own sickness, bravely leading them, as though they had always lived on the waves.

Setting one tentative foot on the pier, Catherine dared a backward glance. The sails that had seemed so delicate when she stood beneath them, ready to rend themselves at the first whisper of wind, sagged heavily against the masts, now massive and thick, where before they had looked thin as toothpickers. She set her other foot upon the wood. It felt thick enough beneath her sole, at least, and that was all she wanted at the moment. The townspeople looked not all that alien. They might almost be from some place in England where she had never visited. Surely the world was not so different here? And Robbie was so close that she could nearly feel him. Her heart quaked in her chest, and she almost giggled.

Their men took leave immediately in search of hired horses, and Captain Simmons strutted onto the pier as the rest of them waited. Ann was leaning on Veronica, while Catherine gazed at the town. Reg was all business, counting their trunks against the list he had made up. The captain said, "The worst is behind you, then? You know your way from here to anywhere, do you?"

"I don't," said Catherine, "but I'll find it." The buildings might have been those in an English town, if she could have taken an English town between her hands and squeezed. If she squinted just a little into the sun, she could keep her imagination away from the rivers running inland. She would keep looking up, at the firm bits, though they seemed then to be drifting away, into the heavens. Reg had a map. Reg always had maps. Or he would make one. "You don't know the road to Wittenberg, do you?" Catherine said to Simmons.

The captain shook his head. "Never been there. They say that it's a mess of politicians out that way. All talk of God and sin and tearing down the Church. Servants don't know their place, I hear. I don't hold with all that. Just put me on the water. I'll make my peace with the Everlasting there."

"I see," said Catherine, closing her eyes.

"Seek out an Englishman for your guide. They're easy to find in these parts."

Veronica was pointing. "I see our men. They have someone with them."

"It looks like the Englishmen have found you already. God keep you, then," said Captain Simmons. "I believe I'm wanted." A few of the sailors had already passed them and were shoving through the assembled people toward a door. The sign above it, a laughing monk, indicated that drink was to be had, but Catherine couldn't read the words.

Reg said, "We haven't been robbed, at least not yet." He tucked away the list and checked the locks on the trunks.

"The captain says our troubles are behind us," said Catherine. "He thinks we can find an Englishman to help us, and, look there, I think we have found one." She smelt something strange in the air, like woodsmoke, but thicker, sweeter. "This looks a bustling place, doesn't it?"

Reg watched their men approach, with some horses and the stranger. They were dragging a wagon behind them.

Their own men were gesturing and the new one was shaking his head.

Ann said, "I think our troubles are just beginning, pardon my saying so."

Two women came sidling down the docks and waved in a friendly way. Catherine thought they, too, looked English, and she walked over to greet her countrywomen. "It's not so different, is it?"

"Every way different," said the elder of the two. "It has no Protestant queen, my lady. Are you newly arrived then?"

"Yes," said Catherine, grateful for the familiar accent. "So many voices here."

"Yes, and foreign ones at that," said the elder woman. "Can we offer you some help? You have left behind the new queen and you seek the comfort of your own sisters. And your church. Am I right?"

"Well," said Catherine. This was more service than she had anticipated. "I'm enjoying the newness. All of this water. A city built upon water. I've never seen the like."

"But you've left an island, have you not? A monstrous island, wouldn't you say? Cities for Satan. And the Whore of Babylon for its queen. All built on the water."

The younger woman stepped closer, almost touching Catherine's arm.

"I wouldn't say monstrous, no," said Catherine. She took a step backward. She heard men and women speaking in tongues she did not understand, but the sound became almost melodic to her ears. People waved to each other. Men slapped each other upon their backs. Women carried baskets and walked together, their heads leant toward each other in private conversation. Small boats, like the barges she'd ridden in London, pushed their ways up and down nearby lanes of water, pushed by men or horses who looked like any other men and their horses.

"But you've fled," continued the elder woman. "We can help you find your way, my lady."

"We'll accustom ourselves," Catherine said.

"But you don't know the words here," the younger woman said. "We come down here to find our countrywomen and offer our assistance."

"God hears prayers in all languages. It looks like a pleasant town." She seemed to note familiar pitches in the voices beyond her, and it put her in mind of the way Anne of Cleves had talked, all those years ago.

Veronica had come up behind, and she said, "It's magnificent! I've wondered what the buildings and people would look like. They're just like ours, Mother, excepting the marshes and the rivers. But such skinny houses, as though they've not fed the walls enough. What do you think of that? And look how they use the water as roads. Roads of water! It's quite wonderful. We'll find someone who speaks English, and we'll make our way."

"My daughter and I speak English," said the elder woman, sliding toward Veronica.

Alice came up behind her. "I want to see the shops."

"I can steer you to the best ones," said the younger woman.

Veronica looked at the mother and daughter and shook her head. "Who are you? We have servants who've already found us a guide. He's English."

The elder woman slipped back to Catherine and murmured, "There's no going back. The Boleyn daughter is back there." She pointed vaguely in the direction of England. "If she hears of your escape, she will cut off your heads upon your return. They still have God here. Let me assist you."

"Elizabeth has no interest in cutting off our heads," put in Veronica. "Those are tales to frighten children."

"She will!" The daughter set herself between the mother and Veronica. "You know what zeal she had against her sister. She is a whore and a heretic and a bastard."

"This is ridiculous," said Catherine. "Elizabeth never—"

"She will!" the daughter said again.

"The English begin to sound like magpies that have learned only one phrase," said Catherine. "I've heard all of this before, and I heard it when Mary Tudor was on the throne. Can we not train our tongues to say something else?"

"Are you not Catholic?" said the mother.

"We're Christian," said Alice. "And we have no need of your help just now."

"Then a coin for your countrywomen?" The younger woman held out her hand. "You look as though you have some silver in your pocket, my lady. Can you not spare a little for two women on their own in a strange land?"

"So that's your trick," said Veronica. "You're just a couple of beggars."

The younger woman said, "Christ teaches us to give." She held out her hand.

"Christ also teaches us to tell the truth," Alice said. "Get your dirty paw away. I'll give you nothing, and that's flat."

Now the elder woman muttered and drew back. "You should have stayed in England. I must not remain in your company."

Alice turned away, blowing out a sound of disgust. "You weren't invited to join us, I don't think. We've only just arrived, and you've thrust yourselves upon us. And you call yourself a Christian?"

Reg came up then. "What's the matter?"

"Nothing but some beggarly countrywomen. They seem to think they can pretend to help us when they mean to rob us," said Alice, a little louder than necessary, and Catherine nudged her, hard, in the ribs.

Catherine pulled out her money bag. "How much do we owe for the horses?" she said.

The younger woman crept close again, like a fox tempted with a little meat, and Reg closed his hand over the bag. "Put that away. We'll pay later." To the women, he said, "Leave us be, now, before I call up the law."

Catherine tucked her money away. "Let's see to these horses." The two women had slunk away and she watched them go. "I'll take a lesson from this to keep my nose pointed forward and not up."

"We've got to get us a bigger wagon," said Reg. "And a better one. Is this best you've got, man?"

The newcomer with the wagon slouched and shrugged. "Men here says you're new-come English and you need a wagon. I got a wagon. It's registered. You're welcome to it, such as it is."

Even piled as high as they could dare, the little wagon would barely contain all of their chests. The horses were too few for all of them to ride singly. The serving men grumbled when Catherine and Ann wondered what they would do, as though to say that they had done their best, here in this land that was constructed of water and indecipherable words.

"It's not big enough," said Reg. "Where can we find a bigger one?"

The Englishman gnawed his lip and combed his beard with his fingers. "You can't hire horses easily for yourselves in Amsterdam. They won't let you ride them through the town if you don't have a license. Wait here. I've got someone who might help." He walked away, leaving the wagon where it sagged.

"Are all of the English here thieves and liars?" Ann fretted. "This isn't an auspicious beginning to a journey."

Catherine looked one way and saw the two women, now with their claws on another couple. She looked the other and saw nothing but a crowd of strangers. No sign of their erstwhile guide. She finally sat on a dirty bench and bit her lip. She would not cry and shame herself, here before her own family. She was meant to be a warrior, she told herself, a pilgrim, like Margery Kempe of old, travelling the world and finding God. But Catherine was just an ordinary woman, and her quests went nowhere. "I am weary to my bones," she said. "I just want to find my son."

From the rear, the wagon's sorry condition was clear: worn and rotted, with the wheels careening every which way. So they couldn't ride? Catherine covered her face with her hands. They couldn't walk to Wittenberg.

When she looked again, she was quite alone. Ann, Veronica, and Alice had wandered up the dock, studying the tall, narrow buildings, and the serving men were edging toward a tavern. Reg was nowhere in sight. Perhaps he had followed the wagon-man. Maybe he was having a drink in one of the taverns. Catherine sighed and, as she did so, someone touched her on the shoulder from behind.

"Madam?" said an old woman. She was short and thick, and she wore a heavy cloth over her head. Her apron was well-woven, and not very worn, and the soles of her boots were old but stout. She spoke in a thick tongue that Catherine could barely understand.

She was surely not English, and for that Catherine was surprised to feel a bolt of joy. She shook her head, pointed at her own breast, and said, "England."

The woman nodded. "England. So many." She waved one hand around, as though seeing dozens of Catherine's countrymen. "Lost?"

"No. Yes. Perhaps," said Catherine. "We have some help. It is only not here with me just now."

"Lonely?"

"I have my daughters to keep me company." Catherine waved toward the buildings where she'd seen them. Alone? Did the woman mean alone? "I am alone just now. They are there." Catherine pointed and the woman's eyes followed.

She nodded. "Where go?"

"Wittenberg. My son—."

The old eyes widened, lifting the hoods of flesh. They were brown. "You go at Wittenberg?"

"Yes. Wittenberg. To find my son. But we have no horses, and I don't know the way." Catherine pointed at the road ahead of them. "The way." She shook her head and waved her hands, hoping to give a sign of her meaning.

"I can show," said the old woman.

"You? Do you not have a family? Children?" Catherine mimicked rocking a baby in her arms.

The old woman raised her chin and laughed at the sky. She scrubbed at her eyes with both fists. Then she pushed back the skin of her face, unfolding the wrinkles. "Old!"

Catherine's face burned. "But grown up? Sons and daughters?" She set her hand high on the air to indicate an adult.

"Nah," said the woman. She flung one hand away from herself and spat. "Nah."

Were they dead? Had they abandoned their old mother to the charity of sailors? She looked hearty enough, and though her clothes were not fine, neither were they patched. Her shoes would keep the winter out. She didn't look like the beggars Catherine had known. Her skin, though it needed a wash, was clear, and she had certainly been eating.

"Hilde!" someone yelled, and the woman raised her hand and beckoned. A young man, with a hefty bag over one shoulder, approached, and Catherine stood, wiping down her skirt. The wagon-man and Reg were behind him. She realized just then that she lacked a hood, and she whisked a length of linen out of her bag and wrapped it over her hair. The man was perhaps thirty and astonishingly fair. His hair was frothy, almost white. His cheeks were wind-smitten, but he was well-fed, tall, and better dressed than the woman Catherine had been speaking with. Close up, he was handsome. Quite handsome. He let the bag fall at his feet and bowed to Catherine, uttering some set of syllables that sounded to Catherine's ear like growling.

"Hello?" she ventured. She pointed at her breast and said, "Catherine Overton Davies. England."

"Ah!" cried the young man. His eyes were bluer than the sky, and he stood over six feet tall. All azure and gold, sky and sun. He said, "English woman! Many English woman here. English man, also. You need help! Hello!"

Catherine had to laugh, and when she did the old woman said something to the man, at which he nodded.

"You are on journey?" he said. "You lose the right road? You go to Romans?"

"Not lost," answered Catherine. "Maybe lost. No, not Rome. Wittenberg?"

"Ah! Wittenberg. The Protesters. Long, long way." He gestured toward the east. "I can show. Make map. But very far. You still wet from sea. You come stay? Need room?"

Catherine didn't know how to both come and stay at the same time. As she tried to form a reply, Ann returned from behind the man and the old woman. She was towing the girls, who were sorrowing over not having bought anything yet. "Mother, who's this?" Veronica said.

"This is—." But Catherine didn't even know their names. "They're offering help," she said lamely. She wasn't altogether sure that this was the case.

"We can make use of that," said Ann, "if they're not another pack of thieves."

The man and old woman had turned by this time to see Catherine's companions, and the man offered a bow and then his hand to Veronica. Catherine could not see his face, but she could see her daughter's—a gleeful expression that melted into wonder. Veronica allowed her fingers be shaken gently.

Ann was greeting the old woman and trying to maneuver Alice forward so that she could say her helloes as well. Alice stepped right up and showed off Toby, who licked the offered hand. Ann turned to Veronica, but Veronica was still staring at the young man. He, in turn, was gazing at her. Ann said, "Do you speak English?"

"Ja," said the man, still looking at Veronica.

Veronica said nothing at all, and Ann slapped her on the shoulder. "Catherine, I think you'd better take control. Your daughter seems to have turned to stone."

"Nonsense," said Veronica, shaking her head. "Do tell me your name, sir?"

"Jan," said the man.

"Far away?" said Veronica.

"Yes, but I am just here!" He laughed. "John is good. You call me John. Easy for your English tongue. This Hilde, my maid. Used to be nurse. Family is De Vries. Much years here. I trade off the boats. Help when help is needed for the foreigners."

Hilde smiled and nodded and chucked Toby under the chin. She glanced at Catherine, and Catherine would have sworn the old woman winked. But John was talking, fast, and she had to strain her ears to understand. Had he said he was the breeze?

"We have farm. Large farm. Not far here. Got horses. You come stay with us. We make you map for travel. I have father and mother there. Brothers. You come stay with us. All you." He pointed behind him, at a couple of men beside a what looked like a small herd of horses and three big, solid wagons.

"We have others with us. Men, too," said Catherine. "Husband and servants."

John said to Veronica, "You have husband?"

She shook her head, and Ann said, "The husband belongs to me. This girl is with her mother." She indicated Catherine.

"Ah! Mama!" said John. He now pumped Catherine's hand. "You come stay with your mens. You have husband? Father?"

Catherine couldn't explain further, not out on these docks with the sun beating her eyes and the wind punishing her face. But then a figure blocked the glare. Reg had caught up to them, and Ann yelled, "Can you help us over here?"

Reg came at a trot, and Catherine noted how stiff he was getting in the legs. Maybe he had too many years on him for all of this. Maybe she did, as well. She walked with Ann to meet him, and pointed back toward John and Hilde as she explained. "Yes, yes, I know," said Reg. "I've hired him. We've got our help after all."

The wagon-man said, "Jan and his family have a house, with rooms to let. They can put you up. You've got luck with you today."

Jan—or John, which was he?—engaged with him in a round of back-slapping and laughter and fast words that Catherine couldn't understand at all. So this countryman, at least, was lending them aid. He said to Reg, "I'll vouch for them. They can show you the best way to your son in Wittenberg. He's got better wagons and horses than I have and they're at your service. Get your men to move your things and I'll take my leave."

"All of us?" said Ann. "Do they own an inn?"

"No inn," said John. "We have farm. Very large. Plenty room." He spread his arms. "We take in lost English. We like the English." This he seemed to find delightfully funny, and he put his head back and laughed.

"A farmer's house?" said Ann.

The Englishman grinned. "You can trust him. You'll have spacious quarters. This is a good man. I know him well. And now God be with you." He helped the serving men empty his sorry little wagon and departed with a gracious bow, leaving them in the hands of this smiling, beautiful stranger.

Chapter 10

John De Vries guided them, on his own horse, through the town, with Hilde beside one of the De Vries manservants on the wagon, which was loaded with bags and bundles on top of their trunks. Catherine's head kept pitching forward with exhaustion, but her eyes wouldn't close. The ground, beneath the hooves of the horse she'd been assigned, gave and shifted like fresh loam, and she was put in mind of new graves. She fancied that they could have hired one of these little boats to float them to Wittenberg. She spied a church and requested a stop, for she felt the weight of eternity in the mass of cold, blue sky and wanted to put a roof between herself and the divine for a little while.

"Ah, that is the old one," said John, pulling his reins up short. "Very pretty. Go on. It opens. I wait with your goods here."

"Is it Catholic or Protestant?" asked Catherine.

"We have the true Church still," said John De Vries. "You can find the Protesters, if you look for them. Not in this place."

Catherine nodded and said nothing. She just hoped that the pair from the docks hadn't found their way here.

Reg waited with John, clearly not fully trusting this sociable stranger. He ordered their men to stay back with him. The women entered through a narrow porch, and stepped into the high, wide light of the interior. Clusters of men and women darkened corners, and lean, long-legged dogs caroused among them, seemingly at home under the vast, arched wooden ceiling. Catherine, with her daughters and Ann beside her, wandered toward the altar, wondering at the clean beauty of the place, like the inside of the most innocent of minds.

"It must be Protestant, don't you think, Mother?" said Veronica. "Look at the people. They are doing business, not worshipping."

"I'm sure he said Catholic," said Catherine. She thought it was not very different from the booksellers and pamphleteers who thronged S Paul's in London. Men shook hands, as though to seal contracts, and the women stood close to each other, either gossiping or making private trades. One lady, folded in fine wools, with a tall hound on a thin leather leash, nodded smartly at her companions and bade her dog to follow her to the door. Veronica and Alice looked tiny, standing alien and alone at the center.

"It's very peaceful," said Veronica. "Come on, Ann, let's walk."

Ann said, "I will sit for a moment, if you don't mind." She took a bench by a whitewashed wall and contemplated the place.

"I feel right well at home here," said Veronica. "It's bright, and the air smells of God."

"As long as you don't try to speak to anyone," countered Alice, sitting beside Ann. "Toby does appreciate a church that welcomes dogs."

"Say your prayers, now, and let's go," said Catherine. "The men are waiting for us." But she couldn't make her own legs move and, instead, stood in awe, gazing upward. Such a solid house of God, built upon a city of water. She said a quick petition for good weather and honest company. Veronica left them to kneel before the great altar, head bowed and palms plastered to each other, at the front of the church. Other women stared and put their heads together at it, and Catherine went to save her daughter from their judgments, even if she didn't see them. The way ahead might be unsavoury enough without display.

Ann and Alice were already outside. "What did you pray for?" asked Catherine, when Veronica emerged into the sunlight.

"For my brother," she said. "That he will be better when we find him."

Ann said, "It seems more a place of money trading than prayer." She spat a small wad onto the ground. "Just like home."

"Jesus destroyed the goods of the traders in the Temple," said Alice.

"Perhaps I misjudged," said Ann. "But they seemed to be looking for each other more than for God."

"God is everywhere," said Alice. "That's what I was taught. I've known it for years." She set Toby in her elbow crook and walked on.

"Out of the mouths of babes," said Ann.

The men were at the verge of the low road, and John was explaining something to them. Reg turned and said, "The entire city has been raised over the water, do you know that? The houses are required to be built of stone, because they had a great fire. They transport and trade over the entire world. It is quite remarkable how it's grown since I saw it last."

Catherine shaded her eyes and let her gaze follow the sky to the horizon. The city was neat, laid out in roads straight as furrows, with the water-roads between, and she felt a longing to wander. But the others were remounting the horses and wagons, and she traded her mare for a seat by one of her men, who had been put to driving the second wagon, and told him to go on. Ann clambered into the back and planted herself on one of the wide trunks. "I can see everything from here," Catherine said. "Let's move on. I'm ready to see more."

They had not gone far before a stench crowded the air, something like a dead cow, or a rotting field of grain. Catherine covered her nose with a handkerchief and called to Ann, "Do you smell that?"

"How could I not?" said Ann. "What's died here, man?"

She got no answer from the men on horseback in front of them, and she called again, "John! Hand!"

At this last, John turned, grinning again. He held up one palm. "Hand! That am I! What do you need?

"The smell!" said Ann. "What is it?"

"Oh, that," said John. "That is just our Old Stinky."

"Old Stinky?" said Ann.

"The windmill!" said John. He launched forth his great belly laugh. "She makes the leather soft and fine, but she sweat like a mule. She stink and we love her." He laughed again. "She is our smelly lady!"

"A windmill!" said Alice. "I want to see that! May I see it?" She was on the smallest of the horses, and she trotted up next to John. "Will you take us?"

"For you, young lady, we will go," said John. "We ride near to that way to my family farm." He pointed ahead. "You smell her before you see her. But she is there. That way."

The stink grew more pungent as they approached, and even Alice, in her excitement, had to cover her face with a linen cloth as they went by. The windmill tilted into the sky above them, and its feet lay near the marshy water, and Catherine almost lost her balance staring as they rode past its placid face. The mill paddled patiently through the air, its broad blades dropping lazily and then swooping back upwards. It was like watching some large bird in a gentle flight to nowhere and Catherine thought that it might be a lesson to her, to let the winds take her where they would. She would find what she sought.

Soon they left the town behind, and flat fields stretched beyond them on either side, clean and low, unending lakes under a skim of grass. Veronica rode up beside John, and they chatted awkwardly. At one point Veronica sang a tune, and John tried to harmonize.

"He may lead us into a hovel," said Ann. "How can we trust this fellow with his stinking windmills?"

"I don't see a choice in the matter," said Catherine. "I thought the windmill charming."

"Charming as a pig in slop," muttered Ann.

Reg slowed until he was riding beside the wagon, and now John was whistling and pointing out something to Veronica, who nodded. "Your daughter seems content with the bargain," Reg said.

"So she does," said Catherine.

Ann said, "But what if we're being led into a thieves' den?"

Catherine could not but admire the tidy cottages and houses that they passed. The way was broad and sunny, and she felt her eyes drooping, just as they turned onto a narrower lane, this one walled with the skeletons of trees just showing their first haloes of green. "Almost home!" called John, over his shoulder, but Catherine could see no house at all.

Hilde turned off at a side-lane and waved as she went. John rode ahead. Catherine had it on the end of her tongue to call for them to turn around and flee when they came through an arch in a stone wall and stopped.

John De Vries lived on a farm, indeed. What lay before them was a massive spread of fields and orchards, with ponds dug into the low-lying places and stables and tenants' cottages dotting the acres. The family home was no mere farmhouse but a stone structure at least as large as Catherine's old lost home in Yorkshire. John threw one leg over his horse and jumped lightly to the ground, and ran to help Veronica before she could dismount on her own. He waved the rest of them forward. "Come see! Come meet my family!"

The family had already noted their approach. The front door had opened and a couple, a few years older than Ann and Reg, stood in the porch. A couple of shaggy shepherds ran out, sniffed around their legs, and set up barking and howling at the newcomers. A smaller dog took its position at Alice's feet and pawed to get at Toby.

"Not a den of thieves," said Ann.

"I would call this a farm," said Reg.

Catherine said, "It's a picture of industry." She slipped from her seat and walked up to appraise and be appraised. Veronica was already curtseying and being raised, her hands in the hands of the woman. There could be no mistake that these were John's parents, both fair as he was, the woman with his arresting blue eyes and the man with his dimpled jaw. Veronica had already been introduced, and the woman was holding Catherine's daughter's chin in her palm, saying "Veronica, eh? A saintly girl!" The man laughed just as John did, with an explosion of unstudied joy.

"You are mother?" the woman said, approaching Catherine.

Catherine curtsied and rose. "I am Catherine Overton Davies. Yes, I am Veronica's mother."

"Such beauty!" said the woman. "From mother to daughter. Welcome in to our home."

John's father said nothing, and Catherine supposed that he knew little English, but he met Reg and they performed the ritual shake of hands. De Vries called out something, and two servants came to tend to the horses and the wagons. Ann stood alone.

"Ann," called Catherine. "My dear friend," she added to Mistress De Vries, who extended a hand. "Ann Goodall. Wife to Reginald." She pointed out each one as she spoke.

"And I Gertrude," said Mistress De Vries, pointing to herself. "This our home. With three sons! Jan is youngest. My baby boy." She had to stand on her toes to tousle his hair, but he endured it. "Older sons have wives already. This one? Will take nobody. Too good for any of them, this one."

The two older De Vries sons were called up from the barns and came through the house from the back. They nodded their greetings and answered "good, good" when their mother told them that the party would stay on. They went on out to inspect the purchases from the town that John had brought. "Some grains for the horses," said John, and his mother added, "Ach, they love horses more than people."

At dinner everyone gathered at an enormous table, almost too large for even the giant room in which the family ate their meals. The brothers, who announced that they were Georg—the same as their father—and Bernhard, were clearly accustomed to visitors and smiled but said little, throwing scraps of meat to the dogs that crowded under the people's feet. Their wives, one hugely pregnant and the other with a babe in arms and a toddling boy on her knee, spoke no English at all. One pointed to herself and said what sounded like "Gertland," but that was no country Catherine had ever heard of and she shook her head to indicate that she did not understand. Then the woman pointed at the other wife and repeated the odd word. Catherine grew embarrassed and gave up the conversation, pretending to comprehend with nods and what she hoped was a winning smile, and fell to the pile of meat and root vegetables before her. The wives replaced words with acts, filling the plates again and again, until Catherine, almost suffocating from food, finally had to say no more as politely as she could with her hands. Veronica, when her plate was taken up, said, "Danke, Gerta und Anne," and Catherine realized that she'd been told their names. She also said the strange thank-you, but her tongue coiled around the pronunciation and she knew she had mortified herself once more.

Upstairs, they were shown two empty bedchambers. Reg and Ann were given the largest as due to a married couple, while Catherine shared the second with the girls. Their servants had already found space in the quarters down by the kitchen, which Reg had been shown to his satisfaction.

"Even all of us haven't filled this house," said Veronica. She was lying across the bed, letting her feet dangle toward the floor. One shoe had dropped off.

"They have more dogs than I have," added Alice.

Ann came in to inspect their room. "At least this place is civilized. And clean. And it doesn't move under my feet. How long do we stay?"

"No more than three days," said Catherine. The bed was soft, and she struggled to get out of her clothes so that she could fling herself onto it. "Longer than that, and I'll have to let out all of my bodices. Did you taste the cake?"

"Too much of it," said Ann. "My guts feel like they've got an anvil in there."

"And to hear them talk!" said Veronica. "I feel like a turnip, Mother, dull and stuck in my own soil. I wish I knew how to speak it. They know English. Why are we such rustics?"

"Your daughter has fallen in love with the Dutch," said Ann.

"Don't mock," said Veronica, rolling over onto her stomach and putting her chin in her hands. "They come from the German lands. John's father was a sailor once and he settled here. They speak the German languages, too. And here I am, almost an old maid, and I've seen nothing of the world."

"You can't be an old maid until you're old," said Ann. "And you're seeing the world right now. When I was your age —"

"Oh, don't tell me again about the world when you were a girl. You've always been a homebody. I want to be different."

"And you will be," said Catherine. "You already are."

"I confess that I find this place very satisfying," said Ann. "And now I'm going to get into a clean bed, free of the endless pitching of that blasted ship."

Catherine slept deeply and long, past the sunrise and almost through the morning. She dreamt weirdly, finding herself on the deck again, but it wasn't upon the water. The ship rocked and heaved on dry land, and the sailors were all nuns. She knew, even in the midst of sleep, that she must get to a certain destination, but whenever she looked overboard, they were on a different kind of land: first arid and poor, like a wasted field, then wooded and loud with the hoots and calls of animals, then abundant with flowers. The dream-Catherine lay down upon a cot which wasn't a cot but a coffin-like box into which she sank, closing her dream-eyes and wondering when she would know where she was supposed to go. Someone lay beside her—how, she could not say—and she was sure it was her husband. She turned, but when she could see she found herself lying next to the corpse of William Overton, her first husband, who said to her, "Get you gone, wife."

And she woke with a start. The room was gilded with sunshine. Veronica, already awake, was giggling and tickling Alice's feet with a feather from her pillow. Catherine thought for a moment that they were at home. But she sat up, and

Veronica said, "Wake up, Alice. Mother's finally back with the living, and now we can go downstairs." Then Catherine knew where she was, but the shreds of the ghostly voice haunted her ears.

Veronica, of course, was already dressed. She hopped about, irritating Alice into a new dress while Catherine forced on her stiff, shabby-looking clothes from the day before. They found Reg at the large table with John De Vries, who was drawing a map. Ann, sitting nearby, looked up when Catherine and the girls came in. "I hope you can wait for your breakfast. These men are going to lead us across to Wittenberg."

"Men?" said Catherine.

"I go!" said John. He grinned at Veronica. "Make best guide. Know how to speak."

"But it's a long way," said Catherine. "Aren't you needed here, to help your father and brothers? You scarcely know us."

"Ach, they can do," said John. "Me? Just other pair of hands. We got plenty."

"We had better get his parents' permission," Catherine said. "We can't be accused of making off with someone's son."

"He's a grown man," said Reg, writing in the directions for north, south, east, and west. "And we can pay him. We can all have an adventure."

John shook his hand over the air, as if to erase Reg's words. "No pay. No, no. I go and you feed me good and get me clean room in the taverns. I pay for room. You feed. That's all. I make some trades maybe."

"We can't ask you to be our guide just for the pleasure of it," said Catherine. "Your parents will expect something in return for your absence."

"I want the pleasure," insisted John. "I got everything I need. Strong hands. Strong back. Strong head for the business. Don't need your money."

Veronica said nothing but shoved a wad of bread, left lying on a platter the men had pushed aside, into her mouth.

"When will we go?" Catherine couldn't stop herself from touching the drawings of lakes and mountains that John had made. Her fingers itched to take the pen herself, and she tried to remember how long it had been since she'd had a quill in her hand for anything other than recording figures in her accounts. "Let me try," she said, and Reg stood aside for her. She didn't know the country, but pleased herself by adding a few small ranges to the edges of a set of lines meant to convey hills and shading in the trees in the lower right corner. She added in a few flowers at the place where she imagined there would be foothills facing eastward and southerly.

John laughed and said, "You are illuminator!"

Catherine blushed at this. In fact, she had decorated many a manuscript in her youth, but those days were far behind her. Where were all of her beautiful receipt books these days? Probably stuffed into the back of a shelf down in her kitchen at home. She would have to get them out when they returned, see if the writing was still legible. She had liked to add pictures of the leaves and blossoms of the various plants she'd grown. When was the last time she'd done that? The pen felt good in her hand, solid, as though it were made to fit up against her bones. She should buy herself a few pots of color, try out her skills again. When they returned. Yes, John would be a fit guide for them, if his parents consented for him to go.

They did. By the time the family had gathered again for a meal, the decision had been made. The brothers poked at John with their elbows, and Gertrude beamed with an enthusiasm that made Catherine suspicious for a few moments, until she glanced at Ann and saw that Ann was watching Veronica. Veronica, in turn, was staring at John with such naked admiration that Catherine gasped a little. Of course, he wanted to go. He was young and unmarried, and he would see some of the world in the company of her beautiful daughter.

And from the look on her face, Veronica wanted him to go, as well.

Chapter 11

Three tranquil nights under the broad roof of the De Vries house. And then three more. And three more yet again. Catherine's muscles began to itch to get on the road, but Ann pleaded the need to stay in one place for a while, and John insisted that he had to gather trading goods. Catherine acquiesced easily, indulging herself in irresponsible comfort. She spent the daylight hours with Gertrude De Vries, who showed her how they made the best cheese, remarking that it was good, good, until Catherine realized that she was calling it by its name and asked her to write it: Gouda, for its town of origin. The kitchens were cavernous but immaculate, more so than any Catherine had ever seen, even in her days with the royal households. Not a speck lurked in the corners, and not a mouse dared flaunt a whisker. Catherine found her memories of grand English palaces cankered with doubts about how clean she had ever really been. She sniffed at her armpits and dug under her fingernails when no one was watching and vowed to become unpolluted.

Ann and the girls wandered about the farm, and the fourth evening they sat at the long front window with Catherine. Ann said, "Have you ever seen such a flat land? Flatter even than the fens. And lower. For miles it goes, so low you think you're going to step into an ocean with every footfall. I fancy that I can see the sea from this very spot." On the horizon, a tiny windmill lazed through its circuit. "Are there any mountains on this side of the water? Any hills?"

"Ah, mountains," said Gertrude, who had come in behind them. She set her knobby hands on the back of Alice's chair and ran a finger down Toby's nose. "Very big." She stretched herself as tall as she could. "Very big." She pointed vaguely eastward. "Not seen those since I was girl. Jan will tell."

Their son seemed indeed eager, finally, to go. "No need for more delay," he said every day, as he ordered the servants to pack up food and clothing, smoked fish and meats, and bags of pepper and nutmegs and cinnamon. He bundled up his maps and bickered with his brothers about which horses would fare best on a long walk and how many wagons they would need. Veronica followed him here and there, asking questions about what they called hay, or bread, or stockings in this land.

"Veronica acts as though she's under a spell," remarked Catherine to Ann, as she observed her daughter from a corner of the great front room the last evening of their visit.

"A spell of love," said Ann. "First love. I wish her well in it. We've both seen love slip away as fast as it came." Ann seldom mentioned her first husband, long dead, much longer than Catherine's first husband. Neither of them ever said anymore that they had grown to despise the men of their youth—too many years had intervened, and it was evil to think ill of the dead. And now Ann had Reg, who treated Ann like the wisest person he could ever hope to know.

And Catherine? Catherine had Benjamin. "I chose badly the first time," she said. "I almost can't see William's face anymore. Except sometimes in my dreams, and then I'm not sure that it's his face at all."

"You chose as well as most young women," said Ann. "You had luck with you that the king let you marry at all."

The king and his laws. The queen and her laws. "Life will be easier for Veronica and Alice."

"Life's never easy, Catherine."

"Perhaps. My daughters have money, though, and a mother who loves them. All the English have seen now that a woman may have her own mind."

"We'll see if that's true. 'Queens is queens, not women,' the man said, or some such," said Ann. "Money may make their choice harder, when it comes to picking husbands, however much you love them. As for their minds, well, they're as good as any. But yours was, too." Ann chewed a thumbnail, and when she bit too hard, sucked at the blood that bubbled from the edge of it and then hid it in her palm.

"Veronica has a good head. And when we get Benjamin home, she'll have a father to look out for her. He's always been good to her."

"And faithful as Penelope to you," said Ann. She rubbed at the snagged thumb.

Catherine had seldom seen Ann agitated so. "I've never been the best judge of men."

"You've been young. But better for you to say it than I." Ann smoothed the injury with her forefinger, then slid the hand under her skirt. "I always tried to be courteous to Benjamin."

"But you thought ill of him?"

"Do you want the truth, or the truth as you'd have it shaped?"

"The unvarnished truth. Honestly, Ann. Tell me what you think."

"I always thought that Benjamin Davies' talk was smoother than a young girl's skin. He was honester than some and loyal when no barriers were placed in the way of his constancy. I think he loved you when you were young and beautiful and he married you when he knew you were carrying his child. I believe he was a faithful husband when you were nearby. But I also know that he lost no sleep in pursuing you when you were married to another man, weak as that man was, and that once he had won you, he often put profit before family. He loved his daughters, but cared less about his children than he did about how fat his account books were and how shiny his public honour. Once Alice came along, he barely thought about Diana at all. As though the one could replace the other." Ann stopped. She put the bitten hand on her breast, as if to slow her heart. The thumb still leaked blood, and it left a red blotch on her breast.

Catherine's head had grown stormy as Ann spoke, and she could barely look her friend in the eye. "Do you say all this? To my face?"

"You asked me for the truth, Catherine. I'll never lie to you, and I won't gild a rusted history if you ask me not to."

"Well," said Catherine. "I asked you and you've told me. And do you know what I must say to this?"

"Say what you will," said Ann. "I can return to England if you want me to go. I've already seen more of the world than I ever meant to."

Catherine put her arms around her old friend. "You are the soul of observation, as you have always been. I have ever been a fool when it came to choosing a husband. But he's my husband in the eyes of God. Life will be as it was when he is home."

Ann clasped the wind out of Catherine. "We are all fools these days, hoping for some anchor to hold us to a place we can recognize. The world shifts too rapidly." She pushed Catherine away and peered at her. "You were raised in a convent. You weren't told who your parents were and you had no one to protect you when you came into the presence of men. How could anyone expect you to know how to choose one, or how to recognize their methods? Men in search of women are cunning, and husbands are ruthless."

"Even Reg?"

"No, not Reg. He's not like other husbands. He's not like other men. Maybe he should have been a king." Ann chuckled and examined her thumb. Then she frowned. "But the ones who circle like hungry dogs? They raise my suspicions. William Overton did it, as did his older brother. Benjamin did it. They're drawn to beauty like cats to cream, and they show their fangs when they're hindered from lapping it up. Good men are rare. They're more like shepherds, tending their flocks and hoping for an honest increase. They keep the wolves off, but they do it with tenderness and attention. And they're seldom noticed or rewarded for it. They're often ridiculed for it instead. They're called womanish or some such thing, to insult both them and all of womankind."

"I can count on one hand the times I've heard such a speech from you, Ann," said Catherine. "Are they tomcats, then, these men I've married?"

Ann laughed. "Pay me no mind. I just talk without thinking. It's the foreign air. It makes me windy."

But Catherine always paid attention to Ann. She knew that Ann was seldom wrong and that she had thought hard on the subject. "And this John De Vries?" she whispered. "What do you see in him? Is he more cat or shepherd?"

"It's too soon to know. I see a handsome youth who has nothing to tie him down. He's full of oats and wants to prance out and see new lands and new people. That's not uncommon. He thinks Veronica is beautiful, and I can't blame him for that. It's true. We'll watch him. And we'll watch Veronica. If he loves her, he can wait and earn her love. If not, we'll pack him up and send him home and Veronica can mend her heart for the next one."

So they started out the next morning, Catherine glad finally to be on their way, and lighter of spirit about her daughter but gloomier about her husband. She now cast her mind over her memories of Benjamin, and they, too, had tarnished. He'd been a kind husband to her, that she couldn't deny. And as they lumbered back down the lane of the De Vries farm, the parents waving them off, and the wagons so loaded and stuffed with bags of spices that she was afraid they would snap the thick axles, Catherine saw no way she could send John home and return to England. He led the train, with Veronica at his side, as though they were already a couple. Ann was right. Her daughter was a woman. If anyone would be turning John De Vries back, it looked as though it would have to be Veronica, and Catherine wondered if she had been as poor an instructor in matters of the heart as her own parents had been.

The first days were slow. John was acquainted with many of the farmers along the way, and he stopped every few hours to visit with neighbors or trading partners, avoiding the houses that he claimed were unsafe. "The protesters," he muttered, as though he weren't hauling an entire family of Protestants. Maybe they weren't, though, not really, Catherine thought. Maybe they seemed as Catholic as anyone to John, and no one had said anything to make him see otherwise.

He pulled hams and embroidered skirts and jerkins, or small containers from the pepper bags and smaller ones of the nutmegs, from the bowels of the wagons as gifts or trades, packing in coins and ale and woolen blankets where they had been. The weather turned cold enough to blister her cheeks in the mornings, and Catherine longed for one of the heavy coverings for her lap. John laughed his big laugh and said that they were for sleeping under, but he dragged one out. As she laid it across her legs, Catherine saw the young man's eyes shift to Veronica, as though to calculate whether she would respond to an allusion to a bed, but Veronica was too busy staring at the houses and people present before her to take note of the future.

The homesteads John chose were as tidy and charming as the huge De Vries farm, and Catherine blushed for her countrymen. Perhaps the light icing of snow they got over the nights served to conceal raggedness, but these people, up close, did not stink of dirty bodies and unwashed linen, like so many of the English did, and the land, though low and often waterlogged, did not appear to be fallow. Homesickness ached in her guts, as though to spite her senses, and when she realized that what she missed was the scent of rancid tallow and rank sweat, she mustered some admiration for the foreigners who had claimed the love of her son. She sat up front in one of the wagons on the third afternoon, watching John trade some smoked fish and nutmegs for fresh bread, when her ear picked up a familiar argument. She shaded her eyes and gazed upward. High above her, in the still-naked branches of a tree she could not name, was a trio of crows, shouting at one another in phrases so articulate that she fancied, if she listened hard enough, that she could make out the words.

She was the foreigner, Catherine thought, and these crows sounded more English than John. But he was the one at home here, in this fresh, wide countryside, and she watched as the birds parted company in their wrath and flew away.

Before the week was out, they had moved into wilder, higher lanes, and John no longer pulled his horse to a stop at anyone's house. He drove them forward, halting only at dusk to search out an inn. Now Reg rode beside him, with Veronica's and Alice's mares tucked directly behind them, and they consulted the map, then the sun, as they rode. The serving men talked between themselves less and gave passing travellers wary stares, all of them in a tight line like grim pilgrims on a march toward martrydom.

The inns were sturdy, dark buildings, not so unlike what Catherine was accustomed to in England, and she was grateful that John could speak the local language, and that made him welcome. Or perhaps it was the money in his purse that put the friendly smiles onto unfamiliar faces.

Within a few more days, however, John seemed almost as much a stranger as the English did, though he could still speak, a little haltingly, to innkeepers and order their food. Veronica learned the tongue quickly, and soon she, too, could ask for rooms and more bread without embarrassment. Alice picked up phrases, as well, and the girls grew bold in their speech, though Catherine couldn't follow what exactly was said. The serving men did not leave their sides.

The mornings continued bitter, but with little snow, and Catherine often pushed back her heavy hood to let the sun touch her face, though its fingers were icy until midday. She wondered if her daughters would take up the style some of the younger women favoured now, the light head coverings that Elizabeth wore. It would become the fashion, surely. The women they passed here wore bulky layers over their hair against the cold, but Catherine imagined summer and the feel of the breeze at her neck and ears.

She did not broach the subject of John De Vries to her elder daughter, though she shared bedchambers with Veronica and Alice as they moved from inn to inn. One evening, Ann left Reg at the table with John. She wanted to see their room, she said, but as soon as the door was closed behind them, she set herself onto Veronica. "Tell me what you think of this De Vries boy. I've held my peace as long as I'm able."

Veronica twittered a little. "What do you mean, Auntie?"

Veronica hadn't referred to Ann as her aunt since she'd worn long skirts. Ann was undeterred. "Go to, child. I see the way you stare at him. Has he asked you to marry him?"

"You'd have heard him if he did." Veronica picked at a bit of loose embroidery on her bodice. "I will have to mend this. It looks wretched."

"I'll do that," said Ann. "Take it off." She helped the younger woman out of the offending item and tucked it under her arm. "I wager he's asked you in Dutch or German and you know enough to make him an answer in kind."

Veronica blushed to her hairline. "He has not!" Then she smiled. "But for all that, he's a handsome fellow, isn't he? Do you see how he sits his horse like a master? It's lovely to watch him studying the map. He knows how to get where he wants to go."

Alice said, "And my sister knows to how to get beside him when he goes."

"I expect she does," said Ann.

"Veronica," cut in Catherine. "Do you love this man?"

"I can't speak of love," said Veronica. "I don't know him enough. But I like his looks, and I like his behaviour, at least what I've observed of it. Is that love? I think not. Not yet. I don't wish to make a mistake in marriage." She kept her eyes on her sister, and off her mother, as she spoke, and when Alice giggled Catherine felt the sting of an unspoken rebuke.

Ann said, "That's wise. You know he's a younger son, younger by two brothers. He won't inherit."

"There's no title in the family, anyway, so what does it matter?" said Veronica. "He'll have a portion, won't he?"

"Perhaps," said Ann.

"And a portion is portable, isn't it?" added Veronica.

"Oh, now I see which way the wind blows," said Ann. "You seek a man who can bring his inheritance back to England."

Catherine had recovered from the jolt of Veronica's slap about errors in marriage enough to say, "I had fears that you'd fallen in love with the countryside more than the man."

Veronica removed her skirt and hung it over a chair. "I like the land well enough. The people are clean, and the cottages are pleasant. The hills are innocent-looking, and the cows are fat." She turned and shrugged. "But it's not home."

"Nor is England John De Vries's home," said Catherine.

"It's too early for such conversations," said Veronica. "I'm having an adventure, and I mean to enjoy it. I'm not so old that I can't find a man if I want one. I'm no queen, and I've no need for babies. Let Robbie marry and have children. It doesn't matter how old he is. He's a man. Let Alice marry and have a litter of children. She can throw them in with her dogs and let them all play together."

"I will not have a litter," said Alice. "I may not marry at all. I don't like men, and that's flat."

Ann roared at this, and Alice said, "Can't we just go to sleep? All this talk of marriage and babies has so upset my stomach I won't shut my eyes again this night. I don't wish to dream of husbands."

"We've disturbed your sister, and that's a fault," said Catherine. "We should all be abed by this time."

Veronica cast a superior look at her sister and sniffed. "Some of us don't desire so much to be old maids that we cannot sit by a candle and gossip a little."

"So you do mean to marry!" said Ann.

"I mean nothing at all, and I'll say nothing more on the subject this night," said Veronica, "lest I shatter Alice's tender soul with my noise."

Ann nodded, and, elbowing Catherine in the ribs as she went, departed with the raveled bodice.

Chapter 12

"Have I really been such a fool in marriage that everyone can see it?" said Catherine, trudging beside Ann the next day. The morning had been silent, everyone's tongues seeming weighed down by their inability to understand the strangers they met. Catherine's imagination had been pestering her all night with the nagging shame of Veronica's barbed speech. She'd brooded as long as she could, but after they stopped for a midday meal and were served by a young couple so recently wed that they were almost on top of each other right there at the table, she had to speak. Ann was the only person she trusted with such a question. She was forced to beg the need to move her legs for a while and a need for Ann to do it with her.

"I don't speak for everyone," said Ann. She adjusted her clothes at the waist and pushed back her cap to let the air reach her hair. "I don't find it wise to advise anyone on their marriage after it's done. Before that? Perhaps."

"Lower your voice! This is serious to me. And that's not an answer," said Catherine. "You talk in general terms. Come, Ann. Tell me truth."

They approached and passed a wooden sign that had "Wittenberg" and an arrow painted on it. "Look!" said Ann. "We must be very close now. Can't we get onto the wagon? My legs are stretched enough."

"Ann."

"Yes. Well. Hmm. Your husbands haven't been the men I would have chosen, either for myself or for you. But there was the matter of the children. William was gone so quickly, to be honest, that I scarcely remember him."

Catherine could tell from the way Ann's eyes stayed on the road ahead that she was buttering the truth to make it go down more easily. She herself recalled how furious Ann often became over her first husband's worries about his position. And whether Catherine's son was also his. Ann had set her lips together, though. She would refuse to remember it. "And what of Benjamin?" Catherine said.

"I've said it before. He has no real human warmth in him. He never did have. He's a man of business, and he has the heart of a moneymaker. Solid gold when it's doing well, just cold metal when it's not. I prefer some heat in a man. He treated you well, and he was never stingy about what you bought or sold. He liked your mind. That's good. He liked your looks. Less good. He ignored his daughters when he had something else drawing his attention. It's no wonder to me that Diana turned out to be such a mouse. She never had a mother until you came into the family."

Catherine saw Diana posed in front of her house in London, framed by the Marys. Straight as a post, as she always stood, and no one on either side of her who would provide conversation or comfort, except to fling curses about Elizabeth. Her hood, still the old-fashioned, heavy kind, had been perfectly pinned on her perfect head. She must have been sweating like a horse inside of that thing. Catherine tried to think of Diana's mother's name. "I've forgotten it," she said aloud.

"What?" said Ann.

"Benjamin's first wife. What was her name?"

"I don't remember it, either," said Ann.

"He never spoke of her after we were married," said Catherine. "I don't even know where her grave is. And Diana never talked of her, in all those years."

"You see?" said Ann. "That's just what I meant. The father shows in the daughter. Gone and out of mind. They lost her, and they found you. They won you over and that was an end to it."

"I wonder if we'll recover him."

"I wonder," repeated Ann. "He might be dead, you know, and then it won't matter."

Catherine settled into herself, now miserable with the prospect she had considered and put from her mind: that Benjamin was buried somewhere and had died without the memory of her face and without regret about it. No wonder he hadn't written. She couldn't bear it, she thought. She would die of the sorrow of it. Why did any woman marry at all? But she already knew the answer: children, and some standing in the community.

She stopped the wagon and dragged herself back onto the hard seat. Lent a hand down to Ann, who boarded and rode silently beside her. Her dearest friend in all the world had been direct, maybe almost cruel, and she was probably wishing she had kept her lips sealed. But Catherine was glad for her honesty, even if it made her hate the idea of the journey ahead. She'd forged this path, though. She'd fought to go. Perhaps they could gather Robbie and return to England, if he hadn't forgotten who she was, as well.

The men stopped to speak to a passing pair of travellers. John De Vries gestured forward, and the strangers turned in their saddles to point the way they had come. All of them nodded and smiled, and Reg leant in close, probably trying to understand what was being said. The men passed on, touching their hats to the women as they rode by, and John whooped. Veronica spurred her horse up to him, and then whirled around to face Catherine and the others.

"We're almost arrived!" she called. "Do you see?"

Catherine lifted her gaze to the horizon. Yes, she spotted the tops of what looked like tall buildings in the distance. Spires, like churches or palaces. A snake of a river. She could see houses, and that was a good sign. And her son would be with her soon. Her heart lifted in her breast. She'd be victorious, after all.

The dwellings were now closer together, and more travellers appeared on the road. Reg suggested that they stop, but Catherine would not, not this close and the sun not yet dropped behind them. Alice rode in circles to contain her excitement, and Catherine urged them toward a long wooden bridge, though once their wheels were on it and she heard it groan and squeak under their weight, she drew in her breath and held it. Even Alice grew sober, and they all crept across. Catherine marvelled at the wide water below them, as crowded as the Thames to her eye. Then they were over, among the buildings. A castle, though she had seen larger ones. Shops and dwellings on both sides, and there, the high palace of someone powerful, looking down its nose at them, and, beyond, the tower of a church spearing the sky.

The girls had halted with John and the wagon pulled up beside them. The man's fair face showed blatant longing, and he said, "It is a whole town of Protesters." Reg had trotted back to them, and he added, "I wonder what they trade in."

"Their religion, if Catherine's son is to be believed," said Ann.

"And books," said Catherine. "They print books." Now her heart swelled and thumped around in her chest. They were in Wittenberg, and Robbie was nearby. It was a clean, orderly place, and, once the river was behind them, as pretty as any English town and less congested with garbage. The streets were narrower than the road they'd been on, but wide enough. They caught some curious glances, but no one paid them much mind as they trundled through, gaping upward and forward. They turned a corner and landed in a square. A large square.

Alice chirped, "We're here!"

"Yes, and now what do we do?" asked Ann. Their wagons and horses were massive and monstrous among the little town ponies and mules, like thick-waisted washerwomen among a throng of elegant ladies. The shoppers glared at them. The streets from which they had to choose all looked the same to Catherine and she had no idea which was the straight or narrow. They all looked crooked. The people were too many, and she feared running over someone's foot if they moved. She dug into the pocket of her skirt and withdrew the letter from Robbie, though she already knew every word by heart. "It says nothing of his dwelling."

"I saw castle," said John De Vries, pointing back and upward. "Castle church will be near. Very famous place. I will find your boy." He dismounted and entered what looked like a tavern.

Catherine watched men and women cross the square. Alice and Veronica reined in their mares, trying to wedge them into a skinny alley that ran from the brick wall behind her, but the horses resisted and Veronica's finally reared, calling more attention to her as an unskilled rider than as a foreigner in town. People stared outright. A couple of women tittered. Catherine got down and sidled up next to her and the horse settled itself. But they were still the objects of everyone's eyes. Their serving men looked bored and hungry and resentful of being watched.

But Veronica, bright as a young hare, said, "Isn't it splendid, Mother?" and then, "What is the matter with this animal that I can't manage him? I believe he is as eager as I am!"

To Catherine, it was not splendid, not just at this moment. The sky was growing dark, and she had no place to lay her head and no one to tell her where her son was. She thought it couldn't be worse, until a couple of men emerged from a flat building nearby and strutted toward them.

The pair stopped before the wagons, just as Catherine had feared they would. They were in important-looking black suits, and one of them was saying something she couldn't understand.

Ann stepped up and brightly said, "English!"

"Ah," said the man. He considered a moment. "Why here? This our, how do you say?, mayor, Thomas Heilinger." Heilinger bobbed from the waist.

"My son," stammered Catherine. She was sure she would wet herself any minute. "We seek my son." Her better angel came to her then and she remembered the letter from court. It was in the bag on her belt, and she pulled it out with shaking fingers. She hoped she hadn't sweated it through. "My passport."

The two men consulted over the paper, nodding and muttering and scrutinizing Catherine's face. Finally, the first one handed it back to Catherine and the mayor now bowed. "Welcome!" he said. "Wagons out of square, if you please." He offered his hand.

Catherine's legs threatened to melt under her, but she managed to grab the offered shake, and nod enthusiastically. "Yes, we are going." And there came John De Vries. He emerged from the tavern with Reg and shrugged. They both joined the women, and John said something that, again, Catherine couldn't understand. "This is the mayor of Wittenberg," Catherine said. "He wants the wagons off the square."

More indecipherable conversation, but it was followed by some laughter and a backslap to John by the mayor, who withdrew, with bows and smiles, alongside his companion, into the building from which they had come.

"They know no Overton," said John. "No one in tavern does, neither. They say a man with the name of 'Lyon' is nearby who keeps English. Could that be where he dwells?"

"I don't know," said Catherine. She could barely see the letters on either of the papers that she had now. "It's too dark. We need to stop."

Reg muttered something, and Catherine knew he was triumphing, in his unboastful way. They should have stopped and come into the town in the morning. But it was too late now, and she said, "I'm sorry, Reg."

"We'll make the best of a sorry condition," said Reg. "Let's send John and Veronica to find an inn. Move the wagons as far to the edge as we can, and I'll wait here with you and the others."

Veronica agreed to this a bit too quickly for her modesty and for Catherine's taste, but off they went. Catherine studied the windows, now lighting up around them with candles. She could imagine her son behind none of them. He had never liked a busy market, so full of things to buy. Frivolity, he would have said. A danger to the soul. It astonished her how easily her mind could cast up his judgments to her.

They did not wait long. Before full dark, John and Veronica returned, beckoning them mercifully down the widest of the streets, plenty wide enough for their wagons, to a solid, two-storey house. It fronted directly onto the street, but there was an alleyway beside it, and they could see the ample stable rooms behind. Catherine could smell cooking meats, and laughter fell onto her ears from the open main door. Perhaps Wittenberg would not be unfriendly, after all.

WORLDS END

Chapter 13

"Veronica looks fatter, doesn't she?" said Ann. She and Catherine had strolled out after dinner, Veronica and Alice staying behind to try out the language with the other guests of the inn. The women had taken the two servants with them, but they stayed a discreet distance away from Catherine and Ann. Ann didn't care who overheard her, anyway.

"It's the food," said Catherine. She'd never seen such quantities of butter and cheese since they'd landed in Amsterdam. And meats—heaps and piles of seasoned pork and joints of beef. "I'm bigger myself." She tried out her waistline with both hands. The women she'd seen had been rather thick, she thought, like so many barrels bobbing along in a stream, and perhaps stoutness was the fashion here. She felt that it didn't suit her, and it certainly didn't suit the clothing that she'd brought. She'd upbraided herself more than once for vanity, but she couldn't dispel the conceit that she bore a tidier figure than the local women. "I'll grow fat if I stay here very long."

"You're slender as a young hound," said Ann, "and you always have been. Englishwomen are no different. Look at me. I don't worry about it. I don't care if men look at me—or women."

The admonishment stung Catherine a little. "Men don't look at me. Not anymore."

"And you regret that as a loss?"

Did she? Catherine wanted to say that no, of course she didn't, but she noticed enough to know it. Men had once watched her. Now they watched her daughter. "It doesn't matter for a woman of my age, anyway. I only need to be able to wear what I have with me."

"No, it doesn't matter. And you can buy new things if you want them. You're healthy and you have money in your purse. It doesn't matter for a young woman, either. But Veronica has always fidgeted the fat off, and that isn't good. She couldn't have gotten any thinner and still be casting a shadow."

"You're saying that this love of hers doesn't worry you?"

"Love always worries me," said Ann. "But starvation in a woman worries me more."

"It's not as though we denied her food at home," said Catherine.

"I know. But you surely noted how little she ever ate. And how she picked at her hair ends in the evenings." She glanced behind them. "And how seldom she had her flowers."

"Veronica's always been a little tightly-strung," said Catherine, defensive now. She had not, in fact, known about her daughter's irregular monthlies. Ann probably thought Veronica had told her. Her elder daughter had seemed healthy enough, though apt to run to fantasies about how large the business of the wool production should grow and how the weavers in Havenston ought to keep their houses. She had never filled her head, or her conversation, with admiration of young men, and Catherine had always put her flighty personal ways down to youth and an abundance of high spirits.

"She's worked herself to the bone and she's denied herself the company of other young people," said Ann. "She won't hear tell of a husband, at least she wouldn't before now. I've feared of late that she was becoming brittle. I'm glad to see her finding fresh air to breathe and fresh folk to talk to. Alice doesn't need to become like her in that way."

Catherine nodded. "Brittle" seemed overly harsh, but Ann had discovered an even livelier tongue in her head since they left England and she let it stand. "I don't want her to lose herself in a strange land."

"Me, neither. Nor do I want her to lose herself to a man we scarcely know, however handsome he may be, just because he's a novelty."

They paused outside of a tavern on a wide street. All was calm and lonely and quiet, except for a sleek dog that padded by, but the lights inside showed men seated around a large table, tankards in their hands or shoved to the side. Most of them were dressed in plain black, from their narrow jackets and hose to their flat, drab hats. A few wore brighter colors, and one of these peacocks was in loud argument with one of the crows.

"What's that about?" said Ann.

"Religion, I suppose." Catherine shook her head. "I don't know. But someone in there is English." She listened harder. "I swear I hear our language." They dared not enter, but they stood awhile, until the argument played itself out. Someone said "God," that was certain. And Catherine distinctly heard the word "Protestant" and "queen." She said, "They might be discussing our Elizabeth."

"What do they care about Elizabeth?"

"Her religion?" said Catherine. "Whatever it is, I'm sure there are Englishmen in there. They'll care about how matters stand in England. And if there are Englishmen about, we might be able to find someone who can tell us where Robbie lives."

"In the morning, you mean. When we have the others with us. When it's daylight."

Catherine had already put one foot out, toward the door. "Of course." She was ready to go back, she said, to go to bed. But she knew that Ann understood what she meant: the earlier they slept, the earlier they could rise and begin their search.

She needn't have bothered, as it turned out. Sleep in the Wittenberg inn meant closing her eyes and trying to ignore the shouting downstairs. Doors slammed and something made of crockery smashed against a wall. The innkeeper raised his own voice, but it wasn't until past midnight that the place battened itself down for slumber, and Catherine didn't believe she would sleep at all until she suddenly woke from a dream of farm animals fighting to realize that it was morning and what she was hearing was a couple of cats outside.

Her eyes felt gluey. She sat up. The others were all gone already, and she threw on her clothes, tying up ends as she went, and found everyone at the table below. Alice said, "Ann has been telling us that the men in Wittenberg are half English and that everyone stays up all night arguing about the state of England. How do they keep the town in such good repair?"

The innkeeper was sitting with them and he said, in shockingly good English, "Bah, religion is the only talk in this town. Luther and more Luther, and then his followers. The university and all of them. God and damnation and good work and faith. They are all for the building, but only if it is in the name of someone or other's notion of God. Giselle, get another plate for the lady."

His wife rose and fetched food, but Catherine had no appetite. "Why do they dress so plainly?" Catherine said. "The ones in black, they look like a pack of grim reapers from the players."

The innkeeper laughed. "Our Lutherans. They scorn the vanities. And does that mean that they also scorn the pleasures of life? Not all. They like to eat. They like their wives well enough." At this, his laugh became husky.

"But they also scorn the monks? They dress very similarly," remarked Ann.

"Ach, do not say so in their hearing. Say nothing at all, if you can. They are quick to anger and quick to lash out. They should calm themselves and be at one with the world. But no, they are much too holy for any of that. They've got to get a pamphlet published every fortnight or they think they have lost their way."

"I heard some English in a tavern when we were out walking last night," said Catherine. "Not far from here."

"Ja, you'll hear the English. There's English. We innkeepers have learnt it good. Here, there, everywhere, the English."

"But you've not heard of my son?"

"Maybe yes, maybe no. Too many of them. And now you have a new queen, they will go back and others will come. These will be monkish in the old way and then they will get hot for the change and be as on fire for Luther as these ones."

Veronica and Alice listened to all of this in silence, and when Catherine, unable to eat and unable to look at her daughters, said, "Who will join me in the search?" everyone got up at once.

The town was up, as well, and the English party found themselves on crowded streets. So many men wore sober black that Catherine began to feel gaudy in her blue skirt, though it was not loud, and her light French hood. Veronica fitted in better, with a neat grey dress and hood, but she would look at no one and pulled her arms in to prevent touching any man who passed her. The women of Wittenberg were out, too, with their shopping baskets and their children, and the whole place looked prosperous. Carpenters were at their rasping, pounding work, somewhere not too distant.

Catherine and Ann led the way to the previous night's tavern, which wasn't difficult and wasn't far. The common room of the place was as teeming as the streets, though, and they fell back for Reg and John to elbow their way into the center. Catherine saw only one woman, and she appeared to be serving table. A couple of men cut glares at her, and she almost retreated into the street. But John shouted over the voices until he could be heard, and she stayed. He was speaking a language that Veronica said was a kind of German, but Catherine distinctly heard the name "Robert Overton." Men looked at each other, shaking their heads. Someone said "a follower of Luther?" and the English women called out "yes" at the same time.

Now the attention of all turned toward them. Catherine stepped up, near to John, and said as loudly as she could that she was the mother of Robert Overton. "I seek his lodgings," she said. John translated, but again the mutterings and head-shakings answered.

Then a fair-haired man at the back stood. "I know him. Knew him, I should say."

Catherine's guts twisted and froze. "Knew?"

The man beckoned them toward the door, and they met again on the street. Catherine, Ann, and the girls surrounded him. Catherine said, "I have a letter from my son, asking me to come here. But I don't know where to look. Is there a place where the Englishmen lodge?"

The man scrunched his eyes. "There's such a place. Up that way, opposite to where they're building the new school." So that was the sound of hammers. Robbie might have made a good schoolmaster. The man raised his chin to indicate the direction. His face was sunburnt, but his clothes were fine, the collar of his shirt trimmed with lace and his cuffs white and soft. He wore a ring with a large pearl nestled in it on his least finger, and when he pushed his hair behind his ear, it caught the sun with a glow like young skin. He was making money in one way or another. "But you won't find him there," the man said. "Not any more. You're his mother, say?"

"Yes," said Catherine. She was desperate to know more, but she squeezed her toes together inside her shoes to stop her mouth. She didn't want to frighten him—or Robbie—off by seeming hysterical. "We've been estranged, since our queen—our queen that was—sent him out of England. You're English, aren't you?"

"Aye, I am. I used to trade in wool. Now I trade in made things, textiles and paper and such. And you are Catherine Davies, am I right?"

"You know my name?"

"I knew your son a little," the man said. "On fire for the Protestants, that one. Talked hellfire and corruption until you wanted to knock his brains out, pardon me for saying so. Honest as the day is long, but not an easy man to have at the table." He appraised Catherine's dress. "I'll venture to guess that you're not as strong in your opinions."

"I have opinions," said Catherine, "but my son grew up in a different time."

"And we have a new queen now, as I hear tell of it."

"Yes. Elizabeth. A Protestant queen. That should warm his heart."

"Kindle a spark, perhaps. She's still a queen, under all that. That won't make your son come running home. I never heard so much talk of women tromping the men beneath their feet as I heard from Robert Overton. It's a wonder he found a woman to marry him at all."

"Marry?" said Catherine. "He has a wife?"

"Oh, begging your pardon again." Now the man looked genuinely penitent. "I thought, from the letter—." He seemed to cast about in his mind for the right expression. "I assumed that you wrote, back and forth, as mothers and sons will do."

"No," said Catherine. "I wrote to him some, but he never wrote me, even once." She pulled the letter forth and flapped it. "Until this. He says he has something to give me. Perhaps he meant the gift of his marriage?"

"Oh, madam, I am very sorry to be the one to give you this news, but his wife died. Poor little thing, barely as high as my shoulder. She'd been a serving girl." The man doffed his hat, without a trace of mockery. "I suppose she was too small to bear a child. Almost a child herself, really."

"A child?" Catherine could hear the echo of his words in her speech. It made her sound simple, but she couldn't hold them in.

The man seemed to have taken no offence. "Yes. They had a child, I think, and she died of it. Then your son went off from here, and I haven't seen him since then. He went off very sudden. Months by now. Maybe a year or more. He was an impetuous man, of that I am sure. I don't believe he could endure being alone."

"You seem to have known Robbie very well," said Ann.

"I knew him enough to see him when I came through these parts. I don't live in Wittenberg. An Englishman in these parts of the world seeks out his countrymen, and there's few places a man can be sure that he'll find them. I can't say that I would seek him out of friendship, to be honest. He often spoke of his father, though, that sent him support."

"His father in Heaven, you mean," said Catherine. "His earthly father is buried in Yorkshire."

"Yorkshire?" said the man. "I know of no father in Yorkshire. No, he meant his father in Lisbon."

"Lisbon?" repeated Catherine. "He has no father there."

"Then I was the more deceived," said the man. "The boy got his money somewhere, and I thought it came from his father. And not his heavenly Father." He bent to speak directly into Catherine's face, as though she was a foolish child. "Your husband, Madam. I've traded in wools, as I said, and textiles. I've been long acquainted with your husband, Benjamin."

"Tell me again what your name is," said Catherine. Her head was windy with worry and confusion. Robbie was gone from Wittenberg. Benjamin was in fact in Lisbon, a world away from here. Robbie had a wife. A child. Were they both dead?

"Don't think I said it the first time," the man said. "Peter White, at your service." He pitched forward, and Catherine thought he had fallen ill until she realized that it was an awkward attempt at a bow. He managed to gather upright himself again and added, "It's not far, to where your son lodged. Nowhere in this town is very distant."

He waved them back the way they had entered town, and Catherine took it as an invitation to let him lead them on. And on they went. The castle lorded it over the town, and they stopped for a moment to admire it. "That's the church," said White with a wave. "That's where it started, all the trouble."

"The trouble?" offered Veronica.

"The destruction. The great reforming. That's where they say Luther stood and condemned his own church." They hesitated, none of them quite sure how to confront the building. Catherine felt the indignation burning her liver, then a wave of sick sadness. "He married a nun, you know," added White. "They had enough children, so I suppose they were blessed. I favour the old ways, myself, but I keep it to myself."

They all turned north before they reached the bridge and skirted the backs of dwellings and shops. It was dirtier here, and Catherine could smell the waste, both vegetable and human, in the rank canal water.

"The other side of the town," said White. He held a cloth over his nose as they passed the water. "It's not quite so ripe as here. New school, too, going up, as I said. Over this way is less of the fashion."

Catherine could see the back of the church in the large central square ahead of them. "Are we going in a circle?" she asked. "Look here, that is where we began." She pointed.

"We're on the other side," explained White. "A bit of a circle, but easier to come in this way. We will go on the Judengasse. It's not far."

One of Catherine's serving men stiffened visibly, as though someone had run a sword down the back of his shirt. "Jews? We are walking among Jews?"

White regarded the man without expression. His face seemed waxy. "No, there are no Jews in Wittenberg, nor no Catholics neither, and yet you are walking with one. I've traded in many places, fellow, and Jews have two eyes and two hands and two feet, same as you. A mind between their ears same as you. I've made many a good bargain with them."

"I expect you have," he murmured, and he sidled to the back of their party.

White seemed content to let the distance grow between them. And then he halted outside of a dilapidated wooden structure stuck between finer brick houses that looked as though they were holding it up. "Here it is," he said.

"This can't be the place," said Catherine. "It's ready to fall on top of us."

"Your son prided himself on plain living," White said. "He could have afforded better for his family. He clothed himself well enough."

Ann recoiled when she realized that this was their destination. Reg was poking at a loose shutter, trying to make it hang straight. Veronica was studying something that had stuck to the bottom of her shoe, and Alice seemed to be saying a silent prayer into Toby's ear. Catherine stepped backward and looked up. Three stories, each narrower and shabbier than the one below it. "Where did they stay?"

"Not right up top," White answered. "Middle floor, if I remember right. Mostly I saw him at the tavern, there." He pointed to a sign with a rooster and a hare painted on it. "The little wife mostly stayed at home."

"Perhaps they know where he's gone," said Ann, "and where he's buried his wife, but you'll have to go inside to ask."

"I'll dare it," said Catherine. "Will you come with me, Master White? You seem acquainted with the local customs. And John?"

John De Vries was gazing at the structure with obvious disgust, but when Catherine spoke he put on a sympathetic expression and said, "I come." He whispered something into Veronica's ear, and she stayed with Alice, who had covered Toby's head with a handkerchief. Ann said, "I'm coming, too. If the ceiling collapses, someone will have to drag you out."

The inside was little better than the exterior. One squat room, its board walls blackened by soot, a dark hallway leading out from it, and a smell of rancid meat and cat piss. Catherine called a hallo and waited. Again she called, and a small girl came running through from the back, wiping her hands on a greasy apron. "Yah?" she said.

John De Vries did the asking, but the girl kept shaking her head. Catherine heard him say Robbie's name, and he pointed directly over their heads. Then he mimicked rocking a baby in his arms, but still the girl would not understand.

A man came in behind them and said something Catherine could not translate. John spoke again, but whether it was the same speech Catherine couldn't tell. She heard "Overton" again and again saw him gesture toward the upstairs. The man nodded mournfully, then shook his head.

John said, "He doesn't know where your son is got to."

"What about the child? Is the child with him?" asked Catherine.

More exchange of words between the men. John said, "He doesn't know. Your son's wife got ill, and so was baby. Wife died, baby died. Don't know."

"How can he not know?" said Ann. "Didn't they live here?"

John glanced at the man. "Many lodgers here. I think they look another way after rent is paid."

Catherine nodded and returned to the street. At least she could breathe here. White was beside her, and she said, "Where is the graveyard?"

"More than one here." He chewed the inside of his cheek, and the skin puckered against the effort. The others were outside now, too, and they all stood, waiting. "I didn't know your son well, but he never spent like a thriving man on anyone but himself. Don't like to say this, but I'll warrant your daughter-in-law's not in the graveyard at S Mary's."

"No!" said Veronica. "My brother wasn't so ungenerous to deny a decent funeral, not to a woman he married."

"Robbie always liked things done right," added Ann, "whatever he might have been."

The others said nothing. Catherine had to be sure. "He would have wanted a good Protestant burial."

"S Mary's has a very big churchyard. That's the one at the square," said Peter White. "We'll search there first."

Their serving man complained of a headache, and Catherine sent both of the men back to their inn. Ann said, "He's sick of Wittenberg already," and Catherine nodded. They were bound to follow her, and she didn't know to what to do if they became discontent. There were other serving men about, men who spoke good English. They might seek out some companions. She watched them walk away. Her men, stout and dependable. But today they appeared dwindled, and Catherine thought they had begun to look like a couple of ghosts. Veronica, there in the sun speaking softly with John, glowed with good health, and the weight she'd gained had softened her face. But maybe Catherine was losing her, too.

"Let's go," said Catherine.

In less than a half-hour, they were inside the graveyard. A sexton was busy cutting weeds back from the stones, and White hallooed him. He cupped one hand around his ear and leant toward them. He never stood all the way up, and Catherine guessed he must have been nearly eighty. But he smiled at them and hobbled as fast as he could, showing no surprise at the English voices. "Overton?" he said to John's question, gazing over his silent city of stones. He shook his head and they talked some more.

John turned to Catherine. "No one called Overton here. Three young married women in last year. None with baby and none married to English."

Catherine put a coin into the sexton's hand, and they trudged away.

"There's another place," said Peter White, "outside the town. It's back the way we came."

Catherine's spine sagged and her head dropped. "My whole pilgrimage turns in circles and comes out nowhere. Is there time today to get there?" she asked White. "I will insist that you join us for supper."

"My duty to a fellow Englishwoman," said White. "And I will be happy to be your guest for supper." He squinted at the sun. "There's time, Madam. Just."

And they followed their guide back once more through the town and out, skirting the street where Robbie had lived. The street became a wide, clean road, and Catherine convinced herself that no one in all of Saxony allowed dirt to stand near their homes, except for the one house her son had chosen.

They walked past a sort of field, with a small church at the end of it. Catherine would have called it a chapel, it was so small. But there were graves, some of them fresh, if the humped and ragged earth was any indication of dwellers within. The trees had battled the wind over the years, and they had twisted themselves away from the stones. "This is it," said White.

"It cannot be," said Veronica. "We're nowhere near the town. It's as though he wanted to hide her. This must be where the poor are buried."

"It's no worse than the town," said Ann. "It's fresh here."

"The church is barely one room," said Veronica.

"God can live in a cottage," said Alice. "Even in a barn. I like the free air."

"In England, we wear out our poor, then we dump them into the ground like last week's meat scraps," said Ann. "And there's your Christian charity for you, Catholic or Protestant. It looks worse because you're unused to it."

"I can see I'm outnumbered," said Veronica.

Catherine passed through the gate and, lifting her skirts, walked a few paces within. Some stones had gone cock-eyed, but they stood fast. She ran her fingers over a few of the names. None of them was Overton. She walked on. Some of the headstones were blank, or weathered to silence, and a few of the mounds of earth were marked by nothing made by human hands at all. She was halfway to the other side when a man appeared at the door of the building and stood there, watching her. She lifted a hand, and he came forth.

John was behind her, and he intercepted the guardian of the place. He asked his questions, and the man scratched at his grizzle of beard. He pointed to a far corner.

"She was laid there," said John. "There was a baby with her. Laid with her."

"Do they keep written records of the dead?" asked Catherine. Her face and shoulders were hot from the sun, but her guts were shivering. She was afraid she might vomit if she had to walk all the way over to that corner. Her grandchild lay there. The daughter-in-law she would never meet. "I'd like to see her name."

John asked the man, and he looked at Catherine. "Overton?" she said.

The man looked at John, who repeated "Overton" and pointed to the corner. He said something more, and John said, "He has the records inside, if you want to see. There are copies in the town."

Catherine walked to the spot alone, over muddy depressions in the soil and raised lumps of fresh dirt. More of the stones here had fallen sideways or, worse, face down, and she stepped around them, through the lanky old grasses. When she saw it, Catherine couldn't stop a weird laugh from coming up her throat, and it scorched her tongue. She knelt in the dampness and touched the simple marker. "Mary Overton and son" had been scratched into the surface. Nothing more. "Earth to earth," she said to no one. "Body of my son's wife. Body that has borne my grandchild. My grandchild."

But only the soft wind had any reply.

She returned swiftly. Veronica was weeping, and John had put his arms around her, as though it was the most natural thing in the world. Catherine could not even muster surprise at the sight of such a public display, as sick as she felt. Why not feel a little love, when one still could? Ann was gazing away, at something on top of a distant house, and Reg was smacking his hat against his thigh. Alice had put her face down into Toby's fur.

"We'll go now," said Catherine. She gave more coins to the keeper of the place this time, hoping they would help to bury another dead girl, and the man shoved them into his pocket.

John said, "Do you want to see her name inside?"

"I've seen enough," said Catherine, and turned away.

White said, "I'm very sorry, Mistress Davies. I would've liked to show you better."

"You have shown me what I wanted to see," said Catherine. "Not all truths are to our liking. And now I will have to see what I can find of the son who would leave his wife and baby in this place with no more remembrance than that."

Chapter 14

They kept a dismal vigil over their meat that night, no one wanting to speak and no one touching the food. The innkeeper's wife fluttered about, worried that the supper was not fit to their tastes, until John said something about death and she brought a fresh jug of ale and retired. The candles wore themselves out, and no one thought to ask for replacements until they were sitting in almost full darkness. Peter White rose then and new light was quietly delivered by a silent maid.

"Where will he have gone?" Catherine said finally. "Alone in the world, and with his wife and child in the ground here."

"He'll have gone to Benjamin," offered White.

"To Lisbon?" said Reg. "It's Catholic, isn't it? I can't imagine Robbie willingly travelling to a Catholic land."

"You perhaps ought to return home to England," said White.

More silence. No one had an answer for this, and Catherine was almost ready to retreat to bed when a knock came at the inn's front door. The innkeeper's wife opened up, and the scruffy girl from the lodging house stood there, still wearing the greasy apron. She offered up a grubby paper and was gone.

The innkeeper's wife looked at the letter in her hand as though it were a dead rat and shoved it at John. He turned it over and brought it to the table. "This is for you," he said to Catherine.

The letters were barely legible, but it was Robbie's hand. The paper was slick and torn in two places. It read something, then "Benjamin Davies. Send all messages," then something else again that was too stained to see. "He's surely in Lisbon," said Catherine.

Peter White studied the paper and handed it to Ann, who could not read at all. He worried his meat around the plate with a slice of bread for a few seconds. "I agree."

Catherine's heart twisted like a serpent in her chest. "But it's Catholic, as Reg has just said."

White's expression constricted. "A young man needs to pay his way, however he prays. He'll go to Benjamin in a time of need."

Reg said, "The boy wasn't fond of the man, any more than he was of the Catholics."

"Maybe not," said White, "but he always took his money fondly enough."

"Robbie has never spoken one good word about the Catholic Church," said Catherine.

White shrugged. "Whenever I saw him, he was always on fire about something or the other. The Pope, sometimes the Lutherans. Women. Queens. But this is a town of debaters, you understand."

Ann said, "How long will it take us to get to Lisbon?"

"You should go home," said White. "Lisbon is a long way away, and its customs are not yours. It's a trading port. You think it strange here? Well, you'll find strange doings indeed when you go there. I can't recommend it. Go home."

"But my son is there," said Catherine. "My husband is there."

White aimed his eyes at Catherine. "You don't know that for a certainty. Who knows when this message was written? Who knows how long that letter you carry travelled before it arrived at your door? Your husband may have moved on by this time. He could be anywhere. I'm telling you, go home."

It made sense, but Catherine's heart hurt, and her head hurt. Robbie hadn't even told her about his marriage and her first grandchild. She would be an utter failure. "If we had a guide, it would be easier. Will you come with us?" she asked White.

"To Lisbon?"

"Yes. You could lead us there. You could lead us to Benjamin and Robbie, if they're there. We'd pay you."

Reg said, "We could use another navigator. It's a long way."

"Not me," said White. "I've some business here in Wittenberg, and I've got nothing to do down there. No, I beg your pardon, not Lisbon. I've led you as far as I can in this matter. England is the best direction for you. Wait to hear from your son again. Wait to hear from your husband. Go home."

"She can't wait," said Ann. "She's waited long enough."

White sighed and stretched his legs out under the table. He scraped at the short beard-hairs under his chin with his fingertips. "You should travel by boat. Land travel is dangerous and the mountains will kill you, if bandits don't do it first."

"We've gone by boat before," said Ann.

"And you were sick the entire way," said Veronica.

"I'll manage," said Ann. She was watching Catherine. "Let's see the world, as your mother has said, even if we never clap eyes on Benjamin Davies again."

"If you're so determined, then God be with you," said White. "The best I can do is to steer you in the direction I know." He asked for a scrap of paper and something to write with. "You've come through Amsterdam, is that right? Go back there, since you know it, and get your passage. Here's the name of a captain I've dealt with. He'll take you."

"We don't even know that Robbie is there," said Alice.

Veronica countered, "We haven't found him here, have we?"

White scribbled at the sheet. "This is the best I can do. Take it or leave it. If your son went to Lisbon, someone there will know how to find him. Or to find your husband."

"Back to Amsterdam? That's where we started," said Catherine. She hated the wailing note in her voice.

"You want to walk? To ride a horse?" said White. "You're mad if you do. Trust me, the water is safer and faster."

"It's coming on summer, and the weather is fair. We've come too far to go home," said Reg. "If you mean to find either of them, we'll have to go. John?"

John De Vries jerked his head toward Reg. He'd been whispering with Veronica. "Ja?"

Catherine said, "Will you accompany us to Lisbon?"

"I will," he said, with a bright note in his voice. "We stop at the farm and tell Father and Mother."

White wrote out a couple more names. "These are other men you might find in Amsterdam if you can't find the other," he said, then he stood and bowed. "And so I take my leave of you, Mistress Davies. I wish you Godspeed in your travel and a sun in the sky as you go, if go you must."

"And a son in your arms when we arrive," added Ann.

"I will say once more, my advice is that you go home. You may not like what you find when you land at Lisbon." White bade them farewell and went, leaving the door open behind him.

Catherine followed to the threshold and watched the sky darken from violet to velvet black. "I wish we could be free of this Purgatory tonight."

"Be careful, Catherine," said Ann. "Some fiery Protestant may take offence at the reference."

"We're sailing into the land of the Pope," Catherine said. "Let them take all the offence they please." She shut the door. "How could anyone walk past that little grave and doubt that we are all in for a spell of fire?"

That night, Catherine woke to the sound of crying. She was sure it was Alice, who had always been an impetuous weeper, but when she sat up, her younger daughter lay quietly in the other bed. Beside Catherine, though, Veronica shifted and sniffled. She was wiping her face with the edge of the sheet.

"What's the matter?" said Catherine.

"It's nothing," said Veronica.

"Are you mourning your nephew?"

"What nephew? I never even met the child. Or knew his name. He and his mother are both bodies in graves. I can't feel a thing about them."

"Has John said something unkind to you?"

"John? No, Mother, John is the soul of courtesy. Shh, Alice needs her rest. And don't wake up that dog." Veronica swung her legs out of the bed and beckoned for Catherine to follow. They stepped into the dark corridor and peered both ways. No one else was awake, and they slipped downstairs. The common room smelt of stale ashes and ale, and the damp had crept in after dark. Veronica had brought a blanket with her, and she perched on the hearth, huddled inside of the woven wool. She looked like a wing-shot bird.

Catherine crouched next to her. "What is it, child?"

"It's Robbie. He's shamed the entire family. To dump her into that little graveyard, with barely a stone to mark her. It's the worst of degradations. He left an innocent child in the ground with strangers for company. It's intolerable in anyone. I feel infected with it. Tainted. I can't look John in the face for the pity I read there."

"Robbie's actions aren't yours," said Catherine gently. "Perhaps he didn't have anything to pay for a larger stone. I don't believe he would have buried his wife in a grave that he thought was showy. Robbie's a hard man, that I grant you. But to be cruel to a wife? No, I can't think that. He did the best he could." Catherine heard a cock crow somewhere outside. The first grey light softened the eastern window, and through the clouds the sky looked feathered and thick. Perhaps it would be a cooler day. "Let John feel some pity for you. It's a sign that he has a warm heart, and that's no bad feature in a man. Remember, my own parents treated me like a foundling until I was a grown woman. Not everyone who has children knows what's best for them. It doesn't touch you or your virtues, Vere. The child is with its mother. That's best for all. We'll find Robbie."

The young woman looked up. "I think I could love him, Mother."

"He's your brother. Of course, you love him."

"I don't mean Robbie. It's John I mean. He sees everything and remembers everything. He wants to be a merchant, he says, with a fine house of his own. He doesn't want to live on the farm. He wants to see new lands and learn new ways. Yes, I think I may be in love with him."

"I'll say amen to that if you do. You've never spoken fair of a man before now."

"I've never met a man who seemed good to me before now. I won't have Robbie ruin my hopes of him."

"If John is a man to be hoped on, then he won't allow all the brothers in the world to say anything against you. There's time, daughter. Be your own self to him, and let the sprout grow if it will."

Now Veronica smiled. "I hope it may. I've never wanted a man before now."

Catherine wiped her daughter's face. "Then be patient. This little rain on our souls won't drown us. Now, shall we dress before the house descends and finds us sitting here without any clothes on? That might shame us indeed."

And so they left Wittenberg, passing by the castle and its church without more than a glance, and settled into the same westward direction they had travelled before coming eastward. Ann lamented that, if they went over water, they would not see Paris, as it had always enchanted her, and Catherine said, "Ann, you've never told me that."

Ann cocked her head at a jaunty, uncharacteristic angle. "A woman might think a thing and never be moved to say it."

John assured them that the return would be swifter as they were travelling lighter and knew the way and the inns. He added that this would be less of a burden on the constitutions of the women and the elderly (at which Reg huffed a little) and make the journey more pleasant for the seeing of the countryside. Late in the afternoon, Ann sidled up beside Catherine and said, "Your daughter is enthralled."

Catherine detected the distraction. She'd been trying to imagine the face of her dead grandson, but now she studied her living daughter. "I think she is," said Catherine. "He seems an honest sort. He might speak to his parents of it when we pass."

"He rides too close to her." It was Alice, who had come up on Catherine's other side. "They are too much in each other's company. She's not ready to marry. She's said so herself."

"It's not as though they're alone," said Catherine. "For the love of heaven, I'm right here, in sight of her all the time. She sleeps in the same bed with me. She's older than you, Alice. You may feel as she does one day."

"It's not good for a girl to thrust herself upon a man," Alice insisted. "She'll ruin her reputation."

"Your sister has never thrust herself at any man," said Catherine. A little knot of defensiveness swelled into a lump, like a large nut, in her breast, and she had to swallow hard against it. Neither of her daughters had ever been in love. Alice sounded jealous. She'd never been a quiet or particularly obedient girl, but now she looked pale with judgment. Her eyes glittered with righteousness, and Catherine was afraid of how much they could grow to resemble Robbie's.

Ann got between them. "What do you know of love, child? You've always kept yourself solitary. If you can love that dog like he's the last thing on earth, then your sister might love a husband. Why take it so hard?"

"For the good of her soul," Alice said.

At this, Ann laughed, a sharp-edged sound. "Your soul is good enough, I reckon. It's practically golden, in my opinion. It's your heart I question. God's foot, child, can't you let a young woman have some warmth in her without making it into the eighth deadly sin?"

Alice glared at Ann with a fierceness that Catherine had never seen on her face before. "It's no new sin, not in this world. It's lust, plain and simple, and she'd do well to guard herself against it. That John De Vries may have pleasant manners, but he's a third son of a farmer. He'll try to grease his way into her affections and then snatch what she inherits because he'll have nothing of his own. It can't come to good, and she'll end up lonely and heartbroken."

"Well, I'm very glad that your powers of prediction are so finely-tuned," said Ann, with a little acid on her words. "Have you been making magic potions that you can see so far into the future and into the hearts of his parents?"

Ann might have been about to slap the girl, her face had turned so red. Alice hissed, "Don't speak to me of witchcraft. I know that it's a heresy. And a felony, too."

"Don't you speak to me that way," said Ann. "I'm your elder, and I'll show you what I have in me."

The two of them had ridden so close together that Catherine was in danger of being squeezed between them. Catherine halted and they took a few steps beyond her, then stopped and looked back. "Stop arguing," she said. "You sound like a couple of fishwives. Yes, I mean you, Alice. You sound like every priggish old woman who's been disappointed in love. You'll dry up and wither like an old apple if you don't give up this wagging of your tongue at every common feeling. And, Ann, don't egg her on."

Ann shrugged. Alice turned her horse so that she faced Catherine. Then she turned it away. Her shoulders sagged. "I don't trust him," she said. She looked over her shoulder. Then the tears started.

"Come here," said Catherine, going to her daughter. Ann followed and they hemmed Alice in. Catherine said, "It's a new thing. And we're in a strange place. You've had a shock, seeing that grave back there. You've lost a nephew, and I've just lost a grandchild."

Ann said, "I was too harsh with you, Alice. I'm fretful and anxious. Will you forgive me?"

Now the weeping began in earnest. Alice leant over to hug Ann, and when her mare backed away, she was left dangling. She fell onto her backside, and Ann dismounted. They held each other, and Alice began to laugh. Toby, stuck in his sling on Alice's chest, wriggled and howled for freedom and Ann began to laugh, as well. Now Veronica, John, and Reg had stopped and were watching. Veronica called, "What's wrong? Is the mare injured?"

Alice sniffed her woe in. Her eyes were bright with tears and her face was red with shame. She had her entire lower lip between her teeth. She breathed heavily for a few seconds, then called back, "No, just ill-tempered. She needed to be brought round. I'm coming." She said softly to Ann, "I'm monstrous, and you've spoken right to me."

"And I'll curb my tongue," said Ann.

Ann tossed Alice back into her saddle, and they rode on.

Chapter 15

Back they went toward Amsterdam, Ann basking in her superior recognition of the places they'd passed the first time and boasting that she would be as good a seaman this time as the sailors themselves. Reg and John set up a lively discussion of how they would lighten their load even more before they set sail, and Alice worked at making up to John, though he didn't know he'd been under her disapproving scrutiny. She rode beside him, pointing out sights with Toby's unwilling paw, and Veronica edged up to John's other side, eager to be included in the decisions. The two manservants kept their own counsel at the rear.

Catherine was sodden in heart and soul. No one mourned the woman and child in the ground behind them. All their talk went forward. Now and then she slouched on the wagon with Ann, and watched her daughters. "See that house, that one just there," Ann said. "We stopped there and asked for directions."

Catherine did not remember, either the house or the request for directions. It all looked more unfamiliar from the east than it had from the west. She had not thought the world so large. England was a speck at the far edge of these miles and miles of field and village, town and river, sea and curving horizon, that they passed through or by or over or toward. She saw strange hats and heard stranger words. John was calling to them now, reassuring them that travel by land would have been impossible, and Catherine felt threatened by the lurking, invisible hulk of mountains she'd never seen. Even the cow-bells sounded alien now, clanging in distant pastures. Two quests and two failings. She'd lost Diana and she'd lost a family she'd never known. They would never find Robbie, or Benjamin either. If Mary Tudor had not lost Calais, all would have been well by now. It would have been easy to catch a small boat to there and claim the men.

They stopped only for private matters and public meals. They rode and collapsed into inns, where even John De Vries could often not make himself understood and had to resort to handfuls of money to secure them rooms. They had surely been cheated more than once, but Catherine felt, some nights, that she would have traded her last stockings for a bed and the silent, familiar darkness in which to misgive herself and brood on her shortcomings. The men sat with maps spread out before them in the evenings, wondering if they would find a captain who could take them all on board quickly. They often asked advice from innkeepers who could not comprehend where they meant to go. The serving men offered one morning a fresh map, drawn by another servant with whom they had shared quarters. He had spoken good English, they said, and had given assurances that they had made the right choice. He had also provided names of boats and their captains that might have English-speaking sailors on board.

Finally, the farmland began to appear to Catherine's eye as she remembered it, and one afternoon the world suddenly fell into place and she recognized what road they were on and knew that the De Vries farm was near. John was fairly trotting, and the wagons could not keep his pace. One of the manservants had the temerity to hallo for him to slow down, and when he turned a circle around them, John's face wore the grin that Catherine assumed would mean that he would be asking his parents for permission to marry. She ventured a glance at Veronica. The girl was glowing like a bride. But she was no girl. Catherine's elder daughter was fully a woman. The temptation rose up inside her to simply book passage back to England and take Veronica with her. If Robbie and Benjamin didn't want her to know where they were, then she could just go home and be done with them both. It would probably make Alice happy.

But that luminous face of Veronica's shone brighter than her own disappointment or sorrow could quench, and Catherine put on a smile, aware that she'd just saved herself from one of Ann's tongue-lashings.

The De Vries family welcomed them as long-lost pilgrims, petting Veronica and asking after Catherine's and Ann's comfort. "We're not decrepit," said Ann, almost rolling from the wagon seat.

Mistress De Vries clucked and brushed the back of Ann's skirt, hard enough to make her straighten up, and Catherine made sure to dust herself off as she stepped down. Veronica was already on the ground, standing next to John. Alice and Toby were greeting the hounds. Reg and Master De Vries had shaken hands like old partners and were already disappearing through the door. John's mother took his hand and said something that Catherine couldn't understand. He nodded and off his tongue raced, leaving Catherine completely befuddled. Veronica couldn't understand them, either, but the expression on her face was asking all of the questions that Catherine was afraid to hear.

The servants took the horses and wagons around the back, and that left nothing more to do except to join everyone else inside the house.

But a welcome entry it was, with the rooms still as bright and orderly as ever. Catherine did feel at home here, she was almost ashamed to acknowledge, even to herself. She wanted that clean, soft bed that she pictured upstairs. She wanted to sleep off some of her worries and woe, and a maid appeared at her side like a benign fairy to spirit her off to what she most craved: a private space. But she had barely touched her back to the mattress when Alice called from below, and so she shoved her feet back into her shoes and trudged on down. John and Reg were absorbed by the men's talk, and that left Catherine, Ann, Alice, and a disappointed Veronica to be entertained by Gertrude De Vries.

"Poor dear," said the woman when Catherine appeared. "Ann say that you have lost the baby before he was ever yours."

"That I have," said Catherine. "And his mother, too."

"Very sad." Gertrude clutched her fists to her breast. "But you will find your son, and that will make the world happier."

Catherine nodded. "I pray that it will."

"So you will travel again," she said. "Away, over the sea?" She spread her arms, as though to warn them how far they were going.

"Yes," said Catherine. She also spread her hands, but it was to indicate that they were empty. "No son. No husband." She showed her wedding ring and shook her head.

"Ach," said the woman. Now she clasped Catherine to her bosom. "Poor, poor dear." She pushed Catherine backward and gazed up at her. "Will find. Plenty places. Jan very, um, um, happy. He likes to go and see the many places. Wants to trade. Make the money."

Ann and Catherine nodded together, looking, she thought, like a couple of doddering old women. "He's a good man," said Ann. "We would be lost without him." She did not look at Veronica.

"Good, yah. Jan good boy." Gertrude De Vries tapped her right temple. "Got big brain."

And here he came, bounding in, limbs flailing, as though he had no wits at all, with Reg, saying, "Father say it's too much sea for women. We must ride." His father wandered in behind him, his nose almost on a map, and bumped into his son.

Reg said, "We must go to the city and ask the captains. We have names. It's much faster to go by boat."

"Trade," said John's father, tapping the map. "Many places by road."

Catherine's mind was tripping over itself. "But what of these mountains? How will we get over them? They say it's too far."

"Ah," said John. "You hear, Father? We go by boat. You must find trunks enough." He almost leapt across the room to Veronica. "Father say not enough place on boat to put trunks for trade. I say yes. We make good trades for pepper and the nutmegs. Good money." John smiled at Veronica.

Reg, a look of alarm playing under his rigid features, said, "We aren't going to buy and sell. We're going to find Robbie and Benjamin."

"But it is Lisbon," said John. "All Amsterdam traders stop in Lisbon for the melegueta. I make fortune."

"The what?" said Catherine.

"Pepper," said Reg.

Catherine realized when she tasted blood that she was chewing the inside of her cheek, but Gertrude laughed. "The boy always want to make the trades. You go. See all the big world. Find son. Find husband. We find the trunks, and maybe Jan go and come home rich. Maybe richer than king." At this both father and mother roared, as though at a private family jest. John also laughed, but his face had gone red as a day-labourer's. Reg stared at the map.

Catherine just wanted to return to her home. She could almost hear the voices of England calling to her from here.

But the others wanted to go. Alice and Veronica were already arguing with Ann about the best methods for dispelling seasickness, and John had dragged his father off to find trunks for storing who-knew-what. And so it was decided for Catherine. They would stay and rest a few days. They would find this captain, whoever he might be, hire their passage, and then, God help them, they would make their way south, farther from familiar England than she had ever thought to go.

Chapter 16

A weary month of backing and forthing, from the farm to the docks, bickering over the supper about chests and clothing, what was required for the journey and what could be left behind. The sun grew fat and yolky, and its weight in the sky would have been a pleasant thing if anyone had had the time to look up. Clothing: as little as possible. Goods to trade: John said yes, his father no. "Why carry pepper to the Portuguese?" he said, as John sputtered about wool and meats, even cheeses. As it turned out, all of the captains told them that men were each allowed to take two chests only. They decided to store in them what little they needed, and then fill them to bring back. For the women, only one each for their personal goods. Reg would have to sell their leftover trunks and much of their clothing for ready money. Catherine reluctantly asked for pen and paper so that she could write to Eleanor and Joseph Adwolfe. Perhaps they'd be glad to have the house and farms to themselves for a while longer yet.

Finding passage proved difficult. No one wanted to carry women, unless they had husbands waiting for them and proof of it. Catherine could not offer any assurance that Benjamin was even in Lisbon, let alone awaiting her arrival, and she didn't much care. Lisbon was a dry word in her mouth. The spring waxed into summer, and, while the men did their searching and bargaining, she walked the soggy fields of the De Vries farm and mourned her grandson. She could scarcely endure the house, with the gurgling babies and happy, plump daughters-in-law to mind them. Ann walked with her sometimes, and they argued, gently, about what to do. Catherine was for England again, but Ann said that Catherine would never forgive herself if she didn't at least look for Benjamin.

"So now you're the one on fire to travel," said Catherine one day. "Can't I just leave it alone? I've already lost two, two that I didn't even know I had. You've said it yourself, that Benjamin isn't worth the bother."

"We've come this far, Catherine," said Ann. "And whatever I think, or have thought, of Benjamin, the man is surely out there. I don't want you to bring yourself to grief by going home empty-handed. And that's what you will do. You're already grieving the loss of your grandson and your daughter-in-law. Don't burden your soul more. The world is changing for women. We've got a second queen on the throne of England. Who'd have thought it possible? Let's go. Come, kiss your old clothes goodbye and let's to Lisbon."

Catherine nodded, unconvinced. Her heart couldn't weigh more, Benjamin or no Benjamin. And queens? She'd been fond of them both, Mary and Elizabeth Tudor, when they were girls, different as they were. She had maybe even loved them. And then they had taken the throne. Mary had grown hard. Elizabeth would, as well. Catherine chewed her cheek. Ann was right. No one had thought it possible before Mary for a queen to rule England. Maybe it had changed the world. A queen was still a woman, after all, whatever men said about it. A knot of grudging respect for Mary and Elizabeth tightened in her throat. But she wouldn't acknowledge it, not out loud. She nodded again and clamped her lips shut.

Catherine had few things to take with her, anyway, so she didn't much care what they packed and what they sold off.

She'd never gone anywhere with such a meager wardrobe and had bought nothing. She'd left her best garments behind in England and mostly wore only one plain dress, brown so that it would not show the grime and mud. Her blue skirt stank so profoundly that she cast it aside without thought. With her greying hair, she felt like a great, dull rodent in the brown, but now she didn't care.

She allowed Veronica and Alice each one change of clothing, which they would carry in their own bags. Alice would not leave Toby, and so the dog would go in a fresh sling fashioned by Gertrude De Vries. Ann didn't care what she took along. She said that her old clothes were as good as any, and she was going to see, not to be seen, and if she smelt bad, well, then, she was no worse than any other woman on her way to somewhere.

But to go somewhere they needed a boat. The captain Peter White had first recommended was nowhere to be found, and the ones with boats big enough to haul them demanded extra money for the passage. "We have to pay it," said Ann one day, strolling beside Catherine, "whatever the cost."

"The cost of it all is too high," said Catherine. "England is closer." She determined that if Ann tried to woo her feelings with any more talk of Benjamin, she would steel herself against it.

But Ann said, "England is farther from your son."

This stuck a wedge between Catherine's opposing feelings. Her heart was prying itself apart, and she gave up. "We'll go, if any of the sailors will have us. But I long for home."

"Home will be there when you return."

"I'm tired," said Catherine. She turned for the house and left Ann to wander where she would.

Slipping up the back stairs, she reached her bed chamber without having to chuck any fresh, pink baby-cheeks or talk housekeeping with the smiling De Vries women. She would just lie down for a few minutes, just a few. But when she opened her eyes, Veronica was stretched beside her, pulling at a hangnail with her teeth.

"How long have I slumbered?" said Catherine.

"All afternoon!" said Veronica. She wiped her finger on her skirt and bounced the mattress. "We have a boat! Didn't you hear everyone downstairs? You've been up here for hours!"

"Too long," said Catherine. "And yet I feel I could drowse the day away." She had not dreamt, that she could remember, and the sleep seemed to have drained away her strength instead of refreshing her. The journey ahead looked as dark as the blank space behind her eyelids when she closed them.

"Well, rouse yourself and come down to eat," said Veronica. "The men are busy loading up those chests, and we have to get ourselves ready to go."

"Those chests," said Catherine. "What in the world does he mean to buy? Can a man carry that much pepper?"

"And other spices, he says. Enough to make him a fortune, he says." Veronica shrugged one shoulder. "He wants to get him some factor or another or something and set up direct trade. I don't understand it all, but he's practically chomping at the bit to get down there."

"Good for him," said Catherine. She disliked the taste of sarcasm in her mouth and rose. There would be ale downstairs and she needed it.

The women's things looked paltry in the pile out front and Catherine was glad of it. Let the sailors insult and throw jibes. The men were the ones with the loads. The women would be small as mice and as quiet. Tiny stowaways that no one would notice. She wanted to shrink into nothing.

Another week had to be endured before they would sail, and Catherine ticked the days by hour upon hour. Gertrude supplied Ann with ginger and dried mint to chew if she suffered sickness at sea. Veronica and Alice slipped extra gloves and stockings into their bags, and Catherine pretended not to notice. They were all shouting and laughing all of the time, dragging her along to the stinking docks, where they could watch the preparations of their vessel. It lay far out in the water, like a small island ready to be gulped down by the waves, and though everyone said it was an excellent choice, to Catherine it looked like an ending rather than a beginning. It would be a boat ride just to get to the boat.

But the day came, as any day might. They downed a hasty breakfast before the dawn broke and said loud, tearful goodbyes and threw good wishes into the air with their waving hands. The travelling party made their way to the water and then onto the small vessel that carried them out of the shallows into the deep. The morning was fine, and the men boarded without hesitation, pacing about the deck and discussing the sturdiness of the hull. Ann halloed until Reg returned to help her up, and Catherine allowed herself to be hauled aboard. This was a ship indeed, and though the wood under her feet was slick and yielding, the passengers and crew made up what looked for all the world like a town on the water. Such strange-faced men, some fair-haired but so burnt from the sun that they looked demonic. A few dark-skinned sailors with black hair they had tied up with bright scarves. They even had a small gaggle of priests to guard their souls along the way. She swayed for a minute, getting her balance, and then followed Alice and Veronica down to a little nook, set aside by a thick curtain, for the unmarried women. The girls demanded to see the coast recede as they went, and Catherine said she would remain below with her thoughts, but within minutes she was discontent with sitting alone in the dark and joined the others to watch their leavetaking from aboveboard.

From here, Amsterdam looked more different and suddenly more dear. They were going away, again, and now Catherine felt the tug of this place. She felt its tone was attuned to her own thoughts, still clinging to the old religion and yet pushed and pulled by the new. She recalled, now that they were almost gone, the various complexions of the people milling around the port and felt a sort of homesickness for a land she had scarcely seen. It was not England, and yet she had moved among the streets and roads without fear, and even the brief moments of molestation or embarrassment had not lasted long, and they had mostly come from her own countrywomen. She had not come away with even a bolt of the bright silks on offer in the markets, and she hoped that Veronica had had the temerity to make some purchases and hide them away without consulting her. Ann was, as always, indifferent to personal vanities, and Catherine whispered to her, "Do you regret that we're leaving again so quickly?"

Ann shook her head. She was gazing over the water to the tiny crowd they had left behind them, and she was smiling. "I've enjoyed seeing what we've seen, and I mean to keep my eyes open and face turned forward. I've seen more of the world this summer than I ever hoped to see in my life, and I will regret nothing now. To think I wanted to stay at home. Why? Do you see how many sorts of men run this ship? What a variety of creatures God has created."

The boat shifted, and Catherine grabbed Ann's hand. As ever, she leant on her friend to keep from falling. "I have barely noted a thing until this moment."

"You've seen aplenty. I've seen you see it. But you've also received a blow and that has turned you inward. It's been ever thus, Catherine." Ann put an arm around her shoulders. "That grandson will haunt you. Of that I'm sure. And I don't know what we'll find when we land again. But look there." Ann led them to the other side, and pointed. "Look at the sun on the water. Have you ever seen such a colour?"

She had not. The sea lay before them, a miracle of azure, and the air sat heavy and golden on it. The sea winds when they had left England had been ascetic, grey, thin and punishing, and they had been cast from the shore as though thrown from the hand of a judging God into a purgatory of cold waves. The water moved here, as well, but the sun was not high and tight but warm as a smear of soft butter on the sky and it seemed to offer itself to them.

"I'm hungry," said Catherine.

"You'd better not eat anything just yet," said Ann. "I filled enough buckets the last time. Let's not have it be your turn this time. Here, have a nibble of this ginger. I'm stocked a-plenty."

They sat in the harbour all that day and laboured outward all the next. They would squeeze through the narrow sea first, but the open waves were before them. They were on their way, and Catherine breathed in the salt air. It was fine and cold and prickly in her nose, like a sudden turn in the season, and she laughed. She imagined herself to be a seasoned sailor now. Ann laughed with her and put her arm around Catherine's waist. "You see?" said Ann. "I am well, and you are well, and we will be there before you can count a hundred."

Yes, Catherine decided. They would be on the other side of the water soon, and then they would be all together again, and almost home.

Chapter 17

To Catherine, everything was looking a long way off. The sodden, green land of the Dutch disappeared in a world of azure and yellow, and she had never felt so treacherously footed. The open sea should have looked no different than the water she had seen from land, rolling away, but this was a place she might have dreamt about in some distant, troubled sleep. The days turned suddenly warmer and as they left England behind, she felt that they had crossed a forbidden threshold. Not even Elizabeth Tudor had travelled this far.

Ann remained stalwart of stomach, chewing mightily at the ginger and putting her face right into the wind if queasiness threatened. She claimed that the sea was healthier as it grew larger, though she stayed beside Catherine, letting Reg wander among the crew. They sailed under fierce sunlight and thrashing, angry rain, John playing the gallant with Veronica by offering a wide-brimmed hat to keep her face unblemished and dry. His spirits showed in his eyes, which had once seemed the most placid of blue but now looked sharded with greens and golds, shimmering with his excitement. Ann mentioned it, too, that she had detected a sprite in him that worried her on Veronica's behalf. She also still noted a coolness in Alice toward John, and Catherine reminded her that there had been no talk of marriage at his parents' home.

"It may all come to nothing. If Alice is a little jealous of her sister, it's nothing more than a girl wanting to be a woman," said Catherine. "Alice and Veronica have been like a pair of twins for years, and now look at Veronica with John. They are almost always side by side." She and Ann were sitting together on a couple of unused barrels, watching the couple lean over the side and wave at something. A saucy fish, probably.

"But she doesn't hold onto him. He holds onto her."

Catherine squinted until a brusque cloud elbowed the sun into its shade. "She knows how to be modest. They are talking regular enough. They must have solved all of the world's problems by this time. If Veronica loves him, then Alice will grow to accept him as a brother. In time."

"If you say so," said Ann. "She has not much good to say on the topic of brothers or husbands."

"My arse is growing numb," Catherine muttered, raising one haunch for a quick rub. "I may never walk straight again."

"Reg finds it all very enlarging," said Ann. "He almost can't sleep for retelling me everything I've seen in the course of the day regarding the sailing of ships. It's as though he never set foot on land. I don't understand a thing he says. He says that each of the sailors is allowed two caixas for their own trading. That's chests in plain English. That's why he and John could take two each."

"I hope you indulge him. Reg is gold," said Catherine.

"Reg never was built to serve with a stooped back," said Ann, chuckling. "Even with your William for a master, he always kept his head up. And now he feels he's among his fellows. Yes, let him enjoy it."

"You've suddenly become sweet-tempered, Ann Goodall," said Catherine. "The Ann Smith I've known in the past would have mocked him into the sea."

"This voyage pleases me," said Ann, "and I don't care who knows it. Reg has a hopeful soul, with a most even temper. And now that he's moved up somewhat in the world, he feels he's done all that God could have dealt him. He's not a complainer, not like some I've known."

It was true. Since the removal of Benjamin, Reg had assumed the position of manager at Catherine's properties, and Veronica, when she came of age, leant on his knowledge and wisdom as she might have a father's. After they had gone back North to Yorkshire, his days had passed without more business in the cities than a few days here or there. They lived a quiet, retired life, one that Reg claimed contented him. Would this John De Vries be so content, with that demon of ambition sparking in his eyes?

"Reg is a blameless man, in everything he does," Catherine said to Ann, "and a good man of business. And he loves you. You played that one well."

"I thank God every night for him," Ann said. "For God knows I made him work hard enough before I consented to marry him."

The trio of priests passed by them on their daily walk. They stopped and spoke to any man they encountered, then nodded and moved in a line past the women without looking at them.

"What do you suppose is their business?" said Catherine.

"God, what else?" said Ann. "Reg says that they're on a mission to the East to save heathen souls. They make me feel as though we've moved back in time instead of forward."

Time seemed to circle Catherine, but she couldn't say that without sounding like a lunatic. "I have no idea where we are. And where's Alice?" Catherine lifted herself and peered over the edge of the ship. She saw nothing but the rolling violet waves, spiked with foamy white. The feeling rushed into her haunches, and her thighs tingled and stung. No one was watching, so she rubbed her legs through her skirt. "I am sore through to the bone."

"Alice is over there, talking to a sailor," said Ann. "Or Toby is doing the talking."

Veronica left John's side and trotted over. "Isn't it like heaven out here, Mother? Blue above and blue below. We saw dancing fish, leaping up into the air!"

"It's beautiful, in its way," said Catherine.

And it was, day after day, though Catherine was not visited by the dancing fish or the angels in the clouds that Alice spoke of in their bed at night. Ann slept with Reg behind another curtain, and Catherine wished she had her friend beside her, even on this infested mattress, to gossip away the wee hours while they scratched each other's backs and complained of lice. Instead, it was Alice and Veronica, who chattered in whispers, the dog nestled between them, almost until the moment they dropped into dream. Veronica never mentioned John's opinions in these nightly huddling chinwags, which struck Catherine as a novelty, and she tried not to allow the worm of maternal concern to make its way to her tongue. Alice was happy enough to listen to everything her sister had to tell her, in the privacy of their little female nook.

The views were surely lovely, with the cloud-shadows racing over the waves, chased by birds she did not recognize. One hazy afternoon, Catherine heard a dog yapping somewhere below, but it turned out to be a large fish with its head out of the sea, talking to the ship. Ann said, "Well, that's the strangest thing I've ever beheld," and Alice, beside her, uncovered her head and laughed.

"I would leave that on, if I were you, child," said Ann. "We are in a more retrograde place here, methinks, and women had better cover themselves."

"Let them think what they will," said Alice, turning her face up to the sun. "The sailors like me and Toby, too, and we can do no wrong." She opened her eyes and caught Ann's frown. "Very well. But a ship is no backward place. It is sophisticated and varied, more so than England." She readjusted her head covering. "I expect the women in Lisbon dress as they please. Mother, may I buy a new dress when we are there?"

"And where do you plan to carry it?"

Veronica had sneaked up behind her sister and grabbed her by the waist. "We'll buy more bags and use them as our bed. They'll be softer. Or John will carry them for me, won't you, John?" Of course, there he was, sliding down the deck toward them.

John winked at Veronica. So the game was on, after all, thought Catherine. The young folk had other things to look at, and when the fish was gone, so were they, Alice running along to keep up with her sister.

"So, Ann, did you hear that?" Catherine said.

"I heard. So why hasn't he spoken of marriage?"

"I don't know," said Catherine. "Look, I think I see land."

Ann raised herself. "What? Where?" Then she sat again. "What a droll jester you are, Catherine."

And yet not far wrong. Reg was the first one to whoop it out, and they all could see, in the far distance, what looked like a spire. It had to be a city. "I see it!" shouted Veronica, and she galloped toward Reg. John gave chase, and then Alice, and they flew down the deck together.

But it was not Lisbon. The ship carved the water westward a little and the land fell away from their sight. Still they travelled southerly, and Catherine set her eye on the eastern horizon, telling herself that each time she spotted land, it would be a good omen. She began to enjoy the sport of it, though there was little enough to see. But, she told herself, it was her own, and, with or without men, she was going, like any queen would, to play it for herself.

Chapter 18

How easy it would be to forget that she was as much on a mission as the priests who would not speak to her. Out upon the open water, Catherine clung to the wale and let her head fall backward to watch the sails sag and belly-out in the wind. She used her hand as a visor to watch for land and when her eyes tired she scanned the waves for fish and skimming birds. She was accosted by neither sailor nor servant and though the space was small she came and went as she pleased. "This boat has become a very island," Ann said once, when they'd slipped below to get a private wash in a corner behind Catherine's meager curtain. Then they sat side by side, as they'd ever done, to mend a tear at the hem of Catherine's skirt, and Ann rocked with the needle in time with the endless motion of the ship and threaded it without a hitch.

Alice got her flowers and spent two full days on the itchy mattress, with Catherine and Veronica scrubbing her legs and dunking the used rags in buckets before taking them up to Ann to be washed with the lye soap Reg provided. "This is no more than a scrap," Ann had complained, holding up one of the soggy cloths, but it was all they could find and Alice became shrill with embarrassment when Catherine said she would demand fresher ones.

Catherine took on the task of following Toby and depositing his deposits into the sea, but a sailor caught her at the job and shamed her by laughing. She was sure that

Veronica had told John, because he kept a decent distance and did not ask questions. Veronica said that she was fine, herself. Her flowers never caused her discomfort and never had and that was the end of that conversation.

After the crisis had passed and Alice returned a few mornings later to the fresh air, carrying herself with sudden rigid dignity and gazing thoughtfully out to sea, Ann plumped herself down beside Catherine, who was watching a seagull that floated along near the ship. "Are you still mourning England?" she said.

Catherine laughed softly. "I believed myself a warrior, Ann, but I'm a house mouse, built for the dismal corners."

"You are not and never have been. Look at the world, how wondrous big it is. What will we see more?" said Ann.

"You," said Catherine, nudging her friend. "You were set against even going out the front door."

"And I was wrong, I see that and say it. Think on your son, Catherine. What do you suppose he'll say to his mother coming so far to fetch him home?"

"I wonder," said Catherine. "You didn't mention Benjamin. Alice hasn't said a thing about him, either."

"Alice prefers the company of women," Ann said, "excepting that dog." She shook her head and stretched her arms out, linking her fingers and pushing her palms outward. "It'll feel good to have a proper walk, with trees over our heads instead of sheets."

"That it will," said Catherine. "Don't you feel any trepidation?"

"Not anymore," said Ann. "I'll live content the rest of my life just to have seen this." Alice called then and she waved, pushed herself to her feet, and strolled away.

Reg was sitting with Veronica and John, pointing out something on a map that was spread out between them, then pointing at the sky. The young ones sat together, not touching shoulders but with their heads so close that they might have been sharing their breath. Both were nodding, and then Reg was folding the map and Veronica rising, smoothing down her skirt. They looked for all the world like a family.

Catherine had lost track of the days. She spied no more cities in the hazy distance, just water, water, and more water. The sun rose up with them and nestled into darkness with them, and they felt the light growing as tired as they. No rain fell now, and Catherine shook out and then beat her clothing every night and raised the only clouds they saw.

Her buttocks ached, and her feet ached, and her hands were stiff as a dead hen's claws. "I'm growing into an old woman on this boat," she groused at the girls one evening.

"But the sea is lovely," said Alice. "I feel that my heart beats to its rhythm."

"Yes, child" muttered Catherine. "My heart thrills at it, too."

"Mother, can't you enjoy the journey?" said Veronica, chirpy as ever. She was filthy all the way through her clothes to her skin, and her face had darkened, despite John's hat, which she now wore almost all of the time, but her smile remained clear, even in the dim, distant starlight. "It's an adventure!"

"Mmm-hmm," said Catherine. It was all she could do to raise one haunch, then the other, trying to find some comfort. Her daughters, meanwhile, still found every tiny fish and swooping bird cause for delight. They pointed here and there and raised raucous laughter at each new turn that showed them another strange shape to a wave or a movement in the sails.

"Look, Mother!" it was, or "See, there, how rich and dark the water is here!" And, indeed, the colours were wondrous and the wind ripe and brisk with the scent of salt, sometimes tasting of freshly-grated spice.

One night as they prepared for bed, Veronica stopped in the middle of her useless washing and said, "Do you think John loves me?"

"If you're as grimy as I am, probably not," blurted Catherine. Her skin felt gritty, even after a scrubbing, and she'd fallen across the bed, as washed as she could be. Veronica didn't respond, and Catherine sat up. "Forgive me. That was cruel. I didn't mean that."

Veronica wiped her eyes. "What do you mean? Am I so gross as all that?"

"You're very dirty," said Alice. "Toby smells better than you do."

"Oh, Vere. You're as sweet and fresh as a spring duckling. Come here." Catherine held out her weary arms, and her elder daughter fell into them. She was not, in fact, clean, but she smelt good.

Veronica said, "He's full of ambitions. He talks to the sailors, to hear of their travels and what goods they've gathered. Sometimes he seems to forget that I'm standing right next to him."

"He's a man. Can't you forgive him a little for it?" said Catherine.

"He wants to see the world," said Veronica. "He wants to see new people and places. I think he wants to get onto another ship and sail away into the sunset."

"So poetic!" said Catherine. "He's a young man, and young men want to test themselves against everything. They want to be knights."

"Don't knights need ladies?" countered Veronica.

Catherine let her head fall on one side, then the other. Something creaked softly in her neck. "Sometimes they do. Sometimes they want to return victorious and then find a lady to suit them. And to be honest, you two have wanted a great undertaking, as well. Aren't you having a grand one just now?"

"Yes," Veronica ventured. "I am."

"And isn't having a new young man by your side part of this adventure?"

"I suppose it is."

Alice said, "Well, I'm having an adventure, and I don't need any man to help me out with it. Is there wash water left?" Veronica handed over the basin and she sniffed at it. "This is muddy. I wouldn't wash Toby in this."

Ann put her head around the curtain. "Wherefore are you still awake this time of the night?"

Veronica shrugged one shoulder. "We've all been talking of our souls. And of cleanliness."

"Vere," said Catherine. "We've only been discussing love, Ann. So little in comparison."

Ann twisted to scrutinize Veronica. "You needn't throw yourself at his feet, Vere. Give it time. You'll see if he grows to love you." She trained a look on Alice. "And not a word from you about it."

Veronica said, "And what if he doesn't love me at all? He's as handsome a man as any I have known, and I think he means to go far in the world."

"Far can mean many things," said Ann.

"He's just young," said Catherine. "I think he sees the goodness of you, Vere. And, Alice, there is no sin in love between two young people. We even have priests here, if we have need of them."

Veronica drew in a little gasp, and Alice said, "I didn't say that love was a sin. But I didn't hear anyone say that he loves you. Maybe he just enjoys your company. I'd rather have a dog than a husband. They're loyal and they smell better." She shot a severe look at her sister, and did not turn her head Ann's way.

"You're jealous," said Veronica.

"Indeed, I am not," said Alice. "You won't see me making calf's eyes at any man."

"You can find a serpent in a bowl of roses when it comes to love, Alice," said Veronica. "The whole world tastes like a rotten apple when anyone speaks of it around here."

Alice harrumphed, and Ann said, "Don't torment each other. You're sisters and that should make you more loyal to each other than any husband will be." She cut another look at Alice. "Or a dog." She left them then.

"Listen to Ann," said Catherine. "She loves you more than any man ever will. We'll keep an eye on your John for signs that he sees more in you than just another sailor on the water with him. Now, sleep, both of you. Have you forgotten all about Robbie and my husband?"

"Ugh," Alice began, but Catherine cut her off with a glance, and they all fell into their beds without another word.

Chapter 19

The days grew grim with heat, and Veronica's borrowed hat grew greasy, so she took to going bareheaded. Finally, Ann could no longer hold in her opinion and told Veronica to cover her hair. "This is no longer Yorkshire, nor Amsterdam neither. You'd better tame that red mane of yours. There's men watching. Men who are not your John. There are priests among us."

Veronica opened her mouth to object, but Catherine had to agree. The sailors' eyes slipped along the bodies of both of her daughters whenever they passed.

"Yes, Auntie Ann," said Veronica. "I hear and obey." Catherine dug out an old hood, and her daughter threw it on. It did make her look like an older woman, but at least the men did not eye her as often.

Ann indulged her with a commending smile, but no ugly headwear could keep the bounce out of Veronica as she trotted back up to John and Reg. She would wear out her feet, thought Catherine, as much as she herself had worn out her backside. She snorted a soft laugh.

"What's the joy?" said Ann. "Has he finally gone down on bended knee?"

"I don't think so," said Catherine. "He's probably afraid of you."

"Do you recall your Margery Kempe?"

Catherine was surprised at this. Ann had detested the book and the woman it revealed, though Catherine had kept her copy despite the taunts. "Of course. Why do you ask?"

"I have in mind that she went on pilgrimage to the Holy Land."

"She did, and had many an adventure getting home."

"And this after many children."

"And a husband she swore to celibacy."

Ann nodded. "Imagine. How far it was, for a woman in those days and no man to guide her. And here we are, complaining as though we've been in a saddle for months. It fills me with admiration."

"You want to go to the Holy Land?"

"I only said that she must have been made of stern stuff to undertake it."

Catherine did not think it kind to remind Ann how little she had thought of Margery in years past. But before she could say anything at all, Ann added, "And I can say my prayers anyplace. Ask Alice if you have any doubts. Anywhere I speak to God is holy."

So it seemed they were in the Holy Land after all, and Catherine had failed to notice. But it lifted her heart to hear Ann's admiration of Margery Kempe, and she mused a while about Mary and Elizabeth Tudor. Mary was vilified all around, but she hadn't been any more brutal in her reign than her father had been. If she'd been a man, she'd be just another king in a line of strong kings. And Elizabeth?

Ann interrupted her thoughts. "Look there. One of the priests is tailing your daughter and John."

The three had mostly stayed together, but the youngest was sidling up to John, like a crow on the hunt for fresh meat.

"Let's move closer," said Catherine.

"You need to make a confession?"

"Close enough to hear better."

Ann took her by the arm. "No, you don't want to become an eavesdropper, Catherine. Let him try to convert them if he will. Maybe he'll be the one to marry them. But leave him be. You've had enough of priests, haven't you?"

"Perhaps," said Catherine. "They're not all bad. That's just the Protestant talk." But Ann had her fast, and she halted, mid-rise, with her rump in the air and had to sit again.

A furrow of concern had creased Ann's forehead. "You aren't going to turn Catholic again, are you? After all that business with Mary Tudor?"

Veronica was speaking to the young priest now, leaning across John, her face in a rapture. Catherine watched her hands fold into themselves at her breast. Veronica stood back then and closed her eyes, breathing as though she were scenting out God himself.

Ann said sharply, "What's that man saying to them?" She gave Catherine's arm a shake. "Let's go find out."

"If you say so," muttered Catherine, but Ann was already up and headed down the deck.

But Reg got there before the women did, and the priest scuttled away like a sun-scared beetle. Ann said, "What was all that about? Does he want to forsake his calling?"

Veronica laughed. "Why would you ask that? No, he just offered to pray with us. The rocking motion frightens him, and he said his fellows have had enough of him. So we did."

"Is that all?" asked Ann.

"Isn't that enough? He's off to convert the heathens, not us," said Veronica, tugging John. "And we're off to find a quiet place where we won't be interrogated. There's Alice. You can catechize her if you will."

And here she came, with the dog under one arm. "Wherefore do you run away when you see me, Vere?"

"We want to enjoy ourselves while the day shines," said Veronica, and drove John before her like a stubborn cow.

"She clings to him and deserts me," said Alice. "I would never abandon a sister for a mere man."

"Never," said Ann, winking at Reg.

"I wonder, will my brother have grey in his hair yet?"

"What do you say?" asked Catherine.

"I spotted a grey hair in Veronica's head yesterday," said Alice. "And she's young. And, miracle of miracles, John loves her. Will Robbie have grey hair like an old man?"

Veronica had a grey hair? "You have a sharp tongue, child," said Catherine. "No wonder she runs from you."

Alice sniffed, for all the world like a woman displeased with some detail in the furnishings, and examined her mother. "She talks to him or she talks about him. I think she's under a spell."

Catherine said, "What's the matter with him?"

"He's clean enough, I suppose." Alice ran a forefinger over the rim of the barrel standing nearby. An inch or so of water had puddled on its top, and she checked her skin in the reflection.

"You look very tidy," said Catherine. "For all that you can be."

"She thinks he's perfect," said Alice. "No man's perfect. I'll have to lash her to the mast to get her home." She kicked off one of her shoes and took great care to check the stitchings at the toe of her stocking, though Catherine knew that Ann herself had finished them and they would be secure. Alice, satisfied with her perusal, looked up. "His talk is all of money-making and travel. He talks of new worlds and new ventures. I don't want him to get hold of her so tight."

Catherine felt an old ache in her guts, like a memory unbidden. She knew what it was to be enthralled to a man.

"You talk nonsense, child," she said. But she'd heard it, too, that song of hope in a man's planning of his business ventures, the unleashed desire for ownership, the communing of spirit, not with heaven but with property. She felt suddenly ill. "Don't be too rigid in your assessment of Vere. There's beauty in her love for John."

"It grieves me, Mother," said Alice soberly.

"I know."

"I wonder what my father will look like," Alice said. "He'll be very grey, too. I hope he knows my face when he sees me."

"I know," said Catherine.

Alice kissed Catherine's cheek and said she would see to Toby's exercise.

"That girl will have to learn to bend her will a little," said Reg, "or she'll never find a husband."

"Perhaps she doesn't need one," said Ann, "or want one. Come on, don't pester her mind with any marriage nonsense. It's bad enough that her sister's gone moon-eyed. She frets about her father, and she doesn't know how to put her fears into words."

Catherine pleaded the need for a nap, and when she was alone, she lay upon the wretched mattress with one arm over her eyes and listened. She was certain she heard birdsong. The cry of a child, playing a game. A woman's voice, scolding. She opened her eyes. No music came to her ears now, and Catherine leant back on the mildewy pillows and let her eyes fall shut again. She saw the dream coming toward her: the sisters of Mount Grace, singing at midsummer. But Diana was among them, as old as Catherine's mother had been. And old Veronica was there, now a woman as young as the new Veronica. They lifted their voices together, and Diana reached out a hand to pull Catherine into their circle. But her fingers were bony and frozen, and Catherine startled awake at the icy touch. She sat up, rubbing her eyes. It was purple twilight, and the air sat cold on her face. She listened, hard, but the only sounds were voices, talking above her. There was no melody in it for her.

Catherine rose and tiptoed up to the deck. Sailors loitered here and there, her own manservants stuck together, and, there, John and Veronica, now with Alice between them walking Toby on a lead fashioned from some leftover rope. Nobody minded her, and she descended once more, pulling the curtain shut.

Catherine fell asleep trying to picture Benjamin, but his face would not come to her. Some hard thing in her chest felt as though it wanted to force tears from her, but she couldn't weep. Her sleep was fitful and hot, already worn away by the long nap, and when she woke, it was broad day again, and the girls were already gone.

On deck, the air was warm enough to make her sweat, and their rut in the waves behind looked like a ravelling ribbon, ragged at the edges and rough beneath. Catherine watched a few birds swirl overhead with a resentment burning its way from her breast to her throat. Ann came up beside her, and she said, "I dreamt of Diana yesterday. Couldn't she at least have written him a letter for us to take? We have no idea where she is now."

"The answer to that is no. Her father could've written her a line or two over the years to send a greeting," said Ann, "but he sent her nothing. I can't be angry at her for it." She looked back the way they had come. "Nor can I want what she wants for myself anymore. There was a time when I believed that the convent was my best hope."

"But now you have Reg."

"Yes. And you. And Veronica and Alice."

"I am as feather-headed as those sparrows," Catherine remarked. Then she blurted, "I'm no longer certain that I care if Benjamin comes home with us." A cloud captured the sun, and Catherine felt the shadow like an accusation upon her. "I mean to say that we may not find him after all."

"You meant what you said," answered Ann.

It was true and Catherine knew there was little point in trying to argue with Ann about it. Ann could tell through a closed door whether Catherine was lying. The sun escaped its veil and glared down. A fear then settled over her. "What if he's dead?" To feel angry at the living was sin enough, and she allowed herself the arrow of guilt in her breast.

"If he's dead, then your worries are at an end," said Ann. "As are his."

"That is an unchristian thing to say," said Catherine.

"It's perfectly Christian. Why not say that he's perhaps dead? We'll all travel that road, won't we? And if we say we hope to see God at the end, then we believe that our travails will be done. So."

"A lawyer and a theologian wrapped in a woman's weeds," said Catherine. "You've become quite the philosopher these days, Ann."

"I have eyes as well as the next woman, or man, and I see more every day. I'm feeling very enlarged by our travels. And I can see the lay of the land as well as your learned men," said Ann. "I've lived enough years to be sure of my own mind. A mind put in my head by God, to be sure. I believe this is some of the most beautiful water I've ever clapped eyes on, and I'll enjoy the day before me, whether Benjamin Davies lives or not."

Catherine looked again, and the way before them had grown brighter indeed. She laughed. The poisonous point had retracted from her and she let the warmth fall like a benediction on her face. "You're a friend indeed, Ann."

"And a wise woman. A female philosopher. A veritable Deborah. Don't forget that." Ann grinned.

Catherine settled against her friend to think. If Robbie had gone straight to Benjamin, she might find them both before the autumn winds blew. They might travel home again before the snows came and celebrate Christmas in front of their own fire. Whatever Robbie had to give her might be sent along ahead, if it were large. A piece of furniture, perhaps, that he could not afford to send. Or a book, precious to him that he wanted preserved with his family but too costly to entrust to a courier. Maybe it was a fine horse, presented to him by a friend or a wealthy patron. That would cost a penny or two to transport, but no matter. She would take it and care for it, and he would know that she was his mother and that she loved him as she had always loved him, even when he spat and fumed like an angry cat. She would have to keep watch on Alice, who shared something of that fiery spirit. It must have come from her, through the womb, she thought, and shame heated her cheeks.

Veronica called out at something, and Catherine watched her older daughter. She was thin, as Ann had said, but she stood lofty and confident, at John's side, though not near enough to touch hands. John would make no bad son-in-law, despite his lack of a farm. He would be granted a portion, in ready money that could be carried back to England. He was sturdy and strong, and he had a sensible way of thought that Veronica could make use of in managing her share of property. They would have intelligent children that would grow tall, children who would care for Catherine in her old age. Grandchildren. She would have grandchildren after all.

"How much longer will be on this boat, do you think?" she said. A headache knocked at her right eyebrow, and she wished she had a broad-brimmed hat to block out the sun.

"A while yet," said Ann. "If I didn't stink so, I would say it's a paradise."

"I don't know if this is heaven or hell," said Catherine. "It's too much of everything for my comprehension."

"And not enough of some, truth be told," said Ann. "You may have dreamt of Diana, but I have been dreaming about Gertrude De Vries's fresh bread. Like a warm cloud."

One of Catherine's manservants wandered by, without his fellow, and she was struck with a blow of guilt. This man had travelled halfway around the world with her, and she had never even spoken his name. "You aren't sick this time, Oswald. Some fresh bread will taste fine after long travel, won't it?"

The manservant smiled. "Yes, Madam. My mouth waters just to think of it. It might wash out the flavour of ginger."

"Have you ever seen such water?" Catherine continued.

He took a step backward. "I have not, Madam. It's a wonder, this. I'm glad to be seeing it all."

"And I'm glad that you're with us." Catherine said. Oswald made a little bow and continued on his way.

"Will you promote him then?" said Ann.

"He has served me for almost his whole life. He's a man, same as other men. Why shouldn't I speak to him as a creature to a fellow creature?"

Ann said, "You'll get your reward in Heaven for it. You see? This venture is changing you, as much as it is me."

And so another day, too bright, fretted with voices, in language strange and lilting, all around her and the sea endlessly churning beyond them. At another twilight, Catherine craved silence and darkness. She descended to her mattress, and said a prayer of thanks for its smallness and for her tatty curtain. Veronica and Alice said they wanted to watch the sun set upon the water, and Catherine bade them go. Finally, she was alone, and she fell across the bed without even removing her shoes.

As she descended once more into sleep, Catherine imagined that she saw Benjamin on the street, surrounded by laughing men and women. He was young, as she had first known him, and. when he spied her, he beckoned her to him. But Catherine did not like the looks of his hangers-on, and she backed away. And then she was dreaming fully. She looked at herself, and she had become a town. Her arms and legs sprouted cottages and rows of wooden buildings, and small people leaned out of windows to shout at one another. Her fingers were pocked with carriages, and the veins in her hands were waterways, with tiny boats floating on their surfaces. Her body was ranged with mountains, capped with ice, and among the peaks twisted narrow pathways and larger roads, with people trudging, laden with packs and pulling animals, toward some destination she could not see. Everyone was talking, and the sound hummed in her ears like hives of bees in spring, and Catherine turned her head to see Ann beside her, looking every bit like Ann. "I am transformed from myself," said Catherine, holding out her hands. "I am as false as anything put on this earth by men, and I am peopled by aliens who cannot speak to me. I am not natural." Ann laughed and plucked a little man from Catherine's forefinger. She flicked him away like a fly, and Catherine opened her eyes.

The space was dark blue, and Catherine lay, listening to her breath. She lifted her hands and stared at their ordinary, familiar forms by the soft starlight. When had she last lifted a plant from her own soil, or dried a bunch of her own herbs? Not since Benjamin's and Robbie's removal from England. Perhaps even before that. She flexed her fingers and pushed her nails into her palms to feel the thrill of pain. She could hear her heartbeat in her ears, which meant that she was still a living woman. But she sought in that beat a skip of love and found nothing but the steady rhythm of a live sinner. She would seek her husband out, as she had set out to do. And if she found him much changed, she would still greet him as a Christian. She was still Benjamin Davies's wife. However she found him, she would practice more mercy and more forgiveness. That she vowed to herself. She did not want to become like Diana, rigid with goodness, but she wanted to feel the touch of the human more fiercely in herself. To be more fully in the world of ordinary men and women.

Catherine rose and went out to find Ann. She'd barge into the corner where she slept with Reg if she had to. But, no, there she was, by herself, gazing at the heavens. She had a bottle of something, and Catherine sidled up beside her.

"Do you care to share that?" she said.

"You're up. Late for you." Ann handed over the bottle. It was wine, and she winked as she drank from an old mug. "You'll have to take it straight from the horse's mouth."

"Where did you get this?" Catherine glanced over her shoulder, then raised the bottle to her lips. Almost vinegar, but welcome nevertheless. It tasted like England, though it had probably come from France. She drank again. She should be grateful to be here, alive and young enough to move where she pleased. She pushed the wine bottle toward Ann, who touched it with her mug.

"City of Ladies," Ann said, and Catherine smiled, recalling her young designs to gather all of the former nuns of England in her household. Ann was closer than a sister, and that design had come to naught, anyway. The women had died or dispersed, and only Ann had remained of them. And then there had been Diana. Catherine might have broadened her search for her ladies, seeking out only like-minded women for company, if she hadn't fixed her despite against Henry Tudor and his church. But now it was Elizabeth, not Henry, at the head of that church, and she was a woman, too.

Catherine's head ached, and she put back her head to drink once more. The stars pushed their light into the darkness above her, and suddenly the sky was sprinkled with them.

"It's like Eden," said Ann.

"Eden," Catherine repeated. "But only at night, when you can't see the dirt."

Ann laughed. "We'll be on land again before you know it. I'll miss this."

She clinked the old mug against the bottle again, and Catherine filled it before tipping up for herself. And so they stood in the friendly dark. Catherine told her about the strange dream and Ann said that she carried multitudes within her and then Catherine could laugh about it, too. It was just a phantom, Ann told her. They listened to the creaking and rocking of the ship. This, if nothing else in this world, was real, and Catherine was free to grasp Ann's hand whenever she chose.

Chapter 20

This ship had become as familiar to Catherine as walking across her own fields, as though she had sailed many times and had become a friend of the sea. The waves opened at their approach, and the sun shone with a benevolent aspect. Catherine turned her attention to the sailors themselves, who kept their distance as much as possible. The darker-skinned men removed their shirts in the heat of the day, and she saw that their bodies were also brown, rich as the earth itself. She wondered to Ann whether these were Turks, or Moors. Ann wondered if they were Ethiopes, hired by the ships that wandered the earth.

"They say that the world isn't flat at all," Ann continued, "but round as any ball, and that men of many hues and statures live over its edge, where the English don't travel. Women, as well."

"Where have you heard such news?" asked Catherine. She had herself heard travellers and traders speak of the round earth, and it troubled her imagination to think of a globe, hung precariously in God's sky, without beginning or end. She had put it from her thoughts, but now the evidence of many unknown kingdoms and peoples, stood before her.

"The same places you might have talked of it," sniffed Ann. "These sailors have seen many a sight and would tell many a story, if a body could hold a conversation with one of them. And have you not noticed yourself how the horizon bends away from us?"

"Ann Smith," said Catherine, forgetting, for the moment, that Ann no longer used her first married name. "How could you talk to anyone?"

"There's more folks that speak a few words of English than you've been willing to acknowledge," said Ann. "A person need only make the attempt, if she wants to talk."

Well. So Ann had succeeded where Catherine had failed again. "What else have you learned? The positions of the stars? The future of our queen?"

Ann laughed. "The stars seem to move as we move, and the future of the queen will depend more upon her guards than anything else. Or upon who she marries."

"Who do you think the choice will be?"

Ann shrugged. "An Englishman, I hope. A Protestant. I am sick to my soul of the changes this way and that. Of hangings and burnings. It makes us beasts. Worse. Not even the dumb animals murder each other for their habits."

"You have no longing for the old Church?"

"I have felt it. Some. It was my home. It was the creed that I learned as a child. I enjoyed feeling its life again among the Dutch. Very much so. But England is an island to itself, and you know as well as I what madness Mary Tudor unleashed for the sake of her Church. We both saw what a tight fist of a woman Diana's faith has made of her. A hard shell, that the Church closed fast around her."

"Your tropes move even faster than your tongue, Ann. Mary had to do what all kings have done. I lost my love for her, but now I begin to feel my old pity for her. Elizabeth may be the same. And Diana may find her peace in the convent."

"Shut up behind walls, doing neither the world nor herself any good?"

"Who says that she will do no one good? I find it tempting, on some days. I'm sure it would do me good, to talk to God all day."

"It's not for me. I'll hold with the Protestants, if I'm to live out my days in England."

"You've forgotten old Harry and his Cromwell?"

"I have not," said Ann. "But Harry's dead and rotting in his grave. Cromwell, too. If Elizabeth turns as bloody as her sister, I'll renounce the church altogether and live in the wilderness. I'll become a pagan, like your father did. Or a hermit. I may sail away to this New World everyone speaks of."

Catherine tried to drag her friend down the deck, away from any listeners. "My father was no pagan. He went mad."

"He was no madman, and you know it," said Ann, shaking off Catherine's hand and holding her ground. "He read and he studied the world, and he believed that the truth peeped out of all books of philosophy, even when it was concealed beneath a load of trash. Do you recall what he used to say of the Romans and Greeks? Wherefore would a God put them in hell for the sin of their time of birth? What logic in that? And if God is not a student of logic, how is it that men can be?"

"You've become a scholar, Ann," said Catherine, "and I'm at a disadvantage. When did you learn to turn arguments so?"

"When the world turned upside down, and then downside up again," said Ann. "We don't know which way we face, nor whether we are God's people or the devil's. I have only one pair of eyes, but they still see well enough."

"Tell me, then, woman of wisdom," said Catherine. "What do you make of my daughter's suitor? Will she have him?"

"I see no suitor at all, if you want my opinion. I see a fair-haired lad who wants to see the world with a pretty girl at his side," said Ann. "Look there! I do think I see a dark line. That must be our destination."

Catherine squinted ahead. Ann spoke right. The line along the horizon became thick and black. It had to be land. A sailor, just then, shouted out the news, and the others came to witness. Ann fell silent, and they both clutched the wooden edge of the boat to see what forms the people might have in this place. Their wait was longer than expected. Instead of moving toward the line, they skirted the land and moved on, the sailors busy about their tasks and short with their passengers' questions. Catherine and Ann might have been unwelcome cargo, for all the attention they received. Sailors stepped past them, sometimes knocking their shoulders or treading on their skirts, as though they would have preferred to walk right over them, or to toss them into the green sea.

"Will we never see a port?" wailed Veronica, coming up behind them. She had been anticipating a landing. "There's a whole country, right there, and we're sailing past it."

"Patience," said John, beside her. "Soon. Trust captain."

"Since I seem to have no choice in the matter, I'll be schooled by you," said Veronica.

"See there," said John. "Land here and more ahead. We will see it and now we see the sea."

Veronica smiled. "Yes, I see the sea. You're happy wherever you go, John, as long as it's a new place."

"New places. New people. I like it all," said John. "I will see more and more."

"Then I will, too," said Veronica.

Catherine tried not to listen to the young people, though she would take a lesson from them. She would not shut her eyes this time. This was a new place altogether, yet again. They were still too far out at sea to see any people, but she could study the blown trees, all leaning away as though repelled by the salt in the wind. Over her shoulder, the water fell away at the far-off horizon, and, under the sinking sun, brightened until it was impossible to distinguish air from sea. "It's all golden out there," Catherine said to Ann. "I wonder how far it is to those new worlds." She shuddered to imagine turning out toward all of that nothing and hoping to discover inhabitable land. "I don't know how men screw their courage tight enough to make such a venture. It's too far."

Ann used her hand to shelter her eyes. "You know right well, as do I. They do it for profit. What else? Our young John would do it, wouldn't you?"

"I would," he said, and Veronica cut him a look that Catherine could not decipher.

"Would you make such a voyage, for a certain sum?" said Catherine, pointing her face at Ann. "If you could take Reg with you?"

Reg said, "She couldn't take this Reg, that's flat. Other men may find it intoxicating to their souls to set off into the unknown, but I'm too old a dog for it."

"And yet here you stand upon a deck, for the second time in one year," said Ann. "You get along well enough among strange folk."

"Yea, I do," Reg conceded, "but only because we have a mission before us, to find Catherine's idols, and that makes the pilgrimage worth the worry."

"Idols?" said Catherine, prickling at the suggestion. "I don't think of my husband as any saint. Nor my son."

"I beg your pardon, Madam," said Reg. He offered a little bow, but he was smirking. "I have touched you in a wound?" Catherine felt her face heat, and she was glad the sun was shining in it. She had used to blush at any bit of nonsense as a girl, and she believed herself to have outgrown embarrassment. Now Reg stood up and took her hand.

"Forgive me. I only meant to tease. I see I've hurt you now, and am truly sorry."

Catherine's eyes burned, and she buried her upper teeth into the soft flesh of her lip. "I know, Reg. Put it out of your mind. I'm grown old and foolish. And I'm afraid."

"Afraid of the water?" said Reg. "This old sea has carried us a long way and has done us no harm."

"It's not the sea," said Ann. "She's afraid of what we'll find on land."

"What? Afraid of Benjamin?"

"Afraid of what he's become," said Ann. "And what we might nor might not find of Robbie."

"I'm not at all afraid of that," lied Catherine, "but he might be surprised to see me. Suppose my letters never fell into his hands? They might have been lost somewhere. They probably started someone's fire on a cold night. He won't expect me. Perhaps he's gone back to England on his own, and is arriving there as we land here. Then he'll think I've abandoned him."

"Then he'll go to Yorkshire and help Joseph manage the sheep until we return," said Ann.

It was a pretty image, two men working side by side. But Catherine didn't believe it, and she turned her face back to the land they drifted alongside, almost hoping that they wouldn't ever make port. But land they would, and she knew that some consummation was near at hand.

Chapter 21

How many shapes, sizes, and colours God's creatures might be, Catherine had never imagined. As the ship eased, finally, into its appointed harbour, she strained to see. Everything was still too far away, but as they waited to be ushered into port, she scanned the neighboring decks. Men wearing cloth bleached almost white, in swathes like robes that covered their bodies, men in bright reds and yellows, silk jackets and breeches that shone as though made of beaten gold. Men in tattered rags, and men without shirts at all. Two men wearing swaddled cloths upon their very heads. They were pink-skinned from the sun, or red, or brown, or black, and Catherine's mind swarmed. She felt she must have a fever coming on. And there—a woman, and another, and another, all in such unusual costume that they might have been queens, or maybe servants of the queen of some vast, distant empire.

She had thought the ship contained the entire world, but it had only been a little nook in a vast globe, and Catherine felt her ignorance pounding at the inside of her scalp.

Their arrival was as slow as their leave-taking, men and goods tumbling out of the ship willy-nilly, Alice frantic about her dog and Veronica hanging onto John. Catherine kept her fingernails sunk into Ann's sleeve until she was almost flung overboard. Her teeth chattered and Ann had to yank her arm free. "You'll shove me into the very water, Catherine!" she cried, but when she looked at Catherine's face, she put the same arm around her and held her until they were moving toward Lisbon.

When her sole touched the dock, her legs wobbled and she slipped to her knees. Shamed, Catherine put her face to the ground and thought she would weep. But, no, here was Veronica, hauling her up and saying "Mother, you'll be trampled."

But it was not just Catherine. Everyone toddled and tripped, and Reg assured them that they would adjust again to being landed, as they had adjusted to the motion of the waves. Alice found it funny, calling herself a monkey and weaving along ahead of them. Catherine envied her for a moment.

But there was no time for jealousy or self-pity. The crowd jostled them forward, Reg fighting backward to keep an eye on their clutch of goods. "That way," he shouted, and they followed his finger toward the buildings, clasping each other's hands to keep from getting lost. So many people, and all of them looking up, up, the hills upon which the city was built, as though they could see their destinations. Catherine gripped Ann and allowed herself to be dragged like a sulking puppy.

They achieved a doorway and gathered themselves into as small a knot as they could. John was not with them, and Catherine's heart heaved with panic until Veronica said that he had gone back with Reg. They had their manservants, who stood in front of them to keep the strangers off, but the door behind them opened and a woman shooed at them with a broom and they had to shift sideways to escape her wrath.

From here Catherine could at least gaze at faces. So many and so alien. So beautiful, some, and others suffering with pustules and rheumy eyes. Some people missing legs and arms. The odour of sweat and unwashed scalp; the scent of something floral and spicy. Hills behind them, rising beyond her vision, and people striding up the narrow streets that cut through them.

A human huddle under the wide eaves of a building nearby looked different yet, their faces smooth and pale, but their hair black and straight. One young woman had such a beautiful countenance that Catherine could not stop herself from staring. No one would notice her at this distance, anyway. "Ann, have you ever dreamed of such an assortment of human beings?"

"Never," said Ann. "Look at all we have missed, hiding in our little corner of the world. We ought to be ashamed of our ignorance."

"There's Reg," said Veronica, on her tiptoes.

He elbowed his way through the throng. "There's a church just there. Let's slide along here and get inside." He led them along the building front and they met John De Vries at the door. They all fell inside and could breathe.

"It's Roman here," said Ann. The church was more a chapel, with a single small altar at which knelt a trio of sailors.

Catherine ran her hand along the damp wall until her fingers discovered a bench. She dropped onto it. The windows were few but all intricate stained glass, and Catherine felt herself back at the old convent in Mount Grace once more. The air was mealy with dust, and she sneezed. One of the sailors turned his head to bless her and removed himself quickly from their company.

"It does my heart good to see this," Ann said, sitting beside her. The other two sailors also took their hurried leave, and, though no priest showed himself, Catherine felt at home and said a prayer of thanks to herself that they'd arrived.

Veronica and Alice wandered the place, fingering the noses and stone robes of the statues and sniffing at the candles. John stood where they'd entered, holding the open door. "We should go," he called. "I can see church at home."

"I have not seen such an old one in its glory," countered Veronica. "The churches in England were all ransacked in the days before our Queen Mary. I want to see them whole, like you have in Amsterdam." She tilted her head back. "This is worth the preserving."

"Ach, I see them enough," said John. "I like the ones at Wittenberg better."

Catherine said, "Can they not both be doorways to God?"

Veronica added, "There are supposed to be many mansions in Heaven, are there not?"

John said, "I have seen enough of this place, I think. My heart does not warm to it. We did not come all this way to pray, did we?"

It was the first true glimmer into his religious leanings, and Catherine wanted to press him on the matter. Veronica was studying him, and she let it lie.

But he went on without prodding. "I prefer to see the remains of the old Romans, their buildings and their ways with moving water. It shows genius, even if they were pagans."

Now Veronica spoke. "Doesn't this show a genius? It is quiet and beautiful. It grows out of the old Rome just as Christians have grown from the old Romans."

John turned as though to leave her there, but he said, "It does. And they do. But this pope has heard the cries of his people, and he has not reformed. Peter was given the key to the church, and the church has given the key to murderers and adulterers." He shuddered a little, though the day was hot. "It does my heart good to know that I do not belong here. I am glad to have come for other reasons."

Veronica nodded and followed him out. Ann and Catherine remained as they were, occupied with the scene before them. Alice had started for the door, but then she turned back, choosing her mother over her sister. Ann said to Catherine, "Do you agree with John?"

"In part. I agree about the corruptions of the Church. I saw them myself. He's reformed, that is clear. It surprises me."

"Would you still accept him as a son-in-law?"

"Shh. He hasn't yet asked to be my son-in-law, that I am aware of."

Reg sat beside Ann. "Are you angling for him for Veronica?"

"Not I," said Catherine. "I've never been a fisherwoman."

"Christ said that his disciples should follow him and become fishers of men," said Alice.

Catherine looked at her daughter. "So he did. But they were fishing for their souls, and I believe that our John keeps his very closely tucked into his breast." She used her hands to push herself upright and called, "What say you, Alice? Shall we see if we can find you a brother and a father? And then go home?"

Alice said, "I think this is very pretty. I like this church."

"We'll have to find transport for the trunks," said Reg.

Outside, the women waited, under the watchful eyes of the manservants. Although they were not full, the trunks were too bulky to lug up such steep passageways. John said he would seek out a cart or wagon and left them, Veronica staring after. Stepping into the broad street, Catherine was set back by a trudging line of people with dark skin and black hair. They seemed to be holding a single rope. Despite herself, Catherine stopped a stranger who walked alone and pointed at the group. "Who are those people?"

The man glanced once. "Ethiopes," he said. "Africans. People buy 'em." The man walked on.

"I don't believe I made myself understood," said Catherine. But, as she spoke, another man, tall and flame-haired and thin as a weasel, stepped from another building and shouted something. He wielded a stick, not much narrower than he was, and as the line of people moved, Catherine could see the ropes that bound them. "What is this place? Where are those unfortunates from? Are they felons?"

Veronica shouldered her way up to Catherine, and, when she came within speaking range, said, "What's the matter?"

"Look there," said Catherine.

The bound men and women were almost too far to be seen, but Veronica squinted in obedience. "What is that?"

"A man who passed by here said they're from Africa. He said that people here buy them. One man can't buy another, can he? What can it mean?"

Veronica said, "Let's go. I want to see. Maybe they come from the other side of the world."

"He said that people buy them," Catherine repeated.

But Veronica was already walking away and she didn't respond. The strangers had departed, leaving her surrounded by yet more strangers in their strange clothing. Ann and Alice followed Veronica, and Catherine took a few steps forward. The smell of fish was nearly gagging, but here, too, were crates of lemons and oranges, and a woman oversaw, nearby, a rickety market stall with a display of riotous colour. That was Veronica's goal. "Look, Mother," she called. She held up something bright in her hand. It was an orange. "Look at these fruits. I have never smelt anything like them. She has olives here for sale, and figs."

Catherine felt dowdy and dull, an old sparrow amidst bright songbirds, and she rubbed her hands over her skirt, trying to dislodge the dirt. Ann had already joined Veronica, and Catherine started toward her daughter, but then Reg and John had joined them, and John had indeed managed to secure them a cart big enough for their goods. The men didn't speak. Everyone was enthralled by the surge of human flesh around them, and the hot scents of spices, and, beneath the rancid fishy air, the familiar smell of baking bread. Horses, too, everywhere, bewildered by the feel of the ground under their hooves again and nickering softly to each other in their common language. Then Alice's dog began to shake his head, and Catherine became aware of the presence of flies and an undercurrent, the smell of decay. A whining at her ear, and she shook out her own head covering and slapped at her head. The flies still came at her, though, and she scrabbled at her hair to chase them off.

"Wherefore all of these flies?" Catherine said. "I'm being eaten where I stand."

They had been left quite alone by the sailors. Not even the captain bade them farewell. No one spoke to them, or inquired about their destination, except for a toothless, crooked man with a wind-battered face who seemed to be trying to sell them an ass to carry their belongings. The animal looked fit enough, and Catherine told Reg to secure it and bargain for the cart.

"And now we must find a tavern with English-speaking folk," said Reg. He searched the fronts of the buildings facing them, and then pointed at one nearby. "Might as well begin here. John, you come along with me."

They emerged a minute later, shaking their heads, and went to the next place that offered a sign of welcome, but came out of that one looking downcast again and trudged on down the docks. The women followed, the serving men leading the donkey, which kicked now and again at the cart, and Catherine put Veronica and Alice between herself and Ann, who had uncovered her hair completely and was waving the flies away. Veronica was eating the fruit and seemed not to have noticed their torment. She turned aside at another offering of fresh lemons, but Catherine pulled her arm and replaced her by the older women's sides. "I won't have you snatched from beneath our noses."

But no one took note of the four women and their men. They were occupied with their own families and goods, with herding their animals and children along. One man, wearing a curved weapon at his side and, on his head, a large hat with a feather, argued in high tones with another man so dark of hue that Catherine wanted to touch his skin and his glistening black curls, to see if they felt like her own, but she beat down her curiosity and felt ashamed after they had passed by.

And who here was Catholic or Protestant? It was all buying and selling, nobody with a care about who sat upon a throne in a faraway little island or whether Henry VIII had broken from Rome over Anne Boleyn. English Catholics had fled the island, and she remembered how often she had heard that they meant to come here or go to Rome. Maybe they had met Romans along the road, fleeing the Pope, all of them saying "Go back, go back" and no one listening.

Was she still a Catholic in her own heart? She tried to feel a warmth in her chest, or the coldness that John had expressed, but her body gave her only its steady rhythm of steady breath. She believed in God, and she believed in Christ. She had knelt for Catholic prayers and Protestant ones and had felt no difference, except among the priests who had delivered them. And they were men, all of them, neither divine nor demonic. She wondered where the priests from the ship had gone.

"What are you studying upon, Mother?" asked Veronica.

"My thirst," said Catherine.

"Here," said Oswald. He had acquired a jug of wine somewhere, and he passed it over.

Catherine accepted the wine, though she didn't really want it. And they wandered on in silence.

Reg and John led them along narrow passages and around unpromising corners. Catherine's shins were quivering from the climb when Reg shouted, "There! I think there might be English there."

It was a ragged shop with a sign of a spinning wheel hanging outside the door. A worm of worry and indecision gnawed behind Catherine's ribs, and she insisted on peeking into the window before they entered. She beheld a large room of spinning women, with not a man in sight. One woman seemed to be the mistress, as she sat on a raised platform to better oversee her charges. It might have been England, and Catherine's heart lifted at the sight.

She went in the door and curtsied, almost falling forward when the others crowded in behind her. The mistress rose and laughed at the intruders. Catherine stepped forward and tried out her curtsey again. "English," she said, pointing to herself "Catherine Davies."

"I speak the English some," said the woman, coming to meet her in the middle of the room. A couple of the spinners had ceased their work, and she snapped out a few sharp words. They bent again to their tasks.

"I seek my husband, Benjamin Davies. He trades in wools."

The woman laughed. "We all of us seek a husband that trades in wools." She gestured over the heads of the labourers.

"No. I mean my husband." Catherine tapped her breast. "Mine."

"Trader?"

"Yes, in wools."

The woman abruptly left the room and returned, dragging a man. He said, "You want an Englishman?" He appraised the group. "You got four here already."

Catherine pushed Ann and Reg together and, with a moment's reluctance, John and Veronica.

"Mine," Catherine said again, pointing to her wedding ring. "Benjamin Davies."

"No, no Davies." The man shook his head. "Know where English go." He left, and Catherine feared they had been dismissed. But the woman indicated that they should wait, and soon the man returned with a scrap of parchment, on which he had drawn a crude picture of a boat with a sheep standing on it. "Here," the man said, punching the drawing with one finger. "Here." He pointed in a southerly direction.

"It must be a tavern or an inn," said Reg. They said their thanks as well as they were able, and the entire party trooped out again, a little dejected but sure that they could find it, or find a drink at least if they could find no one named Benjamin Davies.

Chapter 22

They had worn out the day with walking, and Catherine almost cried when they discovered that the tavern was indeed an inn, with an English-speaking innkeeper. She was desperate to crest the uphill roads, to find some food and a bed, even if she had to sleep with Toby across her chest. John showed the parchment to the innkeeper's wife and got a smile for his effort. "Ah!" she said. And, like the mistress of the wool spinners, she disappeared into the back, leaving them standing there, hungry and hopeful. She returned, with the innkeeper in tow, nodding and waving. The maids followed, bearing platters of food. Yes, they had rooms.

"I'm famished," said Veronica, accepting the offer of a stool. "Come, Mother, you can't sleep yet."

"I can barely stand upon my legs," said Catherine.

"Listen to your daughter," said Ann, joining Veronica at the table.

Catherine sat. "We've become a travelling comedy," she said, allowing herself to be given a cup of wine.

The innkeeper was at the door with the men, pointing and twisting his hands. It looked as though he was about to send them on a perilously long journey yet again, but John and Reg seemed satisfied and came inside.

"He says that many of the English settle in this part of the town," said Reg.

After the meal, the men would not endure talk of sleep, and they set out once more to have a look around.

"I'll go, too," said Ann. "We can sleep after dark."

Veronica and Alice were up, revived from their meal. Catherine sighed. She hadn't even seen their room. But up she got, stumbling to the door after them. "I think I should drop crumbs as we go," she said, looking over her shoulder to commit the buildings to memory. She longed to return, to lie on a soft bed and listen to birdsong. Even a crow would do. Then Veronica cried, "Mother!" She had overshot a turn and almost wandered away from her family.

John stopped three times to look at signs and to listen at open doorways. They went one way, decided that they were no longer among English, and turned back. Catherine felt tossed and overwhelmed by the waves of people, and the second time John bent to a friendly-seeming passerby to ask a question, she thought she might be overcome by frustration. Ann and Veronica and Alice were deep in their joined joy, stopping at the markets offering brightly-dyed cloth, soap, and fresh vegetables. Catherine longed to order them all to turn back, but she bit down on the devil on her tongue that wished it. At every tavern that spilt out English voices, Catherine's stomach lurched. Benjamin might be sitting at a table just inside that wall. He might be within shouting distance. She feared she might vomit, might shriek, but she clamped her lips together and followed the others.

It was a Babel, men shouting and talking in so many tongues that Catherine covered her ears. They entered one well-lighted place where the laughter rode high. She saw only one woman, serving tables, and inched her way along the wall. Ann and the girls marched right through the middle of the great room with the men. Catherine heard English, from English mouths, though after so many weeks even her native tongue sounded alien. But she was not mistaken. The woman spoke to everyone, and Catherine wondered how she kept the words together in her mouth. She hesitated, then placed her hand on the woman's shoulder. She whirled, a curse already forming on her lips, and saw Catherine. "What is it? No women here." Then she saw Ann, then Veronica and Alice, and set her mouth into a hard line.

"We seek Englishmen," said Catherine, attempting the simplest sentence that would form itself in her head.

"Englishmen here, to the right and the left of you. Good men. Get out with your harlotry. This is not a brothel."

"And we're no whores," said Ann, pushing her way through to Catherine's side. "We're looking for this lady's husband, and we need Englishmen to aid us."

At this, the woman leant back to appraise Ann. "No, you wouldn't be whores," she said, with a little sniff of contempt. She didn't need to add "too old." She lifted a tankard and pointed over the room with it. "Very well, madams. You've washed up on the right shore, I wager. Over there. A whole herd of Englishmen."

Catherine's eyes followed the woman's arm to a trio of men in the corner. She took Ann's hand, and Ann took Veronica's, Veronica took Alice's, and they threaded themselves between tables. Reg and John were coming around from the other way, and they all met just as the biggest of the men began talking to the others of the new queen, in terms that would have made Catherine blush if she had been younger.

"You're from England," Ann said.

The one speaking, up close, was a young bear of a man with eyes the color of garden soil and a chipped front tooth. He said, "At your service, Madam. The English go anywhere nowadays. It's the fashion." He laughed, and his companions joined in the jest, whatever it had been.

Reg squeezed between Catherine and Ann. "Reginald Goodall, your servant," he said, extending his hand. "We hail from Yorkshire—with one Dutchman among us."

"Yorkshire?" said the second man. This one was fox-faced and yellow-haired, so skinny in his baggy shirt that Catherine thought she could see the ribs beneath the linen. "You're a long way from home, my man."

"We're all a long way from home," the bear replied, lifting his mug to his lips. He regarded Reg. "We hear there's a young filly on the throne of England who's too frail to bear a stallion. Too prancy."

Catherine knew Reg was wary of spies, as were they all, and he did his best to demur. "Elizabeth Tudor is young indeed, but she's the daughter of Harry VIII, young as she is."

"Well said!" was the answer from the bear, and he invited them to sit. "My partners here don't take up the entire table." It was true that the other two together did not seem to make up the first by himself. Stools were gathered from under windows and along the wall, and enough space was made to seat the Yorkshire party. Catherine found herself between Ann and John. Veronica was on John's far side, with Reg flanking her and Alice leaning against his other side. The servants had elected to remain in the street, so they had no other man to guard Ann's far side, but she invited no intimacies from the wizened little Englishman at her elbow and received none.

"We're seeking my husband," said Catherine. "His name is Benjamin Davies. A Welshman, originally. He trades in wool. We've heard that he might bide here."

"You've heard? Woman, don't you know where your own husband lays his head at night?" roared the bear.

Catherine was certain that everyone in the place had heard the insult. But no one paid them any mind. Maybe they didn't understand the language. She tried not to shout. "He's been an exile since Mary Tudor took the throne. Now that Elizabeth is queen, we've come to bring him home."

"Ah, one queen's as good as another, I'd reckon," said the bear. "He's a broad man? Got a silver beard?"

"Yes," said Catherine. "That might be him."

"I think I know the man. Benjamin Davies, that's the name. I believe he had a son."

It had to be Robbie. The son Benjamin Davies might speak of could be no other. "That will be my son," Catherine said, and to prevent uncomfortable questions, she corrected herself. "Our son. Robert."

"Don't recall the name of the lad," said the Englishman, "just that there was one."

"Do you know where they live?" asked Ann. "It can't be far if they drink in this tavern."

"Don't put your cart before your horse, woman," the man said. "Englishmen come from all over the city to drink here. All over the world. Got to hear your mother tongue now and again. This Benjamin, I don't know where he stays. Know he traded in this and that. We didn't do business. I spoke to the man. I sell wine, and he never bought my products." He waved at his two companions. "These are fresh lambs, trotted in from England themselves."

"Do you trade, too?" asked Ann.

"We're Catholics," said the fox-faced one. The skinny scarecrow beside Ann nodded. "Brothers. Our mother died last year, and left behind her enough for all. Then that Boleyn woman took the throne, and we packed up our portions and came away here."

"Elizabeth is just as much a Tudor as Mary was," said Catherine, not sure which of them she was defending.

"Just the same. She's out of that Boleyn whore, and our mother couldn't never abide her. Wouldn't have her name spoke in the house. Our father, neither, God rest their souls. They had a nice tidy tavern, like this one, with rooms for travellers. My brother here sold it, and the furnishings to it, and said we'd try our fortunes in a sunnier clime. And here we be."

Someone called Ann's name, and Catherine looked over to see Reg beckoning. He had shifted to another table, and over the din of the drinkers Reg shouted again, "Ann!"

"You're being summoned, Madam," sneered the fox-face, and Catherine thanked them and rose.

The bear said, "God be with you. I'll tell the man you seek him if I lay eyes on him."

Catherine hoped for a second that the two men with Reg might turn out to be Benjamin and Robbie, but they were only a couple of transplanted sheep-shearers. They knew of Benjamin, however, and they had worked for him, three summers or more ago, on some building. They doffed their caps and looked Catherine over. Their faces were greasy and their clothes sweat-stained, but their manners were good, even to Ann, whom they clearly regarded as a servant. They tried to get a better look at Veronica, but she was keeping behind her mother until the men were all seated again.

Ann sat beside her husband, and Catherine addressed him when she spoke. "Is Benjamin nearby? Do they know aught of Robbie?"

"We speak English, Madam," ventured the older of the two men. His tone was without resentment, and Catherine turned directly to him.

"Are you English then?"

"We are, though we've been in this part of the world many a day," he said. "We left under our last queen."

"You're Protestant, then?"

"We are. Or were," he continued. "I have a wife now, and a pair of young papists to my name. My young gallant here prefers not to put his neck in the yoke yet." He elbowed his companion, who ducked his head and grinned. He seemed simple, and Catherine wondered how he came to be in the other's care but would not ask for fear of offending.

But she could not hold in the other question any longer. "You know my husband? Benjamin Davies?"

"I do, Madam. Or I did, I should say."

His expression shifted, a slight twist of the eyebrow, or a lowering of the lids—Catherine could not determine where it changed, but cold skittered through her. Ann, beside her, said, "And what's happened to him?" Clearly, she had observed the alteration, too, and Catherine was grateful for her friend's blunt manner.

"Who said aught of any happenstance?" said the man. He now wore a defensive look, and Catherine was grateful, for a second time, that Ann was not a man.

"Has something happened?" said John. He was looking at Reg, but Reg was watching the other Englishman.

"You look as though you'd rather not speak of it," Reg said, scooting closer to Ann. "Is the man still living?"

"Women have too many questions on their tongues," the man answered.

"I have the same questions," said Reg. "We've come all the way from Yorkshire to find him. We're tired. The summer is waxing fast and we're no closer to finding him than we were a month back."

"All I can tell you is this. He said there was work to be done, and we did it. We used to talk about the wool trade. But the last I saw of him, he didn't mention the wool anymore. Don't think he had sheep on his mind."

"What else could he do?" asked Catherine. Her voice squeaked and shrilled, and she was ashamed. And yet she could not stop herself from speaking. "Sheep and wool are all he knows of business."

"There's trading to be done for those that will do it," said the man. "It's not for Christian men to discuss. That's my opinion, and I'll say no more on it. Except this. I think you'll find your husband much changed. He bides at a big house with a sun-sign, not far from here." He stood, and his silent companion stood with him. "I must be off myself. I have work of my own. God be with you, Madam. With you all." He paid his reckoning to the maid, and he left.

Catherine sat astonished. She shivered, even in the swelter of the tavern. She couldn't, for a moment, remember the name of the man across from her. It was John, of course, John, who was perhaps courting her elder daughter. Her daughter, who was shaking her shoulder gently, saying "Mother, let's depart from here." They had all gotten to their feet and Veronica was pulling her to follow them out.

"Should we stop?" said Catherine, rising, and as if in answer, her feet halted. Veronica and Ann lurched a step forward, then faced her. "Should we stop?" Catherine repeated.

"Do you mean return home?" asked Veronica.

Catherine nodded. She could not speak.

"After we've done all of this?" said Veronica. "After we're here and so close?

"We're almost there," said Ann. "Catherine, what do you mean?"

She meant that she didn't want to discover that her husband had become a different man. The world was changing too much, too fast. There was something secret in the conversation, something smeared with filth, and she could almost smell it. She was unsure whether she wanted to see it fully. She didn't know what her son was, or what he believed. Her feet felt stuck in mud, but when she looked down, it was only a coating of dust. "I meant nothing at all. Don't listen to me." She shook her feet clean, and walked out of the tavern.

Chapter 23

The whole party was tired and fretful, and the sky was uneasy. They had been directed to rooms for the night, and Catherine wanted nothing more than a loaf of bread and a clean bed. A few hours to herself.

The room she was shown was not, in fact, tidy at all. It looked as though the previous occupant had fled her own filth minutes before. The sheets smelt of urine and mildew, and the window opened onto a noisome alley, where drunken men shouted in their alien tongues. Catherine and her daughters laid their shawls over top of the bedclothes and resolved that they would sleep, even in the foul stew of other bodies. Ann remained in the common room with Reg and John, unable, she said, to lay her head down in the midst of such excitement.

But though the girls and the poor dog were asleep within minutes, Catherine lay awake in the musty room and studied the patched and stained ceiling above her. Her memory wandered through the many rooms she had called her own. The convent dormitory which she had shared with Ann and the other sisters but where she had had her own private spaces to squirrel away her few things. Her massive bedchamber at Overton Hall, with bed curtains that let the light fall across her body from a friendly remove, and heavy presses for her clothes. Boxes for her jewelry. A husband who often slept elsewhere. The London house she had shared with Benjamin, her least favourite of them all, though her shallow bedroom had been bright and had contained the dark-framed bed and moody fireplace she'd enjoyed. Those now all long gone through Mary Tudor's hands into the ownership of someone Catherine had never seen. Her father's house in Mount Grace, modest but sun-filled, with a room always prepared for her. And then her house in Havenston, built at her own direction, with her bed chamber overlooking her own front gate and the sheep fields beyond.

Homesickness gripped her in the gut. She dreamt of her house, and her daughters began to argue over who would own it when she died. Alice was shouting and Veronica was crying.

"Let her have it," Catherine said, surprising herself when the words came out aloud and she woke to the bright sounds of morning. She even allowed herself a smile at the dream, though she couldn't remember who she'd been talking to as she wakened. Veronica might want the house, but Alice seemed to live more peacefully in it. And if Veronica and John became a couple? Where would they lay their heads? In England or at the farm outside of Amsterdam?

The others were already downstairs, talking, and Catherine heaved herself up. It would do no one any good to have her alone here, foraging in her mind. A cat howled outside, and a couple of birds called out to the early sun, which had fingered its light down the narrow passage and through the slats of their shutters. No human voices intruded, and Catherine lay silent, grateful for the humbler speech of the creatures that people called dumb. She was becoming as sentimental as Alice, she thought, and chided herself for being simple. But just then a woman shouted, and the spell broke. She was in the real world, after all, of fallen mankind and its shattered languages. A sadness welled within her, and she thought she might weep. She felt a wave of jealousy of her best friend. Ann was enjoying a journey that she had thought to despise, and she had grown to love the changes of place and people. It was Catherine herself who was growing tired of alteration, the tilting ways of the world. She felt a hollow desire for their youth, when they had battled the monstrous caprices of old Henry Tudor and stood shoulder to shoulder against his tyranny. The enemy then had been obvious and clear. Now she battled her own mind, while Ann enlarged hers. But Catherine felt it a sin against her old friend to begrudge her any happiness. Catherine had dragged her here, after all. She was almost at the doorstep of her own husband. She should be the one who was brimming over with excitement. She should feel like a bride. But all she wanted was to retrace their steps homeward.

Catherine joined the others at the breakfast table, but her mind continued to wander the streets and alleyways of the city, getting lost and getting angry. Catherine wanted to leave. Today. No, she wanted to remain here, in the inn, alone and unmolested by new manners and old husbands. She didn't know what she wanted.

Veronica looked strained, her eyes showing lines at the corners that Catherine had never seen before. This is how it feels, she thought, to watch your children age. Every bone in her own legs and arms felt creaky and brittle, and she thought she would not be able to take a step into those hilly streets today, even if she knew for certain that Robbie and Benjamin would be waiting. But she couldn't make her fear understood, even to her companions. Her words sounded agitated, like spring crows flying from her tongue, and she finally said she was feeble-minded with exhaustion.

What had the man meant, that Benjamin was much changed? He would be older, of course, and perhaps embittered by his years away from England. But if he was successful in whatever business venture he had put together, he ought to be content enough. He had always said that place mattered less to him than ease of surroundings.

Reg said, "John, are you ready to set out?"

John had acquired a map of the city and he sat, chin in hand, to study it. "See here. Merchants here. I want to visit. Make some trades." He looked up and smiled. "I would cherish the adventure of it." He sounded like Veronica.

"Cherish it, would you?" said Veronica. "You might well love it like a babe in arms, for all the good it will do you. You don't know them. You don't even speak their language."

"Ah, courage, young lady!" countered John. He was still grinning. "I have no fear of them or their words. You see sign of terror in me when you showed up from England? I got two trunks wanting to be filled."

"No, you have no fear of making money. That I see," said Veronica, "but I'd prefer not to walk the streets all the day without any sure destination in sight."

"Thank you," said Catherine. "My bones have rebelled on me this morning. The thought of walking is more than I can bear."

Veronica was looking at John. "What I would cherish is to find our men, if we must go out today. I would cherish that indeed."

Catherine said that her clothing needed adjustment and asked Veronica to join her in their room. She sat upon the bed and said, "What's the matter?"

"What could be the matter?" said Veronica, turning Catherine this way and that. "There's not a thing wrong with you."

"What's the matter between you and John?"

"What could be wrong?" Veronica said. "The summer full high and sunny. The city is full of life and goods I have never seen. I would like to pack up three or four trunks' worth of silk and new boots and gloves, but that would be foolish and

I am not a foolish woman. And, besides, they didn't see fit to allow the women to carry anything."

"My, how you talk," said Catherine, combing out her daughter's hair with her fingers. She turned over a hank and found a solitary white one, but it was growing at the back, so she kept untangling and said nothing of it. After a few moments of silence, she asked, "Were you arguing with John?"

"No," snapped Veronica. "We agree on everything under the stars. Reforms in religion, choice in marriage, a preference for country life over the town."

"Many things," mused Catherine. "So you and he are in perfect harmony."

"Absolutely," said Veronica. "That's enough, Mother, you'll wear out my scalp." Catherine re-tied up the hair, and Veronica slid from her grasp and went to the window. "I told him that he could go looking for his merchants alone. We can find my brother and your husband ourselves. We no longer need his guidance."

"Wherefore would you tell him that?" said Catherine. "He's done us many a good turn with languages. He's brave and he's tall enough to ward off pickpockets. We should be grateful to him for all he's done for us, not send him off like an ill-behaved dog."

"And now who is it talking?" said Veronica. She sat and looked into a mug on the table, but it was empty. "I'll call for a bottle if we're going to sit here all day."

"Now you must tell me," Catherine said, after the wine was brought and poured. "Do you wish to be rid of John?"

"I never said that," said Veronica. "He's kind. He's handsome, at least to my eye. He comes from a good family, as far as I can see. He has a good mind and he uses it without pride."

"Then what's to be said against him?" said Catherine.

"He's a man," said Veronica. "Mother, forgive me for being brash, but you've had two husbands, and I think they were both disappointments in the end. My own father, God rest his soul, was not a good man, though he thought highly of himself."

"How you do go on," said Catherine. "You were still a baby in arms when your father died. Who's told you such tales? Ann?"

"Aunt Ann has answered such questions as I've asked her. My brother spoke of our father, as well, when I knew him. He adored our father. You know that."

"Yes," said Catherine.

"But I know as well as I know my own hand that our father believed Robbie not to be his own flesh and blood. I know that there was an act of violence against you, when you were in the convent. That my father came to blame you for that, to believe that it was not a rape but a seduction and that you were a sensuous creature who fell."

Now Catherine could not speak at all. She could not even swallow, and set down her wine. Her fingers trembled, and she tucked them under her skirt.

"You wonder how I know all of this. I've never spoken of it before, but I've listened. I heard Robbie talk about Father, how noble and honest he was. I heard our grandfather—your father—talk to Benjamin of it, just before he died. I heard Benjamin himself talk of it, to Reg, and Reg talked back to him some. Yes, Reg. Reg admires and loves you above all women, Aunt Ann excepted, and he had many things to say about my father. And me? I played like a child and stayed silent as a post when anyone hit upon the subject of my father, because I wanted to know the truth. Robbie is a dullard who worships a ghost of his own imagination. Benjamin is a man of business, who seeks worldly pleasure more than anything else. Reg is a softhearted, good man with a plain vision of people and a straight tongue to speak of them.”

“And John?”

“John is good and handsome. But he speaks more and more of trading, of hiring a boat of his own and going to this New World. It reminds me of Benjamin somewhat. I haven’t cast him off. I’m just setting him further away for the moment so that I can see him more clearly.”

“And me? What is your assessment of your mother?” said Catherine.

“You’re my mother, and I love you. I owe you my life, my education, and my position. You were raised to be a woman of God, and you knew little when old Harry sent his men in to seize the convents. You were taken against your will, and you married my father in order to set the world right again. But the world was not right, and it never would be, because of my brother’s birth. You blame yourself for that. You married Benjamin because you were weak and allowed him into your bed, and then you were carrying Alice and you needed a man. And then Benjamin and Robbie were sent away by Mary Tudor, and you blame yourself for that, as well.” Veronica took a breath and set her lips together.

“Veronica, you have eyes in your head, I’ll say that much for you. You have a set of ears, too, that hear more than what should be said.”

“Women are not hooks on the wall for others to hang their hats upon. Two queens have ruled England. They’re women, aren’t they? Nobody doubts that they have brains and eyes. And I speak the truth, don’t I?”

“The truth that I know. Others have their own truths, which they believe as strongly.”

“You didn’t love my father, did you?”

“Your father might have been a good man, if he hadn’t blinded himself with his notions. He was a second son, and it weighed on him when his elder brother died. He became monstrous, finally, and he infected Robbie with the plague of his own ideas. I did love him, but I have eyes in my head, as well as you, and I saw what he became."

"Do you love Benjamin?"

"I respect Benjamin. He's a man of sense and he depends upon no one. There's been a great deal of love between us. But I haven't seen him or heard a word from him in years."

"But you told yourself that you loved them both, did you not?"

"I was in an agony when I married your father, of shame, of terror. I was an unworldly girl, alone but for your grandfather, whom I had thought simply the parish priest all of my life. I called it love. It was love, of a childish sort."

"Benjamin?"

"The truth? I enjoyed his wit and his devotion. I loved his body. Does it startle you to hear your mother say that?"

"No. I already knew it to be true."

"So we are speaking woman to woman. What has all of this to do with John?"

"A woman has sat on the throne of England. Another now sits there, as well, and she has no husband. I love you, Mother, but I don't want to live as you have, at the behest of a man, whose will may change with the seasons. I remember how you spoke of your city of ladies. I want to be such a lady, worthy of God and of her fellows of her sex. I have liked you better since Benjamin and Robbie left us."

"You've seen this change in John just now? Is he a different man than you set out with?"

"No. I don't believe so. But now he is set on adventure. He may only require me as part of that adventure. He may only value me as part of his grand plan. You didn't see the change in Father before you married, did you?"

Catherine's heart splintered with shame, and a shard lodged in her throat. Her daughter had a mind as good as anyone and wisdom beyond her years. She had surely learnt that at Ann's knee, not Catherine's.

"No, I didn't," Catherine said, "but I wasn't looking for it. Don't send John away. You may study him further walking by his side. You needn't commit yourself to him in order to do it."

Veronica nodded. "Yes, that's true. I'm having an adventure of my own, as it happens, and he may only be a part of that for me. Very well, Mother. I'll be kind to him without putting myself into his hands. You've spoken wisely."

Catherine let the word sit in the air between them, too hot either to acknowledge or to deny it.

Downstairs, Catherine put a word in the ear of the innkeeper's wife that the room needed a good scrubbing, and the woman, insulted, flounced off in a huff. Ann and Reg had planned the day, having drawn themselves a map of the surrounding area with an X for each inn that might have information. Alice was almost dancing at the prospect of seeing the things that might be for sale. She jingled a little purse at her waist.

Veronica and John stood together by the window and Catherine waited for the young man to leave by himself. Alice tugged at Catherine's sleeve, eager to set out. Their men had become lighthearted and jocund, standing outside singing old tunes. Catherine suspected that they were leaving out some of the verses, as their eyes met too often in laughter as they fumbled their way through the rhymes.

"Are you sure that the map is accurate?" Catherine asked Reg. "Vere, are you coming with us?"

Catherine watched her confer with the young man. They were almost of a height. They were both fair-haired. They made a fine pair.

Veronica said, "John is coming with us. We'll use his map."

And so they set off together, an uneasy family in an unfamiliar city.

Chapter 24

They trudged down streets and up alleyways, across squares spacious and cramped. Faces and scents. Stinking things. The lemon that Veronica had bought from a squint-eyed old woman and was now squeezing to spicy mush. Dead things. Unwashed human flesh. Catherine's eyes skimmed down a side-street, where a boy squatted, relieving himself against a wall. The smell of shit wafted toward her, and she covered her nose. She wished she could block out the sounds, as well, too many languages, too much shouting and singing. Catherine's stomach revolted, and she wished for a cool mug of English ale.

"I'm going to be sick," said Veronica. "The heat and this stench." She threw a scarf over her head to cover her hair and face. "These flies are like dogs at the hunt. Let me sit down."

But there was nowhere to put her, and they were forced to retreat to the shade of one diseased-looking tree. "Have we any ale?" asked Catherine, but the servants shook their heads. "Go in," she said, nodding toward the tavern that Reg and John had just rejected as of no worth in the search, "and buy something to drink." She poured money out, enough, she hoped, and one of their men went off and returned, while they were rubbing Veronica's ankles, with an enormous jug.

"Ale's cheap, Madam," the servant said, "but they gave us no cups."

"Find somebody who will sell you one." Veronica had wilted so much that Catherine put the jug directly to her mouth. She couldn't see Reg or John now at all. At least they wouldn't die of thirst before they returned.

"I saw something. A market, I think, just back there," said Alice, lifting her sister's scarf and wiping her brow with her sleeve. Their clothes were all stained and stiff with sweat already, and her gesture left just one more smear of dark oil along the dirty nap.

"Get me up," said Veronica. She staggered to her feet as the men returned with a single cup and leant against the tree. She drank and wiped her mouth on her own sleeve.

The thought trickled through Catherine's mind that her daughters were becoming coarse. All those weeks on the roads and then on the ship. Despite herself, she looked to see that John had not yet reappeared, though she couldn't say whether John's own manners would have been any better, given the situation. Her eye met Ann's. Ann's head shook, ever so briefly, but Catherine didn't know whether she had been admonished, or her daughter.

"What about this market?" Ann said, after Veronica had drunk another cup. "Is there a trinket that caught your eye? You want more fruit?"

"No, no," said Alice. "It's a way over there. We passed it just now." She pointed backward. "I saw people inside."

"I saw it, too," said Veronica. She closed her eyes.

"It must be a troupe of players," said Ann. "They have them as well as we do, I expect. What were they putting on?"

"It may be," said Veronica. She bit her underlip, in a way that Catherine knew meant she was troubled or doubtful. "It seemed real enough. Didn't you see? Here now, let me retrace the way we've come and I'll search again. I need to see it."

"I don't want to," said Alice.

"Nor I," said Ann. "You're dizzy with the sun, Vere. I won't have you falling upon your head. Where would we find a doctor? The whole place is a market."

"I want to see it for myself, close," said Veronica. "I'll walk by myself, if I must."

Catherine could see no sign of John or Reg. The serving men loitered nearby, and she started to call out. Then she realized that she couldn't remember their Christian names. She said, "Ho, there," and they came and stood before her, waiting for her to order them. "Remind me of your name, please."

The serving man's brows twitched into a momentary frown. He looked into her eyes. "It's Oswald, Madam. You know me of old. And this here is your own Mark."

Catherine's stomach gurgled with shame and she hoped she was too sunburnt to blush. "Yes. Yes, of course. Oswald, will you come with me and Veronica? We'll go and see what's to be seen. Mark, if you would stay with Ann and Alice, it would be most helpful to me."

"I'll stay nowhere," said Ann. "I'll see this play, or this market, or what have you. The men can wait for the men. That's fit enough."

"We can't make our way without a man," said Catherine.

"We will take Oswald and Mark can wait," said Veronica. "Reg and John know his face well enough."

Catherine could see no solution to it. She trusted her servants as much as any mistress, but men were men and there was much to distract here.

"Come apace, Mother," said Veronica, "or I'll see nothing at all."

"I'll stay with Alice," said Catherine. "You and Ann go." She spied a treasonous glance between the servants. She had made an error, to be seen wavering in her judgment. Now she would have to stay, to watch over her travelling family.

Then she saw John step out of a doorway, followed by Reg, and relief washed through her like absolution. She lifted her hand.

"The men here are wild," said Reg.

"Have you found any English?" asked Ann.

"Yes," Reg answered. "We'll walk." He pointed easterly. "That way."

"Vere says she's seen a market," said Ann. She pointed in a north-westerly direction.

"There can come no good of markets in this city," said Reg. But Veronica protested with a snort, and he said, "A minute, no more. Lead on, girl, if you must see it."

When Reg spoke to Veronica, it was always with a fatherly, spoiling tone, and his gruffness halted her for a moment. But she had made the plea and was determined to see whatever had caught her eye, and off she went, her arms out to part the crowd, with all of the others following in her wake.

A raised platform sat in the middle of what seemed an open warehouse, some few hundred yards down, as Veronica had said, but these were no players. The people Catherine had seen earlier stood here and there, now redistributed among various men, and a few women. Veronica said to a man, "What is this place?" and he gave her a disapproving look, almost threatening, that etched fear on Catherine's heart.

"Get away," the man said. He was sun-scorched and angry, his clothing rich but worn threadbare at the elbows, and his stockings were splattered with mud. He was clearly English. "This is no place for a female. Get you gone." He shoved Veronica back with one hand. The other held the arm of a cowering woman.

"Hold off," said Reg. "Don't put your hand on the girl. We're newcomers here and she has the natural curiosity of the young. We're English."

The man, unmoved, grunted for reply and turned away. His companion resisted, and he dragged her a few steps. The woman, up close, was even stranger to Catherine's eye than from a distance. Her hair was black, almost blue in the sunlight, and her skin was fine and dark as ebony. Her eyes were dark, too, as dark as any Catherine had ever seen, but they gleamed with intelligence, and terror. The man yanked her, and she cried out. John looked bewildered, but Reg would not endure it. "Let go that woman," he demanded. "She doesn't belong to you. She's frightened. She's hurt."

The man faced Reg, the woman still in his grip. "That's where you're wrong, my man. She does belong to me. I just paid a good price for her."

"How can that be?" said Catherine. She'd pruned the offence from her words as far as possible, but the question still came out thorny with resentment. "Is she your wife?"

At this, the man laughed, a nasty gurgle in his throat, almost a growl. "No."

Catherine looked about her. Others were being hauled away by other men, talking to one another in various languages she could not understand. She felt rough-hewn, barbed with rage, but her tongue would not form the words that would persuade the man to let the woman go free. She looked at the stage, now empty except for a couple of buckets and a discarded, ragged piece of white linen. "They are selling these people for slaves," she said.

Ann was beside her, and Veronica at her other elbow. Veronica gasped and said, "No!" but Ann murmured, "We've come to a demonish place."

"I knew it," said Alice. "I felt it."

"Is that the truth?" Reg was saying. He sounded cloudy, far-off. Catherine turned to hear him better. He had moved within a dagger's thrust of the other Englishman, and she could see that his hand sat dangerously upon his hip.

"Don't you draw on me, old man," the Englishman said. "You don't understand the customs here. These ones have come a long way to serve us." The man shook the woman, who was now weeping quietly, collapsed against him. "Haven't you? Come here to be taught the ways of the Church?"

The woman continued to mourn, and Reg hesitated. The man scoffed and walked away, dragging the woman.

"Husband," Ann said softly, "don't get yourself killed. We must have you."

Reg came to her side, but he laid his hands upon the boards of the raised platform. "This is a slave market. Look around. You see them? They are buying men and women. God's blood, do they call this a Christian land? Is this where Benjamin has come to?"

But no one answered him. The buyers were now trading among themselves, appraising each other's purchases, sometimes exchanging one for another. They witnessed the separation of a man and woman, who clung to each other and cried out, their words a shrill music, and Catherine saw a woman step between them and wrench their hands apart, then slap the man full in the face. She was not alone, though, but had two other men at her side, who grinned at the spectacle and dragged the unfortunate prisoner away. His companion fell into the dirt, and the man who claimed her lifted her bodily, threw her over his shoulder like a sack, and carried her off.

Catherine let her eyes drift to the door, and then upward, to the roofs of the buildings across the way. Some were plain, others embroidered with carvings and stone faces. The sun gilded their fronts. But Catherine's mood was sodden, and her mind felt mouldy and old. She had been a servant, and she kept servants herself. But never had she thought to see men of God buying and selling their fellows. Never had she thought to hear a Christian man—or woman—speak of owning a slave.

Chapter 25

No one around Catherine's party took note of the sold people as they were led away. No one cared, though plenty of men and women were attending to their dogs with scraps of fish and bread. Catherine's heart kept pounding out the word—slaves—though it was overwritten with another term—husband—and she realized that the dull urgency of the task yet before them exhausted her.

"Which way do we go?" said Alice. "I want to be clean of this place." She was holding her skirts up, away from a filthy puddle, and carrying Toby under her other arm.

"Reg, what did you learn in the tavern?" asked Ann. She was watching a pair of the enslaved women, who remained standing at the rear of the platform where their lives had been bartered away. They were not bound, but they did not move.

"We may have located Benjamin," said Reg. "We go there." He pointed east, the direction he had indicated before Veronica had insisted upon viewing the goings-on of this hateful place, and he was already walking from it as he spoke. "They say he's much known on this side of the town. We're to look for a large-fronted building with the sign of the setting sun over its door."

"And how many have we asked who denied knowing his name?" said John.

"Plenty," said Reg.

Catherine shoved her feet forward, but she couldn't make her mind comprehend what they were doing. Her guts felt loamy, permeable and rotten. One of her servants steadied her arm before she realized that she had listed sideways and almost fallen.

"Madam?" he said, righting her.

"Please tell me your name again," Catherine said, and shame stormed through her. "You're a member of my household. You're one of my own."

"I'm Oswald, Madam. Yes, you know me. I'm one of yours, Lady Catherine."

Catherine stared into the kind, brown eyes and remembered. No one mistook her for a lady anymore. "Forgive me," she said. "I feel ill in my brain. Thank you for being as tall as you are." His hand, still around her elbow, felt like a friendly vise.

Oswald ventured a laugh. "I haven't been little for many a day, but I'll stick beside you." He gazed up, challenging the morose sky with his smile. "My father's been dead this decade and more, and yet he would have called me 'Little Oswald' to this day if he were still alive. The world has its ways, don't it, Madam?"

"It does, Oswald," said Catherine. She was on her two feet again now, and he released her. She felt the heat of his touch lift from her skin, leaving a cool cloud. "You won't leave me, Oswald?"

"That I will not," he said. "I've seen men, my own brother Peter is one, who might be chomping at the bit to make themselves more than what God has done, but not Oswald. No, I like my position and I'll bide with it."

"Mark?" Catherine said, and the other servant turned. "Mark, come here."

The other servant, suspicion and worry creasing his features, moved a step toward them. "What have I done, Madam?" he called.

"Not a thing," said Catherine. Alice and Veronica, up ahead, had stopped, and Ann had hold of Reg's arm. "Mark, what's your father's name?"

"Madam? My father is Mark, as am I. Mark the Wheeler, you know. His father served your first husband, back in those days, and he served you."

"Mark Wheeler. Yes, of course he did." Catherine wondered whether Reg knew this Mark better than she did. Whether Eleanor and her Joseph knew him, too. "And are you content to go on with us, Mark Wheeler?"

The man shot a panicked glance at Oswald, who impassively studied his toe. "What do you want of me, Madam? Have I done something wrong? I am sure I have not." A note of defiance coloured his words.

"You've served me very well, Mark," said Catherine, "and I'm grateful for it. I don't want to drag you around, however, if you find that you would prefer to go another direction."

Mark considered the building behind Catherine. He looked up and down the street. People still crowded about, at their various businesses, and he shook his head. "No, Madam. I see nothing for me here." His eyes fell onto the platform, still visible behind them. "The customs here are strange and I would not be here on my own. I'll go on with you."

"Very well," said Catherine. "Our Reg says that our way lies to the east, and so we'll do as the three Kings did at the end of their pilgrimage: take our way from here and hope it leads us home."

The servant absorbed this curious speech without comment or retort, nodded, and joined the others. Oswald let out a sound that might have been either a laugh or a cough, and Catherine said, "I won't demand service without an understanding between us."

"I understand you, Madam," said Oswald, and Catherine felt that this was true.

The town was overflowing with merchandise, and people carried bags, hauled carts, and led pack animals all around them. They passed by massive supply buildings and districts of houses, built almost one upon the next. Nothing, however large or expensively decorated, could seem grand after the shock of that platform. The sun refused to shine now, and they made their way in the gloom of a day defiled and growing overcast, though no one else seemed to suffer from the loss of light. Veronica regained some of her excitement, but when Catherine heard her squeal over some bauble or sweetmeat, the sound ruffled her, and she felt like a caged bird, full of lice. The sound was too shrill, not the natural joy of a young woman, and Catherine knew that Veronica's mood hovered at the verge of hysteria. Her mind wandered to Elizabeth Tudor, the way her spirits reached the shrieking point too readily. She tried to picture her daughter sitting on a throne, but the image looked treasonous and she beat it out of her thoughts. Then they turned a corner, and another, came out of the end of the steep, narrow street and into a more open space, like a square, Catherine supposed, though the people were so many that it was difficult to see. The varieties of humanity stunned—so many hues of face and hair. Catherine had seen drawings of Moors in books, but here they walked among the pale Europeans, and her hands itched to feel if their skin and hair were as different from hers as they looked. Two men, dark and polished, passed by without so much as flicking a look at the English people. They were conversing, and Catherine strained to hear the tones of their words, as though the lilt might give her some impression of their meaning.

Veronica pivoted and circled back to walk beside her mother. "It's the strangest place I could ever have imagined. Stranger even than Holland or the German towns." Catherine nodded, unable to think of anything more to add to this description, and Veronica went on. "I see many shades of silk, but fewer woolens than at home. I wonder how Benjamin has prospered. Who would want our rough clothing in this clime?"

Catherine said, "They must have clothes for every day. When they're at home, they go less fine, I imagine. Winter comes even here, too, and they surely cover these things with plainer cloaks."

"Did you see the black men?"

"I did."

"Where are they from, do you think?"

"I don't know," said Catherine, wishing she had a map. Reg had one, back at home, that Benjamin had purchased for him. How many years back had that been? "Ethiopia, perhaps."

"Where's that?"

"South," Catherine said, as though she were confident in this knowledge. "In Africa. People who live under the sun grow differently than we do, under the cold clouds." She wondered if she had read that somewhere, or heard it, or if she had simply concocted the idea herself.

""I feel drab in comparison," said Veronica. "Look, do you see? There's a woman."

And so there was. A dark-skinned woman, wearing a skirt of flaming silk, walked along the edge of the crowd. She carried a large basket in one hand, and held a slender dog on a leash with the other. She moved with a liquid grace, and her face, though partly covered by a swath of yellow fabric, shone.

Veronica lifted a fold of her own grey skirt and dropped it. "I'm a field mouse. My skin is dry as old vellum." She wiped at her cheek. "Am I sunburnt, Mother?"

Catherine regarded her daughter's fair skin. "A little."

"And so then I will turn red. And I'll have freckles. Spotted like an ancient sheep."

"You're more like a pup, frisking through the fields," teased Catherine, and Veronica smiled at this.

Then the smile withdrew. "Those others," Veronica said. "Where were they from? Were they also Ethiopes? I've never seen such faces. They looked like condemned prisoners."

"Nor I," said Catherine. She opened her mouth to call to Reg—he who studied maps the way other men studied account books and women—when she saw a head in the crowd. Black hair, curly and thick as lambs' wool. But a white skin at the neck. The young man was tall, and he was striding the other direction, away from them. Away from her. "Robbie!" she called. It was him. She was sure of it. She had seen her son.

Chapter 26

Alice was screeching, "Where? Where is he? Robbie? You saw Robbie?" and Veronica was stretched up on her toes, trying to catch sight of the man, but the crowd was too thick, and Catherine had lost him. Reg and Ann had stopped, and John was looking around, too, seeming unsure exactly what he was searching for. Catherine said, "Mark, did you see him? That was Robbie." She pointed.

Mark said, "I might've seen him," but his words came out mealy with doubt. He was clearly trying to mollify Catherine. He'd been at the rear, and Catherine had probably been barring his ability to see anything at all. "You sure of it, Madam?" he added.

People elbowed past, hemming them in on all sides, and Catherine was no longer certain. "I think I saw him," she said, and the servants nodded their agreement, as they were expected to do. "Never mind," said Catherine. "We're all tired to our bones."

"That we are, Madam," said Mark. "Oswald, did you see aught of a boy that looked like our Robbie?"

Oswald shook his head.

Reg was beside her now, and Ann was the one pointing. Reg said, "Which direction did he take?" but Ann didn't know.

"The streets go every which way," Veronica said. "Mother, where was he?"

"That way," said Catherine. But three narrow lanes spidered away from the square where she had seen the young man. Or was it a young man? Maybe in this land the women cut off their hair when they wanted to. Maybe it had been a much older man.

"We go that way," decided John. "Maybe we find, maybe don't. Won't find anything while we stand here."

The logic struck Catherine like a welcome slosh of water on her hot face. "Yes. If we don't find him down one street, we'll start on another. What was that sign for Benjamin, Reg?"

"The setting sun. I have it marked right here," said Reg, patting his chest. "But it's odd that you should see Robbie, and not Benjamin. It's Benjamin's supposed to be here."

"He must be here, too," said John. "Where else?"

But Catherine could not imagine her son in this place, among all of these jeweled and sparkling merchants, all of these Roman Catholics. She said, "Go," and led them forward, straight across the square and through the waves of people. She almost ran over a juggler with a half-dozen balls of red, yellow, and blue, and he cursed her as she veered around him. His audience joined in the jeers, and Catherine put her head down and blundered on. The sun had broken free of the clouds, and, in the absence of haze, she was blinded, unsure of which direction she had seen the young man go. But Veronica and John now took the lead, and Catherine let herself be drawn ahead by the sight of her daughter's bouncing hood and John's blond hair.

The first lane they chose was quiet but dank. It stank of old cheese and slops, and Catherine had to look downward instead of forward to sidestep the piles of excrement and rags, realizing almost before she was upon it that one of the mounds contained a person. She leant down, unable to stop her heart from knocking the wind out of her throat, but when the man raised his head, he showed a head of unwashed brown hair. He was at least Catherine's age. She started to toss a coin, but it was impressed with the image of Mary Tudor, and she feared he would find no use for it.

They came out onto another large square, this one less fitfully inhabited. A few men, wearing sober black, strolled in pairs and small groups, and Catherine called, "These look like Robbie's sort."

Veronica scanned the open space, her hand leveled against her forehead, but she shook her head. "I say we ask one of them if they know of him." She marched right up to a pair, but they startled back, affronted by the brashness of a young, pretty woman, and one of them scolded her with a shaking finger. Veronica retreated, scowling. "They claim to be a civilized people in these parts?"

"Manners are manners," said Ann. "Best that you keep yours under rein."

"Reg, you might do it," said Catherine. "Mark and Oswald, you walk beside them."

John and Reg edged toward another of the groups of men, Reg hailing them with one raised hand. Catherine and Ann hung back, with Veronica and Alice between them, trying to look innocent and comfortable, but many of the men narrow-eyed them as they went past. Reg was talking with his hands, then the men were consulting among themselves. One of them removed his large hat, scratched his head, and nodded. He pointed south.

"They know where he is?" said Catherine.

"I can't be sure," said Reg. "I said the names, and one said over there, but I may not have understood them altogether. Or they may not have understood me. They pointed this way and said something that sounded like 'all English.' This may be where Englishmen come. Or they might have been laughing at me. I don't know if they meant Robbie or Benjamin."

"Which lane?"

They all looked south. Two more lanes came into the square just south of where they had come out. "We try them both," said Catherine. "We try until we find him or we lose the sun."

Neither of the lanes, however, brought them any closer to finding Robbie, or Catherine's husband, and they had forgotten, in their zeal to see that black hair again, to search out the sign of the setting sun. The real sun, as though to spite them, had set without their notice in a western sky overrun with stormy-looking clouds, and Catherine, as they emerged from the wider street they'd taken into a new square they didn't recognize, sat upon a stoop and put her chin in her hands. "We've wasted an entire day," she said to no one in particular.

"We haven't found him," said Veronica, settling beside her mother, "but that needn't mean he isn't here. He may keep indoors. You know how little joy Robbie takes in the light and fresh air."

If she had meant the remark as a complaint against her brother, Veronica's face did not reveal it. The door behind them opened, and a red-faced, fat woman brandished a broom and shouted at them. They were clearly sitting on her doorstep, another trespass into another woman's domain. Catherine raised her hands in pardon and surrendered the spot. "She thinks we are beggar women." She bowed another apology as the woman looked on, muttering and jabbing with the broom at the place where their skirts had been. Catherine couldn't stop herself from examining her clothes, to see if she was as dirty as this woman seemed to think she was.

"This is an unfriendly city," said Alice, when they'd retreated far enough for the woman to close the door again.

"I wouldn't sit anywhere that I hadn't paid for unless I needed it."

Catherine and Veronica wanted to return to the "English" square, and so they wound their way back the way they thought they had come. The buildings looked familiar, Catherine believed, and Reg said, "This day's done, and unless we want to search through the tavern-goers we should find a place to lay our heads and get a dinner."

"My stomach has been saying the same thing for this hour," said Ann. "And my feet."

Catherine agreed, though her skin was tingling with a sense that her son was nearby. It was silly, a girl's notion, and yet she could not shake off the sense that he was within walking distance. But then she'd seen him, hadn't she? This wasn't some wives' tale of a mother's spirit biding within her child. It was a simple truth, an observation. And Englishmen perhaps congregated here, if her son could be taken for English anymore. She followed along, now aware of her own soles aching whenever she took a step.

"Look there," said John. He'd spotted a place that looked big. Its sign boasted a roaring lion, a very English-looking lion at that, and he left them by the front door and went in to make inquiries.

Catherine scanned the windows and doors but saw nothing of note. Women were hurrying home with their maids and children. Men were together, slipping into the drinking houses. The windows were mostly shuttered or curtained. Then she looked up, westerly. The last crimson fingers of sun lit up the sky, and the buildings lay in shadow, their fronts gloomy and dark. But there. She was sure of it. Almost sure. She saw a figure, standing at a pane. It was a man, backlit by candlelight, or a fire. But not a fire, not in this heat. A candle then. The man had an abundance of hair.

Dark hair? It might be. Was he watching them? He yanked a drape across the window and she could see no more.

Catherine struggled between walking right across the square to knock at the door and keeping what she had seen as her own secret. If it had been Robbie, he might have seen her, even in the gloaming, and could come down and show himself. If it had not been Robbie, she would send her family on yet another hunt for nothing. Reg went to fetch John, who came out smiling, the lion swinging mightily over his head, and said that they had rooms. It was an English-owned inn, as they had suspected, and John seemed very pleased with himself.

Reg said, "We have dinner awaiting us, and rooms in the back for Mark and Oswald. There's a stable. It's clean and we need not share beds with strangers," he said. "I'll send the men to pay our reckoning at the other one and fetch our stuffs."

"Thank God in heaven," said Ann. "I cannot walk another step." She took Veronica's and Alice's arms and steered the younger women, who were staring at people, toward the door.

"Will you come?" said John. He offered his own arm to Catherine, and he spoke in such a familiar, soft tone that she almost expected him to call her Mother. But he was probably thinking about his stomach, as well, and she allowed him to lead her inside.

The common room was spacious, with a few men at tables. No women to be seen, but a young man was laying food on a long empty trestle, and Catherine's guts rumbled at the scent of beef and bread. Vegetables were brought next— piles of bright carrots and a dish of something green. "Is that grass?" asked Ann, and the young man smiled at her but said nothing.

Veronica allowed John to pour her wine while she fished in the bowl with her spoon. "It's the leaves of something," she decided. She put one to her tongue. "They've dressed it with vinegar."

Catherine didn't care, suddenly so famished that she thought she might faint before she could lift a mouthful. The bread was fresh and the wine was sweet, and when the innkeeper appeared to see that they had enough, she almost wept to hear that he spoke English like a Yorkshireman.

"What do you in this part of the world?" he said, wiping his hands on a rag.

"Please, sit with us," said Catherine. "I haven't heard so many words of clear English strung together in many a day, except by ourselves. It does my ears a world of good."

He sat, and for a few minutes they stuffed themselves. The man pulled out a leather bag and withdrew what looked like a pinch of old hay. He stuck it into his mouth and ruminated, his eyes closed. Another pinch and he crossed his legs while he chewed. He looked rather cow-like, content and heavy-lidded. Then he took note of Catherine's stare and spat into a handkerchief. "It's tobacco," he said. "From the new world. Best thing for a man's lungs. Or his mood."

"What is this tobacco?" asked Ann.

"It's a leavy herb," the man said. "Wouldn't be without it. Makes a man feel young again. Wakes me up in the morning, fresh as if I'd slept for three days." He poured some out into his palm and offered it up for inspection. Alice reached a finger to stir it, but he pulled back.

"You break your fast with leaves?" said Veronica.

"Leaves and bread," said the innkeeper. "Gentlemen, will you try?" He held out the bag to John, keeping the handful for himself. "Ladies do not take it in the common room," he added by way of apology to the women. He turned again to

John. "Now, young man, if you mean to trade, here's your merchandise. Nobody needs pepper if they've got tobacco."

"I'm no lady, and I see no other women here," said Ann. "Let me have a bite."

"Have mine," said Reg. He poured his into her hand, and Ann poked the leaves with her finger and sniffed.

"It smells of fruit. Is this from a grape vine?"

"Oh, no, Madam," said the innkeeper. "The leaves are large as your head and yellow as the rising sun. They grow straight out of the ground, they say, and straight toward Heaven." He held out the bag again to Reg. "You'll see." The bag itself he offered to John. "Here's seed-money for you."

Reg regarded his serving with a wary eye, but Ann nibbled on a piece.

"You must take it right into your mouth. Put it under your tongue or against your cheek if you like," said the innkeeper. The other diners were watching Ann with merry expressions, and he frowned at them.

Ann stuffed it in and chomped with all of her might. Then she blew a cough so loud that the tobacco flew from her mouth and into the fireplace. She heaved and gagged, then sank to the floor. Veronica and Catherine were beside her in a moment, sweeping her skirt from the flames.

"That's the very devil!" Ann said, when she could speak again. She scrubbed away her tears. "It's a rank weed, not an herb."

The innkeeper had tipped back in his chair and was laughing out loud. Snorts and guffaws sounded from the depths of the room, and Ann glared around, still coughing. "You think a woman can't bear your magical herb? Well, let me have some more. I'll learn."

"We've all done the same," said the innkeeper, wiping his eyes. "It must be taken more gently, Madam. Like this." He retrieved his bag from John and tenderly drew out a large pinch, which he placed with precision in his jaw. He smiled. "You see? The sweetest physic on God's earth. It cures a melancholy spirit, and it eases all sorts of pain."

"John, you give it a go," said Veronica.

John took back the bag once more, examined a pinch to match the innkeeper's, then laid the leaves on his tongue. "Gently, now, son," said the innkeeper, and John pursed his lips and clamped his teeth together. He blinked, and tears trailed from his left eye. "Do you feel the physic?" said the innkeeper.

John dug the hunk from his mouth with his forefinger and scrutinized it yet again. "Taste bad," he pronounced, laying it down on his napkin.

"Once you're accustomed to it, it's sweeter than honey," said the innkeeper. "Keep the bag, son. I'm telling you, if you have trunks to carry goods home, this is what you want."

"Where does it come from?" said Veronica. Catherine could see that she longed to try it herself but was unwilling to provide the spectacle that Ann had. Ann herself was holding the remainder of hers like a kitten in her palm, putting her tongue to it then licking her lips.

"From the New World," said the innkeeper. "There's a merchant here who keeps a shop. Men come from all over the city to buy his tabac."

"Is this the sort of business that our traders do over the sea?" asked Catherine.

"This and that. This and that," said the innkeeper. "Madam," he added to Ann, "you will have to take it or not. Licking it will do you little good."

Ann tried another bite, this time setting the wad just between her lips. She bit a little and opened her mouth to shove it around with her tongue. She poured some into Reg's hand. "Slowly. Don't chew too much."

Reg tried, his eyes on Ann's. He, too, rolled it around in his mouth. "I wouldn't give a penny for a shipload of this."

"Well. We'll see about that," said the innkeeper. "Once you get the habit of it, you'll want nothing else. You'll feel like a young man again."

"We saw men and women being sold like cattle," said Veronica. "In a big market. Is that a business of the New World, as well?"

Catherine felt her chest wring itself into a knot at the question, but the innkeeper did not show shock. He grew sober and went to a cupboard, where he retrieved a second bag of the weed, before he spoke. "Now that. That's a business I don't like. It's against God, in my eyes."

"So this is a common trade here?" asked Catherine. "To buy and sell souls?"

The innkeeper shook his head. "Not common, but common enough. What did you see? Ethiopes?"

"I think so," said Catherine, unwilling to try the word herself. "What does it mean?"

A man from another table sauntered over and sat beside Reg. "This is not a conversation for ladies." He was English, though so sunburnt that his skin was like cowhide.

"I am not a lady," said Ann. "We're simple pilgrims here in search of our family. This young one wants answers to her questions. We've seen such a sight that I never thought to witness in a Christian land. Tell us."

The newcomer looked at the innkeeper, who shrugged and ploughed through the contents of the second bag and said, "What harm can it do to speak the truth?"

"Very well," said the man. "There's trade in this port, and there's money to buy. Ships come from the New World and they come from the North. They go to Africa and they go farther, to the Eastern countries."

"John here has told us of all this," said Catherine. "He trades in spices, in Amsterdam."

John dutifully nodded.

"Mm, Amsterdam. There's many of your countrymen here then, John. I can lead you to them, if you want. You saw people bought in Africa. Not everyone relishes a voyage farther east. They come here, and they work for their livings."

"They are not from the New World?" asked Alice.

"No, no, my girl." The man withdrew a bag of his own from a pocket in his jacket. "These people come from a very old world, indeed."

"But they are people. Creatures of God," said Alice.

"They're as unlike you or me as that dog over there." The man pointed to a lounging mastiff by the front door. "They need work, and they need a strong hand. This New World. They're needed there, too. They can labour all the day and never feel it. Hard-willed and wily. Must be watched every minute of the day."

Catherine looked at Mark and Oswald. Their expressions closed up, and they sat, with blank eyes, listening to the cruel speech. Catherine said, "We don't buy and sell men in our country. Our serving men have been in our family for generations back. They're our family."

The man laughed. "These Ethiopes may be in their new families for generations to come. Who knows? What difference whether a few coins change hands or not? Some of God's children are born to manage, others to serve. The Bible tells us that we must serve our masters."

"The Bible doesn't require that masters tie their servants in order to force them to serve," said Mark. "It doesn't say that we buy and sell men like cattle."

"Oh, and you've read your Bible, have you? Your mistress here must be one of those reforming types, who keeps her men shackled to her with the Word. Tell me, have you got you curtains for your beds, and slippers by the fire for your feet?"

"Stop this," said Veronica. "Our men are not property. We didn't buy them at a market like a couple of sheep."

"Pardon my tongue," said the man, "but you may be as liberal with your servants as you like. They are still 'your men.' At least the one who buys him an African to cook his meals is an honest trader of flesh."

John's face showed panic, and when Veronica rose, he put a restraining hand on her arm. She turned, in a fury, and said, "You'll defend this talk?"

"Sit, please," he said. "Or I will go with you if you go."

"I must be off to our room," said Veronica. "And you to yours. I've had my fill of both dinner and company tonight."

The man raised his hands, palms out. "I've done. Excuse my presence. I've only sought to tell you the answers to your questions, which you so dearly wanted." He returned to his companions in the corner, who huddled close enough to whisper.

"It seems like time for bed for us all," said Ann, and Reg nodded. They thanked their host, who sat, unable to choose whom to agree with among his paying guests, and removed to their rooms. John held Veronica's hand for a moment, but she said she was tired and needed a bed. Mark and Oswald departed to their errand and then their own room in the back without saying another word.

Chapter 27

Catherine was alert before the sun and Veronica sat up in the thin, grey light when her mother slid from the bed and began to dress herself. "Can't you wait just an hour?" Veronica said. "Wherefore are you in such a rush?"

"Shh," said Catherine. "Never you mind. Don't wake Alice. Go back to sleep and I'll return for you."

"You're going out." Veronica laid back the quilt. "You mustn't go alone. You don't speak the language. It's still dark."

Toby stirred among the covers, and Alice sat up. "I want to come, too."

"Very well. Come on. But be quiet. I want to leave the others here." Catherine helped her daughters into their skirts, and they tidied each other's hair. She listened at the door for a few moments, then they sneaked out together, throwing a sop of last night's bread to the watchful guard dog, who caught it with a single snap and settled again by the hearth.

The square lay empty and silent. A lazy sun cast a sliver of light in the east but was in no hurry to heave itself up, and Catherine went directly across to the building where she had seen the figure the night before and knocked at the door before she could be overcome by fear. A finger of breeze tugged at them, and Veronica pulled a shawl tighter around her shoulders. Catherine had come out without one, and she allowed herself a stealthy shiver.

But Veronica saw. "You're cold. Whose door is this that we must hail them before the dawn?"

Before Catherine could construct a plausible answer, the door opened. A young maid, still in her nightcap, peeked around it.

"I seek one of your lodgers," said Catherine. "Lodger?"

"Lodg-er," repeated the girl in a piping voice.

"Robert Overton. Robbie Overton." Catherine held her hand at the height she figured Robbie still was. She waggled her fingers around her head in what might be taken for a sign of a great deal of hair. "A man. A young man."

"Overton," said the girl. She pointed upward.

"Yes." Catherine nodded vigorously. She pointed to herself. "Mama. Mother."

"Ah, Mama!" This the girl clearly understood. She looked at Veronica and Alice.

"Sisters," said Catherine, and her daughters linked their arms.

The girl withdrew and the door opened wider. They entered a generous hall. It was clean, though shabby, with rugs boasting faded, exotic patterns that Catherine couldn't make out in the low light. The maid indicated a bench, and Catherine sat upon it with Alice. Veronica hesitated, then sat as well. The girl disappeared up a staircase, and Veronica said, "How did you know? He's here? You're certain?"

"I saw him at a window last night," said Catherine. "He was looking out, maybe at us, as we waited outside. I'm sure he could see us. It makes sense. This is where English people stay."

Veronica said, "It can't be. All this searching and then he's here? Right here?"

And there he was, coming down the steps. The maid trotted before, and waved at the women, then whisked on down another set of stairs, probably back to her own bed.

Robert Overton walked into the early light and said, "Hallo, Mother. Sister."

It was hardly believable, that her son stood here before her. After five years, he was older, of course, but how much aged in face and body Catherine could not have imagined. Two lines, deeper than the ones in her own face, harrowed his cheeks, and the skin hung from his jaw like the jowls of a hunting dog. His eyes gazed at her from deep within their sockets, and she saw no spark, either of joy or his accustomed rage, shining there. She was unsure whether to speak or to move, and she lurched forward to take her son into her arms, but the shock of his frailness almost threw her back again. He was insubstantial as a bag of feathers, and he did not return the embrace.

"So it is indeed you. I had some word that you might be coming this way. You've arrived sooner than I expected."

"How did you know?" said Catherine.

He lifted a narrow shoulder. "Word travels. Men travel. I've been watching the harbours. I saw you at the docks. I wondered if you'd have the skill to find me out. Have you hounded me all the way from England then?" he said. His voice sounded broken, refracted, with care, with weariness, perhaps with grief. He set her away from him, and said again, "Have you come from England for me?"

Catherine's own voice cracked in her throat when she said, "Yes," and she had to muster more air into her lungs before she could speak again. "From Wittenberg, more recently, but we started out for you as soon as we were able. We thought we would find you among the Lutherans."

"Mm, the Lutherans," said Robbie. He worried the whiskers on one side of his chin with raw-bitten fingernails. "They might have kept me, I suppose, if they'd wanted to do it. You didn't receive my letter, then?"

"We have the one in which you told me that you had something to give me," said Catherine. "It said that you were in Wittenberg."

"And so I was." Robbie glided around his mother and stood before his silent sisters. "Vere. Have you no word for your brother?"

"I. You," Veronica stammered. "What have you done to yourself?"

Robbie looked down, as though surprised to discover that he still possessed a body. "The will of God. He gives and he takes away. He's taken much from me. A test to my soul."

"Oh, Robbie," said Veronica. She put her arms around him. "God's blood, you're thin as a ghost."

"And here is young Alice, I believe," said Robbie, pushing Veronica aside. He put out his hand and shook hers as though she were any acquaintance.

"Son," said Catherine. "You'll come home with us, won't you? The queen is dead, the queen who banished you, and we'll be a land of the new religion again. You'll be forgiven, I think, your past actions and welcomed again as an Englishman. We'll be Protestant, of that I'm sure."

"An Englishman?" said Robbie. "I've been robbed of my country. I've been robbed of my property and my position. I'm no Englishman, as no man worthy of the name would bear bowing to a woman. It's the sister, isn't it? Elizabeth. She's got the throne."

Catherine stepped backward, and the morning, coming clear at her back, lit his face. It was even more ragged than it had appeared in the dim pre-dawn, and now the old resentment fired in his eyes. He staggered at the light, and Catherine could see through his shirt how spindly he had become. "You're ill," she blurted.

"Not so sick that I'll fall on my face to that harpy," said Robbie. He stumbled backward and sat, hard, on the bench in the hallway. "I didn't to her sister, either. Cut of the same cloth, they are, both women who need a man to cover them."

Veronica stared down at her brother. "How have you come to be so harsh?" she said. "And so foolish? Look at you. You're the shadow of yourself. You've buried a wife and still you will rail at England? You're alive, Robbie. They aren't. And never a word to your family about them, until it was too late? I hardly recognize you."

"Don't lecture me," said Robbie. "My wife was taken by the curse that all women must suffer as the legacy of Eve. That my son was taken, too, is a curse upon me, for what cause I can't say." The hard plank of his expression broke, and he looked for a moment as though he might weep. But weep he did not. He squared himself as far as he was able in such a diminished state and glared at his sister. "But England is still ruled by a woman, and be she Catholic or Protestant, she's the weaker of God's creations, and I won't return to be headed by such a creature."

"Tell me of your son, Robbie," said Catherine. She knelt and put her hands on her son's bony knees, trying to reach through his anger. "What was the boy's name?"

"He's dead," said Robbie, shoving his mother away. "He was the smaller of them, and so he died. He was called William, after my father, for all the good it did him." He finished speaking on a cough, which shattered his composure. He put his head down and retched. A spool of bloody spit uncurled and puddled on the floor.

"What is this?" said Catherine, backing further to see the evidence. "Robbie, you need sleep. You need physic. Have you a doctor here in this place?"

The young man pulled his shirt tighter, with no effort at all. His frame was so withered that the fronts would have overlapped, had it been unbuttoned. "I've no need of doctoring. I'll manage with the will of God. I have no one who depends upon me, and I have no desire to outlive the time allotted to me in the Book of Life. God sees my condition and He wills it."

"You're an even greater fool than I took you for," said Veronica.

"And you're a woman, sister. I don't trouble myself with the words of women."

"Children," said Catherine. "We're reunited, after all of these many years. Must we argue, right here at the first?"

"Don't blame me," said Veronica. "Your son has got himself half into his grave and seems not to care."

"And your daughter has inherited your loose tongue," said Robbie. "And this one here." He threw out his fingers at Alice. "Have you taught her to be a shrew, as well?"

The two Overtons glared at each other, and Catherine almost despaired at a word to make peace between them. But then her mind snagged at something, and she said, "What did you mean, 'the smaller'?"

"I said 'loose,' not 'small,'" Robbie said.

"When you spoke of your son that's dead," said Catherine. "You said he was 'the smaller of them.' What did you mean?"

"Oh," said Robbie. "They were twins. There were two children. And of them, my son died. The other one is alive. For that, I can never be sure whether to praise God or to question Him. May I be forgiven for that. And may you be joyful. You're a grandmother yet."

Twins. Catherine had twin grandchildren. She allowed this to settle in her mind as her daughter and son continued to stare daggers at each other. Veronica had given a little screech at the news of a niece or nephew, and then she had fallen silent. The morning sun opened the hallway with light, and Catherine cast her eyes over the fanciful carpet, which she now saw was moth-eaten or heel-worn in several places. The wooden walls needed a fresher coat of paint, though whoever had done the work had been meticulous in contrasting the colors—red, yellow, and blue—in as pleasing and bright a pattern as possible. The stairs were scooped at their centers with use, but they had been swept and polished. And yet, among these homey comforts, her son's countenance looked as unfatherly in his admission of a child as any she had ever seen. Catherine finally said, "Where's the other one?" She was not sure that she wanted to know.

"It was a girl," said Robbie, as though this answered the question.

"A daughter?" said Catherine. "And so I have a granddaughter? The child is alive and well?"

"Alive," said Robbie. "Whether she's well is God's choice."

"Stop it," said Veronica. "Stop speaking in that sanctimonious way or I'll show you the choice God's put into my mind." She sounded so much like Catherine's mother in the old days of her reign as the prioress of Mount Grace that Catherine almost laughed, but she bit her tongue and let the moment go by.

Robbie had not responded to his sister, and Catherine now sat beside him, saying, as gently as the tempest in her throat would allow, "Where's the girl, Robbie? I'd like to meet this granddaughter."

"I thought perhaps you might," said Robbie. "I sent you a letter, inviting you to come and fetch her. But you didn't respond. My son had died. My wife had died. I was left the sole caretaker of a wailing girl child. What was I supposed to do, without family or land, in a strange country?"

A coldness clutched Catherine's heart. "This is the thing you had to give to me? A living child? The flesh of your flesh?"

"Your flesh, too, Mother, and more like to you than to me."

"But a child is no thing, Robbie."

"What have you done with her?" screamed Veronica. She flew at her brother, and Catherine grabbed her arms to prevent her from scratching his face. Veronica threw back her hands and said, "I've done with him. He's no father, and no brother neither."

"I am a father," said Robbie, "and I've been a brother. But there is only so much misery a man can endure alone and friendless."

"Wherefore friendless?" said Veronica. "Have you given away all of your Lutheran hangers-on, or have you left them in paupers' graves, as you did your wife?"

"That's cruel," said Catherine. "Come, Vere, you cannot mean such a thing."

A form appeared in the doorway, and Robbie raised his palm to his face to see into the light. But Catherine knew the footfall and said, "Ann. How did you know to find us here?"

Ann stepped inside. "I know that shriek. If Veronica shouted at someone in Heaven, I would know it was her. I followed my ears." She came a few steps further inside and stopped. "Well, God's blood. Robbie Overton. So this is where the Englishmen stay. You are a ghost of yourself, boy."

Robbie stood, wobbling and leaning against the wall. "Ann Smith. You're a sight to see. Grey-haired as any crone." But then he laughed, and let himself be folded into Ann's arms. She crushed him close, and Catherine could see in her eyes that she was studying his thinness with her fingers on his back. "How's our Reg?" Robbie said.

"Still casting a shadow," said Ann. She pushed him back but kept hanging on to his shoulders. "We've looked all over kingdom come for you. We saw where your wife and child lie. Robbie, it broke my heart."

His head went down, and Catherine knew he was forcing the tears back. Ann had always had a winning way with him, even with her gruffness. She could cuff him like an old bear and still he would slink back to her side with a smile. She seemed more his mother than Catherine was, and she burned a little, down in her guts, to see how easily Ann won him back.

"He has another child, still living," said Veronica. "But he won't tell us where she is."

"What's this?" said Ann, now standing away from Robbie. "Tell us. It's a girl, is it? A little black-haired girl, a curly-top like her father?" Ann messed his hair with one hand, and Catherine saw her check her fingers afterward.

"Fair-haired," said Robbie. "Her mother's hair was the color of winter straw, and she took after her. Light eyes, as well."

"Your eyes are blue," said Ann, laying a hand on his cheek. "She's yours as well as her mother's. Is she well, Robbie? Have you hired a good, strong wet-nurse for her?"

Robbie turned so that they could all see him. Catherine laid a warning hand on Veronica's wrist, to stop her mouth, and Robbie said, "I know nothing of wet-nurses or girl babies. My son died, and I was crazed." He brushed his hand across his forehead. "I feel I'm still not in my right mind."

"It's the course of nature," said Catherine. She approached her son with small steps, as she might a rabbit trapped in a hen house. "To lose a child is grievous. To lose both child and wife is more than anyone should have to sustain alone. I wish I had been there to give you comfort. I came as soon as I was able, as soon after your letter as was possible. I'm here, Robbie. Let me help you. I'm still your mother, and I'll care for the child as well as I can."

Robbie raised his eyes, and Catherine saw, as she had seen in years past, the boy still there, inside the decayed and angry young man. The boy whose father had never quite loved him. The boy whose father had died at the end of an enemy's dagger. How could he love a child when he had never been able to love himself? She was unsure whether he would run, but she tried one hand, stretched out to him, and, like a miracle, he seized it. "You will condemn me, when I tell you," he said, "but I knew nothing else to do. Wittenberg had become a death to me. I wanted to put the child into your arms, but you were in England, and I couldn't wait for a reply to my letter. I left a message for you. I couldn't stay in that place any longer, so I took her away. And then I gave her away. I've given her away. I have given my daughter away."

Chapter 28

Ann put her arm around Robbie to conceal his weeping. Veronica blazed and cooled, and Catherine steadied her with a hand. Veronica's muscles twisted and hopped under her fingers, and she wondered at how strong such a slender young woman could be. Veronica coiled to move, but Catherine would not free her to attack her brother, and the daughter stilled under the mother's touch. Alice stood separate, unmoving except for her hand, which stroked the dog in the crook of her elbow.

"Robbie, where did you leave her?" Catherine ventured, when she could speak again. "I'm here now. We're all here. We might retrieve the child and keep her with her family. This little girl has aunts and a grandmother who will love her and bring her up." Robbie rubbed his face against Ann's shoulder, and Catherine took that for assent. "If you'll lead us to her, we'll vouch for you that you can take care of her."

Robbie stepped away from Ann, and Catherine could see the shame etched in his features. But the anger that always lurked around his heart flamed out again, and he said, "She's better off where she is. The world needs no more women to head households—or lands."

Ann lifted her hands, and Catherine thought she might rap Robbie about the ears, but she only shook her fists at the air. "When will you stop blaming women for your woes, Robbie? Haven't you done with all of that? No woman sent you from England the first time you went, and no woman made you ride with an army of clodpolls to try and overthrow Queen Mary. If Mary herself sent you out of England, well, she might have done it to keep her own head upon her shoulders. Any man would have done the same. A king might have hanged you and been done with you forever. Mary showed you some mercy, which your religion should make you grateful to have received."

Catherine had to admire the speech. Ann had certainly perfected the art of stringing together her words, and she almost said so. But Robbie, now glowering at his feet, beat her to an answer. "You're a woman, and so you defend your sex. It's the way of the world."

"And that makes me a fit vessel for your temper, does it?" said Ann. "I've heard worse from greater men than you, and I still stand before you with my dignity intact. Your own father would be mortified to hear you speak thus. How can you call yourself an Overton and speak of your own flesh in that way? Here's your mother, who's wandered through Heaven and Hell to fetch you home, and your sisters, who might have remained behind in comfort but who chose to keep her company. And I, who am stiff in the haunches and nearly blind from walking and sailing, even I'm here to see to your homecoming. What have you to say for yourself?"

"I'm glad my father is dead in his grave so that he never had to endure the endless flying of women's tongues," said Robbie. "He never had to bow his knee to a woman who has set a gold crown upon her own head."

"Mary was Queen of England by her birth, and Elizabeth is the same," said Catherine.

"Elizabeth Tudor is a bastard," said Robbie. "And her sister was a heretic." He staggered back to the bench and sat. "I'm unwell."

"In your mind as well as your body," said Ann, but she sat next to him and passed her arm through his. "You have no more meat upon your bones than Alice's pup. Have you a doctor, Robbie?"

"I take the herb," said Robbie. "They say it heals the lungs and increases the appetite."

"Do you mean that vile weed? That one they chew on day and night?" said Catherine.

"The very one," said Robbie. "And the nutmegs. They're cheap and they take away pain."

"It smells like the devil's own breath," put in Veronica. She withdrew from her mother's reach and sat on the other side of her brother. "Robbie, I believe it's poison. Your colour is almost yellow."

"Then I'm like to die," said Robbie, "and I'll go to heaven."

"I'll die myself if I don't get into the fresh air," said Ann, "and I'm not fit yet for heaven. Do come out, Robbie."

He hesitated, but allowed Ann to drag him into the square, where Alice had retreated to be even more by herself. Catherine and Veronica followed Ann, shading their eyes. The sun reigned fully over the paved area, and early shoppers and men of business were already about, in twos and threes. A couple of unleashed dogs trotted by, unconcerned about the crush of humans, though a grey cat eyed them warily from an alleyway.

Robbie appeared even thinner in the light, and Catherine imagined that she could see the outline of bones beneath his threadbare clothes. His complexion was sallow, and now she could detect the flush of low fever in his cheeks and in the glitter of his eyes. Fear mastered her, for a moment, and she thought she would cry out. But she bit the inside of her lower lip and kept her silence. He might bolt at a lecture, at least one from his mother, and he clearly had decided that the weed was physic enough for him. He wouldn't tolerate her appraisal.

"There you are!" Reg shouted from a distance. He was waving, and Ann raised her hand in response. He came puffing toward them, calling for John. "We've looked high and—." He'd seen Robbie, and his mouth remained open on the last word as he approached, more slowly now. He adjusted his expression into something not quite shock. "Robbie. We've found you at last, I see. How are you?" Reg didn't quite bow, but he didn't put out his hand, either. Reg had never been of the forelock-tugging sort, and Catherine thanked God for it.

"I'm as well as any of God's creatures," said Robbie. He offered his own hand, and Reg grasped it quickly. "I didn't expect to lay eyes on you again in this world, Reg Goodall."

"But here I am, older and fatter," said Reg. John came up beside him, and he threw an arm around the younger man's shoulder. "This is John De Vries, who adopted us outside the city of Amsterdam. He's been our guide and our translator, through many a strange land. I think you two may be near in age."

John thrust forth a greeting, and Robbie accepted it, wincing a little at the forceful shake he received. "You are brother to Veronica?" John said.

"Yes," said Robbie. "You're familiar with my sister? You call her by her Christian name."

"Ah." John looked around for a sign of how he was to respond. Veronica looked stricken. Ann was smirking. Reg was still scrutinizing Robbie's decayed form. "Veronica is fine woman," John finally said. "You must feel proud. She teaches me much English. I improve."

"So you've become a learned woman," said Robbie to Veronica. "My simple sister."

"Simple?" said John. "Your Veronica is very wise."

Robbie put on his offended expression, and Catherine feared that an argument was on his tongue, a debate in which John would have the disadvantage. He wouldn't expect the vehemence that was on the verge of release. She stepped between the young men and said, to Reg, "Robbie has a surprise for us. A happy surprise."

"Wherefore 'happy'?" said Robbie.

"Any child in the family is a happiness," said Catherine.

"What's this?" said Reg.

"Robbie was ready to tell us, when we caught sight of you," said Catherine.

Before she could go on, Alice spoke up. "He's got another baby, a daughter, but he's given her away. Mother's trying to pry the location out of him. Perhaps you could give it a go, Reg."

"A daughter? That's happy news indeed," said Reg. "Where is the little one?"

"None of you have let me speak more than three words together," said Robbie, in his pouting tone. "A man can't express what's in his mind when he's surrounded by women."

Catherine pulled Veronica farther from her brother, and Ann crossed her arms. Now he stood with only Reg and John, and Veronica called, "Is that room enough for your mighty thoughts, Robbie? Will you let out the secret now?"

"Hush, you'll agitate him," murmured Catherine.

Reg had stepped closer to Robbie and he said something, too low to be heard, and Robbie responded, inclining his head toward Reg. Reg retreated a step and regarded Robbie, who shrugged and looked away, over the growing crowd. Catherine couldn't contain herself—she would have to call out—but Reg was already with them.

"You won't believe it," he said. "Robbie says that he's put the girl into a convent."

It could not be true. Robbie Overton hated a convent more than he hated the notion of a queen. Or so Catherine had thought. Every time she and Ann had recalled some pleasant memory of their own convent, or Catherine had made mention of her mother or father, he had, since he was old enough to understand the words, snorted or scoffed at the notion of a community of women. "They only serve the purpose of keeping the ears of men free of gossip," he would say. Or "Priests might save more souls if they put the nuns into the hands of strong husbands who might keep them under control." Catherine had heard it more than enough times to cringe at any conversation with her son that happened to wander into the subject of female religious.

"A convent?" she cried out, stupidly repeating what Reg had just told her. Reg would not be mistaken, nor would he misspeak, not about such a topic. "A Roman convent?"

Robbie let out a weird laugh, and the laugh brought up a cough, and the cough overwhelmed him, and he almost collapsed. Reg and John got him, one under each arm, and led him across the square to the door of their inn. The innkeeper greeted Robbie by name. "That's one of yours? Why, he takes the herb for his health. Your people, young Robbie, are of the opinion that our good physic will harm them."

"My people have many opinions," said Robbie. He took what seemed to be his usual seat in a corner and removed from his pocket a leather bag, the twin of the innkeeper's. "I've formed differences with them." He inserted the tobacco quietly into his mouth while the others looked on.

Catherine could stand it no longer. "Robbie, what's your daughter's name?"

"Mm," he said. "We called her Julia, after her mother. "Her second name"Her first name on the gravestone is Mary.Her grandmother was in a convent once, too, don't you know? Isn't the world an unpredictable place?"

Catherine tried out the name on her tongue. "And your son was William."

"My son that is no longer. My son that is dead. William, of course. After my father, God rest his soul. My son rests with him, if an unbaptized child is allowed into heaven."

Catherine heard Ann's breath suck in, but she held her own while this news coursed through her. Ann said, "Didn't you have a church?"

Robbie spat out the wad of weed and retched into a cloth. He looked at it, then wrapped it away, into his pocket. But Catherine had seen the stain. She said, "Robbie?"

"We had church. But I was away when the births happened, and the midwife left them there. My wife was unwell, by my reckoning, and she did not rise from her bed again. The boy may have taken a breath or two, but not much more than that. He was dead when I found them. Infants should not be baptized, anyway. They don't know what it means. They can't assent to it."

"That's monstrous," said Veronica. She would not sit beside her brother, but she took a bench on his far side. "I have no words for this. You found your daughter?"

"She was wailing when I returned," said Robbie. He took another pinch of tobacco. He stroked his thin beard. "Trying to suckle. The girl was the stronger of the two, to say the truth. My wife was baptized, and I pray she will make entrance for her son into heaven. I did the priest's part myself, with the water in the jug, but my own sins likely tainted me for it. The boy was dead. I should not have done it."

Catherine felt a worm of horror creeping through her guts, but he seemed garrulous now, with the weed in him, and she let her tongue go. "And you had the girl baptized before you placed her in the convent?"

Robbie shrugged. "Yes, of course I did. They wouldn't take her otherwise. They will probably smear the poor thing again to make sure that she's completely Catholic." He wiped his eyes and asked for a plate of nutmeg. It was brought, ground, and he stirred it into a cup of ale and drank it down. And then more herb, as his bag was running low. "I couldn't keep her, Mother. She's a girl. She belongs with women. There was only one other place I could put her, and that, I think, you would have disapproved more."

"I didn't say that I disapproved," said Catherine. "I would only like to have her back, now that we're here to take her. We can all go home together. We'll nurse you back to lively health, and you'll have your family with you. All of your family."

"I will never have all of my family," said Robbie. "My family lies under the dirt in Wittenberg. And in England."

"Oh, but son," said Ann. She sat and reached across the planks of the table to Robbie's hand. "We're your family, too. We want you to come home."

"We do," added Veronica, almost sincerely.

Alice said nothing at all.

"And what of you?" said Robbie, looking at John De Vries. "Are you part of this family now, as well?"

John panicked a little, glancing from Reg to Catherine for an answer. "I am here as friend." Then he caught Veronica in his gaze and his expression seemed to ask a silent question. Veronica looked at her lap.

"Then we are friends and family," said Robbie. "How warm. The child is not far from here. I wonder how far you are willing to walk to get yourself a grandchild."

"I'll walk as far as I must," said Catherine. "Haven't I sailed here to fetch you? And worn out my wits with worry in the doing of it?"

"Well answered, Mother, as usual," said Robbie. "We're missing someone, though, are we not? Two someones, perhaps?"

"We'll gather the girl ourselves," said Catherine. "Who else do you mean?"

"Why, Benjamin Davies, Mother. Have you forgot that you have a husband?"

"I have not," said Catherine. "Finding Benjamin has been part of our journey all along. Shall we seek him and return for you?"

"There's no need for that," said Robbie. "I'm like to die before we can walk ten miles, but we needn't go that distance. He's almost within spitting distance. Benjamin is here."

Chapter 29

Catherine's heart misgave with a burble, hearing the name of Benjamin on Robbie's lips. Having discovered her son, she admitted to herself with shame, she hadn't thought of her husband for hours. Still, the surprise of it—both of them here, so near to one another—left her mind tangled and hot, and she could not speak.

Ann saved her. "We spent the whole of yesterday searching for him and losing ourselves in these crowds. You say he's close by?"

"He is," said Robbie. "He was the only person I knew outside of England who would take me in." A nasty smile had crept up the corner of his mouth, and Catherine noted it without comment. So changeable, still, her son, loving and clinging like a child one moment and fierce the next. She had known him to be secretive in the past, and she knew he was holding something in his breast now.

She said, "Will you take us to him?"

"He may not be at his home," said Robbie. "He often travels on his business." His eyes had gone glittery, a little mad, and he called for another dose of the nutmeg.

"He knows you're here?" said Veronica. "You've seen him?"

"Yes and yes, sister," said Robbie. "Wherefore do you think I've travelled to this godforsaken city? I haven't done it for my body's health, as you can plainly see. Nor my soul's." He tossed down another nutmeg drink and coughed mightily. Catherine thought this time the effort was forced, but he managed to bring up some spittle that satisfied his audience. "I had no one in Wittenberg who'd see me buried as I did my wife and son. And so I came here."

"What a wonder that we happened upon you," said Veronica. "Isn't it a miracle, Ann?"

Ann gazed around the room. "No. I think not. This quarter's infested with Englishmen. It's why we found rooms in this square. That lion is no Portuguese beast. It's a sign far and wide that this is an English place. Isn't that the truth, Robbie?"

He nodded. "You know your signs, Aunt Ann. You've always done so. You wonder that I keep my room just there? I'm sick of the Catholic babble, and long to hear my mother tongue." He glanced at Catherine. "As I've not always been to hear my mother's tongue."

"That was cruel," said Reg. "Haven't you learned yet that a sharp word can be worse than a blow? I had hoped your years away had put some wisdom in your head, but I begin to see that it's not so. And you should go easier on the nutmegs, boy. They make a man drunker than wine."

"They ease my pain," Robbie said.

But the blood had rushed into Robbie's cheeks, and Catherine feared, at first, that he would strike. Then he nodded in assent to Reg. The complexion beneath the blush looked even sallower than before. He was ill. Very ill. The weed and spice hardly seemed to have improved him, though he dug into the bag once more and sucked at the pinch of tobacco like a baby at the breast. Catherine searched around in her soul for some grief at Robbie's condition, but she found only a great hollow sadness. Her son had been angry, or hurt, or offended, most of his life, and she had never been able to breach that fortress of mood. Still, he was her son, her only son, and her heart was able to ache at their history. "Do you want aught to eat, Robbie?" she said. "Or something to drink that will soothe your throat?"

"I can't taste anything," said Robbie. "I'll take a cup of wine, if there's some to be had."

There was, to be sure. They were in a tavern, after all, and the keeper brought out a jug large enough to drown a cat. Reg cast Robbie a stern eye, and he took his drink without the nutmeg. No one else had any desire for so bold a glass before the sun was halfway up the sky, and they settled for another jug of ale to break their fasts. Robbie's face had cooled, and after he had emptied his mug a couple of times, Catherine broached the subject of Benjamin again. "You say that we can walk to where he is, if he's at home?" she asked, with an indifferent lilt in her voice.

"Ah, yes," said Robbie. "Surely we can. Or you can. You're fitter than your son, Mother." He extended a withered arm to prove it. "My limbs could belong to a chicken these days."

"You might eat a bite," offered Ann, pushing a platter of bread and cheese toward him. "This loaf is still warm from the oven."

"Eat it yourself," he answered. "I can't touch it. My mouth feels as though it's coated with rancid lard." He stuck out his tongue, and Catherine studied it as closely as she could without calling attention to herself. It was sticky-looking, and covered in white film. She thought she spied an open sore on the side, which he probably found himself biting. She winced, thinking how painful it must be. Wine was perhaps better than nothing. It least it had cleansing properties. She looked at Robbie and saw the death's-head beneath the skin, and she wondered that it didn't move her to sorrow. She feared that she had become hardened beyond the point of humanity, to see her son so and know his likely fate and to feel such a nothing behind her ribs.

"If you can point us the way to Benjamin's house, we'll go and fetch him back here," offered Catherine. "You can rest yourself. Our men might stay with you, for the company."

"Your men? Say, who have you brought along?"

"Oswald and Mark. I think you might remember Mark Wheeler. His father was in our household, too. He was the house manager when we were in London."

Robbie smiled, apparently genuinely happy. "I don't remember Oswald at all, but Mark, yes! Where is he? Bring him!"

Veronica scooted out of her seat and ran off to the back of the building, calling for the servants. She went through the kitchen, and they all heard the back door open and close. "They'll be having their breakfast, no doubt," said Ann.

They waited, Robbie filling his mug again and chatting, now, about how stuffy the house was. Still, they waited. Ann and Reg split the second loaf of bread with John De Vries and shaved more slices from the cheese. The sun inched higher, and the golden light, cast through the windows onto the floor, grew bright yellow. The door opened and closed once more, and Veronica came back through to join them.

"They aren't here," she said. Her hands were open, and she showed her palms, as though someone might have thought she was concealing the men on her person. "I've looked in the stables and in the servants' rooms. Mark and Oswald are gone."

Catherine dashed through the inn and into the small yard, where the outbuildings lay. She entered the servants' quarter without knocking and, to her luck, found it empty of strangers. The beds, rough pallets barely raised from the floor on wooden frames, were made up neatly enough, and beside two of them lay leather bags. But they were not the bags belonging to Mark or Oswald. She saw nothing of the goods that her servants had brought. It had been little enough, though, and she searched under the beds and behind the door. There was nothing to say that her men had ever been inside the room.

She turned to go out, and encountered the surly face of a maid. "What do you do, in this room?" the girl demanded. "This is the servants' room."

"My men," said Catherine. "They slept here. We can't find them. One Mark Wheeler and his companion. They arrived with us."

The girl turned her mouth down, studying the situation. Then she opened her arms, as if to indicate the empty room. "They're not here."

"I can see that plainly enough," said Catherine. "Do you know where they've gone?"

"No one told me," the girl said. She put on a sullen expression, all bunched eyebrows and frown. "I am not a minder of servants."

"But I am," said Catherine. She left the girl pondering whether this demanded a retort and returned to the common room. "Veronica says true. Mark and Oswald are nowhere to be found. Their things are gone, as well."

Robbie put back his head and laughed. "Your men have gone off to make their fortunes, I suppose. Lesser men than Overton Hall servants have done the same, here in the land of opportunity."

"But why?" said Veronica. "We no longer have Overton Hall. We've always treated them well. They're part of our family. Their fathers were part of our family. They don't know the languages here."

"Overton Hall is gone? Well, then, I suppose there is no need for servants. They'll learn fast enough, if they've got brains in their heads," said Robbie. "Men can disappear onto ships and be over the seas before their families know they've set foot out of doors."

"But why?" repeated Veronica.

"Why does any man want to go?" said Reg. Ann cut him a sour look, but he went on. "You know what we've seen here: men roped together like so many cattle. Women sold off like laying hens. It put us in mind of their condition, you know, Catherine. It may have put their conditions into their own minds, as well."

"You were right at the first," said Robbie. "Any man might do it."

"But their condition is superior," said Catherine. "We don't mistreat our servants. We don't put anyone into chains or ropes. We don't buy and sell human beings."

"And why should you need to?" Robbie put in. "You already own them when they enter the world."

Catherine found her mouth stopped as much as the maid's she'd left in the back. Veronica began to cry, and John put his arm over her shoulders. Robbie pointed at the couple and said, "There you see the picture of a happy family. But look at them five years from now, or ten, and what will you see? Not this tableau of charm, I'll warrant you."

"Keep your opinions in your own head, for once, will you?" Alice snapped.

Veronica slapped at her eyes to clear the tears and Ann handed her a cloth to wipe them properly.

"I can speak my mind or not," said Robbie. "The world is the same either way. I only say what's true."

"Is your truth everyone's truth?" said Veronica. "Do you think that your own misfortune, which you have brought upon yourself by being rash and selfish, must mean that everyone suffers?"

"So, I'm rash and selfish," said Robbie. He was cool, though the illness raged red across his skin. "Does that mean Mark and, what is his name? Oswald? They'll appear if I'm silent? I don't see them, and I don't think you will, either."

"You're a mean little man," answered Veronica, "and you were a mean little boy."

"Veronica, stop," said Ann. "This gets us nowhere."

"Let her go on," said Robbie. "The fit will work its way through her and she'll be my sister again. All women have such demons in them. It's the wise man who looks the other way until they've worn themselves out."

"All of this talk is useless," said John. "We go seek the men. If they are run away, we search out your Benjamin ourselves. We are people enough."

"Well said, man," answered Robbie. "You see? A man may cut through the nonsense like a knife through the butter. I like you, John, well enough. Will you be my brother? You're not a Catholic, are you?"

John looked at Robbie with an expression that hovered between amusement and disgust. "I am Christian," he said. He glanced at Veronica and grinned. "Are not we all?"

Veronica's anger broke. "Yes," she said. She took his hand and faced her brother. "Mark and Oswald may go where they will. Are you going to take us to our father or aren't you?"

"I have said so, and I will do it," said Robbie. He pushed himself up, gripping the table's edge with such force that his knuckles strained against the thin flesh that covered them, and called for his reckoning. Reg said, "Put that with ours," but Robbie waved him off, saying "No one will accuse me of leaving my debts for others. Excepting Benjamin, perhaps." He had to dig deep into his pockets, though, to produce the coins. He lifted the remainder of a loaf from the platter, smeared it with butter, wrapped it in a cloth, and tucked it into his bag.

Outside, the sun governed without contest from the clouds. The streets were full again, and Catherine clutched Ann's arm while Robbie got his breath. He walked with difficulty, seeming to need a crutch to stay upright, but

Catherine would not provoke him by saying so. He watched the sky for a few seconds, and with his face turned up, his wasted condition was even more apparent. Catherine could feel Ann squaring up to speak, and she pinched the soft inside of Ann's elbow to keep her quiet. Robbie looked them over and started off, across the square.

Down a narrow street first, then left into an even narrower alley. This stank of stale urine and Catherine held a handkerchief over her nose as they passed through. Then another turn, an odd angle off, again to the left, and steeply descending. The buildings on either side pressed out the sunshine, and the air became as dank as a cellar. They seemed to be among large houses and storage buildings, and few people met them along the way. No women at all. They had walked, by Catherine's calculation, nearly an hour before Robbie halted at a dark door in an enormous wall. A dog set up barking from inside.

"Here," he said. "Do you want to go in?"

Alice said, "There's supposed to be a sign. A setting sun."

"We haven't come all this way to examine the door," said Veronica.

"Very well," said Robbie. He knocked and then cracked the door open without waiting for an invitation. A brown snout appeared and the barking became snarling. The animal scrabbled at the doorframe, and Robbie, holding his knee against the assault, reached into the bag and produced the buttered bread, which he offered to the beast. The offering accepted, the dog retreated, and Robbie opened the door all the way, holding it and waiting as they entered together. He closed it again behind them.

Alice stood behind John. "Are you certain that the dog is under control? Toby is just a wee thing compared to that."

"It's a dog," said Robbie. The animal had taken up a position in the corner, on a pile of rags, where it gobbled down the crust and lay growling softly in their direction. It must have weighed near a hundred pounds. "Now we're inside, we're safe enough."

They stood in what was, to all appearances, a warehouse. Stacks of what might have been sheepskins lay piled against the walls, covered with canvases and old bags, reaching halfway to the raftered roof, but the coverings were filthy, and Catherine saw a rat scramble under an edge of the heavy fabric. A cloying scent of spice, clove and pepper and nutmegs. She could smell unwashed flesh. There was no ceiling between them and the roof, only the open structure above them. The long windows on the walls behind them were grimed and soot-stained, and they warded off whatever light might have struggled down the cramped lanes outside. Two men sat at a table, far at the other end of the room, working at what might have been account books. They had a stack of coins between them, and they were arguing quietly about something. The fetid stink of something dead, mice or rats perhaps, lingered in the air, a little like blood, a little like feces. A lone maid swept at the large open floor in a desultory way, raising more dust than she pushed along. Two large spinning wheels sat unused and webby in the corner beside them. Next to them lay rotting baskets full of mouldy wool. From the edge of one of them dangled a raggedy old skirt that Catherine would not have put upon one of her kitchen maids. No wonder they had vermin.

"Where are the spinners?" asked Catherine. Her voice sounded hollow in the emptiness. "Are there weavers here? Somewhere in the back?"

Robbie coughed and spat on the floor. He smeared the wet spot into the wood with the sole of his boot. "Not that I have ever seen. Maybe before my time here."

"All of this space," said Alice. She walked into the room and looked up. "This is larger than any stable I have ever seen." She looked back at Robbie, who was now perched on the dusty seat of one of the spinning wheels, the dog eying him with half-suspicion and half-longing. "Has he just had a great selling? Wherefore all of this empty room?"

Reg and Ann walked the room together. One of the men at the table looked over at them and back to his companion. Neither of them seemed to care that a group of strangers had come in without leave. Ann called, "This is a very Hell, if you ask my opinion."

Chapter 30

"Where's your master?" Catherine asked the two men seated at the table. Her voice sounded strained and shrewish.

"We're our own masters," said one of the men, without looking up from the table.

Catherine coughed respectfully and tried again. "We're here for Benjamin Davies."

"So you might be," said the man, pushing a couple of coins toward the other man, who set them into his own hoard. "That puts you in good enough company, if the man wants to be seen." He leant back and squared a look on Catherine. "What sort are you needing? We've sold all we got for now."

"What sort of what?" answered Catherine. She realized that he had mistaken her for a trader, or a customer, and her neck flushed with heat. "I'm not here to buy—or to sell."

"You got a whole town there with you," said the other man. "Have you got a letter?"

"A letter?"

"I think there's an echo in here," said the second man, gazing lazily upward and around. He closed the book that lay between them and raked together what seemed to be his half of the money, then rattled it into a cloth pouch. "Yes, he said a letter. Is Benjamin doing business with you?"

"I'm his wife," Catherine blurted. She could feel the others behind her. Ann's hand closed on her right elbow and she leant back into it a little.

The two men looked at her, then at one another. They collapsed into simultaneous laughter. One of them even slapped the table in his mirth. "That's one I've yet to hear," he said. "You got a ring and all of it?"

Catherine extended her hand.

"You cut that off a corpse?" the man said. He stood, all bandy legs and scarecrow arms, and bounded forward, took her fingers, and tilted them into what light he could find. "That'd fetch a nice penny."

"What's the matter with you?" said Ann. "This is Catherine Davies, Benjamin Davies's lawful wife, and she's come to take him home to England. Do you know the man or don't you?"

Another laugh ripped through the building, and Robbie lifted himself with some difficulty from his seat and walked toward them. "Kit, don't torment my poor mother. She's come a good long way to see him."

The man dropped Catherine's hand and said, "Robbie, boy." He peered again at Catherine. "Yes, by God and good luck, this has got to be your dam."

"She is that," said Robbie.

"Don't speak of your mother in such terms," said Ann. She let go of Catherine and yanked Robbie's arm as he came within reach. "Who's taught you to talk thus? You sound like a common vagrant. Your mother is no such thing."

"She's a thing, like enough," said the man.

Ann was bristling for a fight, and Catherine said, "No matter. Words are just hot wind, and I'm a stranger here. Can you tell me where to find Benjamin Davies or not?"

"I expect I can," said the man called Kit. "But this boy of yours might do the same. Robbie?"

"I brought them to the door. That's all they require of me."

Kit raised a disinterested shoulder. "I have my pay right here. Go on, if you will. There's others who need my services."

Reg said, "But where?"

Kit pointed with his head toward the back. The wall was all in gloom, but now that they had been inside a while, Catherine could see a door fitted neatly into it. Kit and his companion headed toward the front, the way they had entered, giving indifferent tugs to their caps as they passed Robbie. The maid had disappeared, out some passageway they hadn't seen. Robbie said, "I'll wait for you here," and took the seat Kit had vacated at the table.

"Is there another dog inside?" asked Alice.

"Not that I've seen," said Robbie. He had opened the account book and was idly reading the entries there.

"On we go, then," said Reg.

The door was unlocked, and it opened onto a small, almost lightless room. Reg left it ajar so that they could find their way. The floor was piled with old instruments and tools —rusty shearing equipment, mouldy harness, and chains and ropes of various degrees of thickness. Tufts of discarded, dirty wool lay here and there, and a few sacks hung upon the walls. Two empty barrels. A pair of down-at-heel boots, looking as if they had been stepped out of and left where they lay.

"Who keeps his corridor in such a condition?" said Reg, kicking aside a matted hank of wool. "I've never known Benjamin to be such a sloth."

"Nor I," said Ann. She sniffed at one of the barrels. "This is surely not where he dwells."

Catherine felt a weight gather and settle in her stomach, as though her insides were pulling together and dropping as one lump into her gut. She couldn't breathe, and when she tried to speak, the mass raised itself into her throat and lodged there. Her scalp itched with fear, but she couldn't raise a hand to scratch it. The wall they now faced was thick, like a second exterior, as though they had passed from one dwelling through to another. She could see light from another, farther, room, at the bottom edge of yet another door, beyond them, and she made for it as though it would open onto her bedroom in Yorkshire, where she could be alone, and safe.

But when she opened it and fell into the next space, she saw only more sights, stranger even than what she had seen behind her. This did seem a different dwelling. Here, the room was bright with sunlight, from long, clean windows. It was not large, but it had been carefully furnished with carved chairs and a table. One throne-like seat, against the far wall, was framed in fine wood and covered in red silk. And sitting upon it, reading a book, was not Benjamin, but a woman, one whom Catherine recognized, more easily than she had her son. It was her former sister in Christ, during their convent years, then her former sister-in-law. And always her nemesis.

"Margaret," Catherine said. "Margaret Overton."

Margaret Overton leant forward and peered at Catherine. Catherine felt a shove from behind as someone—Veronica or Ann—unprepared for her sudden halt, jolted into her back. The chair upon which Margaret sat was large enough for a queen, and every bit as fine. Margaret herself wore a skirt of light, embroidered silk, in a girlish pale yellow, and her breast and shoulders were almost bare. Her hair, fell around her ears like a mane, was surely a wig, such a bright shade of red it was, and Catherine was put in mind of Veronica, whose hair had been nearly that brilliant shade when she'd been in her teens. But Veronica's was fading to a more common brown. Margaret was approaching the end of her fiftieth decade.

Catherine had never seen a woman so ornately made up. Margaret's skin was a sickly alabaster, though wrinkles showed through the heavy layer of whatever she had smeared on her face. Her lips were the color of fresh blood. But there was no doubt who it was. Older by every minute of the five, no, almost six now, years since Catherine had laid eyes upon her, but Margaret was still Margaret, fine in her noble bones. The arrogant expression she'd always worn, however, seemed to have melted away.

"Why, look there. It's Catherine," said Margaret, standing and dropping the book to the floor.

"Margaret? Aunt Margaret?" said Veronica, running forward. The younger woman stopped before she was close enough to embrace, but Margaret met her halfway and rushed to close the distance between them, enveloping Veronica. Catherine could smell the scent on her from where she stood, unable to move.

"How is this our aunt?" said Alice.

Ann said, "God in heaven above us," and Reg said nothing at all.

Catherine found her legs and stepped into the room. She landed on a long swath of sunlight and hesitated long enough to let the heat melt the frost in her veins. But Margaret was already upon her, and the familiar arms came around her in a way she never remembered from before. This was almost sisterly indeed, from the woman who had always acted as though Catherine was a usurper in her household, a lesser form of human creature than those who had been born with the Overton name.

"I have longed to see you," said Margaret into Catherine's ear. Catherine looked over her shoulder at Veronica, whose cheek bore the white streak of Margaret's close hug. "Wherefore are you here? How did you find us, after all this time? And who is this young one?" She curled a finger into Alice's hair and flipped Toby under the chin.

Catherine pushed Margaret far enough away to look at her. The eyebrows were plucked almost to nothing and were drawn in with dark ink of some sort. The perfume was almost suffocatingly sweet. Before she could speak, Ann said, "Wherefore are you here, we might ask. And why are you outfitted like an old punk?"

Margaret let go of Catherine and turned her attention to Ann. "Ann Smith, same as of old." Then she regarded Reg for a moment and added, "But you are not Ann Smith anymore, are you? You are Ann Goodall, the all-good wife to this all-good man." She reached for Ann's hand and held it for a second before she took Reg's.

Margaret had not been in the habit of wit. That had always been Ann's territory, and Ann stood, unable to answer. Reg said, "We're long married, Margaret. You know this."

"There is much I have forgot," said Margaret. She wiped her eyes, and Catherine would have sworn she'd leaked a genuine tear or two. "I live in my memory so much of the time that the present day often passes me by. I need to be reminded to live in the day. Every day."

"What's all of this?" asked Veronica, lifting a handful of Margaret's skirt. "What have you done to your face?"

Margaret touched her cheek and examined the white stain that came away on her fingers. "I'm old. So many women younger than I am, and fewer more aged. I'm not fit for any market anymore." She held out her marked hand to Veronica. "You see what a woman comes to, when she's past desire and unwanted? She wanders about the rooms, unwilling to be seen out of doors and unable to look into her own glass. It's an ugly thing, to grow old."

"You needn't do all this," said Veronica. "Aunt Margaret, you certainly must use a glass to apply this costuming."

"I suppose I do, in the morning when the light is still low and I'm not forced to see the furrows in my face." She did, in fact, have deep lines, both on her cheeks and on her forehead. Two folds of skin lapped from her nose to her mouth, and the substance she wore to cover them only enhanced them, by settling in and creating pale stripes. "When you are as ruint as I am, you'll understand," she went on. "Catherine, let me see your face."

Catherine knew that she, too, had decayed, but she hardly bothered with a mirror in the morning. The household always encroached upon her so early that she hardly had time to dress herself properly before Veronica or Alice or one of the servants was knocking at her bedchamber door. She approached Margaret and allowed herself to be scrutinized.

"Yes, you have some age on you, too, sister," said Margaret. "And Ann." Margaret glided over and looked Ann up and down. "You look much the same, but you always had a hearty glow in your face."

"From honest work," said Ann, "and no time and little cause for vanity."

"You and I are the same age, are we not?" said Margaret.

"Thereabouts," said Ann. "Too old to be making up our faces to look like dolls."

"It's ridiculous, isn't it?" said Margaret. "You see what being far from home and my family has done to me. Who is this lovely child?"

Alice stepped forward. "I am Alice Davies, and Benjamin Davies is my father."

"Oh," said Margaret. "Of course, you are. I'm not your aunt in blood. But I'd be your aunt in love, if you'd have me."

Catherine's heart clogged with pity, despite the years of enmity between herself and this woman. Everyone had fallen silent, and she could hear a couple of birds outside. They sounded like titmice, buzzing in staccato. But she didn't know if titmice lived this far south, and she bent her hearing toward the sound. Her eyes landed again, inevitably, on the broken sight of Margaret. More than her face had decayed. The woman was shrunken, and she looked lonely. Catherine said, "What's become of your maid, Connie?" They all knew that Connie was the illegitimate daughter of the Overton house, but they seemed to have agreed long ago to refer to her by her station. "Is she here?"

"Connie's dead and gone," said Margaret, and her eyes brightened with those tears again, the ones that looked sincere. "She died of a fever the summer we left England." The grief was replaced by sudden red-faced rage, and Margaret's voice thickened. "I should say the summer we were forced to leave England, with no money in our purses and only the clothes on our backs. It was our home. We had a right to defend it—and to defend ourselves, when no one else in the world would."

"Margaret," said Catherine. "What have you done?"

"We did what we were ordered to do. We boarded a boat and we left our land. Our people. Our homes. What can women do, alone?"

A shiver wriggled its way down Catherine's back. "Did you go with Benjamin? My Benjamin?"

"Ah," said Margaret.

"Benjamin Davies couldn't tolerate the sight of you," said Ann. "He loathed you."

"Perhaps he did. Perhaps he does," said Margaret. "I'm not fit for the market anymore, as I have said. I understand that a woman's sale time comes early and doesn't last long. The convent stole my best years from me. Me and all of my sisters. You managed it best, Catherine. But then you always managed to get what you wanted, didn't you?"

"What we think we want doesn't always go by God's plan," said Catherine. "Margaret, tell me, and tell me true. Is Benjamin here?"

Margaret let her head rock to and fro. "He may be. He doesn't set his clock by my rising and setting."

"Tell us outright, without any more sighs and tears," Ann said. "Are you his woman now?"

"You haven't lost your gift for bluntness," said Margaret. "I'm too tired for the games of the young. Too old for the bitterness that burns me. I've done much harm. I've done many selfish deeds. I'm afraid." Her slender fingers dragged at her cheeks, removing more streaks of the ghoulish makeup. "God will not forgive me." She stepped to Veronica. "Will you?"

"What have I to forgive you for?" asked Veronica.

"I meant to have you out of this world, once. It was a long time ago, and you a babe in arms. You were your mother's child, and my brother's child, and I was ravaged with jealousy. It was foul, and I did it with all the intent of an evil spirit. I'm sorry for it and I beg your Christian forgiveness."

Veronica's back straightened into a position that Catherine recognized as disgust. She stepped between them and said, "Margaret, those days are long gone. Have you confessed your sin?"

"Didn't you hear me? That's what I have just done," said Margaret. "I seek no absolution. The time's past for all of that."

"I meant in a church. To a priest," said Catherine.

Margaret laughed, and her rotted teeth showed for the first time. The stench set Catherine back a step. She could taste the memory of having two infected molars extracted a couple of years back, and her tongue found its way to the hole in her jaw. Then Margaret pressed her lips together and covered them with her fingers, leaving white spots that looked like disease. When she opened her mouth again, she was careful not to smile. "Do you still adhere to those old beliefs? You'll find many here that do. But the Protestants say that we need only open our hearts directly to God and we may receive His blessing. Your son believes that. Do you believe that?"

"I know not what to believe anymore," Catherine murmured.

"But your forgiveness is my object. I didn't think to see you again in this life. Or you, Veronica."

"And what forgiveness do you seek?" asked Catherine.

"For everything. For my sins. For my meanness. For Benjamin. For following him. For sharing his bed when I knew he was still your husband."

Chapter 31

The words rang into place with the chime of fear that had been tolling around Catherine's head. Margaret had made such claims before, long, long ago, but the world had been different then. They had both been younger, and fiercer. Catherine had been the object of Benjamin's desire. And now? It had been five years without a letter. Of course, Margaret had been Benjamin's bedmate. She had wanted Catherine's place, whatever it was, since they were young women, and after William Overton was killed, she had wanted Catherine's second husband for her own. Catherine listened to the harmony now in her mind and wondered that it sounded right, neither sinister nor shocking, but what she had known for years must be the truth.

She said, "Benjamin calls you wife now?"

Margaret shook her head. "He's called me his whore, and he's called me shameless. Pitiful, I think, maybe once or twice. But wife? No, Catherine, Benjamin loathes me, as your wise friend here has said so pointedly. He allows me food and raiment and a bed in which to sleep. A chair to mock me." She threw her hand toward the throne against the wall. "He paid to bury Connie in a decent grave. And I suppose if I died tomorrow he might do the same for me."

The weird music in Catherine's head ceased and she listened to a profound silence. Margaret stood before her, a beseeching light in her eyes, and waited. The birds outside no longer sang, and the other members of her family did not move or speak.

But Margaret finally broke the hush. "Before you ask, there was no child. I'm too old even for that. The only children of the Overton house are your own. At least as far as I know. And look. Speak of the devil. There's the heir apparent now."

Robbie stood on the threshold. He glared at Margaret. "Don't talk like that. Your sins multiply on your head every minute you're awake."

"You see, Catherine? What need have I of a priest when I have a nephew to shrive me every day of the week?"

"Robbie," said Catherine, "what have you known of all this?"

"Enough," said Robbie. "I found them all here when I came in search of Benjamin. It's a nest of serpents, Mother, and this one's the Eve of them all, because she's the eldest and ought to know how to restrain herself. But she's a woman and needs a correcting hand."

"How godly of you to remind me," said Margaret. "But if my eyes don't deceive me, you won't be long among us to do the task, and so God has sent my sister to me to chastise me further. A woman to replace a man. What think you of that, young Robert?"

"This is madness," said Veronica. "You're all gone lunatic! Where's my father?"

"Wherever he chooses to be," said Robbie. "And he's not your father, whatever dream you've concocted for yourself. What, sister? You're not delighted to see your long-lost aunt?"

"To hear that she's whored herself with my mother's husband?"

"I was alone, Veronica. I was desperate and poor. Please." Margaret tumbled to her knees and clutched Veronica's skirt.

"Forgive me." She crawled to Catherine and put her forehead on the floor. "Forgive me."

Catherine knelt and lifted Margaret to her feet. "Vere speaks right. This is all a madness. Robbie, do you know where Benjamin is? I must have a word with him."

"Your dear husband? Your loving husband? He's likely at his business, making money. That's what he does best, isn't it?"

Margaret huddled against Catherine. Catherine looked at Ann for some assistance. But Ann was staring at Robbie, and she did not wear an expression of love. Catherine said, "Benjamin always husbanded his profits well."

Robbie laughed. "Yes, he's always been a good husband to money. And if that's the husband you want, then let's go see if he's to be found." He crossed the room, cutting through the amazed group, and went to yet another door in the wall where the throne-chair sat, empty and ridiculous. "This way," he called.

They all followed him through, into what appeared to be a large servants' quarters. The girl who had been sweeping in the supply house had taken up her desultory work here, and two others sat in the corner with a basket of greens between them, tearing the leaves and dropping them into a pot. "Are you hungry?" said Robbie to no one in particular. "The kitchen is down that way." He pointed to a set of stairs leading down, but no one moved toward them. "Into the front, then," he called and passed the servants without acknowledgment.

"Didn't you take us into the front when we first entered?" asked Catherine.

Robbie shook his head. "I thought you should see where your husband makes his living. This building fronts on the street beyond, and you can see that your husband has combined it with the back one. Oh, yes, he's made money.

Much money. It's a large street, and folks who go by know that a grand master lives here. He has many visitors, or so I hear." Robbie led them down a short corridor and into a spacious front hall. It seemed to run the length of the entire storage area in the back, but here the walls were lined with portraits and small tables that held vases and silver platters. Rugs of every color and pattern covered the tiled floor, and the reds, blues, and golds caught the sunlight from the long windows, all paned with new glass, and refracted it in more sumptuous hues.

Robbie halloed with more force than his wasted frame seemed able to muster, but his voice echoed from the painted ceiling and died away. Catherine called "Benjamin?" to the empty room. She heard a ticking of heels, somewhere distant. It was a woman's step, and Margaret backed out of sight, into the corridor through which they had entered.

"Now you'll see a sight," said Robbie. A sprinkle of malicious triumph salted his words, and Catherine felt that worm of fear in her breast again. "Don't run away, Mother. Not after you've come so far to gain your reward."

A woman entered the room, far down at the other end. She had golden hair, fastened on her head by a circlet of gold, and she wore a light dress. Catherine thought it was good linen, and that this would have to be Benjamin's own maid, but for the odd golden ornament on her head. She said, "Hallo to you. Robbie, I see you've brought companions with you. Do come in and sit down."

She was walking toward them, and as she came into better view, Catherine could see that she was not the maiden she appeared from far off. This was a woman past forty years, and she was as heavily made up as Margaret was. Her hair, which had looked fine at first, now looked thin, and it was twisted elaborately to conceal the scalp that showed beneath. Her skin hung slack and had the red-patched cast of a woman devoted to her wine. The fine dress looked tawdry and ill-fitting up close. Catherine wondered what she wore beneath it to heave her breasts up so high. Her neck was spotted and freckled, either from drink or from sunburn.

"Who might you all be?" she said.

"But no," said Robbie. "You must introduce yourself first. We've intruded upon your privacy with no forewarning, and everyone here wants to meet you."

Catherine turned to her son. He was wearing that smile again, the one that put her in mind of his long-dead uncle, the one for whom he was named. Robert Overton had been a selfish and cruel man, and Catherine recalled the moment that her husband William had said they would name the boy after him. The sick twist that had wrenched her gut then came back like a blow to her middle. But perhaps William had been right, after all. Here was the man, and he looked more like an Overton than he ever had, even thin as he was. All the time that William had spent wondering and doubting if Robbie was his own flesh. All that blood when he killed the man who had violated Catherine. And then had been killed in turn. And here stood the boy, become a man, an Overton man, and Catherine did not recognize her son in his face.

The woman said, "Here to meet me?" She put a mottled hand to her mouth, a girlish gesture she should have long outgrown. Then she swept her arm out, as if to engulf them all in her embrace. "Why, I'm Joan Wright. Mistress of this house. Of this entire establishment."

Margaret gave out a little groan that betrayed her hiding place just beyond the door. Robbie chortled, and Ann said, "You're what?"

"I'm Joan Wright, and I'm mistress here." The woman held out her hand for the taking, but no one stepped forward.

"But this is the home of Benjamin Davies, isn't it?" said Catherine. She had gone cold all over, and she clenched her fists to feel her fingers. "You cannot be mistress here."

"But I am," Joan Wright said. "I know Benjamin Davies right well. We are as much as married. Everyone here knows the truth of it. I'm Benjamin Davies's wife."

Catherine's mind clogged with a million bees, buzzing and stinging. Her face was hot and she couldn't catch her breath. Voices keened and lamented about her ears, and she tried to cover them to block out the noise. But on they went, calling out and saying her name, and the light was too, too bright and red-hot. The air smelt of wool and mould. She opened her eyes and found herself on the floor, with her cheek against the nap of one of the precious rugs. Alice was kneeling beside her, crying out for a cup of ale.

"Don't move," said Ann, behind her. "You've struck your head."

"It can't be true," said Catherine. "I've seen a nightmare."

John De Vries was on his knees beside Alice, holding out a drink, and Veronica lifted Catherine to sitting while he held it to her lips. "You fainted away," said Veronica. "I thought you were dead."

"I wish I were," said Catherine. She could see the woman called Joan Wright, still standing in the room and still quite real. The woman wrung her hands and tut-tutted, as though she were worried over Catherine.

"You don't mean that," said Ann. "You've had worse days than this one." She looked up at Joan Wright. "Could you give the woman some air?"

"There's air enough here," said Joan. "What's the matter with her? Robbie, why would you bring an old woman out when she's not fit to leave her bed?"

At this, Catherine's head blazed, and she stood up, pushing her daughters and John aside. "I'm no older than you are. And I'm Benjamin's wife by law."

"What?" said Joan. She backed off a few steps and appraised her guest. "Oh. You're Catherine."

"I am. And I'm still quite alive, as you can plainly see."

"He never said you were dead. This one said that." Joan indicated Margaret, huddling behind them. "He said he'd never see you again."

Catherine turned to Ann and Reg. "Wherefore would he say such a thing? He knew right well that I would keep him in my heart. He knew that he would return to England one day. He surely heard the news that Elizabeth is queen."

"I've heard the news myself," said Joan. "I'm English, too, as you might have guessed. I have a brother in Nottingham or thereabouts. I can tell you that Benjamin was not much moved when he heard that the old queen had died. She lost Calais for her people. A fine legacy. But, as I say, he was not much moved to hear about Elizabeth. A girl queen. Who's ever heard of it?"

Catherine covered her ears. "Don't speak to me." Then she dropped her hands. "No, do tell. Wherefore do you call yourself Benjamin's wife when you know right well that he has a living one?"

"Benjamin was alone. He's not a man who enjoys solitude, except when he's about his business. I was alone, cast out of my home by the same woman who sent him away from England. Your Mary Tudor."

"What crime did you commit, to be sent here?" asked Reg.

"No crime at all," Joan said, with a little pout. "I'm Protestant, and would not abide a Roman Catholic queen. I said so. And then I left. It was more difficult than I had expected, until I met Benjamin. We found that we had common cause, and now we are wed, by the common law."

"It isn't possible," said Catherine. "It hasn't been but five years."

"Five years can feel like a lifetime. Ask your son, there. Yes, Robbie, tell your mother how you came here, seeking out your father."

"He's not my father," said Robbie.

"But you saddled him with that baby of yours anyway, didn't you? You accept his money, don't you?"

Robbie had turned quite pale, the malicious smile wiped clean from his face. He was sweating, and he wiped his brow with his sleeve. "I wanted you to see, Mother, what your husband has wrought out of his new-found freedom. He couldn't have you, and so he's contented himself with that creature. And my own aunt. She has whored herself like a common stale, and now she seeks absolution like the Papist she still is in her heart. And now what will you do? Take them to your breast and forgive them? Use your money to haul them back to England? I assure you that Benjamin has enough money of his own, but whether he'll spend it to good use is more than I can say. Perhaps, though, if you restore his lands to him, and his houses, he'll consent to abandon this place of shame and fall back into your arms like the salamander that he is, shifting his colours for whatever surface he lands upon."

"Have you done speechifying?" said Ann. "I would think, given your complexion, that your time might be better spent in searching your own soul than in leading others into torment. I'm sickened by you, Robbie."

"I'm sick enough on my own without your company in it," said Robbie. "The world is an evil place, and I'm satisfied to be leaving it."

"But whither will you go?" said Veronica. "The pain you've caused here will follow you past the grave, brother. You should be aware of that yourself, with all of your Bible-reading."

"Enough," said Catherine. "All of you. I'll speak to Benjamin on this matter, and to no one else. Until I hear the truth of it from his own mouth, I'll hold my amazement at arms' length."

"That's well said, Mother," said Robbie. He did not add a homily on the wisdom of women, and for that Catherine was momentarily grateful. Joan Wright now came close to examine Catherine, and the two women stood almost nose to nose, though Joan was a head shorter. Catherine wondered if her own face looked as sagged and worn to strangers as Joan's did to her. Age had not been kind to the pale woman. Her eyes leaked a little rheum as she stared, and Joan wiped them with her fingers, breaking the hold between them.

"How have you lowered yourself to be taken for his wife?" Catherine said. "Didn't you suspect that I would come?"

Joan stepped back and sighed. "We heard tales of Mary Tudor. She married Philip of Spain. She was carrying a child. Another child. She fought battles in Calais. The rumours flew, and I thought to be dead before she was. What harm could it do, to give comfort to a lonely man and provide for my own needs at the same time? No, Catherine, I never planned to see your face."

"And Benjamin? Did he think he could simply take on another wife without my knowledge?"

"I never sounded him on the subject of law," said Joan. "He went about, increasing his business, and I kept his house and entertained his companions. I even fed Margaret, though I knew she had shared his bed."

"And how did you know that?" said Catherine.

"Why, he told me himself. Benjamin is not a man to keep unnecessary secrets. He told me how much he loved you, Catherine, and how he pursued you before you would marry him. He had other women, though. He isn't a man to deny himself pleasure."

It was not possible. Catherine had known Benjamin for years before becoming his wife. He had returned to her, again and again, professing his love and his desire. And for that desire, she had risked her own reputation and safety. She had borne him a daughter, and together they had loved that daughter, had built themselves a home. They had joined their monies and their names, and until Benjamin had disgraced himself in Queen Mary's eyes, and that to help Catherine's own son, they had been one in everything. Could he have left her bed to love other women? She never asked him about his life before her, as he did not question her first marriage or the truth of Robbie's father. But after he had begun courting her in earnest? After they were wed?

"You're lying," Catherine said. "You're bitter and resentful that I'm here, and you tell tales in order to wound me."

"Ask him when you see him, if you want," said Joan. "Perhaps he's more honest with his whore than he is with his wife. It's not uncommon. Ask Margaret."

Margaret said, "You shut your mouth, Joan. You're nothing but a bed-warmer, and he'll cast you off like an old pair of breeches. If he's bragged to you of other women, he's done it to put you down."

"So says one of the other women herself," said Joan, a lilt of triumph in her voice.

Reg said, "I've heard enough gossip. Where's Benjamin? I'll speak to the man face to face."

"Do you want to see what he does to make his money these days?" said Robbie.

"I know what he does to make money," said Reg. "He's a wool trader, and he buys and sells cloth."

"Oh ho, Reg," said Robbie. "In that you're wrong. You're in a different place now, and there are new ways for a man to make his way. Wool isn't so expensive anymore, but Benjamin has found himself a commodity that sells higher by the pound."

"Robbie, don't," said Margaret. "It's not to be laughed at."

"I will see," said Catherine. "Show me."

"What day is this?" said Robbie to the ceiling. "I believe this may be a market day." He stared at Reg. "But most days are market days for Benjamin. Will you go?"

"How far must we walk?" said Veronica. "The day is well-nigh on."

"Just into the back," said Robbie. "The morning's work is done, and the second batch of merchandise should be set up shortly."

Chapter 32

Catherine took the position that she would never try to catch her husband unawares at his business and insisted that they return to their inn so that she could change her light head-covering for one of Ann's more old-fashioned hoods.

"Benjamin won't be accustomed to seeing me in the new fashion," she said by way of excuse, but in fact she had determined to conceal her face so that she could see what Benjamin was up to before he saw her. Her dress was travel-worn enough not to attract notice, as were Ann's and the girls'. She asked Veronica to cover her hair, as well. "But wherefore?" Veronica asked, eyeing the heavy thing Ann handed to her, and Catherine confessed, "This business that Robbie is so puffed-up to show us is all too secretive for my liking, and I want to observe with my own eyes before we're observed. Say nothing to your brother."

"Very well," sighed Veronica, "but you'll have to pin it onto me, Auntie Ann."

The men wore their caps low, as instructed, and Catherine searched for Mark or Oswald as they skulked back along to the enormous house, but the two servants seemed to have disappeared for good. John De Vries walked bare-headed, his blond hair attracting many admiring glances from women, and Veronica glowered at them from under her dowdy hood.

The afternoon was fine and breezy, though the smell from the sea was thick with human sweat and fish and the black masses of flies tormented their eyes. The sun was merciless, and Catherine could feel her armpits puddling with heat or fear under its imperious light. But Robbie seemed not to notice, leading them along in a swagger, almost dancing as he turned corners and leapt dung heaps. He even took Alice's hand as though they were any brother and sister. They returned down the alley to find the larger doors flung open and crowds already gathered around, shouting and waving. Catherine had probably not needed to disguise herself at all.

But then Robbie pointed, and she peered into the interior. There, standing upon a wooden platform that had been dragged from the wall, was, unmistakably, Benjamin Davies. He was greyer in the beard, and his muscles had shrunk. He looked much older than he had when Catherine had last seen him, preparing to board ship. His hair, uncovered, had grown thin on top, and it no longer hung in curls to his shoulders. He'd cropped it close to his scalp, and his face looked fatter for the trim. But even in the gloom of the building, she knew it was Benjamin, no doubt of it, and Catherine had to lock her lips together to stop herself from calling out to him.

"Now you'll see your husband at his work," crowed Robbie. He had worn a cap, and he pulled it low on his forehead and stood behind John. "Go ahead, Mother, push your way to the front. I've seen many a lady force her desire when she wanted something particularly fine."

But Catherine hung back, keeping what light there was behind her, and the selling began. It was quiet for such goings-on, and Benjamin himself stood to the side, while another, younger man carried on the exchanges of money. These were obviously purchases made before the fact, and there was no calling of prices or display. These customers were waiting their turn. A woman in a blue silk dress walked right up the steps to the platform, as though it were her daily routine, and spoke, and then yet another man led up a girl to face her. The woman examined the child's mouth and raised her limbs, then bent and spoke to her. The purchaser must have been satisfied, because she put money into the second man's hand and took the child with her, back down into the crowd.

Catherine stepped inside and waited for her eyes to see into the darkness. Along the walls stood men and women, girls and young boys. They were tied together with rough rope.

Benjamin was selling human beings.

"He's one of them," said Alice, beside Catherine. "He's become one of these monsters, that buy and sell souls like cattle. Mother, you must come away, now, and leave him to his sin." She tugged on Catherine's arm.

But Catherine would observe it herself. "No. I'll watch it to the end." She could see, from the edge of her vision, Robbie studying her, and she set her face into an impassive mask. She would not be the object of his ridicule. And she watched, as people came and went, the unfortunates that had been brought for sale unclothed or underclothed, while the buyers circled them and approved or moved on. Men and women, couples, entire families mingled among the tied people, and Catherine could see plainly the difference. The ones who came to buy all looked like her.

"Where do they all come from?" said Reg, and Robbie moved between him and Catherine to speak without being heard.

"These are from Africa, as you can see. They live under the sun all the year 'round and it burns them black. Sometimes they come from the Far East, back on boats with the traders. China. Japan."

"And what's their fate? Where do they go?" asked Reg.

"To wherever their new masters and mistresses take them, I reckon," said Robbie. "I haven't followed one to find out. Nor have I asked Benjamin, who prospers so handsomely from all of this."

Benjamin indeed seemed to be holding a small court at the edge of the platform. Surrounded by paunchy, brightly-dressed men, he was the raven among them in his dark jacket and a plain hat that he removed and replaced, removed and replaced. He held himself erect and aloof, even as he chatted and took money, and he looked every inch a dour king in his cavernous realm. Catherine thought of Hades, and she shivered.

"I know not what to say to him," said Catherine. "Benjamin has always played fair in matters of business. I've never known him to cheat anyone, or to use a man beneath his worth."

"You thought he played fair in matters of love, as well," said Ann.

"They're worth what money he can claim for them," said Robbie. "He even buys them back sometimes and sells them again to more suitable masters."

"I thought you didn't sound him about their fates," said Reg.

Robbie's stern expression relented. "I may have spoken too precisely. I do know that some of them go over the sea and are never heard from again."

"Over the sea to what place?" asked Veronica.

"The farms. You've heard tell of them, I'm sure." Robbie pointed vaguely toward the west. "In the new world. They become tenants, I reckon, or something such."

"We have tenants, and we have servants, and I would never force them into such degradation," said Catherine.

"And yet the two you brought with you have fled just the same, haven't they?" said Robbie. "I have neither servant nor tenant. I serve God and count myself free."

"How can anyone call himself free whose profits depend upon this?" said Veronica. "Don't tell me that Benjamin isn't paying for that room of yours."

"He may be," said Robbie. "But he's called himself my father, and he owes me a living."

"So you're not free," said Veronica. "This disgusts me. I'm going. John, will you take me back?"

John nodded. He was observing the sale, too, and seemed reluctant to depart, but he took Veronica's arm and walked her to the door, where gentlemen parted, with appraising glances, to let them through. Ann said, "Reg, we can follow them, if you've seen enough."

"I've seen all I need to see of this," Reg said, "but don't you want to speak to Benjamin?"

"Catherine, I believe that's your task," said Ann.

But Catherine could not move. She would have sworn that Benjamin had looked directly at her, more than once, but his gaze had travelled right across her without recognition. Did she look that very different? The people had begun to clear out, and Benjamin was in close discussion with his partners. They were counting money.

Ann said, "Will you?"

"What?" said Catherine.

"Speak to the man. He's yours, after all."

"He's not mine. Nor is he that Joan's. Nor Margaret's. Benjamin is his own man."

"This is no time for equivocation," said Ann. "We've come halfway around the world to find him, and there he is. Go say something to him."

Ann gave Catherine a slight shove, and she put a foot forward. The act set her body into motion, and on she went, through the thinning mass of people and up to the edge of the platform. It was not as high as a player's stage, too low to rest her elbows on, and she stood, her arms behind her, and looked upward. Benjamin looked down.

It was easier than she had expected. Catherine's throat opened for her, and she said, "I've travelled a long way to seek you, Benjamin. Will you come down and greet your wife?"

Benjamin did not step down to fold Catherine into his arms. He divided the money in his hands between his two workers, then walked away, hopping from the wooden platform at the back and heading toward the door that opened into the dank storeroom and from there to Margaret's chamber. Catherine stood, unable to decide whether he meant to flee or to lead her, and Ann finally hooked her arm through Catherine's and said, "He won't get away again."

Reg was ahead of them, almost trotting after Benjamin, and the women followed him. Benjamin had left the door ajar, so perhaps he was indicating that they should move to a more private place. But as they entered the dark middle room, Benjamin's voice hit them. He was in Margaret's room, and he was shouting. Reg hesitated, but Ann shoved him in the back, and they went on through.

Margaret stood, in an attitude of penitence, before Benjamin.

"Benjamin, these questions might better be directed to me," Catherine said. "I've come a long way to speak with you."

Benjamin's face had grown purple in his tirade, and he turned on Catherine with a menacing look. "I'll speak with you when I am finished with this harpy."

Margaret shrank at the word, and Catherine felt obligated to put herself bodily in his way. "You've no need to harangue

Margaret. She didn't expect us any more than you did. She's probably not laid eyes on you since we first met with her."

"You come into my house without my leave and direct my affairs?" said Benjamin. At least he was talking to Catherine instead of Margaret.

"I've directed nothing, and it was Robbie who brought us inside," said Catherine. "You see—." But Robbie had not come through with them. "He was here. He was just beside me."

"He hasn't the courage to face the consequences of his actions, any more than he has the wherewithal to face his debts," said Benjamin.

Catherine bit on the inside of her lip and counted ten. "Benjamin, I've come all the way from England to bring you the news that Queen Mary is dead and Queen Elizabeth has granted me leave to find you. I think you'll find that you're pardoned to return home. I remain your wife and have longed to see you."

Benjamin wilted at this and held out his arms. "Catherine. My wife. You have come for me, at last." But before Catherine could decide whether to walk into the embrace, he backed away. "Don't come near me. I'm filthy."

"I've been away from home for weeks," said Catherine. "I'm not worried about your cleanliness."

"No, I mean I'm dirty, here." Benjamin pointed at himself. "You've seen the worst, haven't you? I won't touch you."

"Benjamin," said Ann. "Catherine's your wife. She's here. She's seen you at low moments before."

"As low as this?" Benjamin looked at Margaret. "Have you been inside of the house? The main house?"

"Yes," said Catherine, "and I've met your Joan Wright. She claims to be married to you. Did you know that?"

Benjamin hung his head for a second, then raised up in the defiant attitude he'd shown before. "What can I do about what the woman says? She's here, and she says what she pleases."

"It seems that being your wife pleases her best," said Catherine.

"I am what you see," said Benjamin. "Cast out of my country, cast out of my wife's bed. Did you think I would join an order? Take vows?"

"She thought you would remain faithful to her," said Ann. "It wasn't Catherine who drove you from England."

"What have you to say to me about the way I conduct my life? You had nothing to be taken away from you."

"Reg was stabbed trying to help you and Robbie," said Ann. Her voice was hot now, and she stepped in, almost touching Benjamin. "He well-nigh died being your loyal servant. No, I have no grand houses, and I have no servants, but I do have a husband, and I'd like to keep him well and whole until God takes him, not you."

"You have ever had a harsh mouth," said Benjamin.

"Yes, I have, and here is your wife, come to restore you to your former station, and you act as though she's offered you a spitting viper as a gift."

"My former station? Can she restore my property? Can she restore my houses to me? The servants I had? The furnishings? Will her Elizabeth make me again the man I was?"

Catherine said, "Is that what you've longed most for in these years? Your houses?"

"Yes," said Benjamin. "No. I've wanted you in my bed, but you were sleeping peacefully in your own home in Yorkshire."

"I wasn't at peace," said Catherine, "and the house in Yorkshire went to the queen. I've built another, smaller one, and there I sleep. I wrote you letters, long letters, and you didn't return so much as a sentence to me."

"I did write a few sentences to you. Once or twice. To send to England was a bitter thing. And then it was a thing I could no longer do. I went for a sailor, and I was gone most of the time. I learnt how the world went, and I built a business here. I had to make money."

"I've seen this business of yours. You speak of bitter things," said Catherine. "I can imagine nothing more caustic than to trade in human souls. How could you do it, Benjamin? How can you?"

"It's the custom here. Back in England, we send our own servants hither and yon," said Benjamin. "We bargain away our daughters to the highest bidder. What's the difference?" He looked at the three of them again. "Where's my daughter? Have you dragged her along to behold her father's disgrace?"

Alice stepped into the room then. "I'm here, Father. And I can tell you that I don't expect to be traded off for any man's wealth."

Benjamin gazed at the young woman, holding her dog in her arms, but he did not embrace her. "How grown up you are, Alice. And how quick-tongued. It's fortunate for you, to have a strong-willed mother. Others are not born under such twinkling stars, and they must bear their fates. I am only a trader. I neither acquire nor keep."

"That makes you a Judas, not a man of business," Ann put in. "You've acquired plenty on the backs of those people, as I see it."

"You might consider," Benjamin began, but he could not finish, because John De Vries ran into the room.

"Your son, Catherine. Your Robbie." John was pointing to the door. "Gone to your bed, back at our inn. Much blood. You will come. Come now."

Chapter 33

Catherine was unaware that Benjamin had followed them until they stumbled into the inn, on the heels of John De Vries. Benjamin bellowed a question to the innkeeper, who clearly recognized the voice.

"We've put him in the back. We can't have disease in the open, where guests'll see it. And not on the beds." He beckoned, but John was already leading them. The space in which Robbie lay was a shed beside the servants' room, with a roof that leaked patches of light onto him and a dirt floor. A straw pallet had been pushed against one wall, and Veronica knelt beside her brother, holding a cloth to his mouth.

"He vomits blood," she said when Catherine sat beside her.

John said, "He cannot stand. He fell in the square, coming here, and I carried him inside. And this is where they have kenneled him."

Robbie hacked up another wad of red phlegm, and Veronica caught it in the cloth, wiped his lips, and threw the mess aside. Catherine felt his forehead, expecting the heat of fever, but her son was cold, and his skin had a mossy texture. He was pale, whiter than she had ever seen him, and his eyes, when he opened them, shone too brightly. It was not the sweat. It was not the black death. This was something corrupted deep inside him, a cancer or a rotting of the lungs. She had no cure for it, and did not know what might ease his suffering.

"May I touch you, Son?"

"Mother." He squinted at Catherine and fell back, exhausted. "You may, but there's no need. I'm dying, and now after all of your efforts to find me I'll cost you the burying of me. I've ever been a thorn in your side, and now you may pluck me out and discard me. There will only be the pinch of my remains to worry you longer."

"How can you speak of that?" said Catherine.

Ann was at Robbie's feet, and her face said that she knew the condition was irreparable. Reg stood beside her, and he placed his hands on her shoulders and guided her backward, away from the smell of Robbie's body.

"You've shat yourself, and I'll need to roll you to clean you up," said Catherine.

"The final indignity," said Robbie. He tried to move, but could not, and Veronica helped him. "Sister, don't trouble yourself. I've been enough tribulation to you already."

"Nonsense," said Veronica. "Are you able to lift yourself so that I can take off these soiled breeches?"

"I can do that," said Catherine, and together they stripped the young man. The others had absented themselves in the face of the young man's mortification, except for Benjamin, who removed Robbie's boots.

The wasted condition of his legs was such that Catherine gasped despite herself. His ribs could be easily counted through the skin, but his stomach was distended and he cried out when she placed a palm on him. His body looked as though he had been living a more ascetic life than a monk. This was not disease alone. It was also starvation. Catherine held her tongue and stroked her son. "No more, Mother," he said. "Please."

"Fetch a cup of weak ale," Catherine said to Veronica, and the younger woman left, too.

"If you won't eat, there's nothing I can do for you," said Catherine. "Shall I call a priest, Robbie?"

He laughed, and his bitter mirth dissolved into a cough, and the cough brought up another mass of blood. "No, Mother. I've made my appearances at their church. I've given my daughter to the priests and their nuns. Isn't that enough for one man to slip into Heaven uninterrogated?"

"I can't say," said Catherine. She finished cleaning her son and covered him with Benjamin's jacket. He would not drink from the cup when Veronica brought it, even when she offered to add nutmegs to it. He surely couldn't eat, not in this condition. He would probably refuse an attempt to feed him. He would die here, like a dog in its den, and she would have to watch it. "What's the name of the convent where you placed Julia?"

"Wherefore?" said Robbie without opening his eyes.

"I'll fetch her home," said Catherine. "She ought to see what her father's land looks like, don't you think? She should walk the hills and feel the oily new wool when we've shorn the lambs for the first time. She should sleep in the bed you slept in as a boy. I've kept it, all of these years. Wouldn't it be fine for it to be hers one day?"

The young man's hand fell onto Catherine's. "Yes." His fingers were frigid and hard, and the nails were deeply ridged. "You'll find her in the church with the tower. It's not far from here. I don't remember what it's called."

Every church Catherine had seen had a tower.

"I know where the child is," Benjamin said from the doorway. "I'll get her, if you want her, Catherine."

She imagined the money changing hands, the dirty money. "I'll find her myself if you'll tell me the way."

"I've paid for your son's lodging and his meals. I bought him drink. Do you think I'm too defiled to pay to find your granddaughter?"

"We'll discuss it another time," said Catherine. If Benjamin had paid for food, not much of it had gone into her son. "Was he thus when he came to you?"

"He was thin. He looked weak. He was beside himself with grief and self-loathing. I found him a room near other Englishmen and let him decide what he wanted to do."

Catherine stepped out of the room, backing Benjamin before her. She whispered, "Did he speak of England, ever?"

"Only to spit about it," said Benjamin. "He's full to the brim of rage and hatred, and he doesn't know where to put them. He was born with them."

"Perhaps," said Catherine, "but I think not. He's let them stick in his heart and grow there like some vile weeds and they've choked the life from him." She looked up at her husband. "Had he already placed the baby in the convent before he arrived here?"

Benjamin picked at a thread sticking from a buttonhole on his breeches. "No. And she's not a baby anymore. She's nigh walking."

"So you've seen for yourself where the child is?"

"Yes."

Catherine considered her unmoving son again, through the open door. "He didn't take her anywhere himself. You took her, didn't you? Did you pay them to take her?"

Benjamin made a sound, perhaps grinding his teeth, but Catherine did not look at him again. Then he said, "Yes, if you must know the truth. I suppose you'll find it out sooner or later."

"How could you do it, Benjamin? I know she's not your flesh, but she's mine. You surely knew I would come."

"I knew no such thing. I knew that you were in England, and I received a few letters. But this is a long way, and I expected you would wait for me to return."

"And you had no intention of returning, did you?"

"What should I say, Catherine? Should I grovel here, in the dirt? Should I get on my knees? Should I lie to you?"

"No."

"If you want to go after the child, go, and I'll send money with you to buy her back. I'll take care of the business here when the time comes."

"You will not pay to bury my son, and you will not buy my granddaughter for me. I see it's become a custom for you, to buy and sell God's creatures."

"My money's kept your son alive, and it's not good enough to give him a Christian burial?"

"I have money that we brought with us. It will do for all."

Veronica appeared at the kitchen door, with a doctored cup, but Catherine rose and took it from her. "He won't take this," she said. "Throw it out. He's taken enough of that spice. Come, daughter, we must decide what's to be done next."

"What ails Robbie?" Veronica asked.

"His life," Catherine said. "Nothing but his own life."

Chapter 34

Catherine told Ann and the girls to prepare what they would need, and Reg and John De Vries had gone in search of some man of God. Catholic or Protestant, it didn't matter, just some someone in black. They slept that night in fits and starts, Catherine rising from the bed, more times than she could count, to study the pattern of stars and the moon's path, wondering if she should go back before the sun rose. No, she decided. Let him sleep, if rest would come, and perhaps the world would look different in the morning. A servant of the inn had been set watch over Robbie, and would come calling if he changed in any way.

Benjamin had stayed at his own house, at Catherine's request. Catherine supposed that Joan Wright was in his bed, and she tried to summon up a twinge of jealousy. But at this she failed, feeling only a dismal, drooping sadness. Benjamin would remain in Lisbon, unless she urged his return to England. She might plead Alice's need for a father, the tenants' need of a master on their further landholdings. She might plead her rights as his legitimate wife. She might attempt to shame him into it. The different arguments clogged her thoughts, and she set the need for a decision aside and turned, instead, to imagining the face of her granddaughter. She hoped the nuns had a well-stocked apothecary, or she would face yet another small, strange grave.

She dreamt that she was walking again through the gorse of Yorkshire, and stumbled upon a swollen corpse, alive with maggots. It bloated and bulged and she thought the thing was the world itself. The hideous ball split open, spilled its rotten gore over her shoes, and vanished. She woke with a gasp, damp with her own sweat, and hurled herself out of bed to be sure that she was still among living human beings. As she watched, the sun rose with a fierce light, braving out the threat of autumn, and Catherine dressed herself with dispatch, leaving Veronica to get Alice dressed. She needed Ann to begin counting their moneys for a casket and a funeral. When she came out to the common room, the innkeeper told her that the men had already gone on their quest, and Catherine nodded and, unable to stomach even the look of food, went on back to the sick room.

He lay as she had left him the evening before, on his back. A cup of ale sat untouched, dusty on its surface, and Catherine sat in the dirt at her son's side and placed a tentative hand on his chest. He seemed to breathe, but he did not open his eyes. "Will you drink, Robbie?" Catherine said, and she thought she saw his head move on the pallet. When she held the cup to him, however, he did not move his lips. He was leaving her again, and a resentful knot clogged Catherine's throat. He was willfully taking himself off this time, not being sent away by an angry queen. And even that he had done to himself. What had he thought—that Mary Tudor would simply fall into the rebels' arms and abdicate her throne?

In her son's face, Catherine saw the boy she'd loved, who had wanted his father's love more. The young man who picked and poked at his sister, then grabbed her for a hug. The sullen thug who revolted against a queen, stupidly and stubbornly. No wonder Mary Tudor had sent him away.

Catherine felt the old kinship with Mary rise up behind her ribs, and the rage at her son's cruelty toward women.

Then a hot guilt washed through her and melted the hard places. Robbie had always been seeking some place to belong and some set of doctrines by which to live. England had not given him that—nor had she. He had perhaps suckled the anger from her as an infant, and his turn of mind was her own fault. She felt it now: a creeping bitterness at Benjamin, like a twisting serpent in her blood. Like bile. How could he have gone off with Margaret, and then taken up with yet another woman, while she waited at home, keeping the sheep and the books and sleeping in a cold, lonely bed?

Catherine sniffed at the ale. It smelt rancid, and she heaved herself up to toss it into the dirt outside the door. She stood there, studying the back of the inn and letting the early sun warm her face. And when she turned back to sit beside her son, she found him unmoving. He had soiled the pallet, and when she tried to roll him to one side to clean the spot, she felt the flaccid limbs and knew. Robbie Overton had not lingered on the threshold of death, but had stepped over quickly and in silence.

Catherine leant to him and held her son in her arms. No tears burned the backs of her eyes, and no wail sprang from her mouth. She did not feel the need to flail at her hair or her clothing. She wondered how to get him out without knocking his head or his feet against the rickety doorframe, and managed by bundling the body close to her heart and easing through sideways. And there she stood, in the cramped yard, cradling her son and unable to open the door to get back inside the inn. He felt like a bag of damp feathers in her arms, and his head lolled forward, showing how thin his neck and back were. "Robbie," whispered Catherine. "My son."

And then the door opened. There stood Veronica, and Alice and Ann behind her, and when she saw her mother holding her brother, Veronica shrieked and grabbed at the dead man's ankles. Ann came forward and offered to take the burden from Catherine, but she only nodded ahead, and Ann held the door open. Reg and John had not returned, and the innkeeper turned pale at the sight of a body in his common room. "You will take him into your own room," he ordered, and Catherine obliged without retort. Robbie looked more composed lying in a real bed, and she tucked his feet inward.

"We need linens and water," said Catherine. "Ask the maid if there is a table where we may lay him out for the washing."

Veronica was keening now, and Ann steered her out of the bedchamber. Alice stood in the doorway. Catherine looked at the remains of her only son. So fragile in repose. She supposed Robbie was at peace now, and his slack face showed no trace of his long quarrel with the world. The eyebrows no longer furrowed in disapproval, and the lines worn into his skin had softened. Catherine knelt beside the bed and prayed for his soul, and as she sent her petition to God the natural tears came. She put her forehead onto the cover and let herself weep.

Catherine heard the footstep on the threshold and raised her head. Ann and Veronica stood there with Alice, in silence, Veronica now recovered from her fit and dry-eyed. They held cloths over their arms. Veronica said, "The innkeeper is unhappy that he died here, and he wants us to remove Robbie to his own rooms, across the way. He has given us these cloths in compensation."

"It's a sorry thing, when a man can't die without others feeling that their rights have been violated," said Ann.

Catherine stood and palmed the tears from her face. "How will we manage it? We can't simply lug him through the crowds." The words sounded heartless, and she added, "It isn't seemly."

"John and Reg have returned with a priest," said Ann. "They'll find a way." She gave her bundle to Veronica and went out, returning in a few moments with Reg. "This is a dismal business, if you ask me."

Reg went to the foot of the bed and studied the still form. "He was a good boy, for all that. He had a hard way about him, and the world gave him no quarter. I would that he had come under my wing instead of those damned rebels. I don't suppose he ever wanted a father, though. Some boys won't abide a new one." He chewed on the inside of his lower lip.

John De Vries went to Reg's side. "He was sick? Disease?"

"Sick in his soul," said Catherine. She pointed to her breast. "Melancholy."

"Melancholy?" said John.

"Deep sadness," said Veronica. "Sad unto death. A darkness of vision."

John nodded. Catherine said, "You needn't worry about infection."

John said, "I was not worried. I have before seen death. It does not catch me, at least not today."

"What of tomorrow?" said Reg.

"Eh. Tomorrow is tomorrow and it will keep itself," said John. He turned from the bed and put his arms around Veronica. She was still holding the cloths, and he had to bend across them to embrace her. Veronica inclined her head a little, but her burden kept them apart.

"You are good woman," John said.

It was an odd phrase, and Catherine was not entirely sure what he had meant. Perhaps he meant nothing at all, and the language tripped him up. But he was comforting her daughter, and for now that was all she needed.

The men wrapped Robbie's body in a sheet, and, preceded by the priest, who parted the crowds, carried him as quietly as they could across the square and up to his room.

The landlady tutted as they went by, saying that she knew the lad was not long for the world and that they had better not make a mess of her bedding while they were at their work. The men went up the stairs without responding, and Ann stayed below with Alice, assuring the woman that, yes, she would be paid, and, no, they would not ruin her linens.

The room itself was dingy and small, with a sagging roof and one smeared window. Catherine marvelled that she had not been able to see how cramped the place was when she had spotted the silhouette of Robbie that first evening. The bed looked clean, though, and Catherine assented to laying him there. A bucket of fresh water sat in the corner, and soap, and she had cloths enough to wash him. She asked the men to wait outside while the women did the preparation. The priest looked closely at Robbie and wondered what had caused his death. "A wasting disease," said Catherine, and he appeared satisfied by that.

When they laid Robbie bare, his emaciated condition was horrible to behold. "How is it that his belly sticks out so?" said Veronica. She touched her brother's chest with one finger. She no longer cried out or wept at the sight of him.

"He hadn't fed his body. He spent too much of his time feeding his mind," said Catherine. "The stomach objects to such treatment." She called for Ann and Alice, who dutifully came up. The dog was not in Alice's arms, and she said that she had left him with John. A good girl, thought Catherine, though clearly not much moved by this death.

"He poisoned his mind, and it poisoned his body," said Ann. She ripped a cloth into halves, said a quick, soft prayer, and began cleaning Robbie's feet.

"Do you mean that he starved himself?" said Veronica. "The priest won't allow him to be buried in a churchyard if he's deemed to be a suicide."

"Shh," said Ann. "Don't say it aloud."

But Veronica said, "Do you think the priest knows he's Protestant?"

"He doesn't seem to care," said Catherine. "I expect a holy man in this city sees his fill of all kinds." She had begun with Robbie's face and hair, and found that his scalp was covered with small scabs. She shuffled her fingers through the greasy strands and out dropped lice. No wonder the landlady was suspicious of this family. "We must put another sheet under him. Unfold some of those cloths."

Ann did the job. She had seen the lice. "You are most accommodating of his landlady. He's been sleeping in this bed already. You needn't worry so much over appearances now."

Catherine said only, "I must use the soap on his hair."

"What should I do?" said Alice.

"Refresh these cloths as we use them," said Ann. "We need more water."

So they performed the dreadful task, and as they moved over her son's body, Catherine felt that it became the ceremony it should have been, a duty done that lifted a weight from her. They shrouded him at last, and each woman kissed his lips a final time. He was cold and his limbs were already growing stiff. They had done good work.

The men entered at Ann's call, and the priest managed to convey a willingness to have the body entombed in his churchyard—for a price. There would be no burial in the ground, but Catherine had seen enough of headstones anyway. The parish could hire mourners, if she desired them. But Catherine said no. His family would be sufficient to see him into his resting place. She would pay for men to bear her son to the church, and the priest accepted these terms and left them, saying he would fetch some of his parishioners and return before nightfall. He could lie in the cool of the building until tomorrow. The weather was still warm in the afternoons, and the disposition of the body should not wait longer than that.

They all followed the holy man downstairs and met Benjamin in the doorway. "How dare that son of a whore over there force you to bring him here, in broad daylight with all the city watching your humiliation," he said. "I'll have you all moved out."

"Never mind," said Catherine. "Robbie is laid out and we've made the funeral arrangements."

"Where is he?"

"Up in his room," said Ann. "Don't touch him. We've only just finished laying him out."

The priest slipped away, and Benjamin watched him go. "Where will you bury the boy?" he said.

"In a churchyard," said Catherine. "It's most fitting."

"I'll stand by your side, if you want me," said Benjamin.

"With that Joan Wright on your other arm?" said Ann, and Reg hushed her.

Benjamin flushed a criminal red. If Ann had been a man, Catherine thought, they would have fought right there. But then Reg said, "You've shamed us all with this other woman," and Benjamin did not move toward him at all.

Catherine saw Margaret coming across the square, and she met her halfway. The heavy makeup had been washed off, and Margaret wore a sober matron's head covering. She almost went to her knees, and Catherine held her up. "Don't," she said. "Not in the public eye."

"Robbie's gone?" Margaret said.

Catherine nodded. "We'll take him to a church this evening and put him to rest tomorrow." Margaret sucked in a sob, and Catherine said, "Will you come? He was your nephew." Margaret looked up, and Catherine added, "You could see it as well as anyone, couldn't you? How much he resembled his father as he grew to be a man. He was an Overton, truly."

"He was," said Margaret. "With an Overton's pride and an Overton's temper. Catherine, will you forgive me? Let's not go to our own graves with this malice on our souls."

If forgiveness were easy, it would not have to be commanded by God. It was easy enough to carry resentment, even as heavy as it was, but forgiveness always seemed the more difficult load to bear. And so, it was demanded. She said, "I'll endeavor to forgive, and we'll play at being sisters until the role becomes so common to us that it feels natural and real. And you will forgive me, for my foolishness and stubbornness?"

"I will," said Margaret.

"Then let's go and wait for the priest together," said Catherine. "It will surely be good for Robbie's soul to see all of his family together to send him off to God."

Chapter 35

A desultory little funeral, the church large and the company small. Benjamin did not show himself. Margaret lodged at the inn with Catherine and her daughters, and they moved through the public throngs as though they were companions of old. Robbie was prayed over, prayed for, and prayed along his way to his corner of a purchased tomb, at the end of a line of a family who had died out from plague more than fifty years back. Catherine paid the requested sum, and the meager group wandered back through the slant sunshine without feeling its warmth or light.

Ann walked with Reg, as far away from Margaret as possible, and John De Vries lightly held Veronica's arm. That left Catherine with Alice, at Margaret's side, and she wondered at how familiar it felt, to have this Overton woman as a sister again. All those years ago, when they were in the convent together, they had fussed and nagged at each other, and then the years of rancour and resentment followed. What did it matter now? Margaret had been meek all night, accepting only a straw pallet brought into the bedchamber and refusing the big bed, though Veronica, with a slight air of condescension, offered to take her place more than once. Today, Margaret wore only plain clothing, and claimed she had nothing more to remove to England. It would all stay behind, with her past and her pride. Looking at her feet, she asked Catherine, "What will you do now?"

"Today? I'll grieve."

"You'll grieve longer than one day," said Margaret. "You have much to mourn. I meant to ask, what'll you do about Benjamin?"

"The answer to that lies as much with Benjamin as it does with me," said Catherine. "He has to give up the woman. He has to vow again to respect our marriage."

"And then you'll have him back to your bed?"

The spectre of lovemaking with Benjamin fluttered Catherine's guts, and her ears picked up the twitter of a pair of dust-coloured birds in the eaves of a building. She shaded her eyes to see better. Such a dismal life, stuffing dirt and hair into the sodden underside of a roof and making a nest in the darkness. And yet, they sang. Or perhaps they only cried out, wanting a different sort of existence. Her imagination would not allow a vision of contented sleep next to Benjamin. The sight of Joan Wright intervened, like a wraith in a nightmare.

"I'll decide when I speak to him again."

Margaret walked a while in silence, then she said, "May I stay at the inn with you?"

"Isn't your room at Benjamin's house finer?" Catherine waited for a response, and when none was offered, she added, "Do you really mean to come home with us?"

"If you'll have me."

"You're an Overton, Margaret. There's no Overton Hall anymore, if that's where you intend to go. Mary Tudor took it, and I begin to understand why she did it. But the house is empty now, falling down by the day. I have some of the stones laid into my own house in Havenston. God only knows how much more's been taken since we left."

"You and Veronica are the only family I have left," said Margaret. "I'll come. I can oversee the children. I'll be an aunt to you, too, Alice, if you'll allow it."

Alice shrugged, and Catherine laughed a little, despite herself. "These girls are grown." But then she thought of her granddaughter. "Except for Robbie's Julia. Do you know the way to the convent where she's been lodged, Margaret?"

"No. I wasn't consulted about the decision, and I wasn't even allowed to lay eyes on the child before they took her."

"They?"

"He. Benjamin. With a few servants and a maid he hired to look after her. The maid had lost a child and found the task cheered her spirits. I think the little girl was still at the breast then. Robbie had brought a wet nurse with him, but she abandoned him."

"Reg'll find us a map," said Catherine. "Tomorrow we'll speak with the priest again. He surely knows the cost to ransom the child. Didn't this maid have a husband?"

"A baby in her belly but no man in her bed," said Margaret. "Benjamin said it would be good for her to be in the convent with Julia."

Neither of them commented on the irony. They finally gained their rooms, where the innkeeper fawned over them with guilty solicitousness. Their linens were fresh, and food had been prepared for their return. He had opened some of his best French claret to refresh them.

"How very kind," said Veronica coldly. Margaret glanced over the table and decided upon the bedchamber. She shut the door behind her. John and Reg were already in conference about the location of Julia Overton, and Ann poured wine for Catherine. She swallowed the knot of anguish in her throat and drank.

"I have good news," said the innkeeper. He was wringing his hands like a miser in the old plays. "You'll want to hear this."

"Out with it then, man," said Catherine. Her insides felt dusty and she didn't want to parry wits or solve riddles, especially with this man. Her tone came out rude, and she didn't care. She wanted to rake the table clean of the fine dishes with her arms and folded them to stop herself.

"I've found your men for you and returned them."

At this, Catherine looked up, and there indeed stood Oswald and Mark, just stepped in from the kitchen. They were crushing their caps in their hands and scraping their boots along the floor. "You two are a sight for sore eyes," she said. "Where in the world have you been?"

"We have just today heard of young Robbie's death, from this innkeeper," said Mark. "It's a sorry thing, and we're very sorry for it. We were tempted away, and now we're returned, like the prodigals we are."

Reg said, "You ought to be ashamed of yourselves, leaving your mistress like a couple of scoundrels. She's never done you ill."

Mark Wheeeler said, "We're ashamed, Reg. It was a moment of misjudgment."

"A fine word for a wretched act," said Reg.

"But there's free men all around here," Oswald argued. "They offer wages for work and all the ale a man can drink. There's a captain at the harbour who would have us with him as sailors."

"And they've freed you of all your money, haven't they?" said Reg.

"No," said Mark. "The man offers good wages for sailors."

"So you've returned to swindle more from your mistress, is that it?"

Catherine said, "Leave them be, Reg. Mark. Oswald. Tell me true. Have you come of your own free will or were you brought here by force? You're welcome to return to our family, and I have no pleasure in seeing any man chastened just now. You're not in any man's debt, are you?"

Mark and Oswald said, "No, Madam," in unison. Then Mark said, "We've seen the ships, and heard of a world beyond this one, with riches for men with strong backs and strong wills. And there's other worlds, too, and we could have our own stuffs to sell if we can get them back. Spices and such. A man can make his way. We would try it for ourselves. Or we would have, if not for that man's servants, who spied us out at the dock." He pointed across the room. "It's naught against you, Madam, but we craved some elbow room for our souls. Other men have it."

Catherine considered for a moment. She had the men, and she could keep them if she chose. But she couldn't choose it. Not now. She said, "Go, if you will go. Stretch yourselves however you see fit. Be good men, and God will have mercy on you. Here." She retrieved some coins from her purse and handed them over. "It's little enough for your many years of service to me."

Mark said, "Blessings on you, Madam," and Catherine told herself that she was satisfied with that. Mark and Oswald looked at each other, then threw the innkeeper a scowl and returned to their rooms. They came out again within seconds, carrying their bags. John De Vries said, "I go with you to your new home, to see that it is in order."

"That's kind of you, John," said Catherine. "Can you find your way back in the dark?"

"I can," he said, and the three of them departed.

"You'll let those two run off, just like that?" said Ann. "And pay them for the bargain?"

"My eyes have been shut for my entire life," said Catherine. "It seems a sin to close them again once they've been pried open. Come, let's look at those maps."

They turned again to their consultation, while Alice studied their little account book. "I hope you didn't give them much," she muttered to her mother, and Catherine just shook her head. She didn't really know, but she couldn't feel the loss. She couldn't feel anything but hollow sorrow.

While she mourned, the others made their plan, to set out the next morning, so as not to leave the girl languishing with strangers any longer than necessary. The name Julia on Veronica's tongue brightened Catherine's mind, and she felt herself come alert again. Ann was saying that the convent sisters would come soon to feel familiar to the child, and it would be harder to break the bond the longer they waited. Reg was figuring on a day to find the place and wondered if they should send a message ahead, alerting the house that they were coming. Veronica and Ann approved this idea, but Catherine said no. "We can't be sure how much Benjamin paid them to take her, and they may cheat us of more to regain her if they have warning to make plans."

Margaret stepped into the room. She must have been listening at the threshold. "That's a cold assessment of our sisters in God," she said, and Ann, with a frown that indicated her unhappiness at agreeing with Margaret, said, "It is."

Catherine started to defend herself, but, looking at the other women, she realized that the hardness of her measurement, her lack of belief in the concurrence of honesty and expressions of faith, was her own. She said, "You're right. We'll send ahead, if we can find the place. We'll go and present ourselves at the earliest moment."

Catherine knew that she had to speak to Benjamin before they set off, but she kept her own counsel and waited until everyone had eaten their meal, talked more about Robbie and the tragedy of early death, and finally pleaded the late hour and gone to their beds. Catherine said, "I am fitful tonight and will sit up for a while yet."

Everyone waved and went on, except for Margaret, who said, when they were alone, "You cannot go alone."

"Do you see me going anywhere?"

"I know what's in your mind. You're going to ask Benjamin for directions. You're going to ask how much he gave the convent. You can't walk out in the streets alone, not in the day, and most assuredly not at night. I'll go with you."

Such an unpredictable position to find herself in—consulting with Margaret about her comings and goings, and having her intentions read so clearly and so accurately. Catherine hesitated, weighing the matter, and finally relented. "Let's wait until the others are asleep."

Margaret poured them each another glass of wine, and they sat without speaking until the inn was quiet. Then Catherine and Margaret Overton covered their heads and went, together, in search of the man they had shared.

Chapter 36

"He's not here," said Joan Wright. She stood her ground behind the maid at the front door. She was dressed in a fine, golden silk robe, and her hair was unpinned. Catherine could see now how thin and broken it was, like the woman herself. The maid dashed away, and a man servant, holding a thin torch, replaced her as sentry.

"What's the matter here, Madam?" he said.

"It's nothing," said Joan. "Late-night callers, who ought to be in their beds. Let them come in, since they're here." She turned away and the servant ushered Catherine and Margaret inside.

"Lady Margaret," he said. "Have you been turned out from the back?"

"Don't call me Lady. I've gone on my own and returned on my own," Margaret said, with her old forceful voice. Catherine had not heard the tone since her arrival, and found it strangely welcome and warming. Margaret took a step forward. "I'll go away again when I'm done speaking with Joan."

"Very well," said the man, resting his eyes on the air above their heads. He shut the door and moved back, inside his cone of light, to his private darkness.

"In here," called Joan. She was in the grand room where they had met her before, reclining on a broad chair. It was almost like a small bed, and Joan spread her skirt out to capture all of the space. Two small, straight-backed wooden chairs sat nearby and she flung a hand toward them. "Sit, if you must."

"I'll stand," said Catherine. She wanted to hover over Joan, despite her weary back and sore feet. Margaret took up the position next to her.

"I said that he's not here. What could you possibly want of me?"

"When will he return?" said Catherine. "I need to speak with him about my granddaughter."

"Oh, that," said Joan, sweeping her hand over her eyes. "Will we never be rid of these Overtons and their pups? What more must he do to make you go away?"

Catherine's arms tingled and grew hot. She was afraid she might strike the woman. Or, worse, weep in her exhaustion and resentment. But she bit her lip and counted ten before she said, "Benjamin hasn't asked me to go away. I'm his wife, by law. You know it well enough."

"And you lost him, by your actions," said Joan. She twisted a wisp of the ratty hair and tucked it behind her ear. She looked withered, and Catherine wondered how old she really was.

"I must speak with him."

"Well, come back tomorrow. Or the next day. He's gone away on business. You were cruel to deny him one last look at his son before you put him into the ground. You're shameless in your desires, and you should go home and allow Benjamin to forget about you. Again."

"Robbie was not Benjamin's son."

"Perhaps not. But Benjamin's a man of dignity, Catherine. He won't be brought low by a woman."

"He's brought himself low enough to have you," Catherine said.

"Just the sort of thing I expected from your mouth," said Joan. "You may have played him to a church with a baby, but

Benjamin chose me." She gave Margaret an up-and-down assessment. "When he could have had others."

"You bitch," said Margaret. She slapped Joan full on the jaw and sent her onto the floor. "You gutter trash. You're not fit to clean Benjamin's boots."

Joan lay on the plushy carpet, rubbing her face. She studied the nap for a few seconds, then gazed up at Margaret. "No, I'm not. I'm his bedmate and his wife by common law, so I'm far too high in his regard to clean his boots. We have servants to do that."

Catherine wanted to kick Joan. She wanted to stomp the frail form and grind her into the pattern of the wool. She wanted to beat on the flaky scalp and rip the gown from her body. The woman was grinning now, pushing herself to her feet, and Catherine could see that she had lost most of her back teeth.

Joan said, "I've told him plainly that he must choose. Me or the Overtons. He'll decide when he returns. But I tell you this. Benjamin is a man of honour. He won't cast me off."

"I can bear this no longer. Come, Margaret." Catherine turned to go and saw that the front door was open. Alice stood in the doorway, and Catherine grabbed her shoulder. "You should not have come out alone. We're leaving this house, Alice."

"Yes, you are," said Joan Wright, on their heels. "Benjamin doesn't care for you at all anymore. Any of you." Alice shook Catherine off and stepped up to the woman, close enough to strike, but her arms were filled with Toby. Joan yanked the dog by the scruff and ripped him out of Alice's grasp. "He doesn't care for you any more than I do this cur." She flung him hard, into the street, and they all heard the soft thud and the one yelp. Then a shriek and the stamping of a horse. Alice ran outside, Catherine and

Margaret just behind her. Toby lay in his own blood, with a man, now off his horse, kneeling beside the little body.

Alice wailed and the man began to cry. "I didn't see the little fellow. He was right there before I saw him, and the horse shied. Oh, lady, I beg your forgiveness. I've killed him."

Catherine put her hand on the man's shoulder. "It wasn't your fault." She looked up, but Joan Wright had already slammed the door.

Alice cradled her pet, weeping into his fur, and the man would not move from her side. He wrung his hands and said, again and again, "Forgive me. Forgive me for the little mite," and Alice leant her head against his shoulder. "My mother says true. It wasn't your fault." She looked up at Catherine. "What will I do?"

Margaret got on her knees beside Alice. "Poor thing. We'll have him buried, as the good dog he was." She looked at the man. "These women are travellers here. You're English?"

"Yes. I have a garden, just there," the man said, pointing down the street. "If you have nowhere else to lay him, I'll do it. I was just on my way home. I am very sorry."

And so they went, with the stranger leading the horse ahead of them. Alice snuggled the dog the whole way, and while the man fetched a shovel, they waited in a narrow side yard. Alice laid Toby on the ground and prayed over him. "I know I'm a fool," she said when she was finished. "But he was a good boy."

"He was," said Catherine, and then the man joined them and they waited while he dug a hole under some flowering bushes with his own hands. He'd brought a linen cloth, and Alice removed the collar before she wound the shroud around the body and lowered Toby into the ground.

The man wanted to pay them, but Alice refused and said she needed her bed. He apologized once more to Catherine and Margaret before they left him there, the shovel still in his hands. Alice trudged far in front of the older women, and Margaret said, "She will mourn this for a long time."

"We have much to mourn," said Catherine.

They might have slipped into bed without being noticed, but Alice burst into tears again as they came in, and Catherine could not contain her rage. She left Margaret with Alice and flung herself into the chamber, cursing all the Joan Wrights of the world and their mothers, too. Veronica sat up and said, "What's happened?"

"Joan Wright. She's killed Alice's dog." Catherine yanked down her clothing and slapped a wet cloth around her armpits. She scrubbed her face with a towel. "Your sister is beside herself. We had to bury him in a stranger's yard."

"Just now?" said Veronica.

"Just now," said Catherine. "She threw him into the street, and he was mauled by a passing horse. You need to go and sit with your sister."

Veronica yanked on a skirt. "I can't believe it."

Margaret came in with Alice, who dropped onto a chair. Veronica pulled her close. "I'm sorry. I'm sorry," she whispered as Alice wept onto her shoulder. "Come down with me. I want you to tell me what happened," she said, throwing a robe around herself and dragging Alice out of the room.

Margaret lay on her pallet and sighed. "That poor child. You poor woman."

"Good wives have had bad husbands before now," said Catherine. "Margaret, come get into the bed. It's large enough, and you needn't ruin your back sleeping on that flat thing."

"No," said Margaret. "This is fine." She stretched, as though the meager mattress were fit for a queen.

"So he's gone away while I wait here like a supplicant for him to return," said Catherine. "Who will he buy or sell this time, I wonder."

"Please don't say it like that," said Margaret. "It sounds debasing."

"It's all debasing," said Catherine. She almost prodded Margaret to get into the bed again, but decided against. Let her sleep where she wanted to. She threw herself flat and waited for her daughters to return. In they came, quiet as a couple of mice, Alice just sniffling a little now and slipping into bed without so much as a good-night.

The next morning, the men spent a long hour sympathizing with Alice and grunting with satisfying disapproval any time Joan Wright's name was mentioned. Ann was ready to march to the house and separate the woman from her hair, and when she was dissuaded, stood at the door and shook her fist at the distance. She even cursed with Margaret in her rage.

But there was nothing to do for any of it. To distract Alice from her grief, the men suggested that they walk down to the docks, but that reminded them all of Benjamin, and they turned back toward the city. They found the house where Toby had been buried, but no one seemed to be at home, and so they all wandered to the church to visit Robbie's tomb.

"I'll find a mason to carve his name," said Catherine. That was agreeable to everyone, and it gave the day some meaning. Locating such a man was not difficult, and the price was quickly negotiated. He would do the work the next day, not having any particular tasks at hand, and Catherine could watch him, if she liked.

And so the painful hours were dispatched. Reg pretended to fiddle at a map. Ann and Margaret sat with Alice, who gazed out the window all evening. She did not eat and returned to watch the waning light until the darkness overtook it. Veronica spent her time in quiet conversation with John De Vries, and Catherine in silent conversation with God.

Chapter 37

The next morning, as they all sat at table, unable to decide how to conduct themselves, Benjamin Davies walked into the inn. He was grizzled all over with road dust, his skin and hair peppered with grime. He tossed down his hat and said, "I have her for you, Catherine, and God speed to you with her. I haven't been out of the saddle for more than a half hour these last two days. Bring me a cup, will you, man?"

The innkeeper scuttled off. Catherine strained against the resentment that held her in her chair. She was supposed to leap into his arms, to be led off like a young mother to see her child. She wanted the girl, but she would not preen or flirt with her husband. Ann rose, instead, and said, "Well, where is she?"

"At my house, being dosed with a much-needed bath," said Benjamin. He grabbed the ale from the cowering innkeeper and drank it off. "I expect you can't lower yourself to enter my doorway?"

"We'll see her," said Catherine. "Vere, Alice, and Ann, you come. Reg, could you see to some clean linens? We'll need to make her some clothes."

"She has clothes," said Benjamin. "I bought her a whole case of them. I bought back the nurse, too, so that she's tended by someone she knows."

"Very well," said Catherine. "All's at peace with her, then."

Alice did not move from her place at the table, and Benjamin finally said, "Will you come, daughter?"

"I will not," said Alice. "Your woman has killed my dog."

"What?"

Ann said, "She threw Toby into the street, and he was stomped to death by a horse."

"Oh," said Benjamin. "Well, I'll get you another dog, Alice. A more handsome one, better fit for a girl your age. They're a penny a pound on the market. Come on."

"I hate you," Alice said and left the room.

Catherine said. "We'll follow you at your leisure."

"I've got no leisure, and now I see I've got no daughter. But I've got your granddaughter, so let's be off." He snatched up the hat again, shook it, and stuck it back onto his head. The door still stood open, and he gave it a kick as he went.

Catherine's heart pounded at her ribs, but she smoothed her skirt and checked the pins in Veronica's little head covering. "Let him go on. We know the way." She called into the back for the innkeeper to lend them a couple of men, in case there were things to carry back, and as soon as the servants were prepared, they walked into the square. Benjamin was already out of sight.

Margaret took up the rear with the serving men, and Catherine held onto Ann's and Veronica's arms, to keep herself from running. Tears trailed down her face, but she didn't wipe them away. Why should she? Her son was dead. Her grandson was dead. And yet here, by a miracle, would be her granddaughter. She would weep a while if she wanted to. She sniffed loudly, and Ann stopped and cleaned Catherine's face, then held the cloth to her nose and said, "Blow." Catherine, like an obedient child, blew, and they walked on.

"Do we take the front or the back?" said Veronica, as they approached Benjamin's enormous dwelling.

"The front," said Margaret. "You don't need to hover at the back like traders. I never want to be in that room again." She meant her lavish prison, and they all understood.

Ann did not delay at the great door but pounded it until they heard footsteps within. She set Catherine before her, and when the manservant opened up, he stepped back. "So many of you," he said, "for one scrawny child."

"I'll see my granddaughter," said Catherine, and the man ushered them all inside.

Benjamin and Joan Wright were arguing. They could hear the raised voices from the entry hall. Their feet on the wooden floor sounded like a pack of horses, though, and the rooms fell silent. The man servant waited a few beats, then motioned for them to enter. He did not go in himself.

Joan was stretched across the wide soft chair, and Benjamin stood beside the hearth. Catherine said to him, "I've come for Julia."

"You see?" said Joan. "She cares nothing for you. She wants the child. Let her take it and go."

"I see another member of our family here," said Veronica. "Benjamin. Father, I might say, if you acted the part better. What's the matter with you?" She walked to him, but he did not offer a hug.

"You're tall, Veronica, tall as your mother. You used to be as ginger-haired as your queen, but I see you're fading a little to brown. Have you a husband yet?"

"I do not," said Veronica. She was scarlet-faced, and she backed away from the man.

"Mm. You'd better get yourself one before that hair goes grey."

"I'll get me one when I'm ready," said Veronica. The scarlet had gone blotchy, and Catherine knew anger was seething up, burning out the embarrassment.

"So says your Elizabeth, I hear," said Benjamin. "They say she makes a fool of herself for a married man who's bedded half of her maids. It'll undo her, and then where will little England be? Get you a husband, Veronica, and save yourself."

"I have no answer to this," said Veronica. She backed away, out of his reach. "You're not the man I remember."

"You were a child. Children know nothing."

"You've turned Alice against you."

"You see?" said Joan Wright, in echo of no one but herself. "You're all strangers to each other."

"Will you please stop your mouth?" said Benjamin. "I haven't requested your opinion."

Joan narrowed her eyes, and Catherine felt a little swelling of victory push her under the ribs. Then she looked at Benjamin and it burst into what she thought was sadness but soon realized was nothing at all. Benjamin looked back at her and said, "What would you have me say, Catherine? You see that the woman can't care for herself. Would you have me throw her into the street, too? To starve?"

Catherine didn't know for certain which woman he meant, but Ann said, "She looks as though she's starving right here inside your walls."

"I'm not starving," said Joan. "I'm delicate."

"I said shut your mouth," said Benjamin. He put his hands over his ears. "I can't think with all of the chattering."

"God forgive us for coming here to trouble your serenity," said Ann. "We thought that you'd want your family again. We've been much mistaken."

Benjamin said, "You have new servants with you, Catherine. They look very like the ones from the inn. So you've lost them again, have you? And you question my morals? At least I don't go begging when I need someone at my back. And, Margaret, you needn't cower. I see you well enough. Have you got a brow-beating to give me, as well?"

"What do you know of Mark and Oswald? And what do you care what servants Catherine hires?" said Ann.

"I know that they ran away from her. I found them down by the docks, pockets already full from some ship captain or other. I gave them some money so that they would pay it back and sent word to the inn for someone to get them home. But who'll give me thanks for it? No one. Not one of you. And it seems you've let them run off once more."

"I don't buy and sell men," said Catherine. "I pay for labour when I need it. They were free to go if they desired."

The serving men were stepping backward, toward the door, but Margaret was in their way. They clearly did not want to be at the center of the feud.

"Calm yourselves," said Catherine. "We'll be returning soon." She turned again to Benjamin. "I didn't ask you to do aught regarding my servants, and so I feel no need to shower you with gratitude. They knew where I was."

"You see? It doesn't matter at all what good I do. I am condemned."

"No one here has condemned you," said Catherine.

"I should go get them for myself. They're as much as mine, since I'm your husband. I've already put out good money to rescue them from their own shame. These servants right here could be mine, if I wanted them."

The innkeeper's servants went rabbit-eyed. "We know our place, sir," said the older one. "I'm an Englishman by birth, and I have a master."

"Then you should've stayed with your English master," said Benjamin. "Look at you, shaking as though I've just ordered you to the hangman."

"Sir," said the man, but Catherine intervened. "How much do I owe you for Mark and Oswald?"

"Ah, now you talk like one of my customers," said Benjamin, with an ugly smirk.

Catherine put her purse away. "I let them do as they pleased. They are men, and I'm not you. You've changed, Benjamin. Or you've decided to show yourself in your true light, here under the hotter sun of the south. Do I understand you rightly that you mean to have this Joan with you, when you return to England?"

Catherine watched him retrace the conversation in his mind. All of the women stared at him, and finally he said, "I haven't said that I want to return to England. Or that I don't. I said that I have a duty to her."

"And you have none to me?" said Catherine.

"Will you see this child or won't you?" said Benjamin.

He said nothing else, and Catherine found herself obliged to follow him. Joan Wright stretched and remained where she was.

Catherine's skin felt stuck all over with needles. Like an old bird, being plucked alive, she thought, but she said not a word as they entered the bedchamber. The nurse sat in a corner with the little girl on her lap, and the first glimpse Catherine had of her granddaughter was one pink hand, extended and laid against the nurse's cheek.

The woman rose at their entrance and tried to curtsey with the bundle in her arms. She was young herself, close to Veronica's age, Catherine guessed, but she did not drop the child or mar the curtsey.

"Bring it here," said Benjamin, and the woman stepped closer. "This is Maria, and, Maria, this is Catherine Overton, the child's grandmother."

Maria was small and clean, her clothing neat and plain. She offered the child, and Catherine noted that the dress she wore smelt laundered. The child gazed at Catherine as she gathered her to her breast. Ann and Veronica crowded in to see her face more clearly.

"She's the image of Robbie," said Ann.

"But for the fair hair," said Veronica, pushing back the cap on the child's head.

Catherine held her away and said, "Julia. Julia Overton. I am your grandmother." The child blinked and put one hand on Catherine's lips. She was fat enough, and her skin was clear. She had all of her fingers, and Catherine bounced her a little. "Hello, Julia," she said, and the child pushed backward, her hand against Catherine's face, opened her mouth, and squalled.

"Certainly Robbie's child," said Ann, and Catherine laughed, then wept a little, then pulled Julia close to feel her warmth. At this, the girl squirmed and howled, and Veronica said, "Give her to me, Mother."

Veronica was unskilled in handling small children, and Julia was heavy, and the transfer was awkward, Maria barely containing herself from intervention. The three women seemed too many for Julia, and she kicked and flailed. "I'm your auntie, Julia. Vere. Say 'Auntie Vere.'"

"Give her back to her nurse," said Ann. "That's a face she recognizes."

"How old is she?" said Catherine to Maria.

"Near a year, I think," said Maria. "She walks some steps, and she says a few words. Madam. Overton?" The maid shot a look at Catherine, then at Benjamin.

"Havens," said Catherine. "I'm Catherine from Havenston."

But she was thinking: the first year gone already. The child was already on her own feet and uttering her own mind. Catherine could not give the child back, not yet. She held her more lightly, and Julia quieted, staring up with her deep blue eyes into Catherine's face. She put up a hand again and tested Catherine's skin against her own, and Catherine dared a wet kiss on the hot little palm. Julia accepted this as her due, and Catherine laughed. So much lost time, her son through all of those angry years, the twin to this baby that she would never see. She appraised the child's features, so like Robbie's but with an elegant difference. Finer features. Surely the mother's imprint. Perhaps Catherine would learn to see that young woman through this girl. Had her son loved his wife as sternly as he'd approached everything else he'd seemed to value? Catherine could not think on it. The girl squirmed again, toward Maria, and Catherine relinquished her granddaughter.

"She's hungry, perhaps," Catherine said.

"Why she's just been fed," said Maria. "Little goose." She tossed the girl gently, without ever letting her go, and Julia crowed and said, unmistakably, "Maria." And Maria replied, "You just want to feel yourself against the air, don't you, little one?"

"Maria will need to go with the child," said Benjamin.

"Leave us," said Catherine, and Benjamin left. Catherine sat and allowed Maria to keep Julia on her knee. "Will you come to England with us? We have rooms enough. You'll become part of our family, if you choose."

"England is cold," said Maria. "I've been here for a good many years." She tucked in the hair that had escaped the cap. "My family came here to escape the old king Henry. Am I to go back now?"

"Where's your family?" said Catherine.

Maria put her mouth on Julia's outstretched fingers and nibbled until the girl laughed. "They're all dead, dead of the heat and their homesickness."

"And your husband? Did you have a husband? A child?"

"Had a baby. It didn't live. It had a father, but I didn't have a husband. You see a fault there, no doubt?"

"It's not for me to judge," said Catherine. "How did you come to work for Master Davies?"

Maria lifted a shoulder. "He needed a healthy wet nurse for a child. He put out word and I heard of it. Was working down at the docks." Her neck coloured up, and she said no more.

"That means you hardly know the man," said Veronica.

"He was good to me. Fed me and got me some new clothes." She picked at the skirt. It was good cloth, though plain, well cut and stitched. "He kept me here a while, then we went to the convent. That's not a place where I would want to live my life. All those statues. They look at you like they can see into your soul. I understand why the Protestants smash them."

Ann chuckled, and Maria gazed up at her. Ann said, "Do you know that you're sitting with three women who were in the convent in England? All of us old ones. Not this one." She touched Veronica's arm. "And she is called Veronica, after another old nun, though everyone thinks she is named for the saint. How the world goes round."

Maria shifted on her hips. "Pardon my words. I've got nothing against the old religion. There's many good women in the convent."

"It doesn't matter," said Catherine. "The old church was gone from England, then it roared back, and now I expect it'll be put to sleep again. The new queen is Protestant."

"She's young, I hear!" said Maria. "Barely a woman. They say she's a firebrand, though, and throws her shoes when she gets angry. I think I'd like her."

"Where do you hear such talk?" said Catherine.

"From my gossips," said Maria.

Ann said, "May I hold her?"

Julia went into Ann's arms without complaint, and Ann took her to a window. "She looks healthier than most children who've gone to wet nurses."

"My milk was good, while she needed it," said Maria. "I'm afraid it's my character that's wanting."

"What?" said Veronica. "Are you a thief? Do you lie?"

"No," said Maria. "I as much as told you. I'm a whore. And you, Madam. Are you the gentleman's wife?"

Catherine sighed. "The law of England says that I am, and we took vows at a church. And yet, I also seem to be not. This is Ann Goodall, once Ann Smith. She has a husband, a fine one, who's followed her all the way here from our home."

"I know you," said Maria, looking at Margaret.

"She's my sister by law," said Catherine. "My first husband's sister, and my sister in the convent."

"But you were here," said Maria. "You were here before."

"You're not the only whore in the room, if we must be called such," said Margaret. "Don't trouble your mind with it, Maria, I beg you."

"And you, Madam. You were in the convent, and you've had two husbands? How is that lawful?"

"It's all questionable," said Catherine, "and yet that's how it's been. And here I sit, with a husband I can't call mine and a son in the grave. Here's my daughter, and I wouldn't trade her for the world. And here's my granddaughter, who must be fed and clothed and educated. I've got another daughter, who's not with us. And yet another, by law, who's in a convent somewhere near Rome. I love them all, Catholic and Protestant. I loved the old queen once, and then I let myself hate her. Lately, I begin to understand what made her as bitter as she was. And now we have a new queen, and I once fed her as you've fed our Julia. A whole world of women. So should I sit in my bedchamber and cry upon their sins? Or mine?"

"I think not," said Maria.

"Then I won't cry upon yours, either. Will you go with us?"

"Yes," said Maria. "I think that I will."

Chapter 38

Benjamin and Joan Wright were nowhere to be seen as Catherine slipped to the front of the house. Maria had followed them, and asked, "Am I to go with you now, Madam?"

"Yes," said Ann, taking her by the arm. "We'll send someone for your other clothes." She pulled the wrap from her shoulders and mangled it onto the young woman's head to cover her.

No one prevented them from leaving, and the street outside was almost empty. The landlady across the way from their inn halloed Catherine, and she held up a basket. Robbie's things, it would be. Catherine said she would fetch it and sent the others inside.

"This is everything he left that's clean enough to touch," the landlady said. She set the basket on the paving stones. "He still owed somewhat for the washing up. Left the linens so dirty I had to dip them three times. Then I had to wash the ones you used for him at the last. And that's a good basket, if you want it."

Catherine dug some coins from her pocket. The woman counted them, then went inside and closed the door. Catherine knelt, right there in the open, where anyone might see her. Such a small receptacle to hold an entire life. A Bible, of course, with a cover of leather so worn that she was afraid it would tear. Notes in Robbie's cramped handwriting in the margins of the thin pages. Catherine shook the book, hoping that some note or letter would slip out, something that expressed love or longing. Even grief or regret. But no such paper fell, and she set the Bible aside. A handkerchief, which she put to her nose. It smelt a little of her son. Two pens, that looked as though they'd been chewed at the ends. One threadbare shirt, with stains at the armpits. Benjamin had said that he'd bought clothes for him, hadn't he? She wondered if Robbie had sold them.

She laid the things back into the basket and headed for the inn. The others were passing Julia around, remarking on her beauty and good nature. The girl was laughing for everyone, being as charming as she could be. Veronica took custody of the child, and John stood at her elbow, playing with the chubby fingers. They looked a picture of a happy young family, and Catherine's breath caught in her throat. John had not spoken to her of marrying Veronica. Not yet. That was unquestionably coming before long, she thought. Veronica looked up at John and, raising her eyebrows, nodded. He patted her head.

Ann and Reg bookended Maria and were questioning her. The interview, or interrogation, seemed to be going smoothly. Catherine would leave that to Ann's wiser head. Alice tugged at Veronica's arm. Julia reached for Alice. And so here was her family. It came to her with a start that she had forgotten Benjamin, and then that he had not once asked after Diana. Catherine could almost imagine that she was home again, in England. John and Veronica were maybe thinking of Amsterdam.

The innkeeper came in with a pitcher and a letter, flapping the paper at Catherine. "I have a message for you, all the way from the Dutch," he said.

She must have conjured a spirit. She tore the seal and sat at the table to read aloud for everyone. "It's from your parents, John, but I can't read it." She handed over the outside letter. "But there's another here that they've sent on. This is Eleanor's hand. She says, The wool has all been spun in the village and sold. The hens have stopped laying because of the heat." Catherine stopped and looked back at the date. "This was at the beginning of July. She hopes that we are well progressed in our journey and finding good weather. She and Joseph are managing the farmers, and they are bringing in hay by the piles, with the help of day labourers. The wool profit has allowed them to hire two additional men, and they have almost filled the stables for the winter. Alice, you will want to hear this. Your sheepdog Beatrice has whelped and has three fat puppies, one speckled." Catherine laid down the missive. "They're thriving at home, it seems. I suppose the pups will be sleeping on Eleanor's pillow by this time."

"Does she ask after our men?" said Veronica.

"Not by name," said Catherine. "I'm sure they're in her thoughts."

"We'll have much to tell them," Veronica said.

Alice said, "What's the news from your parents, John?"

"Farm and more farm," he answered. "I must send reply. Excuse me." And off he went. Veronica's eyes followed him, but she kept her seat.

The child now slept in Maria's arms, with Ann stroking her fine hair. "I suggest that we leave this place now," she said.

"How many of us?" said Catherine.

"All who will, those who are family," said Reg. "You will not let him bring that woman to your home, Catherine."

"No, I suppose not. And then Alice will be absent a father, and I'll be a widow with a live husband. How will that fare?"

"He's no longer my father, and that's flat," said Alice.

"Widowhood has done you fine enough for almost six years," said Reg. "I wager that few of your workers would know the man if they saw him. They've grown accustomed to a woman's hand, and they obey you and prosper under your government. Why should they care if you return without him?"

"Hear, hear," said Ann. "Listen to the man, Catherine. He speaks the truth."

"And if he'll leave her behind?" said Catherine.

"Then you'll have a husband and a ghost," said Ann. "How will you put it out of your mind?"

Margaret yelped at this, and Catherine turned to her. "I know what you're thinking. Let it go. You've admitted your fault, and I've forgiven you. You're not Joan Wright, and you are an Overton. You'll be welcome in Havenston, and we'll say no more on the subject. You'll be my long-lost sister-in-law and no one will be the wiser."

Ann looked sour, but she held her tongue. They would be a while mending the torn fabric of their civility. Friendship, it could not be called, as Ann had never found friendship among the elder Overtons. That would be as it would be. They would be family anyway. The child stirred, and Ann said, "Let me try her." Julia went into Ann's arms without a peep, and Ann rocked her as she had rocked Robbie, then Veronica, and finally Alice. Julia settled back into sleep, and Ann smiled. It would all be as well as a human family could be.

Except for the question of Benjamin. Catherine recalled those months, living with Anne of Cleves, when she had secretly been with child—Benjamin's child—and had let her mind question him. He had been loyal, in the end, or so she'd thought, and they'd had more than ten years of marriage without quarrel. But had he sought his pleasure privately, away from their home, so cunningly that she had never suspected it? Yet here sat Margaret, the guilt splattered across her face in embarrassed red, and there was Joan Wright.

Catherine's heart set up an alarming racket, and she knew she could not endure the sight of that woman in Yorkshire. She was not sure she could endure the memory of her if Benjamin came home. "We can't leave today. I'll speak to him tomorrow and see what there is to be salvaged, if there's anything at all."

Chapter 39

She would not speak directly to Joan Wright. Catherine was resolved upon that point, at least. She set out the next morning, with the two manservants from the inn. They said that they preferred to wait for her out of doors, in the fresher air, and she knew they wanted to overhear no more encounters between Catherine and her family. She was allowing it to fester, but she was too old to bargain for a husband. She would do it for Veronica instead, when the time arrived. The thought almost cheered her for a moment.

The same doorkeeper who had attended them before let Catherine into the house. "I wish to speak directly with Master Davies and no one else," she said.

His mouth twitched. "Very well, Madam."

Benjamin was in the back, looking over his accounts. He did not rise when she entered, nor did he close the book. "Sit down," he said, making a mark on the page.

"Is this how you greet your wife now?" said Catherine. "I've been awake half the night wondering how to speak to you."

"I don't lose sleep over conversations," said Benjamin. "You haven't thrown yourself into my arms, Catherine."

"Nor did you take me into yours," said Catherine. "But now I sound like a fishwife, nagging her wayward husband, and that's not a role I've ever relished. Or sought."

Benjamin closed the book and rubbed his eyes, leaving slight wrinkles of ink on his cheeks. "I have a great deal of investment here, Catherine. I never thought I'd be allowed to return to England, and I've built a profitable business that I can't take with me. I have nothing in England. It's all yours. You want me to crawl back, a beggar and a dependent? No. I won't do it. It's not manly."

"How can you call this a business? It's horrid. It's a sin against God's creation. Against Christ's teaching."

Benjamin said, "Others think differently. It's mine, by law and by my own effort. Yours is yours, by happenstance."

"You might think of it as a dowry," said Catherine. "I'm your wife, and what's mine is yours, by law. You know this. You didn't turn down any dowry from your first wife, did you?"

"My first wife brought me some very good pieces of land. Land that your Mary Tudor stole from under me." Benjamin wiped his pen. "It seems I have only one daughter left, too. Do you know how she does these days?"

"Finally, you ask. Diana has gone to join a convent. I saw her, before we left England. I think she was steered toward Rome."

Benjamin considered this. "She's gone, too, then." He regarded the pen, then wrapped it and set it aside. "She never was suited to this world. And now she need speak to no one but her God, ever again."

"Or her priest."

Benjamin blew a contemptuous snort through his nose. "Her priest. For Diana, that'll be the same as God. Well, God go with her, as I never could."

"And Alice? She's a quick girl. Quick to smile and quick to anger. You might try to win her affections again. You would enjoy her company."

"Eh, she's been in women's company, I expect, and is more accustomed to female ways. I'm too direct. You keep her. It's you she wants. And that dog."

"Must we be so harsh?" said Catherine. She sat across from her husband, but did not take the hand that lay on the table. She set her own fingers close enough that he could reach them if he wanted to. "I hardly recognize you myself. This banishment has hardened you."

"It has," he said, without moving. "You don't want a broken man, Catherine. You've seen me in aspects that I always meant to keep from you." His eyebrows rose, and his expression brightened. "You could report my death. Say that I'm gone. Be a widow. Widows are powerful in England. You could find a new husband, and a new father for the girls. Get you a poet, one that can do something better than eulogize his own decay. Buy you a priest. They'll be cheap again, now that Elizabeth is queen."

A cold worm slithered through Catherine. "I never thought to hear you speak with such bitterness. This isn't you, Benjamin. This business you've built, that you seem to love so, it's corrupted your soul. Leave off. Gather what monies you must and come home. Begin again. Stop this, I beg you. You're buying and selling human souls. That's what's unmanly. It's worse than that. It's unhuman. Mary Tudor did what she had to do. She was a queen. Elizabeth is different. Perhaps you'll get on her good side."

Benjamin looked up at Catherine, the ink stains spreading into a sinister mask. "My business is here. I can only do it here, not in England. The throne changes too often, and the people hoard their wealth. I can't begin again with a girl wearing the crown of England. She's fickle and wild. She'll get you into a war. She'll put her head into the yoke with some vile little Englishman, and the country will have a tyrant for a king. No, I don't see a future for the likes of me in England. But don't judge me. I do what other men do, and I know how to turn a profit."

A knot of fury choked the fear out of Catherine, and she stood. "And so you'll remain here, buying and selling men and women? Feeling yourself much abused and keeping your whore in luxury?"

"Whore? You've taken away the little whore I bought for a nurse maid. I don't suppose you'll put her out on the road, either, will you?"

"Maria's not in the same condition as that Joan of yours, and you know it right well," Catherine sputtered. She could feel spit fly from her lips, but she couldn't stop. "You'll throw away your wife and your child to sprawl in sin here, with that woman? I won't get on my knees, Benjamin. I'm your wife. I won't cry out for you from the streets, nor will I plead my destitution and my empty bed. I won't. I will not."

Benjamin smiled thinly. "Rage becomes you, Catherine. I don't believe I've ever seen it from the front. I don't expect you to beg. It's beneath your station. And you're not destitute."

"We're done then, being husband and wife? You're divorcing me?"

He opened his hands. "You see no lawyers here. No writ. I'm providing you with a strategy for your happiness. I won't toss away a woman who's served me and bound herself to me like a sick cat. That would be dishonourable."

"And your daughter? What of her happiness?"

"She has dogs at home, doesn't she? What woman would prefer a father to a good dog? She sounds like a girl of sense. Get her one of those little lap dogs that the ladies dote on and give silly names."

"I'll go right now, Benjamin, unless you ask me to stay, and you won't see my face again." Catherine meant to point at him, to emphasize the threat, but her hands shook and she stuffed them into her pockets instead.

"It is a lovely face, dear to me still, even with the addition of wrinkles," said Benjamin. Catherine could not stop herself from touching her own cheek. "Yes, I see them," continued Benjamin. "You're older, as I am. We're changed. Let's remember our love with fondness. Stay, if you like. You may live here with me, as my wife. I won't turn you out, and I'll love you as I've always loved you. But nor will I put Joan onto the street. If my business so offends you, then go back to England and your mad little queen. It's your choice, Catherine. But I mean to stay here."

Chapter 40

Catherine wanted to storm through Benjamin's house like a fury, heaving the doors and shrieking her good-byes, but the place was empty and the hinges all oiled and heavy. She stomped, but the thick carpets muffled her soles, and she landed in the street without having disturbed anyone at all.

The serving men were leaning against the opposite building, and they straightened when she emerged. Catherine waved them on. "If you want to come with me, then come on. You're free men. Go where you like. Don't put yourself into my service if you think me a tyrant or a shrew."

The two men exchanged a silent alarm, but fell into step behind Catherine. One of them said, "We have caused you some upset, Madam. Please don't give us a bad report. We didn't leave the street here. We heard enough the last time we were inside of that house. It was only a moment's folly, that we remained out of doors, and we didn't leave you alone."

Catherine knew her voice had been shrill, a sound that raked her skin in other women, and she said, "Forgive me. I've had a fretful morning's conversation." She stopped, and the two men almost collided with her. "I want your opinion on a matter."

The two men glanced at each other again, and one of them said, "We're listening."

"Do you think the English queen is mad? Do you think she's too excitable to govern?"

"Ah, Madam," said the talker. "I'm not the man to have anything to say against an anointed queen. No, I have no opinion about her, except that she's the daughter of Henry and has royal blood." He cocked his head. "There's the mother, of course, and they say she had a touchy way about her. She was in France too long, they say, and it did her no good. But the father, there was a king."

His mate simply nodded and stared at Catherine's feet.

"Good enough," said Catherine. "I'll ask no more about it, and I'll give a favourable report to your master." She walked on, and the two men followed, a little too distant for more conversation.

Julia was napping when Catherine entered the inn, and Ann shushed her with a finger to her lips. Maria held the child, and Catherine motioned the others into the street. "He won't give her up."

"What? He means to play the sultan?" said Ann. "He can't do it."

Reg said, "He can't do it in England."

Catherine said, "He's wedded to his business here, and he means to stay. He won't give up his profits, and he won't give up the woman. He says that I can stay here with him, as his wife, and we'll go on as one family."

"He wants the money more than he wants her," said Veronica. "He uses her as a shield for his sin. Mother, you don't mean to remain here with him?"

"No!" said Catherine, and Veronica startled. "If Benjamin prefers this place and this means of making money, he'll have to stay here alone."

"Let him stay alone, then, if he means to stay," said Alice. "I've done with him."

"Not quite alone," said Ann bitterly. "Catherine, you've never had the best sense when it comes to choosing husbands."

It was true, but it stung. "You needn't remind me at every turn. Once daily is sufficient."

"Forgive me," Ann said, putting her hand on Catherine's shoulder. "My tongue has always moved more quickly than my thoughts."

"Well, it's no more than anyone with eyes can see," said Catherine. She didn't know whether she would weep or scream, and she bit the inside of her lip to do neither. She counted ten. "I suppose we can make arrangements to leave. I won't see him again." The tears burned her eyes, and she bit the lip again.

Reg said, "John and I will see to the travel. Benjamin may come around. Give him a few days to consider what he's done. What he's lost. Let him have a hard look at himself, and think you departed already."

"That's good advice," said Ann. "Reg, you go on with John, so that we may go when the time is right."

Catherine looked around. "John. Where is John?"

Now Reg looked around, too. "I haven't seen him all day, now that you mention him."

Catherine said, "Vere, where have you put your man?"

"Ah. Mother. There's a subject on which I need to have a word with you," said Veronica. She put a hand out on the air at Alice. "Just the two of us, if you please."

Catherine hurried into the bedchamber with her daughter, her guts threaded with worry. She would have to give the marriage her blessing, but she didn't feel any warmth toward vows of any sort just now. Veronica went to the table by the window, picked up a book, and stared out.

"Mother," she said, "I have believed that John is a good man."

"He seems very good," said Catherine in a steadier tone than her tongue wanted to use.

"He means to be a Protestant, you know, though his parents remain Catholic."

"I do know that."

"I've been teaching him some English, and he's been practicing. He reads right well."

This was a turn in the conversation that Catherine did not expect. "What, is he a poet, then?"

Veronica turned, but she was not smiling. She was holding Robbie's Bible. She lifted it toward her mother. "John has one of these. It's in Dutch. I don't think his parents know he has it." She regarded the book and set it down. "He's so dedicated to learning English that he bought himself another while we were in Wittenberg. It's much like my brother's. I've wondered now and then if they were bought of the same printer."

"That's very industrious of John," said Catherine. She did not own a Bible of her own. "And you read to each other from it?"

Veronica nodded. "Do you know the passage where Christ tells us that there will be no marriage in heaven? No giving of wives, no masters or servants?"

"Yes, of course I do."

"And Jesus tells the disciples that some of them will see him return. They will not die before it happens."

Catherine murmured a wary "yes."

"I've heard you speak of your father, my grandfather who was a priest."

"He was not a very good priest, by men's measure."

"He liked to read into the ancient philosophers, didn't he? And the poets? Homer and Virgil?"

"That he did," said Catherine. "It didn't always win him renown in his calling. His ideas were thought to border on the heretical."

Veronica's chin bunched in thought. "It was good that he lived in such an isolated place, where his mind could wander freely among his books."

"I suppose," said Catherine.

"What do you make of Jesus's words?"

"They're the words of our Lord," said Catherine. "The Son of God."

"And yet here we are, fifteen hundred and more years after his death, still waiting for him to return. He says that he will return like a thief in the night. John finds it puzzling."

"Be careful what judgments you make about scripture outside of this room," said Catherine.

Veronica sat on the bed beside Catherine. "Listen to me. John and I have discussed this a great deal. Consider that Jesus said he would return, before some of the disciples were dead. Consider, too, that he says he will come in secret. He also says that in his Father's house are many mansions, and he tells the thief who reforms on the cross that he will be in Paradise on that very day."

"You have been in much discussion with John," said Catherine.

"I have," said Veronica. "I think my grandfather used to contend, and I have heard such opinions myself, that the ancient authors had glimpses of the divine truth, that even though they were pagans themselves that God had picked them out to hear what could be heard, that Jesus in harrowing hell plucked them from the jaws of destruction and carried them off to heaven."

"Slow down, child," said Catherine. She put a hand on Veronica's knee. "Many have reconciled the scriptures with the ancient writers. Or have attempted it."

"And your Margery Kempe," said Veronica.

Catherine had not mentioned the name to her daughter in years. The manuscript she had taken from the convent and hidden among her own books. She had opened it a few times and read aloud from it to her daughters. But not for ages. "What of her?"

"She saw the face of Christ in living babies, did she not?"

"So she said. Some are convinced that she was lunatic."

"But not you. You said she had mystical knowledge, that God spoke directly to her."

"I may have said as much," admitted Catherine.

"She had a husband, and she left him."

"She returned to him in old age, when he broke his head. She nursed him until his death."

"But she demanded chastity of him."

"Yes, as I recall it. Where are you leading me with all of this, Vere?"

"I look into the face of little Julia, and I see as angelic a countenance there as any I have seen painted on a church," said Veronica. "And there she lies, in the arms of a reformed whore, a Mary Magdalene, both as innocent as the day is long. It has made me remember the stories of the underworld in the old poems. There is a river there."

"The Styx. One must cross over to reach the last destination."

"But it isn't the last destination, is it? No, the river I mean is Lethe. We forget, when we die, and then we are returned to life to begin again. Perhaps to do better, perhaps to do worse. Perhaps simply to repeat the mission for which God has sent us into the world."

Catherine could hear the echo of her father's talk in Veronica's words, and she chilled at it. "You're confusing the sacred and the secular."

"But God is never confused," said Veronica. "If our church fathers are to be believed, there is truth in those ancients. And Jesus said he would return, and yet who has seen Him? Well, there's the knot I mean to untangle."

"If it is a Gordian knot, you must cut it," said Catherine.

Veronica laughed. "Then here is my blade. I wonder if Jesus has perhaps returned already, and returned many times. He calls to us, but we do not hear, because we are gazing into the blue sky or into the faces on the money we crave instead of looking into the faces of little ones. Look at the seasons. Do they not return? Look at the stars? Do they not wheel into position again? What if Jesus has come again and we have neglected to recognize Him? What if he returned in the guise of a small girl child?"

Catherine gasped and covered Veronica's mouth. "Shh. You must not say such things aloud. This is dangerous talk."

"Then I will whisper it," said Veronica, pushing Catherine's hand away. "What if He has come back? Perhaps as a woman, perhaps as one of the Africans that Benjamin has sold into slavery for his own luxury? And we have spat upon Christ and profited from God's own flesh?"

"Have you said such things to John?"

"I have. More than once," said Veronica. "We've had many deliberations over the subject."

"And he still wants to marry you?" Catherine realized, as the words came off her tongue, that Veronica had not yet mentioned marriage. "Or has he cast you off?"

"No," said Veronica. "He hasn't. I thought when he saw Robbie and listened to him that he would flee, but he didn't. Instead, he studied Robbie. And then he studied your husband. He drew me deeper into speculations about the world and its workings. But we've come to different conclusions." Veronica rose and returned to the table. "I'll have Robbie's Bible, if you'll give it to me."

"It's yours," said Catherine.

Veronica weighed the book in one hand. "I've observed you since we arrived in Lisbon, and I've thought much on Robbie and his family. Such a sorry tale."

"It is that," said Catherine, not knowing if she meant the story of her brother or the story of her mother.

"John has asked me if I would be his wife," said Veronica. "He claims that he wants a thinking woman."

"Good for him," said Catherine, "but he hasn't said a word to me."

"He won't," said Veronica. "I told you that we've come to different conclusions. He's been about the town, and he believes in what he sees. John has concluded that God has ordained degree and order in submission. He's come to believe that God has graded his creatures by different measures and that the Bible condones these differences. Some are meant to serve and others to order and instruct. He's come to believe that he's been brought here to meet Benjamin and to learn how the world is to be settled. He wants to follow Benjamin's example and live by this trade. But not just here. He wants to travel the seas and find these new worlds, where men buy and sell other men and put the money in their pockets. He wants to become rich. He wants a wife by his side who will talk with him as an equal, or so he thinks now, before he has such a wife. He sought out our men after they left us, and he believes that they'll hire on to serve him and travel with him. The idea turns his eyes into glass, and I can see demons dancing within them. But I mean to be my own mistress. Mary Tudor did it, didn't she, even with a husband? And Elizabeth does it. Diana did it, as little as you think of her choice. They're women. Why can't I? Live by my own hands and wits and seek God in the innocent and the poor. And so, much as I have found to admire in John before now, I can do it no longer. I've said no. I have turned down this proposal of marriage."

Chapter 41

Catherine called Ann into the room. Veronica remained by the window, posed in demure reflection, and Ann said, "We will have a wedding before we return to England, then?"

"Vere has cast John off. She's determined to live a spinster's life."

"You had determined upon the same path, Mother, before you married my father," murmured Veronica.

"What nonsense is this?" said Ann. "You have a good, strong man at your feet and you kick him away? You're not growing younger, Veronica. You won't be the prime cut in many markets anymore."

"What? You're the one who told me to be careful in my judgment and—what was it you said?—not to fall at his feet. Well, I haven't fallen."

"I meant to guard your heart, not turn it to stone," said Ann. "You've spent much time with him since then."

"And I've learnt much in that time. I'm not a slab of meat, Auntie Ann," said Veronica. "How old were you when you accepted Reg?"

"I was a widow," said Ann. "Widows are different. They can do as they please, if they have money or a position. You should be so fortunate."

"Oh, you want to kill my husband before I've even taken him?" said Veronica. "That's a fine piece of advice. And your first husband. He was a scoundrel, wasn't he? He played away your money at the cards. A villain, and a rake, too, if I remember the stories. You believed him a fine catch at the time, though. Didn't you?"

"To be sure, I did not," said Ann. "I thought him the best thing that had asked for me, and my father wanted me out of the house. Too many girls." Her colour was up, but at this last she faded, and sat on the bed. "And they're all dead, too, every one of them. You wonder that I went into the convent. I had two babies, you know. They didn't live long, either. You take what life offers you, Veronica."

"No, I won't. You made a bad bargain the first time, and life made you more wary the second time. You didn't marry the first time Reg asked you. Nor the second. He likely asked you a hundred times before you consented. And you, Mother. You left my father standing in the road. You didn't accept him until you knew you had a baby in your belly. Isn't that true?"

Catherine said, "I've told you too much, girl. It's made you foolish."

"Or wise beyond her years," said Ann.

Catherine cut her friend a glare. "You'll take her part in this catechism? I'm her mother."

"I take the part of truth," said Ann. "Listen to her, Catherine. She sounds like a wiser you. And wiser than I've ever been. She has eyes in her head, you know, and you taught her to use them, as your mother taught you, or tried to teach you. She can see what marriage looks like. And she hit the nail about Reg. I expect I made him wait longer than I should have."

"Reg is a good man," said Catherine.

"He is, and I might have lost him," said Ann. "And John seems a good man, and Veronica will lose him. But what if John is another William, and her marriage ends as yours did, with two men dead in the road?"

"You know what all that was about," said Catherine. "Vere's had a different sort of life. But as it turns out, our John has taken Benjamin for his model, and he wants to set up in this hellish trade. If you're right about this, Vere, about your John's newfound love for trade, then you're right to leave him."

"I know it well enough," said Veronica. "I also know the story of my father's death, so you needn't mind my delicate ears."

"What do you know?" said Catherine.

"Benjamin told me all, years back. You may close your mouth before the flies get in. Yes, he told me. My father believed that Robbie was not his child, that you had been with another man, one of Cromwell's men, and it ate at his reason until they killed each other. Benjamin told me that it was a rape, and that my father should have known it. But it killed them in the end just the same, didn't it? Robbie knew it as well, Mother. He knew it all his life, that Father didn't love him."

"He knew nothing of that," said Catherine, but she heard the lie in the words, clear as an owl's cry.

"I won't have my chastity bandied about in men's mouths," said Veronica, "nor will I be mistress in a household that markets God's image. I will live as Elizabeth lives, my own mistress. John's decided that he seeks the life that Benjamin Davies leads, and that's not the life for me. I will never marry."

"I never thought to hear this of John De Vries," said Ann. "I thought I'd come to know the man. But if that's his frame of mind, you're better off settling yourself elsewhere indeed."

"I will never settle," said Veronica. "I'll live single."

"Elizabeth will marry," said Catherine. "She must."

"Then I'll live as your mother lived, and as my namesake Veronica lived, with the women of my family and no men."

Ann laughed at this. "Your grandmother and your namesake were nuns, child. There won't be convents in England anymore. Do you mean to join Diana?"

Veronica bit her lip. "No. I'll live in England. My property is there."

Ann said, "She sounds more and more like you, Catherine. You must forgive her for what she knows about your past."

"I forgive her," said Catherine, "because she's my daughter and because she's spoken the truth, about John and her father, and about me, if I must say it. Oh, the world has changed, Vere, and I wish I could say it was for the better."

"It'll be better for me. I'll make it so, just as our queen is doing for herself. John can do as he wants," said Veronica. "I won't yoke myself to blatant sin."

"So that leaves Reg to see about our journey home," said Ann. "Will you see John again?"

Veronica went white about the mouth. "I will not. He said that he loves me, but I can't return the feeling. We've said our farewells, and I expect that he's already run off to the ship captains to find out what he can about passage abroad. He's taking our men, you know. Mark and Oswald."

"Maybe he's gone to Benjamin as an apprentice," said Catherine.

"If he's done that, then he's run off like a bad dog, and I'm even better schooled in the ways of men."

Catherine heard the echoes of years in her daughter's words. She had left William standing in the road. And now she'd left Benjamin, sitting in that damned room of his. She had loved them both. She'd returned to William, and that had ended badly. But she'd had Robbie and Veronica. Still, she would not return to Benjamin, and that might end badly, as well. But, from him, she had Alice. "Come," she said. "Let's find us a captain of our own and see to going home."

WORLDS END

Chapter 42

Veronica played with little Julia while they waited for Reg and Alice to return with news of their passage, and Catherine watched her. She was patient with the child, and made absurd faces. She bit her toes and made Julia laugh. She put Julia's hand on her breast and said "Vere. Aunt Vere." Instead, Julia said something that sounded like "Mama," and Veronica bundled her close.

Catherine wondered if her own mother, Christina, had looked thus as a young woman, holding Catherine on her knees. She'd have been wearing her habit and pretending that she was being kind to a foundling. Only old Veronica knew the truth, and here was a new, young Veronica, less afraid to speak her mind.

The front door opened and in came Reg. "There are boats if we mean to take them."

Alice came in behind him. "Why must we go home at all?"

Reg threw an arm around her shoulders. "The girl's been at this all morning."

"What's this?" said Ann. "You don't want to go back to England?"

"I do," said Alice. "But here we are, and there's more world to see. We've got a passport. You've written to Eleanor, Mother, haven't you?"

"Yes."

"So we're free to go where we will."

Veronica said, "Please, no mention of this New World. I've heard my fill of it."

"There's plenty of the world we haven't seen," countered Alice. "And here we sit in the midst of it and are determined to crawl back to our corner of cold old England and be done with it?"

"I can't convince her otherwise," said Reg. He threw his hat onto the table and poured himself a mug of ale. "I've spoken to a dozen men this day, and they all say the same. Boats to England are plenty."

"But Alice is right," said Veronica. She looked at Ann and winked. "We aren't getting younger, after all."

"And where is it that madam wishes to go now?" said Ann.

"I think we should see Paris," said Alice. "I've bought nothing on this entire journey. I'd like to see how the women behave in France. I'm in no hurry." She set her chin, and Catherine knew there was no use in arguing. She might as well try to talk Alice out of feeding her pets at the table.

"I've imagined seeing Rome," said Ann. "Perhaps the Holy Lands."

"Yes," said Veronica. "Why not? The queen can't see us. She maybe wouldn't care if she could."

"What's this?" said Reg. "Are you in this together?" He looked around. "And what's become of John?"

Ann shook her head. "The talk of marriage has come and gone long since."

"What marriage?"

Ann said, "Vere says no to any talk of a marriage."

"Who said the word to her?" said Reg.

Ann sat, laughing. "Forgive, me, sweetheart. But you're as absent-minded as our Vere is open-eyed. She had a proposal from John, but she turned him down."

"Aye?" said Reg, and Veronica nodded.

"Well, that explains why he didn't help me this morning. A man doesn't jump in when he knows the water is cold."

Catherine nodded. "Vere means to live as a nun, without the convent. She thinks that she'll be like our Elizabeth, all crown and no king."

"Elizabeth will marry. She must marry," said Reg.

"As I've told her," Catherine said.

Julia had fallen asleep, and Veronica handed her over to Maria. "Will my future be the subject of a public debate? I'm no cow, I've told you, to be sold to the highest bidder."

"I never thought of you as a cow," said Reg. "But you're a young woman. Surely you want a husband?"

"After what you've seen of husbands and wives among my kindred? What fool would put his head into a yoke with an Overton? We're unmade by marriage, every one of us. I've read a wise passage from the Bible. No giving in marriage. No taking of wives. Let me live like the angels, and be perfect."

"I don't want to be an angel. Not just yet," said Reg.

Veronica looked for an ally. "You're all against me. Very well. I'll make you an offer."

"A wager?" said Ann. "Have you become a gambling woman?"

"Perhaps," said Veronica. "You all say that Elizabeth will take a husband. I'll marry when Elizabeth does. On the day they crown Elizabeth Tudor's husband as king of England, you may cry heigh-ho and I will seek me a mate."

"I don't like this wager," said Ann. "She will marry, won't she?"

"Of course, she will," said Reg.

"I'm for you," said Alice. "Let's stay as we are."

Catherine put out her hand. "I accept your wager. And I hope that you get the win of it, whatever comes."

Veronica shook. "John will find another woman he likes better. He wouldn't like me, as I have a tongue and I aim to use it. In Christian love and friendship, of course."

"Here, then. For Christian love and friendship," said Ann. She stuck her fingers into her bodice and drew out a silver ring. "This belonged to another Veronica, the one for whom you were named. I've worn it on this chain for many a year. I'll give it you to wear if you like of it, to remind you. She knew of Christian friendship, maybe more than anyone I ever knew."

Veronica allowed Ann to slip the chain over her neck. "I will. And I'll marry no one before Elizabeth does. That I vow."

"Then we must be content," said Catherine.

"And what of my wishes?" said Alice. "She is loosed of a husband and we're all free as the wind. What do you say, Maria? Would you travel the world a little with us?"

Maria looked around the group and landed on Catherine. "Whither thou goest, Madam, I will go."

Catherine chewed the inside of her cheek. "I'm outnumbered. Reg, you have the ears of the captains at the harbour. Do you think we could find passage toward Rome or the Holy Lands?" She glanced at Alice. "We might go through Paris on our way home."

"Well, I've been a sailor in my time and I suppose I can be so again," said Reg. "Off I go, then, back to the dock with my orders. Wish me luck in persuading them to carry so many strong-willed women."

Chapter 43

"I wonder if Benjamin will come," said Catherine, the next morning over breakfast. "He's had a few hours to think on what he's done. When do we leave, Reg? He may come to speak with me, and we shouldn't go in such haste that he can say he couldn't catch us."

"So that you may say what to him? That we'll squeeze his woman onto the boat for him?" said Ann. "No, let's be gone from this place. Today, if we can."

"I want to see Robbie one last time," said Catherine. "I'll never lay eyes on his resting place again."

"I'll go with you," said Veronica. She was turning the ring, sliding it back and forth on its chain. She said nothing of John De Vries.

"Reg, will you come with us to the tomb?" said Ann.

"Of course," he said.

Veronica removed the ring from its chain and slipped it onto her finger. Then she removed it from there and returned it to its yoke and dropped it into her bodice. Reg picked up his hat, and, since Julia was awake, they all braved the day together. The sky to the north was patched with dark clouds, stained by the waxing sun and bloody-looking at their ragged edges. A breeze freshened the air, though, and Catherine pushed back her hood to cool her neck.

"I see a storm brewing in the direction of home," remarked Veronica. "Will it come this way?"

Reg turned and stopped and regarded the sky. "Red sun in the morning. We shouldn't sail today. But that storm will move toward England." He walked on.

"Your husband seems in a black mood," said Catherine to Ann.

"He frets about Benjamin at night, and wants to challenge him," said Ann. "But Benjamin has been his master, and he sees no opening to go through. It hampers his mind. He'd like to give our John a nice punch in the nose to send him on his way, too."

"My mind is hampered, too," said Catherine. "Some would say that Benjamin is my master, as well, and yet I've walked away from him." She saw a smirk twitching the edge of Veronica's mouth and fell silent.

The tomb was as they had seen it last, the yard surrounding it neatly weeded and mown, the graves well-tended, if a little mossy. The air tasted salty, from the sea Catherine supposed, and she wondered that she hadn't noted it before. Her heart beat its regular rhythm, no jerking in anguish or thudding in fear, and she laid her palm against the flat stone of the grim little building, then her forehead. "God be with you, Robbie, as I could not be. Forgive your mother for her failings. We will look after your daughter." She motioned for Maria to bring the child forward, and she gathered Julia into her arms. "Here's your father, child. He was a man with faults, and he's paid dearly for them."

Reg coughed lightly, and Catherine turned, thinking him impatient with such outbursts and ready to go. But then she saw Benjamin, standing beside the church. Everyone else was watching him, but he did not approach until Catherine gave Julia back to Maria.

"You've come," Catherine said. It was stupid and obvious, but she could think of no other way to greet him.

He stroked his jacket. "It seems that I have. Well, Catherine, will I come with you?"

"I believe that choice is yours." She could hear the others coming closer, her tiny army at the defense.

"I have friends here," Benjamin said, "who might buy my lists of traders, perhaps even my warehouse and home. It would bring me a good pile of money. Your young man has called on me, and he might want to take my place. And there I stood, thinking all the while that he meant to ask for Veronica's hand. I suppose that's not in his cards."

"It's not," said Catherine. "We mean to travel some. Will you be content with that?"

"I might." He examined his right hand and bit off a bit of loose skin at the edge of his middle finger. "There's still the matter of the woman."

"Can't you sell her with the warehouse?" said Alice, standing right behind Catherine.

Benjamin snorted softly. "And you, so offended by the trade I do here. Would you have me still in the business?"

"I've done with your business altogether," said Alice. "And your woman."

"She can't care for herself, Catherine. Did you expect me to be alone all these years, waiting for you? I'm not a Penelope and never have been."

"No, you've been a right Odysseus, stopping where you would and taking your pleasure," said Ann.

"Ann," said Catherine. "Let me think." She had said herself, once, that she would be no patient Penelope, but she saw no mocking light in Benjamin's eyes. "You mean to bring her with you? To have two women for your bed? It's a sin, Benjamin, and it annihilates me."

"We were in a bed together before we were ever in a church together, and you thought that no sin."

"We were as much as betrothed," said Catherine, "or so I thought. And I didn't endure another woman there with me. Perhaps I was the more deceived in you."

"I have never thrust my failings into your face," said Benjamin, "but this one I can't conceal." He nodded at Margaret, who hung back. "You've forgiven that one, and she's done you much greater harm. Joan is nothing."

"I've forgiven Margaret because it's the Christian thing to do," said Catherine, "and she's admitted her fault, more than once. She won't share your bed again. Margaret has committed many sins, but they've rebounded on her head, and she knows it. Isn't that right, Margaret?"

Margaret nodded miserably and retreated a few more steps.

"But your Joan carries herself like a queen in triumph. She scorns me. She thinks herself more your wife than I. No, Benjamin, I won't share my home with a second wife."

"She could serve you," offered Benjamin.

"That's more insult than charity," said Ann. "You men. You believe that your wills are your laws. You think you've become a king."

"I'm her husband," said Benjamin. "She's supposed to obey me."

"Obey you?" said Veronica. "You, who by your rash acts got yourself banished from the country and left my mother to fend for herself alone? She's come halfway around the world to bring you home. I'm with Ann. You men. Women once had only God to obey, and now we have husbands. It's a sorry exchange."

Benjamin pointed a warning finger at Veronica. "Girl, stay out of your parents' business. You've been a daughter to me, but you're not my blood and you're not too old for a whipping."

Now Reg stepped forward. "Sir. I have kept myself out of this dispute for the sake of our long acquaintance and have held my tongue for the sake of the respect I have felt for you. But this. This cannot be borne."

"You've been my servant," said Benjamin. "Keep your place."

"I will keep my place when you hold yours," said Reg. "You bear yourself like a gentleman but you talk like a common villain. You will not bring that woman to Catherine's home. I will not serve her and I will not be in a room with her. I have been your servant, sir, but hear this. I will serve you no longer." He turned to Catherine. "You are a creature of God. You are an educated woman. You might behave with more dignity."

No one spoke. It was an affront no one had ever heard from Reg, mild Reg, always even in his appraisals. A bird sang from a distant tree, and Catherine looked up, but whatever it was escaped her eye. Then it flew, and she watched it—a sparrow, much like the ones in England. It opened its wings, caught the wind, and was gone.

Benjamin tried a new appeal. "I'll get your men back for you. Mark and Oswald are with John De Vries, but I can win them for you again. I'll pay for them out of my own pocket. Mark'll serve me."

"If you come with me," Catherine said to Benjamin, "you'll come alone. No men. No woman. And I'll seek the grace to forgive you."

"I can't do it," said Benjamin. "I won't do it. I didn't forsake you when you carried my child, and I won't forsake Joan. She's too old to bear, and so she's too old to find another husband. I won't leave her."

"Then you must stay," said Catherine.

"And then you must take this," said Benjamin. He pulled a generous cloth bag from his pocket and offered it. "You'll need money along your way."

"I don't want money from your business," said Catherine. "Keep it."

"No. I supposed that. It's all the wealth that I removed from England when I went, to the penny. And it's recompense for your loss of Mark and Oswald, for the care and feeding you've given them. It's as much yours as mine. I don't need it." He thrust it forward.

Catherine took it. It was heavy. It would carry them a good long way.

"And now I've offered all that I will."

"Then we're truly done," said Catherine. She took Veronica's and Alice's arms in hers and, skirting Benjamin, walked out of the churchyard.

Veronica started to speak, once they had left Benjamin behind, but Catherine held up a hand. "You needn't persecute me with your virtue, Vere," she said. "I know right well what you mean to say. You've chosen the better path, sending your man away."

"I meant to say nothing of the kind," said Veronica, but Catherine could tell from the wounded note in her voice that she had and regretted the moment for them both.

Chapter 44

And then it was tomorrow, with promising weather and a boat ready to carry them away, and Catherine followed the others down to the dock for the last time. The rising sun was kind, casting a lavender light over the broken-down crates and people. But the gulls feasted at garbage, and the black flies already fizzed and fussed over the blood smears and fish carcasses. Catherine held a handkerchief over her nose and went aboard. She leant, her elbows on the railing, awhile, staring inland, but Benjamin did not come running, calling her name and vowing to begin anew. No one came but sailors and traders, and she was an alien in a strange land. A breeze caught her from behind and let her breathe. A pair of familiar arms appeared beside her own.

"Reg is a happy man this morning," Ann said. "He needed to speak his mind to Benjamin. Now he's done it, he's lanced the wound and is himself again." She looked up at the sky. "We'll be in another land before you can blink, and you can forget him."

"I won't forget," said Catherine. "Any of this."

Veronica came up on Catherine's other side, holding Julia tight against her chest. "Good riddance to him, I say." Maria appeared on the far side of Veronica, her lips set tight as she gazed around.

"Well, one world ends and another begins," said Ann. "And what think you of us? A congregation of the bitter, the abandoned, the discarded, and the old."

Maria gasped at this. Catherine said, "And which am I?"

"You'll have to determine that for yourself."

Alice ran up to them. "I'm not old," she said "and I feel no bitterness at all."

"Don't you miss your little Toby?" said Veronica.

"I do," she said. "But he lies in a beautiful garden and feels no suffering. He's in God's hands, and so are we."

Catherine felt the mirth rise up in her breast, but it was the wrong moment to laugh at her daughter, and she hugged her instead.

Julia said "Vere," and then Catherine could let out the laugh. "She's one of us. As are you, Maria." Maria offered to take the child, but Veronica insisted that she needed the practice if she were to be a good aunt, and the nurse let her be. Her daughter might have been any young mother, holding her young child, and Catherine patted Veronica on one cheek.

"Mother!" she said. "Don't. Not where people can see. I'm too grown up for that."

"Yes, I suppose you are," said Catherine.

"Think of it, Catherine," said Ann. "You'll have your city of ladies again, after all, and nobody can say nay to it, bloody king or bloody queen or husband. You were once one of the king's sisters, hiding an altarpiece, and now you can be a woman of the world who follows her own inclinations and lives her life as she desires to live it."

Catherine nodded and patted the board under her hand. "A city of ladies on a moving island. And so you're right again, Ann. Worlds do end, and others begin. Let's hope that we're travelling into a good one. I dread to see the practices we have witnessed here spread abroad."

"Not to England, surely," said Veronica.

Catherine watched the water lap below them, this way and then that. "I pray not."

The captain gave orders, and the sailors made ready to sail. The ship keeled against the wind and righted itself. Catherine felt a little skittering thread of fear in her belly, but they were going. Eleanor would keep her house for her, and all her household, and the sheep would be getting fat and fleecy under her watch.

"There was a wise woman at Norwich once," said Catherine said to the other women. "She was called Julian. Isn't that odd? So very close to our own Julia. Well, Margery Kempe once visited her, to get her opinion about her visions."

"What of that?" said Ann. "What are you talking about, Catherine?"

"I recall my mother speaking of her, when I was just a girl. I had injured myself in some childish folly, had fallen from a low wall, I think it was, and I had scraped the skin from both of my knees. I wailed and wept, and my mother put a poultice on me and said that I should remember the words of wise Julian."

"What in the wide world has that to do with anything?" said Ann. "Catherine, have you lost your wits?"

"No," said Catherine. "I was just a child, a spoilt child, and I was cross with God that He had allowed me to skin myself. Oh, I cried at the injustice of it, and the pain, as little as it was. It seemed very great to me, and undeserved." The ship jerked forward, and Catherine lurched. "My mother scolded me for my anger, and then she put her arms around me and said that all would be well. Those were Julian's words, she said: that no matter how far or wide we stray when we try to hit the mark, we will find it at last, and all will be well in the end."

"Then off we go, to see what there is to be seen," said Ann.

"God willing," said Catherine.

They were in full motion now, skidding through the water, and Alice took hold of her mother's elbow. Maria put her arms around Veronica and Julia. Ann clutched Catherine from the other side, and Catherine grabbed the railing of the ship. The queen was dead. Long live the queen, on her distant throne. A sailor whooped, and the sun cleared a stray cloud. It would be a warm day. Catherine braced herself against the waves, and held on for the ride.

THE END

About The Author

Sarah Kennedy

Sarah Kennedy is the author of the novels *Self-Portrait, with Ghost* and *The Altarpiece, City of Ladies, The King's Sisters and Queen of Blood* Books One, Two, Three and Four of The Cross and the Crown series, set in Tudor England. She has also published seven books of poems.

A professor of English at Mary Baldwin University in Staunton, Virginia, Sarah Kennedy holds a PhD in Renaissance Literature and an MFA in Creative Writing. She has received grants from both the National Endowment for the Arts, the National Endowment for the Humanities, and the Virginia Commission for the Arts. Please visit Sarah at her website: http://sarahkennedybooks.com

If You Enjoyed This Book

Visit

Penmore Press
www.penmorepress.com

All Penmore Press books are available directly through our website.

THE ALTARPIECE

BY

SARAH KENNEDY

It is 1535, and in the tumultuous years of King Henry VIII's break from Rome, the religious houses of England are being seized by force. Twenty-year-old Catherine Havens is a foundling and the adopted daughter of the prioress of the Priory of Mount Grace in a small Yorkshire village. Catherine, like her adoptive mother, has a gift for healing, and she is widely sought and admired for her knowledge. However, the king's divorce dashes Catherine's hopes for a place at court, and she reluctantly takes the veil. When the priory's costly altarpiece goes missing, Catherine and her friend Ann Smith find themselves under increased suspicion. King Henry VIII's soldiers have not had their fill of destruction, and when they return to Mount Grace to destroy the priory, Catherine must choose between the sacred calling of her past and the man who may represent her country's future.

PENMORE PRESS
www.penmorepress.com

THE KING'S SISTERS

BY

SARAH KENNEDY

The King's Sisters continues the story of Catherine Havens. It's now 1542, and another queen, Catherine Howard, has been beheaded for adultery. Although young Prince Edward is growing, and the line of Tudor succession seems secure, the king falls into a deep melancholy and questions the faith and loyalty of those around him.

Catherine has found herself in a unique position as a married former nun. Now she is a wealthy widow. She has two children, a boy who has successfully joined the young prince's household and a daughter who lives with her at Richmond Palace, home to Henry's cast-off fourth wife, Anne of Cleves, now designated "The King's Beloved Sister." Catherine also enjoys the attentions of widower Benjamin Davies, and in the festive court atmosphere, she has furtively indulged her passion for him. But England has changed again.

Anne of Cleves hopes for reinstatement as queen—until questions arise about the finances of the houses she keeps. Catherine, as one of the king's "reformed sisters," is singled out, just as she realizes that she is carrying a third child.

PENMORE PRESS
www.penmorepress.com

City of Ladies

BY

Sarah Kennedy

It's midwinter in 1539, and Catherine Havens Overton has just given birth to her second child, a daughter. The convent in which she was raised is now part of the Overton lands, and Catherine's husband William owns the properties that once belonged to her mother's family. With a son, Robert, and her new daughter, Veronica, Catherine's life as the mistress of a great household should be complete.Henry VIII's England has not been kind to many of the evicted members of religious houses, and Catherine has gathered about her a group of former nuns in hopes of providing them a chance to serve in the village of Havenston, her City of Ladies. Catherine's own past haunts her. Her husband suspects that Catherine's son is not his child, and his ambitions lie with service at court. Then the women of Overton House begin to disappear, and though one of them is found brutally murdered nearby, William forces Catherine to go to Hatfield House, where the young Elizabeth Tudor lives, to improve the family's standing—and to ensure, for her own safety, that she is as far away from connections to her old convent as possible.Reluctantly, Catherine obeys, only to find herself serving not only the Protestant Elizabeth but also the shamed Catholic Mary Tudor. As the murders in Yorkshire mount up and her loyalty to the Tudor sisters grows more complicated, Catherine must uncover the secret of the killer and keep her dream of a City of Ladies alive.

PENMORE PRESS
www.penmorepress.com

QUEEN OF BLOOD

BY

SARAH KENNEDY

The Year 1553

Queen of Blood, Book Four of the Cross and the Crown series, continues the story of Catherine Havens, a former nun in Tudor England. It is now 1553, and Mary Tudor has just been crowned queen of England. Still a Roman Catholic, Mary seeks to return England to its former religion, and Catherine hopes that the country will be at peace under the daughter of Henry VIII. But rebellion is brewing around Thomas Wyatt, the son of a Tudor courtier, and when Catherine's estranged son suddenly returns from Wittenberg amid circulating rumours about overthrowing the new monarch, Catherine finds herself having to choose between the queen she has always loved and the son who seems determined to join the Protestants who seek to usurp her throne.

PENMORE PRESS
www.penmorepress.com

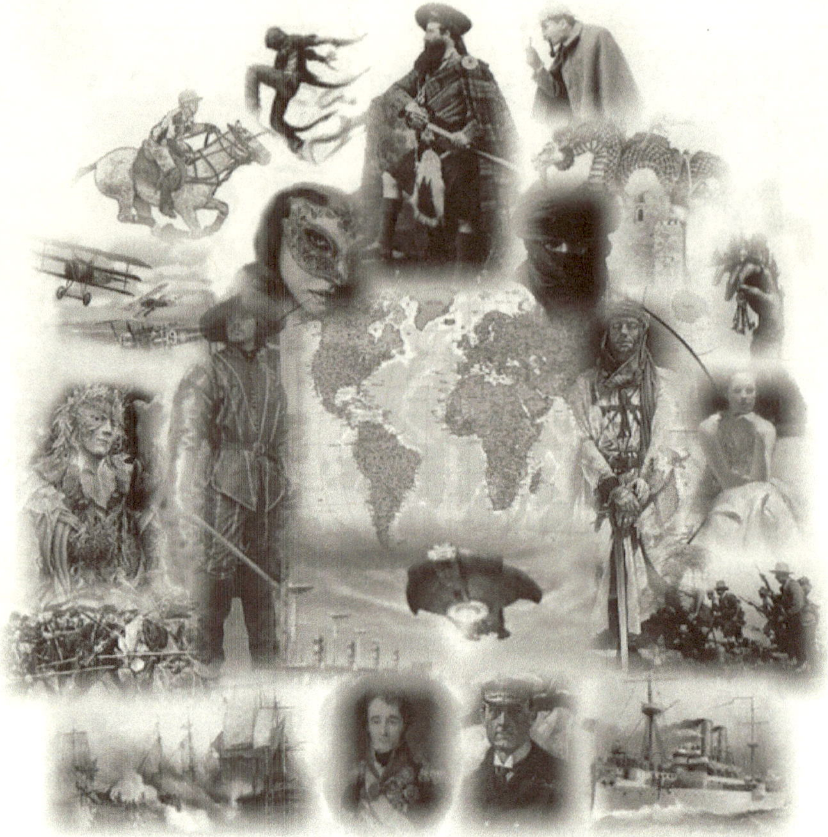

Penmore Press

Challenging, Intriguing, Adventurous, Historical and Imaginative

www.penmorepress.com